The Right Wedding

Frances Chambers

M*Press* Books

The Right Wedding

First published in the United Kingdom in 2019 by MPress Books

MPress Books Limited Reg. No 6379441 is a company registered in Great Britain
www.mpressbooks.co.uk

British Library Cataloguing in Publication Data
A catalogue record for this book is available from the British Library.

Where possible, papers used by MPress Books are natural, recyclable products made from wood grown in sustainable forests. The manufacturing processes conform to the environmental regulations of the country of origin.

ISBN
978-0-9930384-7-1
Electronic book format 978-1-9996531-1-8

Typeset in Minion
Origination by Core Creative, Yeovil 01935 477453
Cover design by Anna Hymas
ePublication produced by MPress Books Limited
Copyright Protected
Printed and bound in England by CPI Antony Rowe

ACKNOWLEDGEMENTS

There are several people without whose help this book would not have seen the light of day. My gratitude is due to three in particular: Andrew Marshall for sticking to his guns during the protracted publishing process and Angela and Tim Devlin for their encouragement and valiant editing. Thank you to each of you – you acted beyond the call of duty and indeed, I think beyond any requirements of friendship (which I hope has remained intact).

AUTHOR BIOGRAPHY

Frances Chambers was born in Buckinghamshire in 1945 and educated in Cornwall and at Oxford University. She has two daughters and six grandchildren. For many years she taught English Literature and Language and various related subjects, latterly at a College of Further and Higher Education.

The Right Wedding

CHAPTER 1

1998 JANUARY

In Cornwall in the woodland surrounding an ancient country house called Trevean the cold weather was keeping most of the badgers underground but on this particular January morning one had nosed his way out of the sett just before the sun rose, in search of slugs or earth worms. He was now galloping back up the slope of the hill to return to his bracken bed, which was warm if flea-ridden. No fresh dry bedding was to be had at this chill turn of the year.

On the same morning in Somerset Antonia Bradford had woken with the thought that she was now, in fact since last Wednesday, officially engaged to Roger Rodmaine. She turned on her radio and hummed along to Celine Dion: 'My heart will go on . . . '

Then she remembered that when they had seen 'Titanic' and she had thought it was so romantic, Roger had said he found it pretty far-fetched from the social point of view, third class passengers would never have got near first class. She stopped humming.

More familiar and worrying thoughts returned. Antonia was desperately possessed by a desire to have a wedding which met her future in-laws' expectations and which would not incur the derision of Roger's critical sister Lizzie.

For this reason she had set her heart, for the wedding reception, on the grandeur of Columb Court Hotel.

Situated in the tidy agricultural countryside but conveniently accessible for the motorway Columb Court was an imposing red brick building in the Edwardian Baronial style, with turrets. Cedars of Lebanon shaded the extensive lawns and there was a rose garden.

Today Antonia and her mother Marilyn were to make their initial visit to the hotel.

The thought of this experience was unnerving Marilyn considerably.

Indeed by the time later that day when they had to set off they were both a bit strung up. The wedding had to be right!

"I wish," Marilyn said several times to Antonia, "that your Dad could have come." For one thing she wouldn't then have had to drive.

But Clive Bradford was away promoting his company's moulded plastic boat fittings at a trade fair in Sweden.

Antonia said, "Oh do watch out Mum, that car behind us is trying to pass!" Although she felt anxious herself she remained resolved of the necessity for this sort of wedding, which must be just like those which she had attended of several of Roger's friends: a country church, a full complement of bridesmaids, a smart hotel reception.

Otherwise she feared that once absorbed within Roger's family she would never hear the last of it.

The Columb Court drive, which ran between trees, seemed even on this sunny wintry day to be dark and gloomy beneath the overhanging branches. Marilyn felt that, impressive though the hotel certainly was, she might have preferred somewhere brighter, lighter and generally less grand.

But Antonia was still determined not to have any such doubts. In the hotel's cavernous panelled hallway she gave their names to the receptionist, identified as 'Lisa' on her clip-on badge, and explained, "We have an appointment, to discuss my wedding reception."

Just saying the words was to experience a pin-prickle feeling of excitement.

The receptionist, who was whippet thin in a navy suit, smiled coolly and asked them to follow her to the Green Drawing Room, where they might take a seat, and the Functions Manager, Mr Peter Fullerton, would be with them shortly.

"Probably she's quite nice," Marilyn tried to tell herself but the receptionist's perfect make-up, perfect hair, perfect nails and nano waist somehow combined to suggest that no, she wasn't particularly nice and she would wipe off her professional smile as soon as she was back through the huge panelled double doors. Sitting again behind her high mahogany reception desk, she would ask herself how such people as the Bradfords managed to convince themselves that their wedding would be suited to the splendour of Columb Court.

Marilyn and Antonia sat on two of the pale green brocade

upholstered chairs and gazed down the great length of the room. Antonia was pleased by what she saw for no-one, not even Roger's sister Lizzie who could be a bit snobby, would be able to say that this was not an impressive venue.

The Green Drawing Room had a high ceiling with cornices, huge gilt framed mirrors on the soft pistachio coloured walls and an enormous fireplace in black marble; French windows opened onto the terrace, where there was a lengthy stone balustrade, with urns.

"This will be perfect for the reception drinks, don't you think Mum?" Antonia said. "And we could have some of the photographs taken outside."

Marilyn murmured uncertain agreement and immediately became distracted. Wedding photographs meant hats. I must, she thought, sort out what I am going to wear. She had already made several expeditions with Antonia to local towns in search of a 'mother of the bride' outfit but so far they had failed to find something suitable.

Antonia was insisting that whatever they chose must tone with the bridesmaids' dresses, which were to be fairy rose pink. "For the photographs," she said. This was a hint which she had gleaned from a wedding magazine. Mops had agreed that this would be a good idea.

'Mops' and 'Pops' were the names which, it had been decided, Antonia was to call her future in-laws, but she wasn't finding it easy to think of them in these rather cosy domestic terms. There was little that was cosy in particular about Penelope Rodmaine, Roger's mother, she was given to organisation and a tendency to recognise the failings of others.

Peter Fullerton, the Functions Manager for Columb Court, now arrived. He was in his fifties, with a full head of elegantly greying hair, a silk tie and the air of someone who has no doubts as to the status of the organisation which he represented.

"Mrs Bradford?" he said. "And Miss Bradford? How nice! No, please – "

Marilyn and Antonia, who had been sitting well forward on the over-stuffed green chairs had started, uncertainly, to rise to greet him; now they subsided again. He himself sat down and placed a file on the low table between them; it was labelled with Antonia and Roger's names and the projected date of the wedding, in late July. The thick cream cover was printed with the Columb Court logo in grey.

"And how are your preparations going?" he asked, smiling inclusively.

"Oh, they're . . . " Marilyn hesitated, transfixed by the elegant, and official, appearance of the file.

"A busy time – " Peter Fullerton suggested, "but especially so for the mother of the bride?"

His tone was sympathetic but from that point on, Marilyn thought, everything got more and more worrying as he proceeded to outline what he called the 'our Columb Court ethos'.

The first problem was shoes. High heels were banned in the actual house by the hotel management because of the likelihood of damage to the wooden floors. A note to this effect should be included in the wedding invitations and guests who ignored the instruction would be asked to remove their footwear.

At this point both Marilyn and Antonia were washed with relief that they were both wearing, as it was winter, leather boots with relatively low heels.

Peter Fullerton continued: both the menu and the floral arrangements must be chosen from a list provided by the hotel, and similar restrictions applied to the musical entertainment. Acceptable would be 'stringed orchestral – perhaps a harp or a cello' during the meal and a local, named, Blues Band or approved DJ in the evening.

Antonia summoned the courage to ask why there were these limitations and Peter Fullerton sighed slightly, adjusted his cuffs and explained that the management wished to ensure that all functions held at Columb Court should preserve the ambience of the hotel.

Pink oriental lilies, their first choice for the flowers, were not acceptable in the house itself although perhaps, Peter Fullerton conceded, they might be possible in the marquee where the wedding breakfast was to be served. His tone suggested that he could not imagine why anyone would want to chose pink lilies. "The stamens," he pointed out, "would of course have to be removed to prevent staining."

One of the tall double doors of the Green Drawing Room was now opened. They all turned towards it.

The nano waist receptionist, entering, apologised for the interruption. "The electricians would like to test the fire alarms," she said to Peter Fullerton. "I could ask them to wait but they say it will take an hour and as it's already after four . . ."

"Ah . . ." he glanced at the watch beneath his immaculate cuff. "Well . . . I think perhaps we have covered most points."

He turned to Marilyn and Antonia. "Would you have any further queries at this stage?"

Realising that they were expected to say no, they both hastened to say it: no, no, they had no further queries.

"Then maybe we can leave things here for now. We will make arrangements for your date to be booked and the further details can be sorted out in due course."

They nodded in total agreement, rose to their feet and were ushered by nano waist back into the imposing hall. The meeting seemed to have taken, and indeed had taken, not much time, barely twenty minutes.

"It being January," Peter Fullerton said as he accompanied them, "we close the hotel to guests so that we can carry out necessary refurbishment. As the building is of national importance all our systems like the fire alarms of course have to be fully serviced."

As they emerged into the huge tile-paved porch and found the winter afternoon had closed in over the wide lawns and the dark cedars a cacophony of sound began to ring out behind them.

They hastened to escape the racket and to get into their car and drive away. For Marilyn the alarms jangled her nerves considerably and seemed to convey an ominous warning that all this was not going to work out well.

Thinking about the whole experience on the way home and hitting the local rush hour, she felt panic envelope her on two levels, at thoughts of all the organisation which the wedding was going to take and more immediately at having to negotiate the heavy traffic. A driver blared his horn at them on a roundabout and twice Antonia cried, "Oh Mum, do be careful!"

When Clive returned from Sweden later that week and was informed of the details of Marilyn and Antonia's interview with Peter Fullerton, he said the whole thing was ridiculous, if you were paying you should be able to have what you wanted, within reason. "And why don't they carpet the place and stop all this nonsense about shoes and floor boards?"

"It's because it's the original décor, Dad," Antonia said, somewhat crushed herself, but determined to defend her choice.

It seemed, unfortunately, that the wedding preparations were not getting off to a good start.

CHAPTER 2

APRIL

James Lacock awoke to the thought that he loathed not having enough money.

He had known that taking on Trevean, this ancient house in Cornwall, would prove to be a disaster.

Life had become filled with people and things with which he couldn't cope, with which in fact he didn't want to cope. His mind formed a familiar, if non-specific prayer for divine intervention. Oh God!

Only Sally his wife was his earthly salvation, for she protected him from the day to day awfulness.

Deep within him he suppressed the thought that if he were not married to Sally he wouldn't be in this situation. He would not be living at Trevean. He wouldn't have to spend his days surrounded by young children, or put up with that awful old harridan Clarissa, his mother-in-law.

Sally stirred beside him in the four-poster bed with the lumpy mattress, her waking mind beginning to fill with details of the numerous demands on her time and energy. James, the children, her mother, the meals, the animals and the garden volunteers, the state of the house, all claimed her attention, along with her part-time teaching job. Also, there was something yet again wrong with the car. However, as she opened her eyes she saw the sun was shining through the mullioned windows and she remembered that she had plans for tackling the kitchen garden. Being positive by nature this thought cheered her up.

Clarissa Seaton, Sally's mother, who lived with them at Trevean, was also awake. She lay thinking how upsetting she found it to watch James being so ineffectual and Sally so overworked. She must move away. But where could she go?

Along the corridor the three Lacock children slept on, for which blessing, had he thought about it, James might have thanked heaven. Frankie, who was aged four, had only recently stopped waking at dawn every morning. When he woke he howled and the only way to quieten him was for Sally to take him downstairs or to bring him into their bed, neither of which possibilities was particularly welcome to James. His own need of Sally's physical presence and exclusive interest was great. He sighed heavily.

"It'll be all right," Sally murmured in automatic response as she glanced at the clock and shut her eyes again.

"I don't see how." James sat up and gazed through the patch of sunlight falling on the dusty Chinese rug which bridged the gap between the bed and the door.

"The garden," Sally said. "It'll bring people in. Make us some money."

"It's a wilderness."

"People like wildernesses. Anyway, we're getting it sorted out, the volunteers are sorting it."

"That Ned fellow's not much use."

"Well . . . he's free labour."

"He eats, he's not free."

Sally realised that she was now awake. "He needs to be directed. We need to tell him what to do a bit more, and a time to get it done by."

James groaned.

"I'll sort it out," Sally said.

James pushed back eiderdown and blankets. These had surely been on the bed when he had inherited the house and its contents from his cousin Lavinia. The blankets had 'Trevean White Room' stitched into one corner in blue wool.

He wore the old pyjamas he'd favoured for years, thick striped cotton with a proper woven cord.

"He's fifty-eight," Sally thought tenderly of James as he shrugged on his mothy camel hair dressing gown and opened the bedroom door. He was eighteen years older than her. In his heart, she knew, he did not wish to be in Cornwall but in India.

James had gone to India after leaving Oxford, a lonely, immature young man, uncertain what to do with himself. There he had experienced some sort of emotional epiphany, falling in love with the country, the life and the people. He had taken a teaching job and stayed.

He was head of department in a private college in Delhi when Sally entered his life, bursting into it like a stream of clear water, carrying him off his feet. She came to teach English in the college for a year, by way of a career break.

James went down the back stairs to the kitchen where he riddled the range which theoretically, but ineffectively, heated the water for the house. He pondered the fact that Sally didn't seem to mind about having a bath in two inches of tepid water, she said she didn't stay in it long enough to mind. James himself knew that he rarely felt really warm in this climate, and here at Trevean even the chance of a long hot soak was denied him.

The dogs got out of their baskets to greet him, all three were spaniels, two-year-old Coal was black and more boisterous than his mother and sister, Tish and Tash, who were both brown and white. James talked to them for a minute or two and fondled their ears. "You are dear dogs," he told them. On the whole, with the exception of Sally, he preferred dogs to people.

He looked in the coke bucket, which was nearly empty. This would necessitate a trip down to the cellar which he disliked, a dark subterranean area divided up into bays; there was no electricity down there and it was damp, with heavy metal grills over coal shoots. In one bay there was a pile of ancient mouldering straw and a chain attached to a ring in the wall, presumably the bed of some long dead mastiff.

"Like the hound of the bloody Baskervilles," James said to himself. He decided against going to the cellar and switched on the electric kettle, the aluminium one on the range would take for ever.

As he waited for the water to boil James reflected that Sally could, and probably would, fetch up the coke. She said she was strong and certainly she seemed to be so, both physically and emotionally. She pulled him through.

He opened the outside door and the dogs rushed out, joyfully evicting Merilla, dowager cat and her off-spring from their cardboard boxes in the back porch and surging, barking into the laundry yard. The cats were of no interest to James, dogs understood you, cats didn't.

James set about making a pot of tea for himself and Sally. He liked making tea; he liked the ordered routine of it: the warming of the pot, counting the tea bags (he preferred leaf tea but Sally seldom bought it for it was more expensive), ensuring that the pot was thoroughly warmed and the water at the correct level of boil, setting the tray with the right cups, the milk and sugar and spoons.

Life was a messy, distressing business by and large, he clung to small routines such as this to bring him fleetingly to oases of calm. Occasionally he thought of the tea plantations running up the slopes of the hills above Shimla where he used to go on leave during the college vacations; the sun and the clear mountain air, and the distant Himalayas.

When the tea was made James let the dogs back in and set off, carrying the tray, along the slate flagged kitchen passage to the hall. Here there was a walk-in sized granite fireplace with above it a stuffed pike in a glass case and two mounted fox masks.

These relics of the chase dated from the time of a Victorian Lacock who had made a fortune from tin mining and married an up-country wife who wished for increased social status.

To please her therefore her husband had begun to upgrade Trevean from ancient barton to gentleman's residence. Sally said that it was fortunate he did not complete his project as the wing he had added, which contained the dining room and the children's bedrooms, was dark and gloomy with much cast iron pipework and pitch pine panel work on view. He had, apparently, wanted to demolish the whole house and rebuild it on this model but died before his plans were fulfilled. The tin mines began to fail not long after, bringing the Lacocks' period of relative wealth to a close.

James didn't look about him, he was concentrating on not

tripping over the dogs or dropping the tray. "On!" he urged them. "Get on, will you!"

Coal bounced around his legs, throwing his head back, tongue lolling and ears flopping. Tish and Tash wove about, more sedately. "On!" James commanded with little effect. "Up!"

All three dogs finally forged ahead, up the wide staircase. This was another Victorian improvement and surmounted by a stained-glass window presenting the Lacock crest, which was based on tin ingots and therefore, as James had pointed out to Sally, unlikely to be of great antiquity.

"Oh well, never mind," she said, "it stops the dust showing up too much."

Sally now heard James and the dogs coming and slipped quickly out of bed to open the bedroom door before the cavalcade crashed to a halt outside it. She had on an old cotton nightdress, so much washed in mixed washes that the original flower pattern had become an all-over dull mauve and there was a tear under one arm. "But we never go away to stay anywhere," Sally thought, "so it doesn't matter."

James put the tray on the table on his side of the bed, negotiating a space for it beside the radio, his vitamin pills, a clock whose dial no longer lit up and some library books, two of which fell onto the floor, bringing with them a small drift of dust. "Damn!" he muttered.

The dogs greeted Sally joyously as if they hadn't seen her for days and then retreated to lie in the sunlight on the carpet by the window. She climbed back into bed.

James, before joining her, poured two mugs of tea, with sugar for him, not for Sally, who had announced a decision to try to lose some weight. "What on earth for?" James asked again now. "Sugar gives you energy."

Then he handed across her mug and switched on the Today programme. They listened for a while to the parade of disasters, global and national, which Sally had begun to feel didn't really set you up for the day. But James loved Radio 4; all his working life in India he had listened to the World Service and the BBC News was the familiar around sound to his day. Like the tea making ritual, it gave him comfort, regardless of content. Sally detached her concentration and thought again about the house. It must, somehow, be made to pay for itself.

James had always known that he might inherit Trevean when his Cousin Lavinia died but there was a sufficient element of doubt for him not to keep this in the forefront of his mind. He had only met his cousin a handful of times, he remembered her as always old, she was in fact older than his parents. When as a child he had been taken to visit her he had been transfixed to find twenty-four hours' worth of meals laid out on the dining room table: today's tea and supper, tomorrow's breakfast and lunch. For him her disturbing presence still haunted areas of the house and this was one reason why they rarely used the dining room, eating instead in the more ancient, slate flagged kitchen.

"More tea?" James turned towards Sally.

"Um . . . yes . . . please." She leaned over to hand him her mug.

Trevean had proved a problematic inheritance, run down and severed from the farm and of course the mines which had formerly supplied it with an income. They had debated selling it and remaining in India until James reached retirement age but after weighing up the needs for the children's education and returning to visit the house on a sweet day in early summer when soft tassles of wisteria covered the shadowed Victorian elevation, Sally had been persuaded that they should come back to live in England. "We should give it a go," she said to James.

"It's an opportunity."

By that stage, although still early in their marriage, James had already abdicated any decision-making role.

Their arrival at Trevean had revealed that a good deal was wrong with the structure of the house and that the 'valley garden', laid out by the Victorian Lacock, had become a morass with a bog at the bottom of it and paths lost in rampant bamboos and rhododendrons. The large walled kitchen garden was claimed by brambles and nettles.

The place needed money thrown at it, in large quantities, which unfortunately they didn't have.

James took a teaching post at the local college, but he found instructing the teenagers a culture shock. The day he was faced, on entering the classroom, by a youth leaning back in his chair with his boots on the desk, his upper body clad in a sleeveless black vest, and engaged in picking dust out of his navel, James decided that he couldn't hack it.

"He also said," he told Sally, "that he had no idea what a verb was." His students in India had been polite and clean and had a working knowledge of English grammar.

Sally, taking the pragmatic view that they needed the money, persuaded the Head of Department, who required someone in front of the class, to take her on as a temporary replacement.

Two years later she was still there while James, theoretically, organised things at Trevean. This involved walking the three children to and from school when Sally couldn't run them there in the car, and coping when any builders they could afford came to patch up the beetle-infested timbers, damp walls or leaning chimneys. Latterly there had also been the Planning Department representatives to deal with, who were interested in listing the house. Generally speaking James referred all these people and their queries to Sally, which they found odd.

He did some cooking, but not much for Sally tried to spare him the domestic role which sabotaged his morale. He was used to a different life, a different world, and servants. Lying now in bed Sally ran over in her mind the various-money making schemes she had come up with: free range chickens, breeding pigs or dogs, growing roses for petal confetti. Although evidence of these endeavours remained, none had proved successful.

Most recently the Garden Volunteer scheme had, like the others, also been her idea. She had discovered an organisation which placed student volunteers in historic but run down gardens, to dig and delve and help to restore. After which the garden could, hopefully, be opened to the public, who would then have the chance to appreciate it and contribute to its future upkeep.

After some months of form filling, photograph taking and a visit from a 'smart Alec' (James' opinion) representative from the organisation, they had acquired two young men as volunteers. They were both nineteen, but otherwise, Sally thought, very different kettles of fish, from dissimilar backgrounds.

Ned Lorrimer was public school educated and his parents were based in the Gulf States while Graham Penhale had been raised on a scrubby local small-holding from which his father made a living growing vegetables to supply the town greengrocers. Although Graham was beginning to make inroads into the brambles in the kitchen garden Ned's impact on the jungle in the valley so far seemed minimal, but Sally remained optimistic that the scheme to open the gardens would work out.

Now the rest of the house began to wake up.

Clarissa Seaton, Sally's mother, who was seventy this year, struggled out of bed and pulled on her threadbare Chinese silk dressing gown. Clutching her walking stick she set off on the risky journey to the lavatory, oddly located on a landing half way down the main staircase, possibly on the site of a medieval garderobe, for this part of the house dated from before 1500.

Clarissa feared tripping but at least she would not be running the risk, as she would if she used the bathroom, of James rattling the door handle and telling Sally loudly that, "Your mother's bagged the bog again!"

Clarissa's opinion of James was very low indeed; why Sally had married him she could not imagine. He was too old and softened up by years of living the colonial lifestyle, and what sort of career for a man was it anyway, teaching foreigners? He had saddled Sally with three children and virtually no income. None of this Clarissa chose to keep to herself: the children, and indeed Sally and James themselves were quite used to hearing Clarissa's monologues on the subject of James' inadequacies.

"There goes Blind Pew," James said now, setting down his cup on the bedside table, as Clarissa's stick tapped on the carpet runner outside their door.

"Don't," Sally said, "please."

"I've got to get some fun out of life."

"I know darling, but it doesn't help."

James sighed; Sally was his lifeline, but her mother was an old witch.

In what was still called the night nursery, three-year-old Frankie and Claud who was seven, woke up and also made a beeline for the lavatory, although in their case this was in the children's green painted Victorian bathroom. The two of them succeeded in spraying wee all over the place. Then shrieking with laughter, they raced along the corridor to fling open the door to James and Sally's room.

"Wee! Wee!" Frankie cried joyfully.

"You haven't been making a mess have you?" Sally asked.

"Not too much," Claud said carefully, for he was a truthful child. "Is it a home day today?"

"Yes," Sally said.

"Swimming!" Frankie shrieked.

"Um. Maybe." Sally tried to gather her thoughts on what she needed to do today On her list were food shopping, the washing, check Ned and Graham's progress in the gardens. College marking could wait . . . Lunch . . .

The summer term started this week at the college where she taught and at the children's school, life would become more hectic.

"Swimming!" Frankie shrieked again, scrambling onto their bed and bouncing.

James groaned. "He's on my feet!"

"Off!" Sally commanded. "Off, now! It's time to get dressed."

The general kerfuffle had roused the dogs and they began to weave around the bed and Coal gave an explorative bark.

"No!" James yelled. "Down!"

"Right, that's it," Sally said, pushing back the eiderdown, "go and find your clothes, I'm just coming."

The boys rushed away to their room and Sally followed, digging around when she got there in the muddle of socks and pants, which she never got round to properly sorting. "Life's too short," she thought.

Claud was beginning to object to various garments, on the grounds of colour or tightness, but Frankie still didn't care what he wore and now trundled downstairs in crumpled green shorts and a pink T-shirt with 'Poppet' printed in spangles on the front; it must Sally supposed have belonged long ago to Perdita, who was now ten.

Sally opened Perdita's bedroom doors and called, "Time to get up!" Then she followed the younger two down the back stairs which were steep and wooden, having been once perhaps the servants' access to the upper floors. Now they formed part of the rackety race track the children took around the house on wet afternoons.

Breakfast happened at the kitchen table, which was massively long, its surface marked by generations' worth of food preparation, and slightly soapy from years of kitchen maids' scrubbing. "Though not so much of that recently," Sally thought plonking two cereal packets down in front of Claud and Frankie. "It's this or this. Which do you want?"

She cleared a space by pushing aside some of the flotsam which as usual covered most of the table's surface. This included an empty dog food tin, the water jug from last night's supper, two plastic toy cars, a quantity of opened and unopened envelopes and some mostly dry laundry.

Frankie up-ended one of the cereal packets. "All gone," he announced.

"Will there be porridge?" Claud asked, with his usual tact, indicating that porridge would be nice but there was no problem if it was not available. Sally wondered sometimes where Claud got it from, this gift for conciliation, and Perdita too. These, her two older children, had an instinctive feeling for diplomacy not noticeable in the youngest. Frankie, aged four, had a demanding personality out of proportion to his chronological position in the family hierarchy.

"Yes," she said now to Claud, "there will be porridge, when I've made it, but if you're hungry have cereal."

"It's yuck," said Frankie, pushing away the other packet.

"No, it's not. It's good for you."

"Tastes like yuck."

"Well then you'll have to wait for the porridge."

Perdita arrived, tidy, hair brushed. "Is it toast?" she asked.

Toast was made on the hot plate of the range and was usually blackened and slightly sticky and metallic tasting. There were often complaints.

"Cereal!" Sally said, suddenly exasperated. "And will someone please take Granny's tray up."

"It's Perdita's turn." Claud said, factually.

"All right." If there was going to be a row about the breakfast Perdita was quite glad to get out of the way, being a peaceable child.

She checked the tray as she carried it up the stairs, for her mother could have forgotten something. Sally dealt in wide sweeps of ideas. Perdita already worried about the details. The sliver teapot, the silver sugar bowl, both tarnished; the china cup and saucer because Clarissa didn't like to drink tea from a mug; the plate with two slices of bread, margarine, (butter too expensive), a tea spoon, a small knife – all were there. Clarissa didn't eat the metallic toast.

"Is it poisonous?" Perdita had once asked Sally, worried by Clarissa's comments.

"We're all alive and kicking aren't we?" Sally had answered.

"No, it's not."

Clarissa was sitting up in bed. Her bedroom had been intended as a dressing-room when the house was revamped in the 1880s. It was narrow and rather cramped, furnished, like her sitting room, with furniture which she had brought with her when she came to live at Trevean.

The reasons why Clarissa had come to live with her daughter

and son-in-law were financial, practical and emotional. She had long been widowed, her income was not now enough to support her house in Kent; she sold it and gave Sally most of the proceeds, which were ploughed into the building works at Trevean.

Practically, Sally had been beginning to worry about Clarissa living alone; emotionally Clarissa craved her daughter and her grandchildren. Her moving into two rooms at Trevean made perfectly good sense, a big sunny sitting room and a former dressing room. Good sense however does not necessarily produce domestic harmony.

CHAPTER 3

APRIL

Clarissa Seaton smiled at Perdita, her favourite grandchild, who had brought her breakfast tray.

"Thank you," she said. "Is everything here?"

It was still the school holidays, , the children and Sally would be home all day, which cheered her.

"Yes," Perdita said. She put the tray carefully on Clarissa's bedside table.

Sometimes Perdita visited Clarissa in her bedroom or her sitting room just to check that she was there. She liked her grandmother to be there, although after they had talked for a while she might start to feel trapped, sensing that Clarissa also needed her, but too much. Then Perdita would make excuses and run away, along the top corridor or down the stairs.

Clarissa poured tea into her cup. "Who made my tea?" she asked. It was too strong; of course, James had made it.

"Mummy," Perdita said, standing by the dressing table looking at Clarissa's ivory backed hair brush with the bristles worn down on one side and the white hairs trapped in it. Clarissa would comb the hairs out daily, wrapping them around two fingers and then dropping them into the waste paper basket. She called this one of her little chores.

Perdita thought how her mother, Sally, did not have little chores, she had Things To Do, of which she sometimes made lists. People's hair would not be high on a list, especially in the school holidays. Sally would only reject a hair brush if it was chock full of hair and nearly unusable and then she might attack it with whatever came to hand, a pencil or the handle of a teaspoon while Frankie, if it was his turn to be brushed, tried to escape.

Clarissa didn't say anything about the tea being too strong. "Can you fetch my marmalade?" she asked instead. She kept her small pots of marmalade and jam in a cupboard in her sitting room for she liked brands with what she described as 'real fruit' in them and not the bulk buys from the cash-and-carry which were now staple fare for the family. The Garden Volunteers Scheme, Sally had discovered, qualified them for a cash and carry card and she bought catering size supplies, jam as well as the marmalade, dog food tins by the box, rice in a woven sack, a huge tin of instant coffee.

Sally regularly collected Clarissa's pension for her and took her shopping list into the village, which was too far for Clarissa to walk. Clarissa would say, 'Buy something for yourself, too' wishing that this could be a magazine perhaps, something like Homes and Gardens, or some nice soap but Sally would if anything buy two pounds of mince for a shepherd's pie or flea powder for the dogs.

Occasionally Sally would drive Clarissa into the village, but then there were problems. James hated being left behind, but if he came too Clarissa would sulk and the children could not be left. Sally was torn between them all.

Perdita fetched the marmalade from the cupboard built under the window seat in Clarissa's sitting room. She considered, as she carried it through to Clarissa, the difference between Granny's marmalade and their marmalade. She held the jar to the light, this was dark orange with thick bits in it, while theirs was pale orange and more solid, with not many bits.

"Can you sit and talk to me?" Clarissa asked Perdita now. She wanted company.

Perdita stood, uncertain. "I've got to have breakfast," she said, but then remembered. "Mummy is still making the porridge."

She sat on the edge of the bed.

"What are you going to be doing today?" Clarissa asked her.

Perdita wasn't sure. "We might go swimming."

Clarissa thought, 'So I'll be left alone.'

She drank some of the acrid tea. "Tell Mummy I need some shopping," she said with an edge to her voice. "This marmalade is nearly finished. And some more face cream." Then repenting, for she could not be annoyed with Sally, she added, "Only when she has time."

She spread the marmalade. "What are you doing in school?"

Perdita considered. "How people lived," she said. "And we've got to talk to a really old person. Can I talk to you?"

"Am I really old?"

"Well – quite old. Aren't you?"

"Yes," Clarissa said. "Quite old."

"Can I talk to you then?"

"What about?"

"What it was like when you were young? What you did in school?"

"We had to practise our writing," Clarissa said. "We had to copy out our spellings. Each spelling mistake, we had to write it out ten times."

"I'm not very good at spelling," Perdita said.

"You have to learn the rules." Clarissa spread margarine on her second piece of toast and wished it was butter, but there was the expense again and nowadays also the fuss about cholesterol. "'i before e, except after c'. Do you know that rule?"

"Yes, Perdita said. "but I don't think it always works."

"Well," Clarissa considered. "Nearly always."

"But you weren't a teacher, like Mummy, were you? You were a nurse."

Clarissa said, "I was a nurse in a big hospital in London."

Perdita knew the stories.

"I worked in the Operating Theatre. I helped the surgeons."

"Cutting people up," Perdita said.

"Yes."

"To make them better?"

"Yes."

Perdita wrinkled her nose.

"What?" Clarissa asked.

"It is a bit yuk."

"Not really." Clarissa said. "Do you want to lick this spoon?"

"Yes please." Perdita tasted the marmalade on her tongue.

Clarissa thought back to her younger self, in her nurse's uniform. The aprons, the caps, the cuffs she wore then. She remembered Sister Daniels on the Maternity Wards, she was always critical, one nurse or another was permanently in tears. It upset the patients, all new mothers, they used to cry too partly from post-natal depression, partly in sympathy with the weeping nurses.

"I've got to write it down," Perdita said. "What you say."

"Maybe later." Clarissa finished her cup of tea. "I must get up now. Can you go and see if the bathroom's empty?"

Perdita jumped down the two steps outside Clarissa's room and went along the corridor far enough to see that the bathroom door was open.

Returning to her grandmother she said, "Yes, it is."

Clarissa put her feet out of bed. Perdita looked at them, seeing the dry, mauvish skin. She wriggled her bare toes in her sandals and wondered if her own feet would look like that one day and hoped they would not.

"I better go now," she said. "Because I expect the porridge is ready."

Clarissa said. "Say thank you to Mummy for me." When Perdita left she felt bereft.

Breakfast was still underway in the kitchen although James had removed himself to his study, the hurly burly was too much for him.

Graham Penhale, one of the Garden Volunteers, had arrived with a copy of a book on growing organic fruit and vegetables which Sally had leant him. He was familiar with most of the information it contained but he used it to provide protection from the Lacocks. He had fathomed that at Trevean it was acceptable to read at breakfast although not at any other meal.

When Sally had discovered that Graham's father had a small holding and produced vegetables for sale, she told Graham that he was manna from heaven. She took him up to the walled kitchen garden, opened the wooden door onto the acreage of grass, weeds and brambles and said, "It's all yours."

James found Graham uncommunicative to the point of deliberate surliness. "He's less than mono-syllabic," he said. "For all we know he might be the silent axe murderer."

"Spade murderer, maybe?" Sally said. "I think he's harmless, really. And if he can grow us some veg, well 'Alleluia!' say I, he's welcome."

James considered. "Asparagus?" he suggested hopefully.

"I think that takes several years, darling, and probably a team of under gardeners, mulching."

Sally, thinking about Graham, reflected that he hadn't a hope of going to a smart Agricultural College as Ned Lorrimer, their other volunteer, was supposed to be doing in the autumn, for Graham lacked A-levels and, as James pointed out, interview skills. Socially, she sensed, he felt totally out of his depth at Trevean. And yet Graham had far more feel than Ned for the garden, and caring for plants; life, Sally thought, was indeed not fair.

Now Graham sat spooning porridge into his mouth and staring fixedly at a page in his book which described, with diagrams, the pruning of fruit trees.

Sally turned her attention to Frankie who was objecting to lumps in his porridge. "Horrible!" He pushed his bowl away, slopping milk onto the table.

"Eat it up, please," Sally said, pulling a tea towel off the back of her chair to mop up the mess.

"Don't like it!"

"Yes, you do, it's just the same as it always is."

Claud, being the sweet natured child he was, said encouragingly to Frankie, "I'm eating mine, look! It's nice."

Frankie glared at him. "Go away!"

"I'll make a bargain with you," Sally said, getting fed up. "Eat this bit – " she divided the porridge in his bowl into two. "Just this half, see?"

"Jam." Frankie stared down at the table, steely eyed.

"You don't get jam with porridge."

Frankie howled.

"Oh for heaven's sake!" Sally fetched the cash and carry jam from a cupboard and dolloped a spoonful onto Frankie's plate. "Now get on with it please, I've got things to do this morning."

She looked at Claud, who was watching, spoon poised. "Do you want some too?"

"Yes please."

"Perdita?"

"No thank you, it doesn't look very nice."

"Don't say that about food. We're lucky to have it."

Graham shuffled his feet and turned the page of his book, moving from details on training espalier apple trees to pruning pears. The meal time arguments put him off his food. He usually took sandwiches up to the kitchen garden for his midday meal; he liked a bit of peace and quiet when he was eating. Two meals a day with the family were as much, he reckoned, as he could manage. The Lacocks didn't eat cooked dinner at midday as he was used to at home, but supper in the evening.

"Granny said she has a shopping list," Perdita said.

"Oh." Sally sighed. She was watching Frankie eat his jammy porridge. "Good boy, well done."

When everyone had finished eating and the table had been pretty much cleared, the children dumping their bowls and plates in the sink, Sally noticed the empty bucket beside the range and went down into the cellar to fill it. In the process she noticed that they were nearly out of coal. She thought, 'I ought to order in a load for the winter while it's on summer prices.'

But this, at the moment, was not an option. How much simpler life would be if they had some spare money.

She put a shovelful of coal into the stove and then went up to see Clarissa. "Duty visit," she instructed herself as she climbed the front stairs. "Don't get rattled."

She tried to visit Clarissa in her sitting room at least twice a day, in the morning and the evening. She knew that her mother clung to her emotionally.

Clarissa was dressed and tidying her hair. She remembered, and sometimes told the children, that before she was widowed, before she sold her own house, before she moved into Trevean, she had been considered well dressed. She still received Harvey Nichols and Harrods catalogues but now she did not buy anything from them. Perdita believed that her grandmother's well-dressedness manifested itself in her always wearing stockings, while Sally went bare legged all summer.

Clarissa was still smarting with the knowledge that she was to be left at the house while the rest of the family gadded off to the beach.

"Good morning, Mother," Sally made her voice determinedly bright. "How are you?"

Clarissa sniffed. "I'm out of marmalade and face cream. But I gather that you won't be going into the village."

"Yes, I will. I've got some food shopping to do."

"Oh. Perdita said you were all going to the sea."

"Maybe this afternoon, but I've got lots of things to sort out today."

Clarissa, slightly mollified, reached for her handbag. "James will be playing golf I suppose?"

James' love of golf was fairly high on Sally's list of things to worry about, because of course they couldn't afford it, the club membership fees were increasing each year. Already James had stopped going to the Club House bar after a game because of the cost of standing a round. But he had a low handicap and he got on with one or two of the other members, some of the few locals of whom this could be said. Golf, or the prospect of it, was the only thing which on a bad day could lift his spirits. So Sally knew that the money to pay for it must be found.

Clarissa thought differently. What right had James to be spending money and time on golf when Sally had to work to pay for the food on the table and the clothes on the children's backs? She knew Sally was upset by criticism of James, but irritation and anxiety gnawed at her and flared in a scattering of spiteful comments. Even if she managed to hold her tongue Sally could interpret silences. Recriminations and denials followed, sometimes tears.

"Oh mother," Sally said now, "please don't start all that again. Anyway, it means I can take the children swimming."

It's not, Clarissa thought, that I grudge the children going swimming. It's that I'm excluded, left behind again.

She sniffed. "Of course."

"It's all James has really got, that he enjoys," Sally said, feeling her exasperation levels rising. "You know that."

"Well, why can't he find a job that he enjoys?" Clarissa demanded, resentment curdling like acid lava below her ribs. "If he can't teach, why can't he do something else?"

"Please Mother, not now. James is very good at teaching, but just not the sort of teaching that's needed here. I'll get your face cream."

"And the marmalade. There's some money in my bag."

"All right."

Sally picked up Clarissa's tray and then went along the corridor to the playroom. Claud and Frankie were here, building a tower of lego from bricks which formed part of the layer of toy debris covering the floor. Crayons, colouring books, some pieces of a plastic tea set, pots of dried up poster paint, small toy cars, a ramp for the cars made from cardboard boxes, several toy animals – all these lay scattered over the worn carpet.

"I'm going to the village," Sally said. "Do you want to come?"

"Yes!" Both boys scrambled to their feet and surged towards her, squashing jetsam underfoot.

"Go up to the top yard then. Run, don't keep Daddy waiting. He's already gone up with the dogs."

Their current car, which was an old Volvo, chosen for its size and cheapness, was garaged in the former cart shed, beside the kitchen garden. It wouldn't start.

James sighed, leaning back in the passenger seat, as Sally several times tried the ignition. "It's flooded," he said, defeated and despairing. He preferred Sally to drive, which pleased the children for James himself was a nervy and erratic driver on the rare occasions when he drove them somewhere himself.

Claud, Frankie and the three dogs began to shift around restlessly on the back seat.

"It may be out of petrol," Sally said. Money again. She hadn't settled their account with the local garage for the last six weeks and had often been driving on a wing and a prayer, the indicator hovering on red, while she avoided the garage proprietor and bought a few pounds' worth of fuel elsewhere. "Or maybe it's the starter motor. We're going to have to try to settle Jack Richards' bill and get him to have a look at it."

Typically, Sally approached problems by talking about them and then she would propose how they might be tackled. For James the mere acknowledgement of the difficulty gave it a horrible validity which he would prefer to ignore.

Now he fell back in his seat; evidence of their poverty constantly demoralised him. He didn't deal with the practical demands of life at all well but he had been in the position before they came home and took over Trevean of being able to pay other people to deal with them for him. With this option removed he was sunk.

"You steer and I'll push," Sally said, climbing from the driving seat. She opened one of the back doors of the car. "Come on boys, go and stand out of the way."

For James this was hideous. He had a dodgy back; of course Sally shouldn't push, he couldn't push. Why was life so bloody awful?

Claud and Frankie had been through all this before. "Oh no!" they chorused together, scrambling out and running off, shrieking and laughing. The dogs followed them barking.

Graham coming up the steps from the laundry yard was startled to find Sally pushing the Volvo, the more so when he saw James, despondent, now in the driving seat. His opinion of James sunk even lower, what sort of man expected his wife to push him in a car?

Sally, catching sight of Graham, waved to him to come and help. They both shoved while James, grim faced, put the car into second gear. The engine hiccoughed a couple of times but then died. In the end Graham fetched jump leads from his own car, a Vauxhall of sufficient age for him to be able to do the maintenance himself.

The Volvo clunked eventually into life. Sally called to Claud and Frankie who were jumping on and off the old mounting block and told them to get back in the car. Then they drove slowly out of the yard.

"Tash's standing on me!" Frankie wailed. The dogs liked to stick their heads out of the window and let the wind blow in their ears.

"Can you sort them out?" Sally asked James, she was concentrating on keeping the revs of the engine up in case it stalled.

"Sit down!" James twisted his head round. "Good dogs, sit down!" He ignored the children. The dogs barked joyously and Coal crashed through the gap between the seats to reach James' lap. Claud and Frankie both yelled.

The car headed up the back drive, in reality a farm track, which lead to the road to the village.

When James and Sally had first arrived at Trevean the shopkeepers in the village had hoped for large orders from the Big House but after a few months they realised that the old lady's nephew and his wife were either skinflints or broke. The latter seemed the most likely for it was known that they did not do mega-shops at the local town supermarket. Mince, sausages and a piece of pork for Sunday; sliced bread, margarine, cabbage and a whole sack of potatoes told the butcher, grocer and greengrocer how things were with the Lacocks. It was noted when they started going to the cash and carry.

None-the-less their shopping expeditions to the village, car rattling, dogs barking, usually with several of the children in tow, was always an interesting sight to the locals and worthy of comment.

Today as usual James quailed at the prospect of being stared at and cross-questioned in the street about what was happening to the gardens up at the house. Sally looked at him and saw that he was going to hate being dragged around the shops.

"Come into the newsagents and pick up the Telegraph," she

said, "and then you can go to The Lion and I'll meet you there in half-an-hour."

"Where are you going?" James' heart rose a flicker at the prospect of a quiet drink, though he would have preferred Sally to be with him.

"Nowhere much – butcher, a couple of things for mother."

James sighed.

Sally said, "I won't be long."

In the post-office-cum-newsagents Ivor Morton the proprietor pulled a hard-backed notebook from beneath the counter and stated that their account was owing for four copies of Country Life and sixteen copies of the Telegraph which were delivered to Trevean along with the post.

"Have you got any money?" Sally asked James.

"No," James said with finality.

"Sweets!" Frankie announced standing four-square in front of the shelves which held wine gums, jellytots, fruit lollies and a wealth of other temptation.

"No," Sally said. "No sweets now."

Ivor Morton squared up the notebook on the counter and pursed his lips.

"When we've finished the shopping," Sally said to Frankie. "Maybe. If you've been good."

Frankie picked up a packet of fruit pastels.

"No, I've said no." Sally grabbed his hand and returned the sweets to the shelf. "I'll come back in quarter of an hour or so and settle up," she called to Ivor Morton as she made for the door, propelling Frankie who was now howling, through the queue of people waiting behind them.

They exited the shop, James' face expressing his fatalistic acceptance of the ghastliness always to be expected on family outings.

Claud, distracted and vague, followed behind. He had seen a plastic water pistol on the circular rack of cheap toys by the window and was wishing he could buy it. He turned the idea over in his mind but knew it was no good asking now. Claud was a noticing and accommodating child. Frankie swung from Sally's hand and continued to yell.

"I'll get some cash in the grocers," Sally said to James. "From the machine. Perhaps we ought to stop Country Life. Do you read it much? I never really get the time."

"Another," he thought. He had taken to counting coffin nails, awarding one to every small blow dealt to his favoured way of life, working towards a score of five hundred, at which point if reached he would pop his clogs. This idea amused him, but he kept it to himself; Sally laughed at his jokes, but possibly not at this one.

CHAPTER 4

APRIL

At half past seven on this bright, early summer morning Clive and Marilyn Bradford were eating breakfast in their kitchen. Most unusually their younger daughter Imogen had decided to join them.

The Bradfords lived in a modern detached house on a private suburban development, it had been built long enough ago to allow the Leylandii hedges which separated their garden from those on either side to grow to a height of about twenty feet. This was an on-going source of annoyance to Clive; he would have liked to cut the trees back but their neighbours resisted the proposal, citing loss of privacy.

Called The Rowans although there was no rowan tree in the garden, the house was identical in plan to the others in Glebe Road, and indeed to most of the houses which made up The Glebe estate. In some cases owners had added a degree of individuality to their properties by the addition of a kitchen extension or a 'sun room'. In one case a hot tub had been added on the back patio, but the people who put this in had not stayed long and the next owners, having more sensitivity to what suited the neighbourhood, had it removed.

The Bradfords had been living at The Rowans for two years now but so far they had not made any real friendships on The Glebe.

Imogen Bradford, aged seventeen, sat sulkily stirring skimmed milk into her slimmers'cereal.

"I hate this stuff," she said.

Her parents did not respond. Marilyn wished that Antonia was here to counter Imo's complaints, for the ongoing arguments wore her out. Clive, scanning a plastics trade journal, already had half his mind on the details of shipping containers which awaited him at the factory. He tended, in point of fact, to agree with Imo about the muesli but was attempting from long habit to support Marilyn who could far too easily get upset.

Antonia, who was older than Imogen by three years, was responsible for the muesli. She had got the idea into her head that the whole family should go on a diet in preparation for her wedding in July. It was necessary, Antonia insisted, that she, Imogen and their mother Marilyn should each drop at least one dress size before the wedding day.

Antonia also wanted her father Clive to look 'distiguished' for the walk down the aisle. Everyone suspected that she meant 'thinner'.

"The Diet," she said in the tone of voice which gave the words initial capitals and indicated a chronic edge of panic, "won't work unless we all do it!"

Antonia however did not live at home but in a shared flat in

London with two other girls and also she had a job in catering. Imo suspected that Antonia's version of The Diet was nicer and surely more varied than theirs, for Marilyn was not an imaginative cook and had been producing unexciting salads and fat free yogurts for the past month.

Butter, full milk, jam, biscuits and baked beans were off the shopping list, oven chips forbidden and also bread except for one slice of toast for breakfast. In fact, no ingredients for a quick snack were now available in the kitchen and with these Imo had been accustomed to feed herself, so avoiding as far as possible having to eat with her parents. She got quite a lot of satisfaction from replying to a summons to meals, "No thanks, I'm not hungry."

Clive Bradford had initially been pleased, proud even, when his elder daughter became engaged to Roger Rodmaine who worked for a firm of City investment analysts, but lately he had found his enthusiasm decreasing. The Diet and Marilyn and Antonia's total preoccupation with wedding plans were beginning to grate on his nerves. The two of them talked lengthily and almost daily on the phone of invitation lists, church service sheets, ivory versus white for the wedding dress, pale pink or dark pink for the bridesmaids, vintage or not for cars to the church, flowers in the church, flowers for the bouquets, flowers in the hotel, seating plans and menus.

Marilyn, whose nerves frayed easily if she was faced with unfamiliar or taxing situations, had become prone to flooding bouts of tears.

Clive frequently travelled to promote sales for his small plastics moulding company, in Europe and Scandinavia and increasingly in the Middle East. He wanted to provide well for his family and had sent Antonia and Imo to a fee-paying girls' school with a nice uniform which had pleased Marilyn but he also believed that he knew the value of money and was beginning to feel that this wedding was going to cost him an arm and a leg.

He had been further disconcerted to discover that the Rodmaines, Roger's parents, were not planning to contribute to that cost. Antonia made it sound as if they would be quite shocked by the suggestion.

"Roger says that they expect the bride's father to pay for the wedding," she said. "Because it's traditional."

"Tradition that needs changing, if you ask me," Clive had said.

He continued to think about this and increasingly to suspect that the Rodmaines did not consider his family were good enough and regretted their son's engagement to Antonia, whose parents did not know how things should be done.

It was not a propitious start to the wedding preparations.

Now, eating toast and cholesterol busting margarine, Clive pulled a face. "This doesn't taste of anything, Marilyn. Find the marmalade, can you Imo?"

Most of the time Imo felt that she came second in both her parents' affections to Antonia, their golden girl, and this added to her dissatisfaction with her life and to her sulks. Recently however she and Clive had formed something of an alliance against Antonia's imposition of The Diet.

She went now to look for the marmalade which had been banished to a shelf in the utility room.

"But it's got sugar in it," Marilyn protested; her eyes lingered wistfully on the jar, for she had a sweet tooth.

"Too bad," Clive said. "And a spoon, Imo."

He glanced at his wife's anxious face and said, softening,

"Look – one spoonful's not going to do much damage."

Marilyn was wearing her pink velour dressing gown and had not yet sorted her hair or her make-up for the day. Perched rather uncomfortably on her stool at the kitchen's island unit, she had still an early morning rumpled look. As a young girl she had been pretty and giggly, which at twenty-one Clive had equated absolutely with femininity.

When he first saw Marilyn, they had both been employed by a light engineering company which manufactured valves. She was a junior in the admin department, he a graduate trainee, having just completed his degree at Sheffield University. He had proposed after the firm's Christmas Dance.

Antonia was born a year after they married and Imogen three years later; each of them named for the heroine of one of Marilyn's favoured historical romances.

Antonia took after her mother, soft skinned and fair; she always, as Marilyn put it to herself, looked nice. Antonia had never suffered from the afflictions of teenage appearance, like spots or a desire for unattractive personal adornment.

Imo was different. For two years in her middle teens she had to have braces on her teeth and now she wove coloured wool and beads into her hair, which made it unbrushable. Occasionally she herself wondered if she was a changeling, or the names had got muddled in the maternity ward; she rather wished this was the case.

"So, when my results come – " Imo had decided to grasp the opportunity of her parents being both together in one place and unable to plead alternative distraction, like watching something important on TV. This was the only reason why she had come down to the kitchen so early. "If my grades are good enough, then can I go to Art College?"

She wanted to take a degree in Fine Art, an aspiration which neither Clive not Marilyn, although for different reasons, supported.

"Slapping paint around and making useless objects out of chicken wire and lumps of clay is a waste of three years." Clive swallowed a mouthful of toast. "And money. We've been through all this before."

He felt it was quite enough that he had been persuaded, against his better judgement, to let Imo take a two-year Art Diploma at the local Sixth Form College, instead of the far more sensible A-levels. The chicken wire was a reference to a student installation which he had viewed with disfavour at her end of year show.

Imo felt her heart contract. After her stuffy private school where she had not shone, either socially or academically, Sixth Form College had proved a place of difference and excitement. Especially the Art Studio, where in the company of a rag bag collection of would-be individualists she had first felt that she actually belonged, that she was at last in the right place at the right time.

"Oh, don't start all that again, please Imo," Marilyn pleaded. "You'll be much better off doing something practical."

"Like what?"

"Well – something like Antonia."

Antonia had taken a catering course and had now landed a lovely job with Directors' Lunches, based in the City. She talked impressively about creating smoked chicken and mango blinis and salmon en croute for fifty.

"And look where it's got her!" Marilyn exclaimed.

"Where?" Imo asked irritatingly, for she knew quite well what Marilyn meant.

"Meeting nice girls, and now Roger!"

"I don't want to meet nice girls."

"She's going to have a lovely life!"

"And I don't want – "

"Don't argue with your mother." Clive looked at his watch and pushed his stool back. "Think about getting a job, that's my advice to you, Imo. The sooner the better. Or perhaps I can find something for you to do with us. In fact – " he stood up, "I might see if they could do with some help in Distribution."

"Oh, no – "

"I've got a Rotary meeting tonight Marilyn." Clive headed for the kitchen door.

"But you said you would look at the sample menus!" Marilyn's light voice rose in plaintive reproach.

"What menus?"

"The hotel wedding menus! It's not Thursday, why have you got to go to Rotary?"

"Carnival Committee meeting," Clive said, checking his jacket pocket for car keys. He enjoyed the company of other men with interests similar to his own. Plus, contacts were good for business. Plus an evening at home was currently no way to relax, with Marilyn's continuous requests that he approve florists' estimates and wedding cake designs. Imogen's presence, as she flopped around the house insufficiently occupied was also beginning to irritate him.

Clive kissed Marilyn in passing and left. Outside he pressed the remote for the garage door, got into his three-year-old Jag and drove to work, consciously leaving all thoughts of weddings behind to swirl amongst the pink hybrid tea roses and busy lizzies in the front garden.

He passed Julia Prentice biking up the road to help Marilyn

with the housework and gave her a wave, but he had forgotten her too by the time he reached the first set of traffic lights. Emptying your mind of extraneous distractions was one of Clive's favoured stratagems for successful business management; he saw this ability as a necessary strength.

Behind him Julia Prentice, forty-seven and overweight, pedalled with increasing difficulty up the slope of Glebe Road heading for The Rowans. Eventually she had to dismount. When she reached the house she parked her bike in the narrow passageway between the garage and the hedge and went round to the back door.

"Morning!" she called cheerfully, pausing to draw breath as she came into the kitchen.

Julia had been 'helping' Marilyn twice a week since not long after the Bradfords had moved into The Rowans, when it had dawned upon Marilyn from one or two comments from her new neighbours that doing your own housework was considered inappropriate on The Glebe. She had been invited to a coffee morning where one of the women had actually said to her, "I thought everyone had someone to clean."

Appealed to, Clive had initially said that this was rubbish and she should take no notice but Marilyn had became tearful and protested that she would never make friends here unless she could fit in. Clive had capitulated, saying all right, if fitting in meant getting a cleaner, then get a cleaner. It was fortunate as Marilyn wasn't sure how to go about this that Julia, who had cleaned for the previous owners of The Rowans, had called a couple of days later to see if she would be needed.

Sadly, however, even with Julia turning up visibly on Tuesday and Friday mornings, Marilyn had still not sensed a welcome in The Glebe coffee circle. She felt lonely, and increasingly lately what she described as 'jittery'. She did not know what to do with herself while Julia was engaged in the cleaning, to the extent that she was usually obliged to leave the house, with no purpose other than to occupy the time.

None-the-less Julia possibly provided more comfort and support in her willingness to listen and comment on Marilyn's anxieties about Antonia's wedding than did Clive or Imogen or any of her neighbours. Had this been pointed out to her Marilyn would have been quite upset.

"Hello!" Julia now greeted Imogen, for Marilyn had retreated upstairs, not happy to be found in her dressing gown.

Imo, obeying her natural instinct to avoid unnecessary conversation with the older generation, also rose from her stool and headed for the door.

"And how are you today?" Julia called over her shoulder as she went to hang her bag in the utility room; she was well used to the anti-social habits of teenagers. "Got your exam results yet?"

"No," Imo said. She had tried explaining before that her diploma course was project based, she hadn't taken any exams and was now only waiting for confirmation of her final grades. She couldn't be bothered to go through this again.

"Our Gary's still waiting on his results," Julia said.

Imo knew this too, although what results these were, exactly, she wasn't sure. The only fact that she had taken on board about Julia's son Gary, who was a year younger than her, was that he had lost his magazine delivery job when it was discovered that he was dumping most of the magazines behind a block of garages.

"We're not expecting too much," Julia said, heading for the J-cloths under the sink. "Your Mum'll be in the shower will she?"

"I don't know," Imo said. "She was here."

"She'll be down," Julia said. "I'll just get on."

Imogen slipped quietly from the kitchen and Julia moved the plates and mugs from the kitchen island to the dishwasher. Then she set to, with cloth and spray, on what she and Marilyn called the surfaces.

Up in her bedroom Imo stood staring at a pencil study of hands, which she had completed for course work at college, and which was now stuck with masking tape to her wardrobe door. Sticking anything to the floral wallpaper was guaranteed to give Marilyn hysterics.

After a while she sat down on her bed and allowed herself to slip into despondency. What had her immediate life to offer? A summer job sticking labels on boxes of boat fittings or roof bolt covers at Dad's factory and longer term a course in cooking, word- processing or nanny-ing, with a view to meeting and marrying someone like Antonia's Roger, who looked like a giraffe.

The colour of life was black.

When Marilyn came downstairs looking, she thought, quite nice in a new pair of cropped linen mix trousers in a sort of pale lime green, Julia was arming herself with a squeegee mop to tackle the kitchen floor.

"Good morning," Marilyn surveyed the aspen beige floor tiles.

"It's not wet," Julia said, "I thought I'd just get on."

"Oh, yes . . . " Marilyn always felt that Julia knew more about the house and the details of its cleaning needs than she did herself for Julia after all had been cleaning it for longer.

"I saw Imogen," Julia said. "She said you were upstairs."

"There was something I just had to finish."

Julia nodded without comment. She leaned on the mop. She was always up before six in the morning as her husband Alan left for work with the Council Highways at ten past, but at present she was usually woken even earlier. Their daughter Sharon, plus two-year-old Nyle and the baby were back in the house until such time as the council came up with some accommodation, or Sharon moved back in with her boyfriend. The children were at an age to wake early.

Usually Julia would tell Marilyn about her life which was full of exhausting incident, and Marilyn was very interested and offered comments. Today however Julia was a bit tight for time, as she was going with Sharon to the baby clinic with Finn who needed his injections.

"Better be getting on then," she said, "because you can't count on the buses."

"Didn't you come on your bike?" Julia asked.

"Yes, but to get us all to the clinic."

Feeling deflated, Marilyn stepped back from the tiles and said she had to go into the town. "Will you do the lounge through?"

Julia always did the lounge through on a Tuesday and Marilyn usually went into the town while she was doing it. The routine was familiar to both of them.

"Right you are. Hoover it shall I?"

"Yes please." This involved shifting the cream leather settees around and Marilyn never knew whether she should, or should not, help. She found the uncertainty jangled her nerves.

Pausing in the hall it occurred to her to call up to Imo and ask if she would like to come into town with her. They could perhaps have a look for some favours to be scattered on the tables in the wedding marquee, one of several commissions which she had recently received from Antonia. However, her heart quailed.

Undoubtedly Imo would start arguing again about the Art College idea and anyway shopping with her was not much fun for she made it clear that she wasn't interested in the wedding or anything to do with it. She had even stood like a puppet to have her lovely pink bridesmaid's dress measured, raising her arms when instructed as if they were attached to strings and getting back into her jeans at the first opportunity.

Marilyn, truth be known, increasingly missed Antonia since she had gone up to London. They both liked doing the same things.

Now she set off walking briskly towards the town centre but with nothing specific to do when she got there.

Lately she had taken to going into The Lemon Tree on Julia's mornings. This café had not long since opened in a side lane off the High Street, called inaccurately a Mews. Julia liked it because it was quiet and she always found a table.

The Lemon Tree's proprietor and manager was Jamal Akbar, who was from Pakistan. This had set Marilyn back a bit at first, but she had now got used to him and she liked the way he had pictures of his little boy, who was nearly three, on the wall behind the counter. The family lived above the café.

Her first visit had been in the company of two women from one of the early Glebe coffee mornings to which she had been invited She had found them dithering outside the window of The Lemon Tree, then newly opened.

They had been examining the menu and egging each other on to try the cakes; somehow Marilyn's turning up had tipped the balance of decision and they all went in together. Marilyn would not have gone in alone.

There was a waitress, Tanis, who had just completed her

GCSEs at the local school, and had been a classmate, Marilyn later discovered, of Julia Prentice's Gary. "Though he wasn't there much," Tanis had said with a shrug.

Tanis was now on Work Experience, she wore a yellow apron and had her hair scraped back in the style of an old-fashioned shaving brush, it was anchored in place by about six coloured clips.

The first time Marilyn had come into The Lemon Tree, with the other two women, Jamal had welcomed them and they had told him it would be nice to have a café open at this end of town. He smiled and said he hoped they would become regular customers and that The Lemon Tree would be specialising in homemade cakes and be open from nine to five, except on Sundays.

When he went with a slight bow back behind the glass topped counter the other women had looked at each other and said, "Well – " and raised their eyebrows.

At first Jamal had called Marilyn 'Madam' but now he had discovered her name and Tanis, still there, knew that she would order a coffee which came with a small spiced cake, or lately lemon tea because of The Diet. It pleased Marilyn to get this recognition although it would be even nicer to have someone to meet up with. She had never got to know the other women well, the ones with whom she had come in on that first visit, she didn't even know their surnames and she hadn't seen them again in The Lemon Tree.

"We've lived here nearly two years," Marilyn thought now, finding a seat by the window, "and I still don't really know anyone."

Today she asked Tanis for coffee and added a quarter of a spoon of sugar and felt guilty.

CHAPTER 5

APRIL

Marilyn sat in one of the two leather arm chairs by the front window of The Lemon Tree café and opened the complimentary copy of the Daily Mail which lay on the low table in front of her.

Jamal acknowledged her arrival with a nod and a smile from behind the counter where he was preparing coffee for the only other customers who were two women seated at one of the tables and engaged in looking at some photographs, perhaps of a grandchild's birthday.

Tanis the waitress who hated her yellow apron, stood bored by the counter waiting for the coffee to be ready. Tanis' hair was now streaked and her eyes fiercely and blackly outlined. Fed up with Work Experience she was dreaming of being a travel rep somewhere hot.

Marilyn began to read on the front page of the newspaper of the extra-marital affair of a football star. She looked at the photographs: the footballer, the girl and the wife were all glamorous and smiling, which seemed strange. She didn't relate to them, not even the wife. Part of her mind was still trapped in thoughts of how empty her life seemed, how empty the house seemed now Antonia had gone.

Then another woman came into the café alone and looked around; she turned towards the vacant arm chair by the window. Marilyn hastily moved her bag and the newspaper to make more room.

"Is this seat free?" The woman sounded friendly; she wore an enviable pale suede jacket.

Marilyn said that yes, the seat was free, quite free and the woman settled herself and said that she had been shopping for a wedding present for a friend.

"Second marriages," she said. "It's impossible, isn't it? They've got everything and two of most things. It was so much easier first time round, wasn't it? Then everyone had lists."

Marilyn felt a flicker of hope. This was perhaps a chance to talk to someone about Antonia's wedding, someone whom she felt instinctively would appreciate her difficulties, and the frightening need for everything to do with the wedding to be perfect.

But then Tanis had brought Marilyn's cappuccino and the woman had said that she was meeting a friend and would wait to order until this friend arrived, which she shortly did.

The two of them moved to a table further inside the café and ordered Darjeeling tea and pistachio biscuits. Jamal had a new menu with an Indian Extra Specials section.

Marilyn slid back a little into the brown leather chair and wished very much that someone would come through the door of The Lemon Tree and say hello to her and maybe, "I've been hoping to see you. Now we can have a good chat."

No-one did and this was not surprising, for indeed she could not think who that someone would be.

She turned the pages of the newspaper, skimming an article about how immigrants were stealing all our jobs and moved on to an interview with a woman who had been jilted five times by prospective husbands and had finally found love with the sixth. There were a whole two pages giving her story. She said it was meant to be and she and her new husband were all in all to each other.

Marilyn's eyes were blurred. Very slowly she sipped her coffee and nibbled the almond biscuit which came with it, both of which of course must break The Diet rules, but you were allowed 'treats' sometimes weren't you? And anyway, somehow just now she didn't feel able to care.

When the first two customers began to gather their photos and purses and ask if they might have the bill and then each of them claim that it was, surely, her turn to pay, Marilyn looked at her watch. It was eleven o'clock and Julia Prentice must have finished the hoovering by now and so it would be all right for her to go home.

But there was nothing to go home for. Ahead of her stretched seven hours of nothing until Clive returned from work and then he would leave again shortly afterwards for his Rotary meeting. Imo would probably stay in her room most of the day or go up to the top of the garden to sunbathe, not wanting to talk, or if she did talk it would be all about why couldn't she go to Art College and how it wasn't fair.

Meanwhile back at The Rowans Julia Prentice had indeed finished the hoovering. She was now engaged in the bathroom, spraying shower cleaner on the shower tray and anti-smear on the shower panels, chrome gleam on the taps, a disinfectant which killed 99% of all known germs around the toilet rim and glass shine on the mirrors. She thought to herself that half a capful of bleach in a bowl of warm water would do most of these jobs just as well; her Nan had used vinegar. But she didn't argue with her employers, it was their choice how they chose to spend their money.

As she was stashing all the cleaning materials back in the unit beneath the twin hand basins, she heard the telephone ring. She waited to see if Imo would answer it but no sounds came of her leaving her room.

Julia picked up the cloths which needed washing out and set off downstairs as the answer-phone in the hall clicked in to record Antonia's voice on the other end of the line.

"Mum! Those rose petals for the confetti have come and they're the wrong colour!"

Julia paused; Antonia sounded stressed.

" . . . I ordered Dusky Pink and it's important for the photographs because we really want one of them to be of Roger and me and confetti, those petals, sort of falling all round us . . .

"And they say it's because of the rain last summer, the dark ones got mildew or something, but they should have told us before! Now what are we supposed to do? Mum! Please ring me back. Where are you?"

Julia picked up the phone. She had, after all, known Antonia since she was studying catering at the local college. "Hello," she said, "it's me, Julia. Your mum's gone out."

"Where?"

"Probably just down the shops." Julia was pretty much aware of Marilyn's hang-ups about having a cleaner and also of her coping strategies. Another woman she cleaned for went out to the gym as soon as she came through the door.

Julia was blessed with the sort of voice which calmed emotional people and animals. "Something to do with your wedding arrangements, is it?" she asked.

Antonia paused but she had to tell somebody. "It's the rose petals, we can't have the colour I want," she said, sounding slightly less panicky. "For the confetti."

Julia sympathised; it went with the job, it wasn't just the cleaning, you had to be a good listener. People told you all sorts when you mopped their kitchen floors and cleaned their toilets. And in fact she knew just what Antonia was on about because Marilyn gave her old copies of her magazines to take home and recently these had been exclusively to do with weddings. Petals were what everyone wanted these days.

"That's a pity," she said, leaning on the phone table so she could ease her left leg which was playing up a bit. "There was something in one of your mum's books she gave me about a farmer growing petals, but they weren't from roses, I don't think."

"Was there?" Antonia said, a spark of hope in her voice. "I think there's delphiniums. Were they delphiniums?"

"That I'm not sure," Julia said. "I'll see if I've still got it, if you like."

"Oh, "Antonia said. "Yes, could you? It might have an address, because otherwise if you have to buy them from a wedding shop they are so expensive and anyway I want this particular colour."

"All right then." Julia shifted her weight to the other hip; it was the biking that did it and all the doctor suggested was Ibuprofen which didn't seem to do much.

"But can you leave a note for Mum, and ask her to ring me? Say, can she use my mobile number because I'm at work. Or I'll try texting her at lunch time, but I can't stop now."

"Right you are then."

"Thank you."

With some care Julia wrote the required note on a page from the floral message pad by the phone and left it where it could easily be seen. Then she took the cleaning cloths to the utility room and put them into the washing machine.

When Marilyn arrived back, coming into the hall still wearing her dark glasses, she asked Julia if she had had her coffee.

"I think I've got some grit or something," Marilyn said, "in my eye . . . "

"Could you wash it out with cold water?" Julia suggested, looking at her. Been crying, she thought, oh dear.

"Oh, it's getting better," Marilyn went to the kitchen and switched on the kettle

"Antonia phoned," Julia said. "It's her petals."

On her walk home Marilyn had felt the evaporation of the slight lift in her spirits, which she had gained from her visit to The Lemon Tree. Now she wondered if she could cope with yet more wedding problems. Thoughts of the wedding gave her an anxious, clutching feeling below her ribs. She poured boiling water into Julia's mug of instant coffee and chose a Diet friendly sachet of camomile tea for herself, trying not to think about the frothy cappuccino and the almond biscuit.

Julia found it uncomfortable to sit at the kitchen island, for the stool seat was a bit too small and there was not enough room for your knees, but none-the-less she settled herself to commiserate with Marilyn about the wedding, The Diet, family life. Anything really which allowed her mid-morning coffee break to be extended a bit, and gave her a chance to rest her feet. Though she had to keep an eye on the time today because of Sharon's appointment at the clinic.

"Children," Julia offered, "they're always giving you grief aren't they? No matter what age they're at."

Normally Marilyn might have defended Antonia against such a charge but thinking about the petals crisis made her feel that yes, it was true, both her children had indeed been causing her grief lately.

"The trouble is," she said sadly, "Antonia and Imogen are just so different. Antonia has always liked clothes and Imo never has, or not – " she paused considering Imo's razor ripped jeans and the hours she had spent tie-dying T-shirts in one of the saucepans, leaving its inside permanently stained, "not nice clothes."

"But for the wedding?" Julia prompted, knowing something of the ongoing saga of Imo's bridesmaid's dress. "She'll be wearing something nice for that?"

"But she's being so difficult."

"Well, Antonia will look lovely I'm sure," Julia said, trying a different tack. "She's got the colouring for it, hasn't she?"

Marilyn's heart lightened a little. "Yes," she said and smiled. Antonia would look lovely, although there again she had started making a fuss about the wedding dress, and wanting to alter it.

"Having it made, isn't she?" Julia prompted.

Yes, Marilyn agreed that Antonia was indeed having her wedding dress made. The dressmaker Maddy with whom Antonia had been at school had now started her own business. It was Maddy who had suggested catching the silk over-skirt of the dress up at each side. She had shown them a picture of a pretty china figure, a girl in a bonnet with some sheep, quite old fashioned, to explain what she meant. They'd all agreed on it and now Antonia wasn't sure. Again.

"She keeps changing her mind about everything," Marilyn said, "and it's so unsettling."

"You have to live through it yourself to understand," Julia said, she was regretting that because of The Diet Marilyn had stopped offering her a biscuit with her coffee.

Marilyn, pensively stirring the camomile tea bag in her mug for it didn't seem to be giving out much flavour, agreed that yes, you did. Although what situation there was, similar to her own, that Julia Prentice had lived through wasn't too clear. Not certainly an offspring's wedding for her Sharon had not so far married her boyfriend despite the arrival of the baby. And Julia's son Gary, although he sounded older than his age in some ways which would have worried Marilyn if she had been his mother, was still only sixteen and wouldn't hopefully be getting married for some years yet.

"Our Sharon's Nyle is in trouble again, at the Early Start," Julia now said, thinking that she had earned this change in conversational direction through showing a sympathetic interest in Marilyn's anxieties.

Marilyn felt her heart sink half a notch lower. She had never liked to ask about Nyle's father who was 'not around' but Julia had been preoccupied with the toddler's difficulties since her daughter and the children had moved back in two months ago.

"Oh dear," Marilyn tried to suppress her desire not to hear anything about it.

"Biting," Julia said. "And then he threw his juice mug at the new Nursery Help, he doesn't like her."

Marilyn had met Julia with Sharon and the children in the town. Nyle had looked a bold child and demonstrated quite a turn of speed when he let go of the buggy strap and headed off for the pedestrian crossing. "He likes to do the lights," Sharon had said, hauling him back by the hood of his anorak.

Marilyn mostly tried not to think about Julia's home life although she regularly heard about it. Julia's husband Alan who worked with the tarmac gang on the county roads had to have his dinner waiting for him, meat and veg, when he came in from work. When Julia broke her wrist and couldn't peel potatoes or make pie pastry, he was out of sorts for the duration of the time her arm was in plaster.

After his dinner he liked a bit of peace and quiet, during which he could look at the paper or watch the sport.

At the moment, as Julia had told Marilyn several times, peace and quiet in the house was not easily achieved. Sharon, now nineteen, had a volatile relationship with her boyfriend and they had broken up on several previous occasions, the last reconciliation resulting in the birth of Finn, the baby. Currently Sharon and both children were back in her old bedroom and the house was littered with plastic toys and used disposable nappies in poopa-scoop bags. These details upset Marilyn.

"I have to take the children to the play park, let Nyle run it off a bit, in the evening," Julia said.

"Can't Sharon take them?" Marilyn asked.

"She's not feeling too good at present," Julia said. "I think it's that post-natal myself, but she won't go to the doctor."

Marilyn gazed at her in despair.

"Well," Julia picked up their mugs and took them to the dishwasher. "I best be getting on. I did the bathroom and the cloths are in the machine.

"I left your money in the envelope," Marilyn said weakly. "On the side. In case I didn't get back to catch you."

It was what she always did.

Shortly afterwards Julia was on her way down the hill,

freewheeling on her bike.

Imogen meanwhile was indeed, as Marilyn had suspected, still up in her bedroom. She was searching the Student Union magazine for holiday work advertisements. She had suddenly decided that she couldn't stand being stuck at home and hearing nothing but wedding, wedding, wedding right through the summer. Her search had led her to the Garden Volunteers.

CHAPTER 6

APRIL

At Trevean garden volunteer Ned Lorrimer sat alone at the kitchen table.

Ned yawned; he had rejected the congealed remains of porridge left in the saucepan on the back of the range but had made himself a mug of instant coffee. He had no idea where anyone else was, but he wasn't particularly bothered. In fact he was quite pleased for he was in no hurry to start work.

The most noticeable thing about Ned was his looks. Even now, not long out of bed, unshaved and indeed unwashed, his physical beauty was remarkable. He was eighteen years old.

The kitchen was in a mess but Ned didn't notice. He had never had to concern himself with domestic detail having spent most of his life so far abroad or in boarding school where such matters were looked after by other people.

His parents were currently based in the Gulf States where his father worked for an international oil consortium. When staying with them Ned's cast-off clothes were removed to the laundry by the Philippino maid, housework had been accomplished by the time he got up in the morning, and there was a cook. There had been much the same arrangement at school.

Clarissa came downstairs. Today she was feeling bored; from past experience she knew what state the kitchen would probably be in, surely she could make herself useful to Sally by tidying it up?

When she appeared in the doorway Ned, looking up and registering who this was, was momentarily disconcerted. His mother and school would have expected him to stand up in acknowledgement of an elderly member of the Lacock family. He had recently decided to free himself from the restrictions of home and school rule at least for the summer but now habit forced him to push his chair back and half rise to his feet.

Clarissa was charmed by Ned.

She responded positively, as people tend to do, to golden youth. She thought that he was very good-looking and forgave him for not standing up properly. His fair hair flopped boyishly over his eyes, he was tall and well put together. From her window she had watched him swinging easily down the slope to the bamboos and regretted the stiffness with which she herself now seemed condemned to move.

"Good morning," she greeted him.

Ned was glad it was Clarissa for she was the only person at Trevean who treated him as rather special. Sally didn't seem to differentiate between him and Graham, the other volunteer, which was odd. And irritating.

James so far as was possible ignored both of them.

The children had pretty soon discovered that Ned wasn't

interested in them and did not want to play cricket on the lawn or make bows and arrows, so they too tended to leave him alone.

Clarissa observed the kitchen, the pile of dirty plates, cups and cutlery sliding across the draining board, the open jam pot and tub of melting margarine on the table amongst the books, pieces of paper, the empty tin of dog food and a jar of drooping buttercups.

"This is all a bit untidy," she said, picking up the two grubby tea towels hung over the back of one of the kitchen chairs.

Ned looked round vaguely.

"Where is everybody?" Clarissa asked.

"I'm not really sure."

"They may have gone shopping," Clarissa suggested.

"Maybe . . . " Ned wasn't terribly interested, but if Sally was out she wouldn't be coming to tell him it was time to get down to the bamboos. This idea cheered him.

Clearing the bamboos was hard work, their cut off stems, still upright in the ground, became sharp spikes on which he ripped his jeans. They threatened the soles of the expensive working boots ordered for him by his mother.

Ned was at Trevean to help him make up his mind whether he should go to Agricultural College to study Estate Management.

He had started by working with Graham, who had since been re-deployed to the kitchen garden. Although Ned's days were now passed in solitude, hacking and stacking the bamboos, he in some ways preferred this as Graham was not a very congenial companion; he worked stolidly and he didn't talk.

Clarissa sat down at the table and she and Ned settled to a discussion of Ned's current situation and future prospects, for Clarissa as usual felt starved of conversation and human interest. Ned was always happy to talk about himself.

"Do you think you might work abroad like your father?" Clarissa asked.

"Perhaps." Ned was uncommitted to any particular career path. Estate Management had been his parents' idea, picked from a range of options suggested by the school when he didn't get offered a place at Cambridge. His father had not been pleased about the Cambridge business, telling the Headmaster he had expected more for his money.

"The climate would be better?" Clarissa suggested. "Are they in the Middle East?"

"Yes . . . " Ned paused reflectively. "And the sport."

"And the social life?" Clarissa said wistfully. She remembered her time as a corporate wife, lots of afternoon bridge and tennis and drinks at the Executive Club. "What is your sport?"

"I played rugby and cricket at school."

"And were you good?"

"Pretty good, yes." There was no necessity to be falsely modest, he had made the school first teams.

"Really? But I don't suppose you are getting much opportunity for sport down here are you?"

This was true. The routine at Trevean had turned out to be more work-based than he had anticipated and the location made getting around difficult, buses to the local town ran every two hours and seemed to stop at five-thirty.

"I'm thinking of doing more surfing," he said.

"Really? Do you have a board?"

Ned hadn't got a surfboard, he had been borrowing one of the Lacocks' old bodyboards, a necessity which irritated him. He hesitated slightly. "I'm probably going to buy one."

But in reality this was an idea rather than a fact, for financial reasons. He wasn't earning anything much above his keep at

Trevean and his father, whose annoyance about the Cambridge rejection encompassed Ned himself as well as the school, was unlikely to stump up.

Clarissa sensed the cooling in Ned's mood and changed the subject, wishing to keep the conversation going for as long as possible. "And what are you doing in the garden at the moment?"

Ned explained about the bamboos and he felt that Clarissa rather shared his opinion that such heavy manual labour might have been more suitable for Graham.

"Of course, when the garden was laid out there would have been plenty of staff to maintain it properly," she said.

She made a point of saying this to people because although James was an unsatisfactory son-in-law in so many ways, not least in age, it was important to establish his family's social credentials which showed that Sally had not been totally remiss in choosing to marry him.

Ned's mother would have understood exactly where Clarissa was coming from but the Lacocks past and present didn't concern Ned beyond their influence upon his own situation. He had got the impression that they were currently short of money, but so what? He was only here for the summer.

He was however happy to continue talking with Clarissa because she seemed suitably interested in him and it provided an excuse for not starting work. He got up to switch the kettle on again, asking as an afterthought, "Would you like some coffee?"

Clarissa hesitated, she didn't usually drink instant coffee. "Thank you. That would be very nice."

Watching Ned look around doubtfully for a second mug, she had a sudden thought. "Have you had some breakfast?"

"No." Ned gazed at Clarissa, this was a turn in the conversation which held promise. Maybe she would produce something.

Clarissa looked in the fridge, which made her shudder slightly – what were those bowls of shrivelled remains lurking at the back? But there were three eggs in the door shelf.

"An egg?" she suggested. "Boiled or fried?"

Ned agreed with alacrity. "Fried."

"And fried bread?"

Ned smiled his charming smile and Clarissa also found some cold potatoes to fry up.

Meanwhile in the village James was entering The Lion pub with Coal, top dog, beside him. Dogs were permitted in the public bar under sufferance, which basically meant if they were local and didn't cause trouble. James anyway considered that Coal had near human qualities. Tish and Tash, as a gesture of co-operation with the pub rules, were left in the car.

Zachariah Williams, known as Boy Zaccy by the people with whom he had gone to the village school and those others who dared, was landlord of The Lion. He had joined the merchant navy in his teens and been away from the village for thirty years which gave him, in popular opinion and his own estimation, a certain clout.

James, had he realised it, suffered similarly to Clarissa from lack of congenial company. He liked to talk to Zachariah about India, of which Zachariah had some knowledge from his naval days.

"You can," James told Sally, "at least have a sensible conversation with him."

By which he meant basically that at least Zachariah was a man, women's conversation with the exception of Sally's was often trying.

"Morning, Sir. And how does the day find you?" Zachariah indicated, in query, the relevant beer pump and then proceeded to draw James' usual pint of bitter.

James felt his spirits lift a bit. "Not too bad, is it?" He sat at the polished bar counter; Coal gazed at him fixedly in hope of crisps.

The bar was nearly empty. There was only a couple of old men in their usual seats in the corner. James nodded to them and they nodded back without enthusiasm. He felt an antipathy in their glance. He had complained of this to Sally on previous occasions; she said he was imagining most of it. "They may expect us to do more social stuff in the village," she said. "I expect your Cousin Lavinia did."

"Can't afford to," James had said gloomily.

Zachariah, his shirt straining in the middle button area, presided with professional bonhomie. "The lady wife not with you today?"

Lunch time trade was pretty slack, food was supposed to be the answer according to the Brewery, food would widen the clientele, bring in the families. Zachariah however was not convinced that families were what he wanted. He drank brandy and lovage and preferred a traditional pub patronage.

"Shopping," James said, feeding Coal crisps.

"Oh, indeed," Zachariah said. "Can't stop them, can you; born to it."

James nodded and then felt a twinge of guilt because Sally could hardly be accused of shopping indulgence, she rarely bought anything for herself and this morning's expedition with Claud and Frankie in tow would be no more her idea of fun than his. He wondered if Zachariah's wife Nancy had an uncheckable inclination to buy, say, tea towels? She spent a lot of time, when behind the bar, using them to polish glasses.

"Many people around?" he enquired.

"Fair to middling," Zachariah said.

"Visitors?"

"A couple of mini buses of surfing types in earlier."

"Oh, yes." James didn't know much about surfing, other than that Sally took the children down to the cove with their body boards when he played golf.

"Wouldn't know what to do with a surf board if it stood up and banged them on the nose, which it probably will," Zachariah said, watching one of the old men make his way slowly to the bar, clutching his glass. "Top up, Alec? Yes, from up-country, all the jargon and all the gear. Well, good luck to them, as long as they spend their money and don't go drowning themselves, because that gives us a bad reputation."

"Seems to be getting more popular," James said.

He hadn't been into the sea since they moved back to Trevean. Too damn cold, too many years in a hot climate.

For a brief moment he was in Shimla, gazing across the foothills of the Himalayas, dark green with Deodar pines and the valleys scalloped with terraced plots of tea bushes and rice, seeing in the distance the snow-covered peaks. His heart contracted, India!

Sally arrived.

"I've left the boys in the car," she said. "How are you doing?"

She looked at James' glass, assessing if he was ready to leave.

"Will you have a drink?" he asked hopefully. Opportunities to have Sally to himself were rare and he clung to them.

She knew this. "Just a half," she said. "And I better take some crisps to the boys."

She patted Coal's thrusting head, his short plumed tail beat.

"How are you, Zachariah?" Sally asked when she returned from the car, and having told Claud to make sure Tish and Tash didn't get Frankie's crisps.

"Well as can be expected," he said. "When you get past fifty you just keep going, don't you? Downhill momentum."

"That sounds cheerful."

Zachariah thought Sally had more go about her than James. Years younger too, as Nancy pointed out. Why had she married him? Maybe for the house, but that was falling to bits by all accounts.

Zachariah moved down the bar to draw her half a pint of local bitter, odd drink for a woman, though not his to reason why.

Sally drank bitter partly because she didn't subscribe to the idea that men drank beer and women didn't and partly because it was, like James's pint, cheaper than a lot of other things.

"I've cancelled Country Life," Sally told James.

He nodded, despondency claiming him.

"Never mind," Sally said, "when we get the garden open things will start to pick up."

"Will they?"

"We could do with some more volunteers."

James sighed, the idea did not appeal to him. "Have to feed them," he pointed out.

"But if we're going to get into the garden guides we ought to have more for people to see. We could open the paths up, get the lake cleaned out. And the rhododendrons in the woods need clearing – it's a jungle in some places."

"Take years."

"No, months, darling, I'm sure."

The whole thing defeated James.

"I'll sort it out," Sally said. "I'll have more time when this term finishes." She turned to Zachariah who had placed her glass before her. "Oh thank you, Zaccy."

Nancy Williams, Zachariah's wife, now made her morning entrance behind the bar. She gave the impression of taking her professional presence seriously.

There was Sally thought something reminiscent in her appearance of a ship's figurehead, that forward-leading bust with no natural contours, whatever did she wear underneath? On top Nancy favoured machine-knit suits in cheerful colours, today a vivid mauve.

Nancy was gratified to see the Lacocks for they came from the big house of the village which still counted for something. However, Sally's lack of effort with clothes she found deplorable, along with James' worn cords and the disreputable unreliability of whichever was their current car.

Nancy herself believed in the obligations of position and did not appear in public unless her make-up, hair and jewellery had received her full attention.

She scanned the bar, calling good morning to Alec Sancreed and Bobby Grose the old regulars seated in the corner and then joined Zachariah to adjust his arrangement of drip mats and cast a sharp eye over the optics.

"Good morning," she said to James and Sally, taking in what they were drinking. For that was another thing . . . half of bitter, not appropriate.

Nancy however was a professional, her glance betrayed nothing. She smiled. "And I see you've brought some of the children."

Sally looked at her. "What are they up to?"

"Oh God, they haven't let the dogs out have they?" asked James.

"I just caught a glimpse of them as I came down," Nancy said, "in the car."

Her eye had in fact been caught by flailing arms and legs inside the Volvo for Frankie had dropped his crisps and the dogs were eating them.

Sally wondered whether Nancy Williams made her feel inadequate. Although she told herself that she didn't have the time or inclination to give attention to her appearance she could still feel unsettled by women who clearly thought this was important.

She noticed the splodge on her skirt where Frankie had slopped a spoonful of cereal and felt that perhaps she ought to start making more effort to look, at least, clean. She gave a half sigh but stifled it so that James wouldn't notice. Get a grip, she told herself, I'm not the mauve worsted and red lipstick type.

After some brief further discussion with Zachariah and Nancy on the arrival of summer visitors in the village, which led onto the garden volunteer scheme, and the activities of Graham and Ned at Trevean, Sally suggested to James that they ought to be getting back.

Zachariah said as they left the pub. "Going to take more than a couple of teenagers who don't know what they're doing to turn that place around and make something of it."

In the car Frankie was howling.

CHAPTER 7

APRIL

The car wouldn't start. Frankie, who had been cheered by Sally and James's return and the prospect of not being stuck in the car much longer, started to howl again.

Despondency claimed James.

Sally felt her nerves would snap as she repeatedly turned the ignition key and the engine clunked and failed to turn over. In the end she got out and walked to the garage at the end of the village main street. Here in a dark and oily cave she found Jack Richards together with his mechanic Peter, examining the underside of a Masda.

At first Sally had thought that the workshop was empty but then she located voices at foot level and a dull glow shining from between the Masda's wheels.

"Hello," she called, bending double and addressing the hole in the ground.

"Lo?"

"It's me, Jack, Sally Lacock. I can't get the car to start."

"Oh?" There was a pause while Jack Richards conferred for a couple of minutes longer with Peter about the state of the Masda's exhaust before climbing the concrete steps out of the pit and emerging, in blue boiler suit and wool hat, both much stained with grease and brake fluid.

"'Morning," he said.

"Good morning." Sally found Jack reassuring. The cars he dealt with were usually older vehicles in variable degrees of unreliability, driven by the locals. He knew their individual quirks and those of their owners and approached any mechanical problems with cheerful fatalism.

The Lacocks' Volvo required a new starter motor, he had started it for Sally a couple of times over the past month with jump leads from his pick-up but this was a waste of his time and the call out fee.

"Where are you now?" he asked, wiping his hands on a rag.

"The Lion car park."

"Right on."

"Can you – will you be able to come out?" Sally tried to keep the fret from her voice.

"I can."

"Oh, brilliant!"

"But I need first have a word with Peter about this other problem here." He slapped the Masda's wing and turned back to the pit.

Sally watched as he disappeared again underground, knowing there was absolutely no point in pushing for speed. She gritted her teeth and stared hard at the operating instructions on the wall above the emissions checking machine. Diagrams of dials blurred; life could be a pain.

Jack drove Sally to the pub car park in his pick-up. " Morning," he acknowledged James, still sitting despairing in the front seat. Then he backed the pick-up alongside the Volvo, hitched up both bonnets and linked up the jump leads to the batteries.

Now that there was a man on hand who was capable of sorting the problem James got out of the car, leaving Claud and Frankie and the dogs churning around inside. This was how life was supposed to be: when something wouldn't work you got hold of someone who knew how to fix it. This made sense. You didn't try and botch it yourself.

James respected specialist knowledge. During his teaching career he had been trained to acquire such knowledge and then disseminate it. He wouldn't expect Jack Richards to instruct students in the fine points of English grammar or analysis of the nineteenth century novel, similarly he himself should not be expected to sort out non-starting car engines.

Sally unfortunately, much as he loved her caused him anguish on a regular basis by hurling herself at problems when every instinct he possessed screamed at him to stand clear.

Money. That was the root of it all, they never had enough bloody money. Trevean had been a ghastly mistake, he should have got rid of the place as soon as he inherited it. Oh God!

The car engine sprang to life.

"You're a miracle worker, Jack!" Sally cried joyfully.

Jack unfixed the jump leads. "Starter's on the way out," he observed.

"I know," Sally said. "I know. We really ought to get a new one."

She looked at James, conscious that Jack would expect this to be his decision.

James sighed. Of course they ought to get a new starter, if that was what the problem was. The whole thing was ridiculous. Here they were living at Trevean, considered the 'big house' of the village, with probably less monthly expendable income than Jack Richards himself.

"Jack could get one for us," Sally suggested. "What do you think?"

"Yes? I suppose so." James felt wretched. "Yes." He shrugged, absolving himself of the decision and its financial implications.

Jack nodded. "Right on, then. Be in early next week."

"Are we going home now?" Claud asked hopefully as they drove out of the car park.

"Yes," said Sally. "We are. Home and don't spare the horses!" She put her foot down a bit. Now the car problems were going to be sorted she felt positive again.

Back at the house Ned and Clarissa were still comfortably seated at the kitchen table, Ned having been appreciative of the fried egg and potato and the two pieces of toast Clarissa had made for him. Neither of them were very lit up by the sound of Claud, Frankie and the dogs cascading into the hall.

As she sometimes did Clarissa felt uncomfortable to be found involving herself in the domestic matters of the house and now she also had a pang of doubt about feeding Ned. Ned merely regretted that the family's return meant he would have to start work in the bamboos.

"Hello!" Frankie bounced into the kitchen.

"Hello!" Clarissa was always cheered by the children for they brought an active present into focus, otherwise things seemed to have been better in the past. "What have you been up to?"

"Nothing! Frankie shrieked. "Tash ate my crisps."

"Crisps?" Clarissa said, pretending excitement. "Did you

bring some back for me?"

"No! Tash got them all."

"Oh dear, never mind." Clarissa got to her feet, cautious of her hip. She pulled Ned's plate across the table and made her way carefully over to the sink. "Remove the evidence," she thought.

Sally arrived with the shopping bags which she dumped on the kitchen table and started unpacking. "Here you are Mother, face cream, and marmalade." She opened her purse. "How much did you give me?"

"Oh, it doesn't matter," Clarissa said. "Really."

She wished that she had the money to give freely to Sally, to try to take away the constant financial anxiety which dogged the household. But she had done that and the money had disappeared into the maw of Trevean and now she was stuck here and really Sally had not been helped. She was still having to work too hard, still having too much to cope with, was still broke.

Sally fished some change from her purse. "There," she said, "I think this must be yours."

"Thank you," Clarissa closed her hand round the coins and unhooked her stick from the back of the chair where she had hooked it. "Maybe one of the children could bring my things up?"

"Yes, of course," Sally said and turned her attention to Ned who was making for the door into the back porch. "How are you getting on with the bamboos?"

"Well . . . OK." He didn't try to sound positive, in fact he was pissed off with the bloody things. He was being used as a human rotavator, why couldn't the Lacocks get a real one or at least put Graham onto the job?

"Good," Sally said, "because we ought to get on to clearing

the rhododendrons as soon as possible."

Ned gazed at her in mute astonishment. Wasn't he supposed to be getting an insight into the different aspects of estate management? That was how his father had presented the three months at Trevean and presumably this information came from the Garden Volunteer Organisation which had set up the placement. But now a dark thought entered his head – someone had not been completely honest. The organisation, his father or the Lacocks had sold him up the river, to be used as slave labour.

Coming out into the yard he decided to try to ring his parents, but as usual he couldn't get a signal on his mobile. Benighted place. His face clouded sulkily.

He remembered his surfing plan and decided to go, on the quiet, up to the kitchen garden and put it to Graham. He would deserve something to look forward to if he was going to have to spend hours hacking at bamboo canes.

Graham was checking rows of carrot seedlings for root fly. He was not best pleased to see Ned step cautiously through the wooden door in the high brick wall, scan the garden and then saunter nonchalantly across.

"Hi," Ned said on arrival beside the carrots. "What are you doing?"

Graham straightened up reluctantly. He paused; he rarely responded instantly to requests for information, in his own mind weighing up the purpose of the request. This would obviously affect the detail required in a reply. He rarely deliberately withheld information but it could appear like that.

"Root fly," he said. This made sense, why waste words?

Words for Graham were slippery things which he struggled to pull together into orderly sentences or at least into the sort of sentences in which the Lacocks and Ned spoke. At home or with the boys he had grown up with he 'spoke broad', using a differently constructed English which harked back to an older language yet. With other people he preferred to keep his mouth shut.

Ned was none the wiser for the answer he had received but as he wasn't actually interested in what Graham was doing it didn't matter much.

"This is all looking good," he said, glancing round at the orderly rows of beans, peas and beetroot which Graham had planted in the area he had cleared of brambles and nettles. Ned was not sure what he was looking at but it made sense to be conciliatory.

Graham was suspicious that Ned was taking the piss, but he was deprived of anyone showing a sensible interest in the kitchen garden except Sally and she was usually in a rush and distracted. Despite his natural caution he responded to Ned.

"Soil's good," he said. "Been cared for, see, for years till it was let go."

Ned nodded. "Like the rest of the place, I suppose. But it'll take more than you and me hacking our way through the jungle to sort it out."

Again Graham didn't rush to reply. Eventually he said, "Me'be."

Really, Ned thought, any attempt at conversation was a waste of time. He decided to come to the point. "I fancy getting down to the beach later on."

Graham returned to his examination of the carrots. He did not respond.

Sod it, Ned thought, why try to be subtle? "Can you give me a lift?"

"What – drive you?" Graham asked, glancing at him briefly.

"Yes. This afternoon."

"Where to?"

"The cove. To look at the surf."

"No," Graham said succinctly.

Ned felt a rush of fury. Why was a car wasted on this clod? "Why not?" he asked.

"I'm fetching down a load of manure."

"What?" Ned stared at him.

Graham was getting increasingly irritable; he might, he thought, have guessed that Ned was on the scrounge, and now he was being slow to get the message that he wasn't welcome.

"Fetching down a load of manure from the riding stables," he said. "Been fixed up all week."

That surely was plain enough even for an arrogant fool like Ned who was making a lash-up of clearing the bamboos by the lake. Mentally Graham tested an initial 'h' on 'arrogant' and rejected it, but the uncertainty added to his frustration.

Ned thought Graham was incomprehensible, why would he spend his free time and use his own car to cart horse shit around the countryside? He stared at Graham's back, now bent again resolutely over the carrots, and raged inwardly.

"So you won't drop me down at the cove?" he said finally.

"Can't," Graham said. How many times did you have to tell one of these people something? And yet they carried on like they were superior. "Makes you laugh, quietly," he thought, moving on down the carrot row.

Ned felt a strong urge to kick something. "Right," he said after a few moments of breathing deeply, during which Graham continued to ignore him. "Right."

Then, teeth clenched, Ned walked back down the path and

out through the door in the wall. As he passed a cold frame which still had enough glass in it to protect a melon plant which Graham had planted he landed the kick on the bottom course of brick work. A brick fell out, but Ned also stubbed his toes and the pain shot up through his foot.

"Shit." He slammed the door in the garden wall and several large flakes of paint drifted down onto the path.

CHAPTER 8

APRIL

"Imo!" Marilyn called up the stairs. "Do you want some lunch?"

She wished Imo would reply, "Yes! Yes!" and come bounding down from her room, cheerful and chatty as she might perhaps have done when she was little. But this, lately, seemed increasingly unlikely to happen.

Imo was torn. She was hungry but she didn't want to have to talk to Marilyn for of course this would be all about the wedding. Why had Antonia chosen to marry Roger Rodmaine, he was years older than her and surely she couldn't fancy him? He had a long thin neck and laughed a haw haw sort of laugh at his own jokes and other things which weren't funny.

Marilyn watched Imo coming down the stairs, bored reluctance radiating at every step. Why, oh why must she insist on wearing such dreary clothes when some girls could look so nice? And her hair! It seemed to have yet more coloured wool woven into it.

Wistfully Marilyn remembered clothes shopping expeditions with Antonia. How could the two girls be so different? She never found answers to these questions.

She opened the fridge door. "Would you like cottage cheese?"

Imo pulled a face. No, she wouldn't like cottage cheese, she would like a plate of chips, or possibly a chocolate muffin and a packet of crisps. She missed the junky food that she used to eat at college.

The phone rang in the hall, distracting Marilyn for it was Antonia agitating about the rose petals. "Mum! How about delphiniums . . . ?"

Imo moved swiftly through to the kitchen, found the bread and retrieved a jar of peanut butter from the utility room. As she slapped some sandwiches together she looked through the window at the patio where it would be good to go and sit in the sun but if she did so Marilyn would certainly come out and recount the whole of her conversation with Antonia and Imo knew that she simply couldn't bear it. I don't care about boring freeze-dried petals, she thought. I just don't care.

She therefore returned crossly to her room, conscious of Marilyn's reproachful glance as she retreated up the stairs.

She continued checking out the Garden Volunteers advertisement, encouraged to see that the people shown in the photographs looked mostly around her own age. They were variously engaged in wielding bill hooks in heavy undergrowth, sloshing around in the ornate basin of a giant fountain and planting trees. They appeared to be enjoying themselves, they smiled at the camera. One group was having a coffee break and they sat swinging their legs over the edge of a flight of stone steps; they raised their mugs in salute. 'Join us to rescue an historic garden and have some fun as well!' the text suggested.

Imo scrolled down the screen to the Application section for Garden Volunteers and she began to fill in the required information.

Downstairs Marilyn's voice was rising in anxious query in response to whatever Antonia was telling her.

Antonia was in fact now worrying about the wedding invitation list, which was getting exponentially out of control. Apparently, some of Roger's cousins had small children who could not be left at home and for whom provision must therefore be made.

Marilyn could imagine Clive's response to a proposal for ten more expensive places at the reception, for under fives who probably wouldn't eat the food anyway.

"And Roger's parents think a crèche would be a good idea so the children can have something to do during the speeches, toys and things to play with and their mums and dads can have a break . . . " Antonia was consumed with anxiety. "Mum, can you find out if the hotel can do a crèche?"

"A crèche?" Marilyn felt her own anxiety levels rising; all this organisation, all these details.

"Yes!" Antonia said. "Some hotels do. They have a nursery nurse or someone to look after the children. And they may do a children's menu. Please find out, Mum! Roger's parents have been asking about it."

Roger's parents intimidated Marilyn. She and Clive were to meet up with them shortly to 'talk through the wedding details' as Penelope had put it; remembering this now made Marilyn feel worse.

Antonia returned to the petal crisis. "Can you see if anyone knows where else to get them? Real roses or maybe delphiniums?"

"Well – " Marilyn could not think whom she might ask.

"It's really important! Deep pink – they're for scattering on the tables as well as for the photographs. Please Mum! Julia said there was an article in one of the magazines you gave her."

"What about some of your friends who have got married?" Marilyn asked plaintively. "Wouldn't they know?"

"Mum! I'm working and there's so much to do! Please can't you help? I had it all sorted and now everything is going wrong."

Antonia was not usually so demanding, but the wedding filled her thoughts.

When she rang off Marilyn shakily switched on the kettle to make herself a cup of camomile tea and stared, despairing, at the opened jar of peanut butter and the loaf which Imo had left on the work surface, almost directly beneath the pinned-up diet sheet which specified bread for breakfast only, wholemeal, one slice toasted and thinly spread with margarine. Imo had not cut the loaf straight.

Later Marilyn decided to ring Clive at work.

But Clive was not in the right mood to discuss the wedding. A large order for moulded roofing panels, destined for Qatar, was running late for shipment.

He was normally supportive when Marilyn got as he thought of it 'het up' about the details of their domestic life or some problem to do with the girls, because basically he thought that was how women were – inclined to be over-emotional. Currently however he had a serious business problem to sort so yet more wedding decisions were necessarily way down his list of priorities. He did however note that this crèche business, which Marilyn was trying to explain, would obviously cost and the reception looked increasingly like going over the budget they had agreed.

"If they can't control their kids they shouldn't bring them," he said, "it's simple."

"But what can we tell the Rodmaines?"

"Well, if they must have a crèche, let them pay for it," Clive said. "I don't see it's our problem. None of our side have got kids have they?"

"But otherwise the children will have to come to the meal!" Marilyn was staring at the insoluble and trying not to cry. "And the speeches."

This was a point; Clive paused at the prospect of kids turning up their noses at salmon with dill mayonnaise at the ludicrous price per head which they had been quoted by Columb Court.

"Ring the hotel," he said.

"But what shall I say?"

Marilyn wanted him to sort this out and he knew that he would have to in the end. He stalled: "Ask them if they can do a crèche, and for how much. And ask them for a kids' menu, fish fingers or something, get them to give you some quotes. I've got to go."

"But – "

"Listen, I've got a real problem on my hands here with an order now. It's urgent. Just get on to the hotel It'll be all right."

"Oh – "

"It'll be OK," he repeated, relenting from habit. "Don't worry. It's sortable."

"But – "

Clive said. "I'll see you later." He added, "Love you" and rang off.

Marilyn found that she had not drunk the cup of camomile tea which she had made earlier, the truth was she didn't really like it very much. She switched on the kettle again to make a cup of coffee. If Imogen had been more approachable she might have talked it all through with her but she could imagine Imo shrugging her shoulders and saying, "So what?"

None of the wedding details, which had so completely occupied Marilyn and Antonia's thoughts for the past six months, seemed to hold any interest for Imo whatsoever.

Marilyn looked round the kitchen which they had had re-done last year in Scandinavian Aspen laminate. Usually the units and the sparkly white work surfaces lifted her spirits but today they just seemed to offer reproach for her not being a more enthusiastic cook. The kitchen had an under-used look about it.

She took her coffee outside where there was a table and chairs on the patio. The garden was quite large by estate standards, large enough anyway to provide a potential building plot had there been any access from the road, which there wasn't unless you demolished the garage. At the moment there was also a planning embargo on any further development on The Glebe.

The sun was warm on the patio, Marilyn sat in the shade of the table's central umbrella and steeled herself to ring Peter Fullerton at Columb Court Hotel.

Clive had originallysuggested that the local golf club would do very well for the reception; they would put on a good meal, he could probably get a deal on the wine and there was a wide view across the links. But Antonia had wanted something else.

Initially Marilyn had supported Antonia's wish, expressed with pleading, for Columb Court. Apparently one of Roger's sister's friends had had her reception there, it had been a Christmas wedding and there had been venison and holly garlands and mummers.

Antonia was wide eyed and impressed when she told them this.

"Mummers?" Clive had questioned.

"Sort of actors," Antonia said, "With music. Oh, please Dad! Please! It's only five miles away and everyone will expect it."

"Our family won't expect it," Clive said.

Marilyn had gazed at the beguiling hotel brochure which spoke of champagne cocktails in the Green Drawing Room and photo opportunities on the sweeping staircase.

Eventually Clive had agreed, thinking that the business was doing reasonably well at the moment and there might be some mileage in advertising this fact.

Since then however Marilyn had suffered from increasing anxieties.

She had been severely unnerved by the initial visit which she and Antonia had made to the hotel. Clive had said that he would join them for this consultation but as the date of their appointment approached it had looked more and more unlikely that he would be back from abroad. Antonia had said, "We're just going to have to go without him, Mum."

Thinking over all this now a few weeks later Marilyn quailed at the thought of phoning Columb Court to speak to the daunting Peter Fullerton and raise the question of a crèche and fish fingers. She wondered whether it really might not have been possible to have had a marquee in their garden as some people further down the road had done for a party, but Antonia had said precipitously, "Oh no, Mum!"

Marilyn was uncertain about the reason for this reaction but feared it was, as Clive had suggested, because Roger's parents would think The Rowans was not grand enough.

But Clive had also pointed out that the lawn sloped too

steeply and the marquee would probably have to enclose the water feature.

This, the water feature, inspired by TV gardening programmes and a video loop promotion at the garden centre had by and large not been a success. It was supposed to be a natural pond encouraging wild life which turned out to be mostly water boatmen and toads. Marilyn didn't like the toads at all, they clogged the water with glutinous masses of spawn in the spring and had a habit of migrating round to the front of the house and getting squashed under the car wheels.

Meanwhile Imo, gazing down from her bedroom window, longed to be outside in the sunshine. Also she still felt hungry. She listened to locate Marilyn's whereabouts, and came to the conclusion that she was on the patio, which meant that it might be possible to get another sandwich without provoking her objections.

Through the open kitchen door Marilyn immediately noticed Imo rooting in the bread bin. Imo saw her head turn.

"I can't do anything without Mum seeing," she thought crossly as she slapped the peanut butter onto slices of bread. "Why don't they just leave me alone and let me go to Art College?"

She glared as she made off towards the upper lawn, clutching her sandwich and challenging Marilyn to say anything. "You don't understand me and I don't understand you," she thought. "I hate it here, I'm going to die of boredom, totally."

Watching her stalk away up the grassy slope Marilyn felt her heart contract; once more she remembered Imo as a little girl. She had managed to look scruffy however she was dressed; her hair was so soft and fine that slides, grips or ribbons simply slid down to ear level or fell right off. She lost things all the time: cardigans, belts, socks, gloves. And if there was anything which might get smeared on her face or her clothes, it did.

"Oh, why can't she be more friendly?" Marilyn thought, getting up and going back into the kitchen. "Why does she have to fight against everything we try to do for her?"

She looked at the loaf which Imo had again left on the work surface and a ripple of irritation passed through her; Imo wouldn't even co-operate about The Diet which was so important to Antonia.

"I wish I had someone to talk to," Marilyn thought, yet again. But yet again she couldn't think of anyone in the neighbourhood of The Rowans with whom she could discuss family problems. Mostly she and Clive socialised with couples connected with Clive's work or The Rotary Club, but even they weren't real friends.

Imo disappeared from view, to lie in the grass among the apple trees at the top of the garden. She left behind her, invisible but potent, the impression that she did not wish to be disturbed.

Marilyn eventually summoned the courage to ring the Columb Court number and ask to speak to the Functions Manager. When Peter Fullerton came to the phone he said that, although ideally he would have liked notice with the initial booking, the hotel could indeed offer children's entertainment. This would be in a separate marquee, with picnic hampers, nursery nurses and Coco the Clown, at a price so alarming it took her breath away.

CHAPTER 9

APRIL

Antonia's anxieties about the wedding were compounded by her sharing a flat in London with Roger's sister Lizzie and another girl called Petra Colyton.

Lizzie and Petra had been at boarding school together and had chosen Antonia to flat share from several applicants because, mostly, she could cook. Also, they thought that she wouldn't stand up for herself – they needed to be able to get their own way in the flat as the third bedroom had once been the larder and it had a view of the fire escape coated with pigeon droppings. The reduction in rent which Lizzie and Petra were proposing for this room didn't really equate with the difference in quality between their bedrooms and the one on offer.

The cooking was desirable because they wanted to give dinner parties.

Antonia was new to London and new to her job as a junior

chef with Directors' Lunches. She was excited by the realisation that here she now was, an independent city girl. It gave her a tingle of excitement to be minding the gap, hearing her heels click on the pavement as she walked back from the tube.

A girl about town. She hoped that she looked the part although inside she still felt unsure.

In the flat Lizzie and Petra continued to do things their way and for the first few months all went reasonably well.

As Antonia became less in awe of them, however, she couldn't deny to herself that she increasingly found the other two girls to be thoughtless and untidy.

The flat was on the first floor of a large mansion block and was approached through a high ceilinged, dark hall with its original black and white tiled floor and bottle green paintwork. Numbered doors, left and right, led to other flats and similarly upwards, where the layout was repeated on each landing of the wide lino covered stairs.

It was old fashioned and Antonia could never quite convince herself that she was living there. She hardly ever met anyone else on the stairs, although the number of dustbins in the alley beneath her bedroom window regularly filled and somebody put a lot of gin bottles into the re-cycling.

Lizzie and Petra liked to have a flat dinner party if they were stuck in London at the weekend and if no more exciting date offered.

It was, in fact, at one of these dinner parties for which Lizzie and Petra had bullied Antonia into cooking sea trout and a chocolate soufflé that things had begun to change, for on this evening Lizzie asked her brother Roger to make up the numbers.

"I know he's your brother – " Petra said, "but he's – "

"Boring?" Lizzie said. "I know. But all the men we know are

boring." She stared hard at Petra. "Or married."

"Oh, OK," Petra said hastily.

Roger had just gained a promotion with his City finance firm. He was very pleased with himself.

The Senior Partner with whom he had discussed his future had intimated that an appropriate parallel move could now be to get married. "There comes a time to hang up your shield," the Senior Partner said, maintaining his attachment to the myth that Roger was 'a bit of a lad with the girls'.

Roger agreed jocularly but felt as usual that the Senior Partner had got him muddled up with someone else.

That evening at the flat dinner party, having drunk several glasses of the champagne which he had brought with him to celebrate his promotion, he looked across the table at Antonia warm cheeked from the heat of the oven and thought, "Why not?"

Happy with his decision he made one of his jokes, about hoping it was a young trout he was eating and not an old trout, which made everyone except Antonia groan.

When Lizzie discovered which way the wind was blowing she was hopping mad.

When Roger took Antonia on a second date Lizzie flounced into the flat kitchen where Petra was drinking a papaya smoothie and reading the Daily Mail. Petra said her bloody brother must have lost it; what was he doing going out with Miss Apple Dumpling?

Petra laughed, and as Lizzie got crosser she laughed more. "Oops," Petra said, "apricot toilet paper in the en-suite. Lucky Roger!"

"He can't be serious," Lizzie said.

But Roger was serious. After all, he thought, Antonia came

pre-vetted by his sister and Petra so she must be suitable or they wouldn't have chosen her to flat share. The girls were pretty hot on that sort of thing.

The guys he played squash with thought she was pretty, she giggled at their jokes which like the trout one she didn't always understand. And the cooking was very good news.

When Roger and Antonia got engaged Lizzie went into a sulk which lasted for a week and since then relationships in the flat had become increasingly strained. Petra, now that she realised the situation was real and not a joke, sided with Lizzie. Antonia did not have the right parents, had not been to the right school, used the wrong vocabulary and didn't live in the country. She would be a hideous embarrassment as a sister-in-law.

So now, after a day at work and worrying about the rose petals for the wedding, when Antonia turned her key in the green painted door of the flat she felt as usual slightly anxious. Roger had told her that she was exaggerating things and that Lizzie and Petra were quite jolly when you really got to know them. "Which you will," he pointed out, "now we're engaged."

Today Lizzie and Petra were back before her and flopping on the sofa to watch a game show on television. Between their feet, which were resting on the coffee table, stood a bottle of red wine left over from the most recent dinner party; they each had a glass in their hand.

"Hi," Petra said, glancing briefly at Antonia. Lizzie kept her eyes fixed on the TV.

"Hello," Antonia said. She saw the pages of the Evening Standard sliding onto the floor, the wine glass rings on the coffee table, the trail of shoes, jackets and handbags cast aside by the other two when they fell through the door earlier and she felt a stab of annoyance. She liked things to be nice and tidy, which they knew.

"Are these people for real?" Lizzie said still staring at the screen. "Or a sub-species?"

Antonia went into her pokey bedroom where she had tried to brighten things up with a peach coloured duvet cover and valance, and matching pillow cases. Over the window she had hung a lace curtain which hid most of the depressing view of brick wall and fire escape.

She shook out the duvet over her aired bed, which was a single divan, this being necessitated by the lack of space.

Antonia and Roger had never shared this bed, the flat seemed so much Lizzie and Petra's place that Antonia didn't think she would have felt comfortable. Instead she stayed twice a week at Roger's small house in Fulham and here their quite adequate love-making took place.

Now, taking off her shoes she put them in the white canvas shoe tidy on the back of the door and then sat down on the bed. She stared at the photographs on the small chest-of-drawers: a picture of her parents on holiday in Tossa de Mar, one of herself and Imo aged eight and five playing in the garden of their house before they moved to The Rowans, and one of Roger in his squash kit. He had written on the back of this 'To Dumpling from her Own True Knight' but she was quite glad that the wording was hidden now she had put the photograph in a frame.

Lizzie and Petra had picked up on Roger's choice of nickname and, she knew, made fun of it.

As she sat there she was aware of a shaft of doubt which slid into her mind and manifested itself elsewhere as a nasty feeling of sickness in the pit of her stomach. For the last couple of weeks she had sometimes found herself feeling a bit queasy when she looked at Roger's photograph. An article in one of the wedding magazines talked about pre-wedding nerves and she was trying very hard to relax as they instructed, with breathing control and cutting back on caffeine.

Of course she loved Roger. He was protective, well off and clever, he had a good job and his own house and he said he loved her but sometimes she felt that the organisation of the wedding was draining her initial pleasure in her engagement, day on day.

She also thought sometimes that she would be happy to leave all the arranging to someone else, after all she did have her job and that could mean working weekend shifts. The wedding magazines' problem pages regularly dealt with complaints from brides whose mothers or mothers-in-law kept interfering with their wedding plans but Antonia now felt that she might be quite relieved to let Marilyn or Penelope sort out the myriad details.

Then on The Day she would be able to walk serene and happy down the aisle in a mist of white veil between pew ends decorated with sweetheart rose buds and trails of ivy . . . or maybe organza bows instead of the ivy . . . oh no, another decision!

Quite early on however she had become aware that some of the ideas which she and Marilyn had for a lovely wedding were not meeting with approval from Roger's parents. There had been that initial awkwardness when Roger had driven her up to the Rodmaine's house, The Old Granary, in Worcestershire for the weekend at Easter.

Antonia had brought with her the design which she and Marilyn had chosen for the wedding invitations. This featured, on the front, two linked gold hearts.

There had been a silence when Antonia first laid the invitation on the gilt-legged and glass-topped coffee table in the sitting room. George then had raised his eyebrows and Penelope had drawn a short breath and said, "Well – I think we were expecting something more traditional."

'More traditional' turned out to be embossed black lettering on thick card, formal wording and no decoration. The price of these invitations was considerably more than that of the gold hearts, which would have been, Antonia secretly remained convinced, nicer.

Now she felt forlorn. She did not want to spend the evening alone in her room but Lizzie and Petra often made her feel uncomfortable if she joined them in the sitting room. They would talk about people who she did not know and giggle at jokes in which she was not included and often did not understand.

When Petra had gone for what she described as 'a filthy weekend' with Jeremy, who Antonia suspected was, shockingly, already married, she had brought back a pink china ashtray with 'A Present from Hove' painted around the rim. Lizzie had laughed till she choked and fell off the sofa.

Although Antonia was in the kitchen when this happened she suspected that the joke was partly directed against her. She examined the ashtray later and guessed they were laughing because she didn't know about things which they thought were smart. Or not smart.

Now she decided to make herself a mug of raspberry tea and as quietly as possible opened her bedroom door and made her way to the kitchen.

The evening sky over London was becoming paler and the distant drone of the rush hour traffic was lessening. The warmth which had been generated in the streets during the sunny early summer day radiated back from the pavements and walls.

Newly unfurled leaves hung limpid on the plane trees and in this up-market residential area the wilted daffodils in the window boxes were being replaced with mostly blue or white trailing plants, occasionally an arty mixture of miniature aliums, ornamental cabbages or DIY herbs.

Sadly the flat carried no rights to the garden at the back of the building, which the kitchen overlooked. This was a rather sooty and uncared-for space but it possessed a strip of grass and a double white cherry tree, now in full flower. Antonia, standing at the window waiting for the kettle to boil, gazed down onto the billowy mass of snowy blossom and thought of her wedding dress.

Petra's laugh reached her from the sitting room. An unsettling thought slid into her mind: was her dress going to be too cherry-blossomy . . . too frilly? Lizzie had incomprehensibly said that she wished the cherry tree had been something else, maybe a monkey puzzle.

This was not the first time that Antonia had been gripped by doubts about the design of her dress. Maddy, the dressmaker, was getting a bit fed up and even Clive had said that it was time she made up her mind and stuck to it or the dress would never get made.

Antonia retreated with her raspberry tea to her bedroom.

In Fulham Roger walked home across the Common carrying his briefcase and wondering whether to get a frozen chicken korma for his supper, perhaps with a balancingly healthy mixed leaf salad.

It would certainly be nice to have Antonia's home cooking to look forward to when they were married. That and other things; he had a unsettling mental image of Antonia's creamy white breasts and nicely rounded bottom and himself climbing joyfully on top of her. He had to stop for a moment to take his thoughts elsewhere: the owner of a West Highland Terrier was pretending that she had not noticed the dog was depositing a small pile of turds under a chestnut tree.

It occurred to Roger that he could say something to the woman about cleaning up her dog's mess but he decided he wouldn't. He walked on, firmly fixing his mind on the report in his briefcase, which he had to read that night. As he reached the door of his house his mobile rang.

"Roger!" Antonia sounded as if she might be crying. She had started crying quite a lot lately and although girls did of course cry, as he knew, he was beginning to find it a bit wearing. More effectively than his deep breaths on the Common this acted to dispel any lingering feelings of desire.

"Hullo, Dumpling," he said with a note of caution in his voice.

"Are you at the house?"

"Just," he said, turning the key in the lock and pushing the door open

"Oh – " she paused and he heard a small quivering intake of breath. "Are you busy?"

Roger felt the tug of conflicting impulses. One was to say, "No, I'm not!" and go and pick her up in his Porsche and listen to her worries about the wedding and claim his reward in bed (or on the bed, or on the sofa). The other alternative was to sit down with a glass of wine, read his report notes and eat his chicken curry in front of the tennis on TV.

He stooped to pick up the letters and junk mail lying on the mat.

"Roger – ?"

"Uh, huh," he said, shuffling the letters in one hand.

"I miss you."

He heard a distinct sniff.

"What's the problem, Dumpling?"

"I feel so lonely."

"Isn't Lizzie there, or Petra?"

"Yes, they're here," Antonia said, she was keeping her voice down, "but – "

Roger decided he was feeling tired and the image of Antonia's breasts melted away from the edges of his mind. She just didn't seem to be able to hit it off with Lizzie and Petra, who could be a bit 'girly' sometimes but were really quite jolly.

"Well, why not have a chat with them?" he suggested. "That'll cheer you up."

"It won't!" Antonia wailed. Why couldn't Roger see how horrid Lizzie and Petra could be to her? "Can you come over?"

One of Roger's letters was a bill for the repair of the rear lights of the Porsche. Some oaf had reversed into it in the street outside the house and done a runner. To save his No Claims he was going to have to pay and the amount was upsetting. As he opened the garage bill he thought he felt intimations of a headache; he'd had a tough day at the office and he hadn't even managed to get a drink in his hand yet.

"No," he said. "I'm afraid I can't. I've got this report to read. Antonia, you are going to have to get used to this when we're married. I have my career to think about."

Antonia felt tears slip down her cheeks. She tried to brush them away with her hand which was not holding the phone. "But – " She wanted to try to explain her nagging worries about the wedding and specifically the new intractable problem of the crèche, however a sob caught at her throat and the words were lost.

Roger frowned.

"Please – " Antonia gasped soggily. "Roger? Can't you come over?"

If the time and place were right he found her neediness when she was feeling vulnerable rather feminine and attractive but now standing here, holding a handful of bills and with the front door still not yet latched behind him, he experienced a stab of irritation.

"No, I'm afraid I can't," he said. "This is what being a Finance Analyst means, I have responsibilities, there is the chance of a Senior Partnership with the firm within three years, you know." He paused to let this sink in. "It's important for both of us."

Antonia had to accept defeat. "Goodbye then," she whispered. "You do love me, don't you?"

"Yes," Roger said. "Of course."

"I love you too."

"Of course you do."

He paused for a moment and she didn't add anything.

"So, bye now," he said and with a definite feeling of relief rang off. Poor Dumpling, she got in such a state about nothing, really. When the wedding was over things would of course settle down, meanwhile he was just going to have to be firm. His career was at a critical point at the moment and he must remain focussed on that. After all it was going to provide for her and their children. The idea gave him a sense of worthy satisfaction.

When she realised the call was ended Antonia cried for five minutes and then looked up and saw her pink and blotchy face in the mirror on the chest-of-drawers. She couldn't, possibly, face Lizzie or Petra like this but she couldn't sit on her bed all evening and have no supper. Her stomach was rumbling already.

She opened the door of her room cautiously and listened,

trying to ascertain if the girls were still in the sitting room. Then she slipped out and locked herself in the bathroom and splashed her face with cold water. Lizzie and Petra heard her and looked at each other, in delightful anticipation.

Antonia sat on the edge of the bath with a wet flannel over her eyes. When she removed this she noticed the plastic doll with a frilly crocheted skirt on the shelf opposite. With a nasty stab of suspicion she picked it up; the skirt concealed a roll of apricot toilet paper.

But this time Lizzie and Petra had gone too far, for although Antonia now felt totally miserable and stayed in her own room all evening, she possessed a latent stubborn streak. She might not fully understand the girls' jokes but she knew they were intended to upset her.

In succeeding days she became less accommodating about doing more than her fair share of housekeeping in the flat. She 'didn't see' notes left in the kitchen asking her to pick up extra bits of shopping and she stopped cleaning the bath and the shower unless she was using them herself. She even managed to leave the others' dirty plates in the sink and not stack them in the dishwasher.

And the next time she stayed with Roger she was just a little less pliable and less willing to listen to his reflections on the impression he was making at work. He was slightly puzzled and couldn't quite figure out what was different about Dumpling, but whatever it was it was probably down to hormones.

In her new mood of defiance Antonia also dug her heels in about the crèche. She didn't want Roger's parents to have any excuse to be disparaging about the wedding. There would have to be a crèche for the children and her dad would just have to understand.

CHAPTER 10

APRIL

After some bureaucratic chasing up of references and an up-to-date tetanus injection Imo was accepted by the Garden Volunteer organisation and shortly afterwards received the offer of a placement at Trevean.

Marilyn was anxious but Clive phoned Sally Lacock and reported that she seemed sensible and was a teacher, so Imo should be safe enough.

"But what about the wedding?" Marilyn protested. "Imo needs to be here for dress fittings! And . . ." anxiety made her voice rise. "Shoes!" They still hadn't got Imo's bridesmaid shoes, she had such large feet.

"She's not going to Africa," Clive said. "Only Cornwall. There are trains, and buses." Indeed, Sally Lacock had suggested that Imo come down by coach and she would meet her at the bus station in the local town.

Clive was pleased that Imo had got a job, if only a temporary one. It would hopefully take her mind off the Art College nonsense.

Marilyn drove Imo to catch the coach, both of them were on edge. Imo had never been away on her own before except on school trips. Also, she was refusing to take any clothes with her, other than her jeans, a pair of combat trousers and some T-shirts; this, particularly, upset Marilyn.

"It's a gardening job!" Imo stared ahead, her sunglasses down like a visor as Marilyn backed the car out of The Rowans' short brick driveway and into the road.

"But you'll be living in the house!" Marilyn's voice hit a note of anguish as drivers coming in both directions hooted furiously. "Won't you?"

"I don't know."

"But your Dad phoned them. He said -" Marilyn struggled to straighten up the car.

Imo refused to respond It felt as if the muscles in her jaw had locked tight; her mother was so annoying she could not bear to talk to her.

Marilyn, from the scrappy fragments of information which she had gathered from Imo and which Clive had acquired from his phone call to Sally Lacock, pictured Trevean as a large and imposing country mansion, something along the lines of Columb Court Hotel. A mental image of Imo sitting at the dining table in grubby jeans and a T-shirt with the sleeves cut off, made her feel so distressed she could cry.

"But you've got some nice clothes . . . skirts and dresses. Why do you never wear them?" Marilyn braked as she reached the bottom of the hill. The driver behind her, who had assumed she would continue through the junction, which was clear, flashed his lights.

"I'm going to be digging!" Imo said furiously. "Of course, I won't wear a dress!"

"But not in the house -"

Imo turned her head away and stared through the side window at the knobby pollarded lime trees whose roots were doing severe damage to the pavements on The Glebe. She saw the houses set back tidily behind their front lawns, each just like The Rowans and she thought, "I can't wait to be out of here!"

When they reached the bus depot, she dragged her backpack out of the car and said, "Thanks. You don't need to wait."

"But I want to -" Marilyn started to protest.

Imo shut the car door with finality to avoid hearing the rest of the sentence "- see you safely on the bus".

Marilyn sat disconsolate at the wheel for a few minutes until eventually she registered the sign 'No Parking except for Buses'. She drove round a mini-roundabout and returned looking for Imo, meaning to wave, but couldn't see her.

This was because Imo had deliberately gone into the newsagents beside the bus station to avoid seeing Marilyn again. "Leave me alone!" she thought furiously, standing in the queue to buy a bottle of strawberry flavoured water and a box of tic tacs.

She paid at the till and muttered to herself as she pushed everything into her bag, "Just stop interfering with my life!" The girl on the counter stared at her.

The Cornwall coach drew in, Imo climbed aboard and parked herself in a seat towards the rear and stared fixedly out of the far window until they had passed the bottom of Glebe Road.

Back at The Rowans Marilyn stood for a while in the hall,

then went upstairs and opened the door to Imo's room. The air of abandonment made her catch her breath as she stared at the tossed back duvet, the wardrobe door left open and the bits and pieces of clothing, clean and dirty things muddled up together, lying on the floor. Photographs of teenagers, most of whom she didn't think she recognised, were stuck around the mirror and inside the wardrobe door.

Marilyn gazed at the photographs; they were mostly of groups of girls with their arms wrapped around each other's shoulders. Were they friends of Imo's from her Sixth Form course? She looked at their bright, outlined eyes, their thick shining hair, their laughing mouths with the startling coloured lipstick and felt desolate, excluded. Her own eyes pricked with tears.

Meanwhile at Trevean relative peace had descended upon the house by the middle of the day. The Lacocks were occupied with their individual daily routines: James was in his study with the newspaper, Sally marking essays, Clarissa in her sitting room, the children at school, or in Frankie's case nursery.

Later on, Ned wandered up from the bamboos to find himself some food and, the kitchen being empty, he removed five cold sausages and a large chunk of cheese which he found in the fridge, together with the remains of the loaf from the bread bin. He took these down the slope below the house to sunbathe for a while; he wanted to consider the possibility of asking his grandmother to buy him a car. Lying in the sun he had to break chunks off the loaf as he had forgotten to bring a knife.

Graham was as usual in the kitchen garden.

Sally, tossing the last essay onto the 'marked' pile – they were an A-level batch on 'Much Ado About Nothing' – realised that it was past one o'clock. She decided to cobble together some soup for lunch and going to the kitchen she searched the fridge for the cold sausages which she had thought she might add to it.

Later when she took a bowl up to Clarissa, she explained that she was collecting the new girl from the bus station.

"I hope she'll be some use," Clarissa said.

"I'm sure she will be," Sally said firmly.

"There isn't any bread?" Clarissa suggested.

"No, sorry," Sally said. "We must have used it up at breakfast. I can get some more when I'm out."

Coming down to the hall she stuck her head into the study to repeat the information for James. "Lunch? I've got to go soon to pick up the new volunteer."

"Good." James said to lunch, he followed her to the kitchen. He didn't want to talk about the new girl, someone else to claim Sally's attention away from him, and female too, so potentially yet more irritation.

"Maybe we could take the dogs across the fields later to collect the children from school?" Sally suggested as they ate the soup. This was the sort of thing which James liked to do, a peaceful walk together without distraction, the dogs enjoying themselves.

James nodded agreement; the soup had cheered him up. He breathed out, a short break perhaps from the wear and tear of what life threw at him each and every day.

"Oh hell!" Sally glanced at the clock on the shelf above the range.

"What?" James felt an instant stab of anxiety somewhere just below his ribs.

"The girl's room," Sally said. "I haven't looked at it."

I knew it, James thought. The girl was intruding, and she hadn't even got here yet. And why should Sally spend any time on her room, dear heaven the girl was coming to work wasn't she, surely she could sort out her room herself?

"Why do you need to look at it?" he asked.

"I've got to make her bed up," Sally said, pushing her chair back.

A further unwelcome question occurred to James. "Where are you putting her?"

"In the attic," Sally said.

James was horrified. "What, in the house?"

"Yes," Sally said, "she can't share with Graham or Ned, can she?"

"I don't see why not," James said morosely. "They all share everything these days, don't they?"

"I don't think that would be acceptable to the Garden Volunteer people," Sally said. "There's a bit more soup if you want it. I don't know what's happened to Ned, he's usually hanging around waiting for food." But it occurred to her that this might explain the missing sausages.

James didn't care about Ned. "No bread?"

"No," Sally said. "Sorry. I'm going to get some."

She went to collect bedding for the attic room but only managed to unearth a Thomas the Tank Engine duvet cover which she decided would have to do and hung it over the airing cupboard door to get some of the creases out while she rummaged for sheets.

She hadn't been up to the attic room for a while and now

climbing the narrow brown painted back staircase and opening the low door she found the room hot and stuffy with three dead flies on the window sill. A Victorian wooden towel-rail was propped on one of the two single beds, draped with a coverless duvet and various towels and bits of clothing which looked as if they might have come out of the washing basket. Across the floor was a scattering of toys and blue glitter dust, clearly Claud and Frankie had been building a den.

"Oh drat!" Sally exclaimed, exasperated. She opened the casement window, scooped up the flies and tossed them out into the leaded gulley which ran between the slate slopes of the double roof. Then she turned back to the bed but gave up in despair of having time to sort it out.

Leaving the room, she made a mental note to tell the boys off for going where they shouldn't be and making a mess, then she shut the door on it all and hurried down the stairs.

The girl's bus was due soon.

"I'm just going!" Sally called to locate James as she came into the hall. He had, as she had expected, sought solace with Coal in the study. He had put his soup bowl beside the kitchen sink as a gesture towards domestic co-operation which he felt, at an emotional level, made his having to suffer further disruption because of this girl sadder yet and more unfair.

At first James didn't answer Sally, hoping that she would come and find him and see how much he was in need of cheering up. Then, however, he heard her open the front door and knew that she was actually leaving.

"I'm here!" he called.

"I'll be about an hour. A bit less if the bus is on time."

"Hello?" James called again, and then more urgently, "Sally!"

She came back and appeared in the study doorway. "I won't

be long. Then we can take the dogs out."

He nodded glumly, Coal at his feet looked up and thumped his short plume of a tail.

"It'll be OK," she said. "This girl. She won't get in the way. She'll be a help."

James sighed. Sally must realise how difficult all this coming and going and people in the house was for him.

Sally did realise and her heart contracted but she steeled herself to be resolute, Trevean must somehow start to be financially productive. James' pension, Clarissa's pension and her part time teaching salary were not going to be able to keep the place afloat much longer. Her contract anyway was up for renewal for it was nearly the end of the college year but this fact she had pushed away from the front of her mind.

Imo's bus had arrived early. She stood on the pavement beside the stop with people milling around her backpack, watching for a car of superior status to her father's Jaguar for after all the Lacocks were the owners of an historic garden. She therefore didn't register when the old and scruffy Volvo drew up beside her.

Sally stuck her head out of the window and called, "Are you for Trevean?"

Imo stared, then nodded.

"Right," Sally jumped out, leaving the engine running and ignoring the double yellows. "Can you put your bag in here?"

Imo understood this, correctly, to be a request not a question. She pushed her back-pack into the car boot to lie on top of a layer of general detritus, bathing kit, odd socks, biscuit wrappers and scrunched up plastic bags.

"Quick," Sally said, "I think I'm causing an obstruction." A bus was waiting behind her and an elderly couple wanting to board it waved angrily.

Imo climbed into the front seat. Sally sighed. "Why they have to get themselves so worked up at having to wait for two seconds I do not know, and why there is no-where sensible to pick anyone up here I also do not know." She waved at the angry couple and then glanced across at Imo, "I am Sally Lacock. And you are Imogen Bradford I hope?"

Imo nodded. She was feeling rather disorientated.

Sally drove out of the town. "How was the journey?"

"OK." Imo wasn't sure what else to say.

Not very chatty, Sally thought, is that good or bad? Remembering James, waiting for her to get back, she put her foot down a bit and hoped she wouldn't meet a tractor where the road got increasingly narrow. Branches of hawthorn and sloes and the flat white heads of cow parsley knocked against Imo's side of the car.

"Have you had some horticultural experience?" Sally asked, trying to remember what she knew about Imo. The garden organisation had forwarded details of several applicants, most of whom had not materialised into actual volunteers.

Imo still felt a bit odd, now with a sinking feeling above her stomach. In her desire to escape the wedding preparations at home she had largely overlooked what exactly she was going to be required to do at Trevean.

"Not much," she said cautiously. At school she had planted some crocus corms in pots for the Christmas sale but that was when she was in Year Six; more recently she had occasionally watered the rampant spider plants in the Art Studio at College, where they were supposed to remove the toxicity of the paint and fixatives from the atmosphere. Occasionally her parents had prevailed upon her to turn the hose on the tomatoes or de-head the front rose bushes, but in honesty gardening wasn't her thing.

Faced now with Sally's question she was daunted. The watering of the spider plants had been largely by default, for despite the lecturer's remonstrances the students used to empty the dregs of their bottled water into them.

"Oh well," Sally made herself sound positive. "I'm sure you'll pick it all up easily enough. It's quite basic stuff we need really, mostly clearing undergrowth and weeding. We've got two other volunteers here already, and they can show you what to do."

Imo nodded.

They reached the main gate of Trevean, propped open and hanging lopsided from its granite gatepost as one of the hinges was cracked. Sally drove up the drive and stopped the car in front of the house, thinking as she had thought before, I must sort out the weeds here Dandelions, chickweed and beech seedlings were encroaching across the gravel.

As Imo climbed out of the car, she found a piece of paper had stuck to the bottom of her trainer. It was a child's drawing which looked a bit like a potato with twigs sticking out of it; she bent to peel it off.

"Oh, that's one of Frankie's art works," Sally said, glancing down.

Imo saw that it had been stuck to her shoe with a squashed jelly sweet.

"Swap," Sally said lifting Imo's backpack from the boot and holding her hand out for the drawing, which now had a trainer sole print across half of it. "I think it's a hungry monster. We've got several of those. Frankie likes me to put them up somewhere."

Imo picked up her backpack and gazed at the house. It didn't look as big as she had expected, but possibly it was very old. She considered the small irregular mullioned windows and low granite arch over the front door. The flowerbeds at the base of the walls were overgrown and there were children's toys sticking out of the vegetation, plastic spades, a small blue lorry and a three-wheel trike with convolvulus twining around its frame.

Following her gaze, Sally said, "Well, there's plenty to do, all those lupins and irises should have been lifted and split last year really but what with one thing and another it didn't happen."

Imo realised that she was still feeling a bit odd; she wondered if she was actually going to be sick. She remembered feeling like this before when she went on the French Exchange from school and ended up staying with Miserable Monique who had cried in England but sulked in France and would not talk to her.

When they went into the hall, which was dark, she stared at the stuffed fish and birds in glass cases and the enormous fireplace which contained a half-burnt tree trunk, while Sally talked round a door to someone who did not come out to greet them.

Imo dropped her backpack on the dusty carpet.

Then they went upstairs, along a corridor and up again to a room which seemed to be full of children's stuff. Sally bundled most of this up in a rug from the floor and pulled it out onto the small landing. "I'll bring you up some bedding," she said. "I'm afraid I haven't had a minute to get it sorted."

Left alone, Imo crossed to the small window. She wondered if it was possible to get out and sunbathe there, in the gulley between the roofs; this idea cheered her a little because it promised privacy.

When Sally came back, she brought a pink flannel sheet, two yellow and orange flowery pillow-cases and the Thomas the

Tank Engine duvet cover. Imo, jolted, momentarily half closed her eyes.

"Can you sort yourself out with these?" Sally said. "Sorry about the colours, but at least they're clean."

"Does it matter which bed?" Imo asked, preferring the one beneath the window, from which it would be possible to see the sky.

"No," Sally said. "Have whichever you like. This room's all yours, for the moment anyway."

She turned to go. "When you've sorted yourself out come down and have a look around. I'll introduce you to the family later and Graham and Ned, you'll be working with them. I'm afraid I've got to go now; my husband is waiting – we're supposed to be collecting the children from school."

As Sally's footsteps hurried away down the stairs Imo continued her earlier examination of the room. In the way of furniture, besides the two beds with battered brass frames, there was a pine chest-of-drawers painted cream, with on top of it a wooden framed swing mirror. The single bentwood chair had a seat decorated with punched holes. A cupboard, which proved to be of no great depth, was built into the wall near the door.

The ceiling sloped and so, Imo soon realised, did the bare floorboards. It was really rather a pokey little room, but Imo decided that she liked it anyway, liked it better in fact than her room at home with its floral girly bits and pieces chosen by Marilyn. Even on reflection she decided that the eclectic mix of bed-clothes had a sort of comforting, childhood feel.

On the wall above the beds there was a faded reproduction of Botticelli's Venus, rising in her shell from neat, crimped waves. The white paint on the wall was peeling slightly.

When Imo looked round for her back-pack she realised that

it must still be downstairs in the hall; she decided to go and find it. She missed the turn, however, onto the main bedroom landing and so ended up continuing down the lower flight of the stairs and was lost in the back half of the house where Sally had not taken her.

Uncertain, she stood in the slate floored corridor, having no idea which way to go. Around the bottom of the back stairs, at her feet, there was a welter of children's flip flop sandals and Wellingtons and tumbleweed balls of dog hair.

Everywhere, at first, was quiet.

She was startled then, after a minute or so, on hearing a door open in a further room and what sounded like someone pulling a chair across a hard floor and a heavy box dropped onto a solid surface.

Imo realised that she could feel her heart beating but after a moment or two of hesitation she decided that she was going to have to ask this person, whoever it was, to tell her how to find her way back to the front of the house. Cautiously she walked along the corridor in the direction of the sounds.

Graham had brought down the box of potatoes, peas and beans from the vegetable garden; now he leaned over the kitchen table writing on the back of an empty envelope. When, looking up, he saw Imo standing in the doorway he was as much caught out and discomfited as she had been. He hadn't grasped that she was arriving and girls threw him off balance at the best of times, even when he was expecting to see them. Who was she?

"Hello," Imo said doubtfully, gazing at Graham's muddy jeans and rolled up shirt sleeves and uncut hair.

Graham nodded, frowned slightly and returned his gaze to the envelope on which he had written for Sally's benefit BEETROOT READY.

Imo expected him to say something else, but he didn't. She stood, at a loss.

"I'm Imo," she said at last. She tried to remember the names Sally had given her. "Are you . . . Ned?"

His face flickered displeasure. "No," he said, his head still bent as he considered the note he had finished writing. He propped it on top of the box of vegetables and then turned towards the door.

"I think I'm going to be working with you," Imo said, anxious to get some information.

Graham paused "Oh?" His tone was not encouraging.

"I'm a garden volunteer."

Graham did not respond.

"Are you?" Imo asked. "A volunteer too?"

As ever Graham was reluctant to release personal information, he considered his reply. "Eh?"

Then on reflection, with the aim of ending the exchange he added, "Yeah."

Imo did not know what to say next. Might he offer to show her the garden where she would be working? But he didn't. He went out into the back porch, pulled his boots on and then paused. His head re-appeared in the doorway. "More rhubarb if wanted."

Then he went away across the cobbled yard.

They both recognised that this had been an unsatisfactory meeting. Imo realised that she had forgotten to ask for directions to the front hall and this person hadn't even told her his name. Graham was annoyed with himself for not adding the rhubarb to the note he had left for Sally. The girl turning up like that had put him off.

Imo, left alone in the kitchen, looked around. It was totally unlike the kitchen at The Rowans which was always so clean and shiny with its ruched blinds and jars with gingham mob caps.

She came forward to stand beside the wooden table, unvarnished and huge, with at one end the vegetable box left by Graham. She read his note about the beetroot, written entirely in capitals.

There was a Marie Celeste air about this room as if a number of people had got up recently from the table and exited at speed, leaving behind them dirty bowls, a plastic container of milk, a quantity of junk mail and some toy sheep. Imo lifted her gaze and looked round; there were children's paintings stuck on the walls, on backs of doors and stuffed into bowls amongst fresh fruit, withered fruit and vegetables. One or two of the paintings she picked up and examined; they were similar to the one she had trodden on in the car, potato monsters.

There was a large cream coloured range in the chimney alcove, the paint marked by much burnt-on spillages from cooking, and a scattering of shoes, boots and clothes, mostly children's, across areas of the floor.

All in all, it was a room where life clearly happened, ebb and flow.

Imo's glance passed over the general clutter. Like Ned she was not used to getting involved in domestic details, these were of interest to Antonia and her mother, but basically boring. However, the impression of activity and people and the degree of chaos appealed to her.

She continued to stand for a while, looking around, uncertain. Then she remembered her backpack and decided to see if she could find it. There were two doors in the wall opposite the range and cautiously she went across and turned the handle of one, which opened into a small room with wide slate shelves and a metal grill over the window. The second room contained rows of oil lamps. Both rooms were cold and smelled unused and musty.

Giving up on these she retraced her steps into the corridor and followed it to a green baize door which she pushed open and so found herself finally back in the front hall. Here was her backpack lying where she had left it beside the huge fireplace. Seeing it was a surprising comfort in this strange, unfamiliar place and she lugged it up to her room and dumped it on the bed by the window.

CHAPTER 11

APRIL

In the kitchen garden Graham had finished thinning a row of lettuce seedlings and was debating whether to start clearing a further area of brambles.

He was steeling himself to ask Sally about more planting, but he found it painfully difficult to communicate what was needed. And she would talk, and ask questions.

The Lacocks all talked, at each other but also at him. On and on, questioning, putting suggestions, interrupting, expecting comments.

Graham had made a list of the vegetables he wanted to plant, more French beans, lettuce, spinach. The winter stuff needed planning too, he wondered if Sally would give him the cash to go to the farmers' market to buy leek and cabbage and cauliflower plants, main crop potatoes. If the greenhouses were in better shape he could grow more from seed.

He stared across at the original wooden framed greenhouse by the south wall, it was slewed at one end where the structural timbers had rotted and the glass roof panels had avalanched over the edge and lay smashed among the nettles and grass. Another job to do – clear that lot up.

What was needed was more manpower. Over half the garden was still uncultivated, the soil should be turned over to let the weeds start rotting down. He considered the girl who had turned up in the kitchen; it was unlikely she'd be much use but like the others she would probably talk.

He went across to the old potting shed to examine again his list of seeds. He liked this small building which was sited in a corner where two walls met. It was stone built with a roof of small hand-cut slates. Inside on the cobweb coated shelves were stacked clay pots, ranged in size; tools, mostly old and rusty, were hung between nails against the wall.

Below the window there was a long bench for sorting seeds and potting out. A snail eaten planting schedule from 1915 still hung from a nail. Sally had pointed this out to Graham.

"So sad," she said. "The village boys who worked here would have all left together to join up for the First World War. Most of them were probably killed in France. And if they did come back times had changed and there were no Lacocks left either, to run things."

Graham felt the presence of 'the old men' who had worked in the local tin and copper mines, or on the land. The men, particularly, who had looked after this garden when it would have been properly managed, when tasks were tackled at the correct time of the year with the correct tools and the correct knowledge. He would have fitted in then, talked the right language.

For this was part of the trouble, not that he couldn't talk, but that the language which he had been raised to use was different from the language he met here, different and by implication, inferior. He was well aware that James and Ned thought he was ignorant, and all of them made him feel awkward, even the kids. The new girl would be the same.

He stared bitterly at the seed packets he had sorted on the work bench. He was nineteen years old and he didn't know what he was going to do with his life. He could work on the small holding with his father, which was what his parents wanted. But there must be more going on out there.

Well, there was, of course. Ned for instance would not be hanging around, he'd be off with the movers and shakers. This, Graham thought, was what got to him the most, that for some people it all came so easy.

They'd had everything on a plate, the likes of Ned. You could see that by the way they behaved, like they were owed.

For Ned was no practical use. He didn't know how to use tools; when he first came to Trevean he had been set to clear the overgrown flower beds in the small formal garden but all he did was take out everything, weeds and flowering plants both, and scatter earth and root clumps on the surrounding gravel.

While Graham brooded in the kitchen garden Ned was in fact feeling an equal measure of frustration. He was back clearing the bamboos, but he wanted to be in the sea. Sod it, this place was within three miles of the beach. Yet again he was faced with his need for a car.

Fallen bamboo leaves rustled, dry and papery around his feet. For an hour or so he continued hacking and dragging the thick canes to the stack he was creating; Sally was supposed to be finding out about selling them to a garden centre. The air in

121

the valley was dusty and humid, on an impulse he tossed down his billhook so that the blade embedded into the ground where he left it as he headed up the slope towards the rear of the house.

The laundry yard was still and empty, sunlight lying over the cobbles and the dandelion flowers opened wide in the warmth; mosquitoes danced above the sludgy water in the large slate tank beside the laundry house wall. Ned fetched out a wooden chair from the kitchen and sat in the sun to consider the car problem further, which might necessitate getting somehow to Sidmouth where his grandmother lived. She would probably help him with the money, a more real problem was that his parents would kick up a fuss if they discovered that he had asked her.

He stared at the dust motes floating in the air and let his mind wander around the unreasonableness of his parents. This whole Garden Volunteer thing had been their idea, not his. Why couldn't he have gone travelling like most other people or at least spent the summer in Oman with them to take in some swimming and tennis and have a break after the A-level stress? But no, he had been packed off to this back-of-nowhere place to slave away with virtually no money on the basis that it would be useful for his career.

Some while later, thinking he heard a movement, he glanced up. A girl was standing in the doorway of the back porch of the house, he stared at her in surprise.

"Hi," he said.

"Hi." She sounded uncertain.

Ned stayed where he was. "Are you looking for someone?"

Imo shifted her feet. "I'm a new garden volunteer," she said. "I'm Imo."

Ned felt a stab of regret that she was not, as he considered in this first moment of assessment, one of those stunning girls. She was wearing combats and a sleeveless brownish T-shirt, her hair was a bit of a mess. He stood up only after a moment's hesitation and came across the sun hot cobbles.

When he saw her face more closely however with its hopeful smile he decided that she was after all quite pretty and anyway anything was better than nothing. Under the T-shirt she had, he could see, breasts.

He said more positively, "I'm Ned."

"Oh – " Imo gazed at him.

"Have you just got here?" he asked.

"Yes. Mrs Lacock fetched me from the coach."

"Sally," Ned said. "It's OK to call them by their Christian names. Sally and James. But James doesn't get involved much with the garden."

"Oh."

She didn't have much to say. Possibly she was shy which he thought would be good on the whole. And she was looking at him as if she might fancy him, or fancied him already, which was definitely good.

"Where've they put you?" he asked.

Imo looked blank for a moment and then grasping his meaning, she said, "Oh . . . at the top of the house, in the attic."

"I'm in there," Ned nodded over his shoulder at the Laundry House. "And so is Graham." His tone was disparaging.

Imo flushed, wondering if it was Graham she had met in the kitchen.

Ned felt there was perhaps some need for justification if he was to retain her favourable interest in him and said, "He's a bit . . . rough I suppose."

He chose to smile, which had upon Imo the positive effect he had intended. She felt her heart beat.

He then had a sudden thought, "Is Sally here?" Perhaps Sally would drive him to the cove, he might offer to make the time up later. Possibly.

"I think she's gone to collect the children," Imo said. "But I'm not sure. I haven't seen anyone else."

"Oh sod it. In the car?"

"No, walking, I think. She said she was going with her husband. Is that James? And the dogs?"

"The dogs," Ned stared displeased across the yard, considering. "They smell."

If he walked to the bus stop at the bottom of the drive and if a bus actually turned up, it would take him most of the way to the cove. He could hire a body-board from the café on the beach for an hour for he certainly wasn't going to carry one of the Lacock's battered body boards all that way. This was looking increasingly like his only option.

"I've got to go, actually" he said.

"Oh – " Regret sounded in Imo's voice.

"Need to catch a wave," Ned said and then thinking she might suggest that she came too, he turned abruptly and went into the Laundry House to collect his wetsuit. She would expect him to talk to her and possibly look after her.

Imo hung about hopefully and was disappointed when Ned reappearing with his back-pack slung over his shoulder gave her only a brief nod and set off without pausing, around the corner of the house. She gazed after him and stood for a minute or two wondering what to do next, until she eventually took the same path, past rampant camellia bushes and the beds of the small formal garden.

Here Sally had got Graham to put in a few dozen wall flowers, to repair the ravages of Ned's weeding work. She had an idea to make an Elizabethan Physic Garden in this area, which bordered the oldest part of the house but time and money as she said to herself, precluded. Time and money. As they so often did.

Beneath the magnolia which reached the buds of its giant porcelain flowers up past the first-floor windows, Imo stood sadly on the weedy gravel. There was no sign of Ned. Eventually she decided to find her way back up to her room and to unpack; she wandered to the front of the house and inside.

"Who are you?"

Imo paused on the top step of the main staircase and turned to gaze, startled, at the figure standing at the end of the galleried landing, an old lady with an accusatory manner.

"Imo . . . . Imogen Bradford."

"And what," Clarissa asked her, "are you doing here?"

"I'm – " Imo decided to stick to the immediate, "going to unpack."

"You," Clarissa told her, "are the new garden girl."

"Yes."

Clarissa was headed for the lavatory. As usual these days she wanted to get there with a reasonable degree of urgency but having dozed after lunch in her chair with her rug over her knees she was stiff.

"Help me," she said to Imo. The girl might as well make herself useful.

Imo advanced towards Clarissa with reluctance. She didn't know any old people; they were different from normal people. Her grandparents had died when she was little, or before she was even born.

Clarissa held out her hand, "Give me your arm."

Together they proceeded along the landing towards the

bathroom. Increasingly Clarissa felt the need to arrive in time, she bit her lip. "Open it please," she said when they reached the door.

Realising where they were and repulsed by the thought that she might be expected to stay here while this bossy old lady actually used the toilet Imo hesitated in the doorway, but Clarissa got her to accompany her to where she could lower and raise herself by hanging onto the hand basin.

As Imo then headed immediately for escape, Clarissa called after her, "Wait outside!"

"This wretched arthritis," Clarissa said to herself, as she struggled with skirt and underskirt. Sally had suggested getting some elasticated trousers, but Clarissa had reacted explosively to this idea, life was undignified enough already as old age claimed you without surrendering entirely. "I'm not totally decrepit yet," she said. "I don't need to look like a cleaning woman."

"I didn't mean – "

"And not senile."

"Of course not. Please don't, Mother. I was only trying to think of something practical."

"It's not necessary."

Now Imo stood on the landing, aware of Clarissa's huffing and puffing in the bathroom and wondered what would happen if she just slipped away and pretended she hadn't heard the command to stay. But it was too late, for the door was opened and Clarissa emerged and demanded again to hold her arm. "That lavatory is far too low," she said. "The one on the stairs is more convenient."

Imo could offer no comment and so they made their way, negotiating the two shallow steps up to the half landing outside Clarissa's sitting room.

Once she was seated in her chair by the window and had got her breath back Clarissa looked at the girl standing in front of her. She appeared to have strands of coloured thread in her hair, which presumably indicated that she was interested in her appearance but really the results were not satisfactory. Her clothes, dull and unfeminine anyway, were scruffy and creased.

"So," Clarissa said, "what did you say you were called?"

Imo told her again.

"And you're here to work in the garden?"

"Yes."

"We have two young men here already. Ned is charming, he is going on to study estate management."

Clarissa's eyes travelled over Imo's T-shirt, which seemed to have had its sleeves ripped off, with the arm-holes left frayed. What was the girl thinking of?

"Sit down for a minute," Clarissa said. "You're making me crick my neck, having to look up at you."

Imo sat on the edge of the chintz covered Victorian nursing chair opposite Clarissa and wished she was somewhere else.

"And there is also Graham," Clarissa said. "He works in the kitchen garden."

"I've met him," Imo said, making the connection. "He was in the kitchen, bringing in some vegetables."

"I hope he had taken his boots off," Clarissa said. "Sally doesn't have time to chase after them all the time."

Imo instinctively looked down at her trainers. "And Ned," she said. "I saw him too."

Clarissa fixed her with a sharp gaze. "Where?"

"He was outside, he's gone to surf."

"Oh," Clarissa was still looking at her. "I'm Mrs Lacock's mother. My name is Mrs Seaton."

Imo nodded, uncertain.

"Tell me about your family," Clarissa said. "What does your father do?"

Imo very much disliked being cross questioned; also she wasn't actually too sure what Clive did, he didn't discuss his work much at home for no-one was interested in injection moulding.

"Dad runs his own company," she said doubtfully.

"What kind of a company?"

Imo squeezed her hands together in her lap, the chair was very low, now she had to look up at Clarissa. "He makes things out of plastic," she said. "Bits for boats and roofs and stuff."

"Oh?" Clarissa sounded non-committal. "And what about your mother?"

"She – " Imo paused, checked by a fleeting unexpected feeling of loyalty to Marilyn, "she cooks and . . . does the plants in the garden and sometimes . . . changes the curtains and things."

Clarissa nodded, "Makes the house nice." This information at least seemed to meet with her approval.

"What about your grandparents? Grandparents are important."

"No, they're – " Imo hesitated, looking at Clarissa, so old. "Dead".

"Really? And you are at school?"

Imo frowned slightly. "I've just finished at Sixth Form College."

"Hmm, well it won't be book work here," Clarissa glanced away dismissively. "You can have too much education in my opinion."

"I was doing Art," Imo said, stung. "I want to go to Art College."

Clarissa was undaunted. "That's not much use in real life, is it?"

Imo thought, why do I have to have this horrible old lady being rude to me? She found embarrassing tears gathering in her eyes and blinked to try and get rid of them.

"Never mind," Clarissa said, "you're young, you'll survive. It's not the same when you get old, there's not things to look forward to anymore and your problems don't go away."

Imo thought. "Being old is gruesome. I won't let it happen to me. I'm not going to have someone take me to the toilet. Yuck."

The sound of voices and running feet on the stairs announced the return of the children from school. Clarissa's face lit up. "Careful, careful!" she called as the door swung open and knocked against a polished wood bureau; Peridta and Claud arrived panting in front of them.

They crashed to a halt on seeing Imo.

"This is Imogen," Clarissa said. "She has come to help in the garden."

"Like Graham and Ned?" Perdita asked.

"Yes," Clarissa said. "Say 'How do you do?' and be polite."

"How do you do?" they both said.

"This is Perdita and Claud," Clarissa said.

"Hello." Imo felt outnumbered.

Perdita pushed a straggling lock of hair behind her ear. "How did you get here?"

"By coach."

"We didn't know you were coming," Claud said and then added, trying as ever to be kind, "But it's nice."

"Nice of you to come and help with the garden," Perdita explained. "We did, actually. Know you were coming, but we forgot."

Clarissa wanted to reclaim their attention. "How was school today?" she asked.

"We did wax," Perdita said.

"Wax?"

"Yes, beeswax and sealing wax on letters."

Clarissa said. "Why? Schools are so odd these days."

"It's a project."

"And we did Growing Things," Claud said. "Our beans are growing. Up poles."

"Well," Clarissa said, "you'll be able to show Imogen what to do then."

CHAPTER 12

APRIL

Imo looked at the children, their school uniform was crumpled and indeed rather grubby for Sally sorted out a clean set on Mondays and that was about it.

"Where are you going to sleep?" Claud asked. "Are you going to share with Perdita?"

At this Perdita appeared slightly anxious, flicking an end of hair into her mouth and chewing it. Clarissa tut-tutted at her reprovingly.

Imo said, "I think it's the attic."

Claud considered. "I wish I could sleep in the attic."

"Why?" Clarissa asked him. "It's a pokey little room and gets far too hot in the summer."

Imo looked at her, startled.

"But you see," Claud said, speaking slowly as he did when he was working out how to explain things to people, "I could have my things up there and no-one would get at them."

Imo remembered the children's den and the toys in the attic, which Sally had removed.

"I'd better go and finish un-packing now," she said, wanting to get away from Clarissa who wasn't, she had decided, particularly nice and didn't seem to like her.

Perdita followed her along the landing. "Can I come too?" she asked.

Imo looked at her and saw a skimpy child, a grip sliding down her hair. "All right," she said, "if you want."

Perdita was prepared to be captivated by Imo, or more precisely, by the difference of Imo. She was familiar with mothers, grandmothers and middle-aged female teachers but Imo was none of these. She was a grown-up girl; she brought with her knowledge of a life which one day would beckon to Perdita herself.

Perdita looked at Imo's torn T-shirt and multi-zipped trousers and the purple wool in her hair and wondered.

Imo lacked awareness of what impression she made upon others. She did not understand Perdita's interest and she had no idea what Clarissa thought of her, or Graham come to that; in all three cases she would probably have been surprised.

In fact, she had caught both Clarissa's and Graham's attention and basically for the same reason that she intrigued Perdita: she was different. Since Clarissa had come to live at Trevean she had not had much chance to meet as she called them 'the young', other than lately Ned and Graham and they weren't girls.

Graham found all girls unsettling.

Now, on this first meeting, Clarissa told herself that Imo seemed to have a spark of something about her, hopefully she would not prove to be too self-satisfied, as even quite moderately attractive girls so often were. They did not realise that it was their youth which made their life charmed and let them see their specialness reflected in others' eyes.

Graham was irritated with himself for feeling a jolt of interest when he saw Imo. Girls were disturbing and Trevean with its inhabitants caused him enough bother already, without bringing more problems into his life there. Steer clear of trouble, he thought as he made his way back up through the laurels to the kitchen garden. Easier said than done, a voice in his head pointed out, if this girl was going to be working with him on the veg. Slim she was, but a girl's shape all right, and yes probably she would talk but she was not, perhaps, too pushy. He frowned as he tried to put the image of her out of his mind.

Imo and Perdita stood in the attic bedroom and looked around.

"Is that Frankie's duvet cover?" Perdita asked.

"I don't know," Imo said.

"I think it is," Perdita said, "but he probably won't mind. He mostly likes dinosaurs now. Have you got any brothers?"

"No," Imo said, "just a sister."

"Is she older than you or younger than you?"

"Older but she's not very interesting. Well, not now anyway." Perdita considered. "What's her name? I'd like to have a sister."

"Antonia."

"Why's she not interesting?"

"She only talks about getting married."

This did indeed seem rather strange and maybe not interesting to Perdita. She nodded in agreement. "I think that might be a bit boring," she said.

"It is," Imo said. "Especially when she's going to marry someone like Roger."

Perdita was again nibbling her drooping lock of hair. "Roger?"

"Yes," said Imo. "He's got a long neck and he laughs Haw, Haw, Haw."

Perdita's eyes widened as she tried to visualise this.

But Imo was beginning to feel overwhelmed now with new experiences and new people. "I need to sort my things out a bit," she said gazing round.

Perdita looked at her. "Do you want to be by yourself?" she asked.

"Yes, really."

"All right," Perdita said quite cheerfully for this was something she was used to with grown-ups especially James who seldom found the children's company congenial for very long.

She said, "Later on we'll have supper. Not Frankie, he's supposed to go to bed earlier."

"OK," Imo said.

"I will see you later," Perdita said, standing in the doorway and formal in her adopted role of hostess. "When you've finished sorting your things out."

"Yes," Imo agreed, nodding.

When Perdita had disappeared down the narrow stairs Imo fished around in her backpack and found her sketch book and pencils and box of paints and placed them on the chest-of-drawers. Her few clothes she bundled into drawers and hung her cotton jacket in the cupboard on a hook as there was no room for hangers.

She wondered if the room was pokey as Clarissa had said and decided that she liked it anyway. After a while she climbed out of the window and sat on the outside ledge with her feet above the roof gulley and the sun warm on her head.

At lower levels in the house life moved forward.

Imo heard somewhere below her voices come and go and later, more faintly, Frankie's shrieks as he resisted spaghetti hoops for his supper. "No! No! It's 'gusting!'"

Finally, as the sun had almost disappeared behind the right hand roof and the gulley was slipping into shadow Perdita reappeared in the room behind Imo to tell her that supper was ready.

"I've got to show you the bathroom," she said, "because Mum says that she forgot."

She led the way down the narrow stairs.

Imo thought the children's bathroom, which apparently she was to share, was rather chill and unattractive. It was painted a clinical pale green, with brown lino on the floor. There was no shower and the cast iron bath stood on legs, its interior marked with ancient tide rings and rust marks, thin and soggy towels were flung over a wooden towel horse. There were plastic toys, boats and frogs, some with bits missing, in the bath and on the floor.

"Shall I wait outside?" Perdita said.

"Yes please."

It wasn't until Imo had seated herself on the lavatory that she realised there was no toilet paper, she fished in her pocket for an old and crumpled tissue. The hot tap in the basin ran barely tepid. Being used to Clive's insistence on domestic appliances which were well engineered and Marilyn's liking for baskets of apricot double layer toilet paper and Country Garden potpourri, she was surprised by the general disregard for convenience here.

She followed Perdita down the back stairs to the kitchen where supper was happening. Much of the debris which had covered the table when Imo had seen it earlier had been shoved up to the far end.

"Hello," Sally said. "Come and meet everyone you haven't met already. This is my husband James. Who else don't you know yet?"

James was serving stew of some sort from a large casserole; he paused to look hard at Imo. "Hello," he said, "I hope you'll get on all right here with us."

Wan hope, he thought, but manners of behaviour dinned into him in his youth had stayed with him. What did this girl look like, she had a bird's nest on her head?

"Hello," Imo said uncertainly to James. She looked round the table, seeing Graham gazing at his plate; Ned, his hair wet from his recent return from surfing; Perdita and Claud.

James had continued dealing stew onto plates and handing them to Sally who sat next to him. Imo thought he looked old; old and rather cross. Could he really be the children's father?

She sat between Sally and Perdita. Opposite, Graham stared fixedly at the water jug directly in front of him. When James now passed him a plate of stew Graham registered this with a slight shake of the head as if he had been deeply engrossed in some weighty consideration.

"Wakey, wakey," James said. "Sally, am I supposed to be giving some of this to your mother?"

"Yes please," Sally said, tolerant of James' question although of course he knew the answer. "Perdita, will you take Granny's tray up?"

Imo, again feeling a stranger here, kept quiet and spoke only in response to requests to pass vegetables or plates. However, she watched Ned whose suntanned skin had a glow about it in the fading evening light in the kitchen. His damp fair hair fell across his forehead and he pushed it back with a gesture of not unstudied casualness, for he was aware of her interest.

As was Sally. I hope, she thought, that we're not going to have trouble here.

"I would like," Ned said turning to James and Sally when he had eaten his stew and was waiting in hope of being offered a second helping, "to go and see my grandmother."

"Oh?" Sally said, for James didn't respond. "Where does she live? Claud, please eat that carrot."

"Sidmouth," Ned said. "She hasn't been well, my parents are getting rather worried."

He had no concrete evidence for the accuracy of this statement, but it made sense. His grandmother was old, all old people were ill quite frequently; probably his parents were permanently worried about her. Also of course he had to say something which would get him the OK to go.

Sally said. "When would this be?"

"Actually, I was thinking about tomorrow," Ned's glance moved to James, who wasn't looking at him, and so he turned back to Sally. Both of them knew that officially the volunteers only got half of Saturday and all Sunday off a week.

"Friday?" Sally said. "How would you get there?"

"Oh – " Ned said, for he hadn't thought about it, "by train?"

"I don't suppose you'd be able to get there and back in one day." Sally moved the water jug to get a clear view of Claud slicing his carrot into very small pieces.

"Well . . . no," Ned paused, to convey regret. "Maybe I could stay for the weekend?" A weekend was likely to prove more productive for his car acquisition plans than half a day. Also there was the possibility, surely, of some nightlife in Sidmouth? It couldn't be as dead on a Saturday night as it was round here.

We can hardly say no, can we, Sally thought. Although I'm not one hundred percent convinced by this sick Granny story.

She looked to James, who was contemplating the middle distance along the table. "What do you think? Is there a problem with Ned taking this weekend off to visit his grandmother?"

"What?" James asked, reluctantly returned to the current discussion, for he preferred to disassociate himself from decisions regarding the volunteers. But to pre-empt Sally repeating the question he added quickly "No" in answer to it.

He poked the serving spoon around in the stew bowl. "There's not much of this left."

"Maybe split it between you and Graham and Ned, they've been working outside," Sally said. "Graham, would you like some more stew?"

Disconcerted at finding himself the focus of several people's attention Graham shook his head, although in fact he could have eaten more, being used to the solid plateful of meat and pastry and vegetables which his mother dished up for the main meal of the day.

Afterwards they ate stewed rhubarb.

"This is very nice, Graham," Sally said and he raised his head briefly to nod acknowledgement.

"Graham grew this rhubarb for us," Sally said for Claud and Perdita. "Straight out of the garden, everything tastes so good." She turned back to Graham, "How are the runner beans coming on?"

"'Ez, they're ... " Graham said and then stopped. James stared at him and sighed.

"Will they be ready soon?" Sally prompted.

"'Ezzz," Ned murmured under his breath and Graham glanced at him with loathing.

"When we get the gardens open," Sally said, "we will be able to sell some of the vegetables."

At the completion of the meal there was a general pushing back of chairs, wood scraping on the huge, unsealed slates of the floor. Perdita and Claud were detailed to clear the table.

Imo stood uncertain as everyone else dispersed and Perdita sloshed water into the casserole dish in the huge enamel sink.

Claud ran up to Clarissa's room to fetch her tray, Sally went to spend time reading the paper over a cup of instant coffee with James in the study – a sacred time, not to be disturbed and to which James clung.

Graham melted swiftly to the Laundry House and the sanctuary of his own room and Ned followed more slowly to collect his mobile and try to find a signal somewhere in order to ring his grandmother. He would have asked to use the house phone, but this might have revealed that he had not, as yet, actually been in touch with her.

After a few minutes Imo wandered out into the cobbled yard. The evening air pooled soft and still warm, scented by the pale lilac which was flowering, straggling and untended, against the wall of the yard. Swallows looped across the fading blue of the sky. Imo felt a ripple of an uncertain longing in response to the sweetness of the evening and then a more specific ache sharpened when Ned came from the Laundry House.

He had in fact seen her already through the open door as he came down the stairs from his room and he was not displeased. She was probably waiting for him.

He walked over. "What are you doing?"

"Nothing really," Imo said, "just sort of . . . getting used to everything."

Ned turned his phone over in his hand. He hesitated slightly, he was not sure whether he wanted to do anything about this girl. It was getting darker and a bat flew low above their heads.

139

"I'm going up the hill to see if I can get a phone signal," he said.

"Oh – " There was a wistfulness in her response which encouraged him to say, "Come too if you like."

He spoke with deliberate casualness, but her face brightened so immediately that this caused him again to hesitate. "It might be colder up there," he said, not wanting to commit himself to the suggestion.

"Oh, I won't be cold," she said quickly.

They set off round the side of the house across the lawn where the grass was dampening and small pale moths were fluttering above it.

They didn't talk. Things were progressing well enough as far as Ned was concerned, which made the effort of making more conversation unnecessary.

Imo was afraid of saying the wrong thing.

Mixed up with her wanting to go to Art College was the hope that there she would find a boyfriend. Indeed, not a boyfriend but The Boyfriend, special, different; he would be confident and good looking; he would hold the key to life being much more interesting, much more fun.

He would not hang around in gangs of mates like her fellow students at Sixth Form College, being sick in the hotel toilets on trips to London galleries. He would not wear clothes like her dad and make stupid jokes like Antonia's Roger.

For the past two years at least, she had been hoping to find him, or not so much to find him as for him to find her; find her and tell her she was the one girl he wanted.

And now here was Ned.

He was surely the embodiment, physical and real, of the insubstantial figures with whom she had spent so many recent hours wishing herself in love. By contrast the images and the memories of the couple of boys she had briefly thought she fancied at College vanished into the pollen laden air.

She must not make a mistake, say anything which would spoil this chance, so suddenly, miraculously offered.

Beyond the lawn the two of them crossed into a field which rose up before them towards a circle of beech trees, black on the edge of the sky above, and they climbed in single file up the series of narrow tracks trodden by cows around the side of the hill.

At the top Ned moved away and bent over his phone. Imo wandered into the circle of trees and stood gazing up at the leaves against the pale sky. Her every sense seemed sharpened, the breeze was cool on her arms and she heard a last bird singing close by. Ned's voice rose and fell, carried from her by the moving air. She turned away, savouring a small thrill of power in the thought that he might come to find her. When he did so she caught her breath.

Ned was irresolute, standing beside her.

"Did you get through?" Imo asked and there was a thrill in talking to him and having him answer her.

"Yes." Ned pushed his phone into his pocket.

But explaining what his grandmother had said which had involved some reproach for his being so irregularly in touch was effortful, and in truth he couldn't be bothered for he was now preoccupied with wondering what he should do about Imo.

He had been wanting a compliant girlfriend. Someone to relieve him of the ridiculous burden of not having had proper sex. This lack of experience was clearly not what was his due and increasingly an embarrassment. It was the result only, obviously, of incarceration in a segregated boarding school and spending the holidays under the overly vigilant eye of his mother.

Here possibly was a willing girl but she wasn't quite what he had had in mind. She didn't seem sophisticated enough, probably not experienced enough, not casual enough.

Still she was a girl and the only one around.

As they came back down the hill and crossed the lawn they disturbed a badger which was rooting for leather jackets in the un-cut grass. It moved off at speed, startling Imo and giving Ned the opportunity to take her by the hand.

CHAPTER 13

MAY

Marilyn woke with a headache. She was finding herself becoming more and more anxious and unsettled as the days of early summer passed and the momentum of Antonia and Roger's wedding preparations increased.

Today she and Clive were to meet Roger's parents for dinner . . . or supper? Marilyn toyed with the words anxiously for lately Antonia had started correcting her about this sort of thing. Certainly it wouldn't be 'tea' as her parents would have described an evening meal. 'Tea' according to Antonia was sandwiches and cake in mid-afternoon.

They were to meet in a hotel not too many miles away and it was the thought of this which had woken her early.

George Rodmaine, although now retired from his legal practice, retained a few elderly clients around the country whom he would visit at home. This arrangement had the advantage as

143

Penelope explained it to Marilyn of justifying their taking a few days' holiday 'in your part of the world.' Marilyn wondered if she was imagining the suggestion that otherwise their choice would have been different.

"The hotel is rather old fashioned," Penelope said, "but they look after us very well and we always stay there. It will be a good opportunity to see you to talk through The Arrangements."

She meant the wedding arrangements, the importance of which was implied in her tone, excuses and attempts to get out of the invitation were not on.

"You won't be late?" Marilyn said anxiously to Clive. "We've got to be there for half-past seven."

Clive was sitting on the edge of the bed pulling on his socks. "Yes, I know," he said, "No, I won't be late."

He refrained from asking why, yet again, they must meet up with Roger's parents to discuss the minutiae of wedding arrangements, because he knew that this question would throw Marilyn into a complete tizz.

Clive felt that he had tried and would continue to try, for Antonia's sake, not to find Penelope and George Rodmaine irritating but their attitude got to him. Bluntly, they behaved as if they thought their family was better than his.

Now Marilyn had reported Penelope as saying, "Of course I know that these days young people will have their way, but I do think we should keep an eye on things. A wedding is such an important family occasion. We wouldn't want any surprises."

The implication Marilyn thought was that anything unwelcome of this sort was more likely to come from their side than from Penelope and George's.

Antonia had been absorbed into the Rodmaines' circle where much was made of her Directors' Lunches job and her sharing a flat with Lizzie, Roger's sister, but Marilyn had got the feeling that she and Clive were somehow not quite so acceptable.

When Clive had left for work Marilyn opened the doors of the walk-in wardrobe in their bedroom and tried to make up her mind, yet again, what to wear that evening. She felt fidgety and miserable and nothing seemed suitable. In the end she picked out a dress and jacket which she had worn once for a wedding two years ago, then she remembered that the matching shoes had got grass stained, for it had been a wet day in June. She wavered.

In the end, hearing Julia Prentice arrive, calling, "It's me!" from the kitchen, Marilyn decided that her white high heeled sandals would have to do. She went downstairs. Catching sight of her hair in the mirror in the hall she thought it looked a mess and she must try to do something about it.

"I wish," she thought, "that I had some money."

She meant money to spend, money for emergency visits to the hairdressers, for purchases of confidence boosting shoes, money to do what she liked with. Clive wasn't really mean, but he didn't understand; if she said she needed more housekeeping money he would probably give it to her but by the time she had explained what else she wanted money for all the impetus would have gone out of the idea. With the shoes he would undoubtedly say, "But you've got about fifteen pairs already."

Julia Prentice was emptying the dishwasher. Marilyn was faced with her familiar quandary of deciding what to ask her to do, with relief she remembered Imo's room. She hadn't felt up to tackling the scattering of clothes, the tumbled bed, they made her sadness increase.

"Could you do Imo's room today?" She said to Julia's large backside.

"Still away, is she?"

"Yes," Marilyn said. "On this summer job. Down in Cornwall."

"Enjoying it?" Julia straightened up holding a couple of plates.

Marilyn thought that Imo had barely communicated with them since she arrived at Trevean, she had said that her mobile didn't work there.

"Oh, yes – "

"They're all the same," Julia said, guessing the situation. "Teenagers. Tell you nothing but they're in touch quick enough if they want something. Do the bathroom too shall I?"

"Oh, yes . . . "

"Our Gary's been up the college after the electric course." Julia put the last plate away and closed the dishwasher door.

"Oh good," Marilyn was used to hearing about Gary's progress through, and now beyond school. It had been erratic.

"They say he can have a place but it's waiting on his exam results."

"Yes, I suppose so . . . " Marilyn felt a stab of anxiety, remembering Imo's stubborn refusal to consider a business studies, or a catering course.

"So we're not holding my breath," Julia said.

"Well, you never know." Marilyn hoped for both herself and Julia.

"No, that's right," Julia was now in the utility room fetching bathroom cleaning materials and rubber gloves. "We're nearly out of this lemon one. And Sharon's had to be up the Nursery again about her Nyle."

Marilyn found herself not wanting to know, she repressed a sigh. "Oh?"

"Yes. Now they're saying he's got a problem." Julia reappeared, holding cloths and plastic bottles. "Personality."

146

"But he's only two, isn't he?"

"Yes, that's what I said. How can he have a personality problem at two? They're saying he doesn't talk, well he doesn't need to does he? If he yells loud enough Sharon always gives in to him; I've told her. And he won't play with the other children."

"Oh dear – "

"And his biting of course."

"Oh. Yes."

Marilyn wasn't sure whether hearing about Julia's family made her feel better, on the basis of her own life being, at least, not so awful as theirs. Or worse? How would George and Penelope Rodmaine react if they knew that she had a cleaner whose grandson had a personality problem and bit people? She suspected this would be added to the increasingly long list of things which Antonia had warned her not to mention to her future in-laws.

While Julia set to in Imo's room Marilyn also returned upstairs to worry again about her choice of dress for that evening. What would an 'old fashioned hotel' be like?

Her experience of hotels was quite limited, to all-in-one deals for dinner dances organised by Clive's Rotary Club or to airport hotels on the way to family holidays to Spain.

Were the dress and jacket too dressy? She thought of asking Julia for her opinion, but it did not seem likely that this would supply convincing encouragement. Julia, trying to be helpful, would probably say yes to whichever garment was shown her.

As usual Marilyn could not settle to anything while Julia was cleaning, which was why she usually made an excuse to go into the town, but today she felt too jangled even to do this. She opened Clive's half of the bedroom wardrobe to check that his dark suit was there and his most likely choice of shirt was ironed. As she already knew perfectly well, they were. She gazed in the mirror, worried again about her hair and decided to spend time, when Julia had gone, with her electric tongs to see if she could give it a bit of lift.

She stood, uncertain what to do now, gazing from the window up the slope of the garden where the grass was getting a bit thin in the continuing dry weather. There had been a hosepipe ban for the past three weeks.

Remembering Imo's obvious reluctance to share any information with them was saddening. People had said when their second baby was also a girl, and perhaps feeling that a boy might have been the preferred option, "Well, with two girls you will always have someone to talk to." And indeed, before Antonia became engaged to Roger she had been happy to shop and chat and keep Marilyn up-to-date with gossipy details about college and later her job and living in London.

But since all the hassle of the wedding plans had filled her horizon Antonia was not the comforting companion she had been. In fact she could be, on occasion, downright critical of Marilyn and Clive's views, their clothes, the house, their food and lifestyle generally. She had asked one day if they must have pink busy lizzies in the pots by the front door and petunias in the hanging baskets; she had also started pouring the tea into the cup before the milk.

Marilyn suspected that this was the influence of the Rodmaines and began to fear that they might take Antonia even further away from her once she and Roger were married.

As for Imo, despite what kind people had wished at the time of her birth she had not proved to be a companion for Marilyn, even as a little child. By the time she was ten she preferred to spend a lot of her time at home alone in her room drawing her pictures, reading her books and lately of course, endlessly on her computer in a web of teenage communication.

This day had not started well and really it was getting no better. Marilyn found that she was looking forward to Julia's coffee break for a chat to distract herself from her thoughts which seemed to centre so much lately on the disappointing things in life.

The two of them sat at the kitchen island and pondered the inability of men to adapt. Julia remarked that on her birthday Sharon had suggested ordering in a Chinese, to be eaten once the kids were in bed. "She thought it would be a bit of a treat for me, no cooking."

On two grounds Alan, Julia's husband, had vetoed the idea. Firstly the familiar one that he wasn't eating any foreign muck and secondly that he liked to eat when he came home off the lorry, that is at five o'clock, and not half way through the bloody night.

Marilyn remarked that Clive's favoured choice whenever they ate out was steak and chips while she herself would like to try something different sometimes.

The conversation proceeded along these quite comfortable lines for a while until Marilyn suddenly remembered the meal they were having with the Rodmaines that night and the possible hurdles posed by the menu. Would it, for instance, be in English?

There had been a horribly embarrassing occasion when they had been invited out for a meal in London by a Greek client of Clive's when the food had been unidentifiable and the waiters threw plates at the wall.

The discussion then flagged a bit. Julia went to start on the bathroom and Marilyn, staring at her hands, decided to re-do her nails to be on the safe side for the evening. She turned on Radio 2.

Later in the morning when Julia came downstairs with the hoover, she also brought a couple of pairs of pants and a coffee mug which she had found under Imo's bed. Marilyn gave her her money and saw her off with regret; now the house would be empty until Clive's return. She stood at the dining room window and watched Julia disappear on her bike down The Rowan's short brick drive and into the traffic which largely consisted of locals avoiding the dual carriageway into town. The council did its best to discourage this practice by clogging up the road with mini-roundabouts and humps and carriageway narrowing chicanes, but people doggedly continued to negotiate around each new obstacle.

Marilyn wondered what other members of her family were doing right now. She ate cottage cheese with pineapple and two Ryvita for her lunch and the long afternoon stretched ahead of her.

Clive didn't arrive back from work until after six, by which time Marilyn had spent a second forty minutes trying to get her hair right. She sat in front of her dressing table mirror with the electric tongs. "I've put your clothes out," she called down as soon as she heard him come through the front door.

Clive mounted the stairs slowly. He had had to spend a lot of time on the phone to the agent he used in Norway, pursuing various snagging problems with orders for ceiling cornice mouldings recently despatched to a Norwegian cruise line; he was feeling tired.

"Just what I could do without," he thought as he looked at his suit and striped shirt hanging on the wardrobe door. "Battling around the motorway to listen to Penelope Rodmaine bang on about seating arrangements at the wedding reception."

Seating had featured in the conversation on the last occasion when the Bradfords and the Rodmaines had met. This had been lunch at The Rowans, a barbeque because Marilyn's nerve had failed her at the thought of cooking for Penelope who, Antonia told her, had last year been President of her local WI branch.

That afternoon had not been a relaxing occasion although not so wearing as the weekend Clive and Marilyn had been invited to spend at The Old Granary, the house to which the Rodmaines had recently retired in rural Worcestershire. In Clive's recollection Marilyn had nearly been reduced to tears by George and Penelope's descriptions of disastrous weddings which they had attended, so often spoiled by the folly, ignorance or presumption of one or other family involved.

All in all neither Clive nor Marilyn had much hope of an enjoyable evening as they drove into the leafy streets on the outskirts of the local town where they found that the Rodmaines' hotel was small and there was no available parking. This hiked Clive's irritation levels up another notch.

"You go on in and I'll sort the car out," he said to Marilyn.

"No – " she protested.

"Yes," he said firmly. "You've got those shoes on, haven't you?"

Her anxious presence was winding him up and they were running late already.

Marilyn entered the foyer of the hotel with a degree of trepidation, trying to smooth down the back of her skirt which she feared might have creased.

The décor was dark, with maroon patterned carpet and a grandfather clock and a wide mahogany reception desk from behind which an elderly man in a navy jacket asked if he could help her.

"I'm just waiting for my husband." Marilyn was uncertain who she was talking to, was he the receptionist? Or maybe the manager? Standing awkwardly in the foyer she thought how hotel staff could seem so superior, she pictured briefly the disparaging expression of Peter Fullerton manager of Columb Court when she and Antonia had enquired about possibilities for the reception.

Surely this person must be the manager? After a few minutes during which he examined some paperwork on the desk, he looked up and asked if Marilyn and her husband had a reservation?

"We are meeting some people for . . . " Marilyn hesitated.

"Dinner?" he suggested.

"Yes," Marilyn said, with gratitude. She was still haunted by Antonia's strictures on the naming of meals. Supper? Dinner? What had Penelope called it?

"And the name?"

"Oh – "

"For the table booking?"

"Well, perhaps . . . Mr and Mrs Rodmaine?"

"Ah, yes. And you are Mrs Bradford?"

Marilyn agreed that yes, she was.

"Mr and Mrs Rodmaine are expecting you," the manager said, glancing at the grandfather clock with surely a hint of reproof. You are late, the glance told Marilyn, late for our hotel guests. "In the salon. Shall I let them know that you have arrived?"

"Well – " Marilyn gazed helplessly at the hotel entrance. No Clive.

"Allow me to introduce myself," the man emerged from behind the huge desk. He was shorter than she had expected, perhaps he had been seated on a high stool. "I am the Head

Porter. Edward Skimmins"

"I thought you were the manager – "

"Oh no," he said reprovingly, "our manager is Mr Larkspeare. Perhaps you would like to take a seat."

Marilyn sat well forward on one of the carved dark wood chairs which were ranged beside the wall while Edward Skimmins disappeared through a door opposite. She glanced at the table beside her on which were copies of Country Life and Hare & Hound and the county magazine.

At this point Clive arrived saying that he had had to park two streets away. Marilyn, although she was relieved to see him, suffered a stab of anxiety for he looked rather wind-swept. She raised her hand instinctively as she stood up, to straighten his tie.

"What's the matter?" he said, frowning.

George Rodmaine came into the foyer. He was wearing a three-piece tweed suit, his grey hair parted and combed with some care and just slightly longer than might have been expected.

"Here you are," he said. "We were beginning to wonder what had happened."

CHAPTER 14

MAY

Greeting the Rodmaines was still, at each meeting, a trial to Marilyn. Whether to kiss or not to kiss? They didn't know each other well but they were to share their offsprings' wedding. On the few occasions on which they had previously met there had been slight muddle and confusion at this point and the question was not satisfactorily resolved.

However, George dealt with the immediate quandary by ushering them immediately towards the door to the salon, without inclining his head towards her or indeed taking Clive's irresolutely proffered hand. Was this, Marilyn wondered, to indicate his displeasure at their lateness?

"Here they are," George announced loudly to Penelope, who rose from one of four arm chairs grouped around a low table.

The few other people seated in the room turned their heads.

Penelope, although relatively short, was a woman of presence and a well supported bust. Marilyn was relieved to see that she was wearing a dress and jacket, in a pale pinkish grey.

"I expect the traffic was dreadful, wasn't it?" Penelope did proffer a lightly blushered cheek to them both. "We think we're so lucky not to live in a built-up area, we simply don't get a rush hour at all. How bright and summery you're looking this evening, Marilyn."

"Nowhere to park," Clive said. "You'd think they would have more spaces."

Penelope gave him a sharp look. "Well, it's not a large hotel. We prefer the personal service."

"Where do you put your car?" Clive asked, still irritated.

"Oh, Edward takes it away for us. Did you meet him? Of course, all the staff here are absolutely marvellous. And so loyal; they stay year after year. It's one of the reasons why we keep coming back. Do sit down. George will organise a drink. George!"

Clive and Marilyn sat, as she indicated they should, side by side on two of the red and navy covered armchairs, which were stiffly upholstered and not very comfortable. George went to summon a white wine spritzer for Marilyn and a beer for Clive.

The other people in the salon returned to their own conversations.

"We got them to arrange the chairs for us." Penelope glanced down, spreading the fingers of one hand on the chair arm. Her nails were varnished a pale pearlised pink and she wore two rings which Marilyn noticed and felt she should, perhaps, admire.

"What lovely rings," she said.

"Oh – " Penelope's tone of mild surprise hung in the air making Marilyn fear she had made a mistake. "Thank you. This one was my mother's."

"Are they sapphires?" Marilyn still uncertain, gazed at the deep, dark blue of the stones.

"They are, yes."

"And obviously worth a packet," Clive thought. He shifted to lean back slightly in order to stretch his legs beneath the table.

"And this one," Penelope turned the second ring slightly to catch the light and to look at it with a certain satisfaction, "is an opal which I like very much although I believe some people consider them unlucky."

"Isn't that because they shatter?" Clive asked.

"Well I think you have to be careful with them." Penelope's tone was discouraging. "It was an anniversary present from George."

There was a moment's pause.

"They're both very nice – " Marilyn twisted her engagement solitaire diamond to the back of her finger, she felt it was out-classed. Roger had given Antonia a ruby.

"By the way, this is on me," George, returning and taking a seat, made this sound like an announcement. "they're bringing the drinks. We've already had a look at the menu."

"While we were waiting." Penelope folded her hands in her lap to signify the close of the ring discussion.

"And we think the lamb shank or the skate should be pretty good." George picked up the menu from the coffee table. "Have a look." He handed the menu which was inside an embossed maroon cover to Clive who was seated beside him.

What Clive saw was that the lamb shank and the skate wings were the cheapest dishes on offer.

"I think I fancy a steak myself," he said.

George Rodmaine's glance froze slightly. "We've always found the fish very good here," he said, taking the menu back after a moment or two when Clive didn't comment, and handing it to Penelope to pass to Marilyn.

"It's always nice traditional English food," Penelope said. "We're not fans of undercooked vegetables, or meat, I'm afraid."

"No," George said.

Marilyn gazed at the menu doubtfully, relieved that she could at least read and understand it. She thought the skate wings sounded nasty and favoured the poached salmon because of The Diet but in an attempt to follow George's direction she chose lamb, as did Penelope.

George with a certain coolness picked the skate. "And perhaps we had better go through to the dining room. We did say seven thirty."

In the dining room where an elderly waiter hovered, moving back their chairs and shaking out the starched linen table napkins, the discussion moved to starters. "We find two courses are quite sufficient for us in the evening these days" George said. "And I think I will be having my favourite dessert here, crème brûlée. I expect you'll be the same Penny?"

"Yes, I think so," Penelope looked at Marilyn and Clive, "but if you would like to have a starter – "

"No, no," Marilyn said hastily, she was fearful that Clive would said yes, he would.

George turned to the wine list.

"I'll order a bottle of the hotel red as most of us are eating meat," he said without enthusiasm. "It's very palatable."

Everyone remembered that he was eating fish.

"Why don't you have white with the skate?" Penelope suggested. "They will serve it by the glass."

George shook his head. "No, I don't think so."

"That's Henry," Penelope named the waiter rather too loudly as he retreated with their order, "he's a treasure, they all are. The staff make a hotel, of course."

She turned to Marilyn. "And now you can tell us how are the wedding arrangements coming along?"

Marilyn felt her stomach begin to knot.

"Have you made a decision about what you will be wearing? Mother of the bride, so important."

"Well . . . not quite – "

She read 'How inefficient' in Penelope's eyes.

"I'm rather pleased with my choice," Penelope said. "So clever of Antonia to decide on the colour scheme idea."

"I think she got it from a wedding magazine," Marilyn said doubtfully.

"Yes, well, I didn't suppose she'd thought of it herself. But quite clever of her to pick up on the idea."

"What's yours like?" Marilyn asked. "Your outfit?"

Penelope pursed her lips and frowned slightly. "The dress," she stressed the word, "is slub silk, and with a longer line jacket." She paused as if considering whether to divulge further information. "And rather an unusual colour: 'Blush."

Marilyn was unsure, but didn't like to ask, what colour blush might be. Pink? "And have you chosen your hat?"

"Yes. A little darker."

"Oh – " To have these weighty problems sorted, Marilyn was impressed and envious. "And where did you get them? Your dress, and the jacket and . . . hat?"

Penelope's expression again flickered discouragingly. "From a very clever woman who runs a local boutique, she knows just the sort of thing which suits me. And her seamstress will alter anything."

"That's so nice, isn't it?"

"We're very lucky to have her near. We all go straight to her for weddings and garden parties and that sort of thing."

Henry, the waiter, now approached with dishes to serve their main course. George stared hard at Clive's steak and gave his own skate a slight prod.

"We were so pleased to hear that you've managed to sort out the crèche for the children," Penelope said. "It would have been very difficult for some of our young marrieds – having to arrange child-minding for the whole day. Or maybe the whole weekend if they had to travel far. I'm sure yours are pleased too, aren't they?"

"Well – " Marilyn glanced at Clive anxiously.

"There aren't any children on our side," Clive said.

"Really?" Penelope was dissecting her lamb. "Could I have a little more redcurrant jelly? I think Roger's cousins all have at least one child now. Girls these days seem to leave having babies until quite late don't they? And then there they are, popping up all over the place."

Marilyn didn't know what to say, she still hadn't told Clive the price which Peter Fullerton had quoted for the crèche. She felt that she had now quite lost her appetite and she began to cut a potato into very small pieces.

"I hope Roger and Antonia won't leave it too long to have children," Penelope continued. "I know girls take their careers more seriously now than we had to, but I still think it's nice to give time to your children and husband."

George looked at her mildly surprised for Penelope had been a secretary in the solicitors firm where he had trained and she continued working for some time after they were married. Admittedly she stopped when Roger was born but this was only after some years and the expensive intervention of Mr Fenn-Gresham, gynaecologist of Wimpole Street. At eight Roger had gone to board at Prep School and Penelope as far as George remembered had not seemed to miss him unduly, bridge and the WI began to take up a lot of her time. For various reasons the arrival of Lizzie had been rather a surprise. However he did not comment.

"If you can afford them," Clive said. "But kids don't come cheap."

"Quite," George agreed poking some bony bits out of his skate.

"There are just one or two other things about the wedding which I wanted to check with you." Penelope nodded to the waiter, now hovering. "That was delicious, thank you Henry. I'm sorry I couldn't manage to finish the carrots. We do like them quite well cooked, terribly old fashioned I know."

"I will mention it to the chef," the waiter inclined his head. "And have you also finished, Madam?"

"Yes, thank you," Marilyn had laid down her knife and fork. "I'm sorry I don't seem to be very hungry."

She had only managed to eat a portion of the lamb and was aware of George's disapproving glance as Henry gathered up her plate.

George himself had made a point of pushing the skate bone to one side which then left his plate clear. "I don't always like fish," he said, "but that was very palatable. A good choice."

"I'm glad you enjoyed it," Penelope smiled to indicate a united front. "My lamb was very good too. Tender."

Marilyn felt herself to be doubly reproved.

Clive thought that if George had enjoyed his skate, he had shown little evidence of it.

He himself was annoyed that the Rodmaines had managed to assume that the crèche was necessary but that the organisation of it, and presumably the paying for it, was not their responsibility.

"Steak was good," he said, hoping to needle George a little. In this he was successful; the sirloin had been the most expensive item on the menu.

Spending money unnecessarily was anathema to George, a fact of which his family, which now included Antonia, was well aware. Also waste, as in food left on your plate, upset him a lot.

Penelope over the years of her marriage had found ways round difficulties which this character trait presented. Some of these ploys verged on the deceitful, but she was pragmatic about the basic problem for after all a large part of why she had married George was to do with his money and his attitude to getting more of it, and having got it to hanging on to it.

"The flowers for the church and the hotel – " Penelope now changed the topic for discussion. "Is your florist totally reliable?"

"The hotel sorts out most of the flowers themselves," Clive said. "Isn't that right Marilyn?"

"Well – " Marilyn remembered Peter Fullerton's reaction to the pink lilies

"But for the photographs?" Penelope said. "And on the tables for the reception?"

"Antonia wants lilies . . . or maybe roses . . . " Marilyn found her voice had dropped strangely to almost a whisper. "But – the hotel has a list," she tried to explain. "Of flowers – "

She was aware that they were all gazing at her.

"Well, these decisions do have to be made," Penelope said briskly. "And if it is to be roses in the church it's worth remembering that they can be tricky, especially the older varieties. They can droop or drop their petals. Who has Antonia chosen to do them?"

Antonia had chosen Sarah of Sarah's Flowers, who had recently set up her own floristry business. This choice had caused yet more difficulty with Peter Fullerton at Columb Court for he had intimated that he would prefer a florist who was 'familiar with the hotel and our style preferences'.

"She's a friend of Antonia's, they knew each other at school . . ."

"This person is properly trained, I hope?" Penelope said, after a moment's pause.

"Oh, well, yes. She's called Sarah – she's just setting up her own business. Antonia thought it would be nice . . . to help her get started? With weddings."

"Oh. Isn't your dressmaker newly set up too?" Penelope looked at George. "What do you think?"

George's expression indicated that he didn't think anything about flowers. "Not really my area," he said. "More your sort of thing, Penny. As long as this girl's had the proper training, should be all right, I suppose?"

"Well," Penelope said, "I hope she's going to be able to cope. People do notice the flowers, I think, at a wedding. What sort of thing is she doing?"

Antonia had shown Marilyn pictures from one of the bridal magazines of rosebuds, the pink lilies and maidenhair fern. She had agreed that the flowers themselves would be quite expensive, but Sarah would make the displays as a wedding present and as promotion for her new business.

"I think they'll be very pretty." Marilyn felt anxious just remembering these flower photographs which had seemed worryingly elaborate but Antonia had set her heart on them. Sarah, a bouncy blonde girl, had encouraged her. In fact she had sung, "You've got to have a dream . . . " while sticking carnations into oasis for a corporate marquee at the county show when Antonia and Marilyn had visited her workshop, which had turned out to be her parents' garage. They had all agreed that carnations lacked romance, for a traditional wedding you needed something trailing. "And frothy," Sarah had suggested. "Stephanotis."

"Well, cream and pink roses," Marilyn now told Penelope, "and lilies . . . pink . . . and . . . ferns . . . "

"Oh, ferns?" But Penelope was distracted by the dessert menu. "There's our crème brûlée George, and treacle sponge, fruit salad – what shall I have?"

George felt a surge of irritation. He had a sweet tooth and he suddenly had a sharp longing for treacle pud, with cream. He owed it to himself, in fact, after the experience of eating skate wing while paying for Clive to munch his way through prime steak.

Henry departed slowly with choices of two treacle sponges (George and Clive), crème brûlée (Penelope) and fruit salad (Marilyn).

Clive decided at this point to tackle the question of paying for the wedding. It needed sorting, in fact sorting it was long overdue.

"This wedding," he said, by way of introducing the subject, "as I see it, will be joining our two families."

George and Penelope looked at him with a certain coolness and not as if this idea appealed.

Clive felt that he was trying to be fair and reasonable. "It will mark the start of Antonia and Roger's life together." He paused and then to make the point clear he added, "Our daughter and your son."

Marilyn twisted her fingers in her lap. Clive sounded as if he was making a speech. She was afraid that he was going to mention money, which would be embarrassing because hadn't Antonia explained several times that people like the Rodmaine's expected the bride's parents to pay for the whole wedding? Clive still maintained that this idea was outdated and unreasonable. She knew that she had been right to dread this evening.

Clive was trying to think of a straight forward way of putting his point across. "We, Marilyn and I, are of course prepared to pay for . . . towards the cost of this wedding. Antonia is our daughter after all. But these days, I'm sure you'll agree, it is usual for the other party to contribute. Sometimes the couple themselves put something into the pot."

Yes, he thought, after all Roger must be earning a good salary, London accountants don't come cheap. Even Antonia had now been working for two years. Was it reasonable that he alone, trying to run a small company with all the hassles and costs involved, not to mention the mortgage on The Rowans and Imo still not off their hands, he and just he, should be expected to cough up for this one-day extravaganza?

Clearly the answer to this was No, it was not reasonable.

A silence settled over the table. Marilyn felt ill. Eventually Penelope glanced at George who was staring into the middle distance with a fixed, and not positive, expression on his face.

Even Clive's resolve began to waver. "It is something to think about," he said.

And what is more, he thought, it should have been thought about before, when Roger and Antonia first got engaged.

"Well," Penelope said eventually, folding her napkin and placing it on the table. "We will discuss it, won't we George?"

"Yes," the word was heavily laden with disapprobation.

"Do we want coffee?" Penelope continued briskly. "I won't. It will keep me awake. Marilyn, what about you?"

Marilyn felt that her throat had suffered some constriction. "Oh, no. Thank you."

"And Clive?"

Clive realised that the discussion, one-sided, about the wedding costs was at an end and so was the meal. "Oh . . . no, then. No."

They moved from the dining room back to the hotel foyer. The evening sun was still slanting through the glass panels of the double mahogany doors.

"Well, thank you for coming through all that awful traffic to see us," Penelope said. "I hope it will be better going back. Of course, the rush hour will be over now."

Clive, used to driving to London and the midlands, and indeed on the continent on a regular basis, couldn't make much sense of Penelope's insistence that their journey from home had been exceptionally difficult.

"Do you want to wait here while I fetch the car?" he asked Marilyn when they found themselves being attended by Edward Skimmins, the porter, who emerged from a dark cubby hole behind his reception desk to enquire whether they had brought coats and to express the opinion that it was a very pleasant evening, warm for the month.

But Marilyn did not want to be in the hotel for a moment longer than was necessary, she wanted to go home. "I'll come with you," she said.

The evening was at an end, George and Penelope said goodbye and Penelope hoped the traffic would not be too bad on their way home.

Clive and Marilyn thanked them for the meal and escaped

into the cool air beneath he pollarded chestnut trees along the pavement.

Clive was distracted by annoyance. In his view his suspicions had been confirmed, the Rodmaines had little or no intention of contributing financially to the wedding, even now. The cost of the meal they had just eaten, emphasised he felt by George, was like a drop in the ocean.

"If they were helping Antonia and Roger to get a roof over their heads I could understand it, but Roger has already got a house," he said walking fast so that Marilyn was hurried along in her heels.

Roger had bought the small Edwardian terrace house in Fulham when he joined his London firm. At the moment the décor was rather masculine and minimalist, but Antonia was hoping to effect a bit of make-over.

Marilyn, dodging other pedestrians and feeling the toe straps of her sandals beginning to rub, didn't answer.

"Don't tell me they can't afford it," Clive said. "George owned that firm of solicitors before he retired, didn't he? Both children have left home and are working. It's ridiculous."

They arrived at the car and Marilyn got in and kicked her shoes off with a sigh of relief. "Penelope did say they would think about it," she said.

"Think about what?" Clive said, manoeuvring the car away from the kerb. "How many more kids to invite, or the right sort of roses?"

"About helping with paying," Marilyn said, clasping her hands as Clive shot through the amber lights.

"Fat chance," he said.

Back in the hotel Penelope said, "Shall we sit in the salon for a while?"

"I think I could do with a whisky," George said. He had been unsettled by Clive's insistence on raising the question of wedding costs. Unacceptable.

"Well, really," Penelope said when they were settled with their drinks, "I do think that was all very peculiar, Clive Broadhurst behaved most oddly. All that business about wedding expenses was quite uncalled for, when you had invited them to dinner."

"I agree," George said.

"And that dress Marilyn was wearing, I suppose it was a dress, under that jacket, the colour didn't suit her."

They drank their drinks and considered.

"I hope Roger has thought very carefully about this marriage," Penelope said.

CHAPTER 15

MAY

At Trevean Sally told herself that life was being a pain. This was, as usual, for financial reasons; she was trying to stay upbeat, but the situation wasn't good.

The builders who had repaired the roof at the back of the house were, after protracted requests for the payment of their account, threatening court action. They had originally been called in to replace some of the long narrow slates which were slipping and looked set to slide over the edge of the lead guttering, possibly decapitating anyone passing in the Laundry Yard below. However further inspection had revealed rotten roof timbers and the job had escalated in time, labour, materials and so inevitably in cost.

With minor bills Sally usually tried to keep the details from James as they inevitably depressed him. In this case however the amount involved was too large for her to have any way of sorting it out without his knowledge.

"Oh God!" James said when Sally came to him in the study with the news. "What do we do now?"

He had been sitting in his chair reading the Telegraph and now he dropped his hands to his knees, some pages of the paper slid to the floor. He gazed at her without hope, for what solution was there?

This was as it always was and as always Sally's automatic reaction was to try to come up with something positive. She said, "We'll sort it out somehow."

"How?"

"I'll phone the bank."

James groaned. "Oh no."

"It'll get sorted," Sally repeated.

"What about the last loan?" This had been to replace ancient lead pipes which were possibly poisoning the water supply.

Sally said, "We've put in for a grant for that, remember? Which should cover it."

"If we get it, which is doubtful."

Sally rang the bank and made an appointment for a couple of days' time. "Forget about it till then," she told James.

James habitually chose to follow instructions for this meant it wasn't his fault if things went wrong. He picked up the Telegraph again and sat glumly concentrating on the details of some Government department's inadequacies.

Sally kissed the top of his head, she loved him dearly, but she couldn't always cheer him up however much she wished it. "I'm driving the children to school and dropping Ned at the station if he's ready in time then I'll take the new girl, Imogen, up to the kitchen garden," she said. "she can start working with Graham."

James sighed. This meant that Sally would be out of the

house, out of calling range. It made him feel unsettled. "What if the phone rings?" he asked.

"Just leave it," Sally said.

Imo had slept with the window open and the thin curtains drawn back to let in the cool night air. Gazing upwards she could see far more stars than she remembered seeing at home where the sky was washed out by the orange glow of street lights. Waking, she thought immediately of Ned, wishing that he was not going away to see his grandmother. Thoughts of him brought a ripple of excitement; for months and months there had been nothing to bring excitement, she had barely felt alive.

But now here was Ned and he was different, different from the Sixth Form students with whom she had been mixing, different from any other boys she knew. He was more grown up, he had lived a different and surely a more exciting life. And he was gorgeous looking; he was, wasn't he? For a moment she longed for confirmation, she was unsure of her own judgement for it seemed so unlikely that someone as different and glamorous as Ned should be here on this gardening job, and that he should notice her. He had taken her with him, up to the hill and talked to her, to her alone. He had held her hand. Her heart sang.

Perhaps she could see him before he left? She pulled on her clothes and ran down the back stairs to the kitchen.

Graham sat there alone eating cereal with a Victorian book on vegetable growing open in front of him on the table, Sally had found this on the shelves in the back hall. It was old enough to have wood-cut illustrations but when he noticed Imo he attempted to give the impression of being engrossed. And indeed he was interested for he believed the old men knew what they were doing and there was plenty could be learned from them still.

Having waited in vain for him to recognise her presence, Imo asked, "Hi, have you seen Ned?"

Graham frowned, the question irritated him. Ned, the arrogant arsehole, had he already got this girl interested in him? He shook his head.

Sally, arriving, said to him, "Will you take Imogen up to the kitchen garden with you and when I've dropped the children at school I'll sort out some work for her to start on. You can show her round."

Graham felt he was being got at, he glanced up briefly and nodded without any sign of enthusiasm. After a pause as they were both still looking at him he said, "Right."

Sally sighed slightly, he really didn't make communication easy. She looked at Imo's trainers, "Did you bring some boots?"

"No," Imo said.

"Didn't the Garden Volunteer people send you a kit list? They said they would."

Imo did vaguely remember something on the website about wet weather clothes. She shook her head doubtfully.

"You'll need some," Sally said, "you'd better borrow someone's wellies." She went into the back porch and rooted around in the pile of boots and shoes heaped around the cats' cardboard boxes.

"I think these will be all right," Imo said looking at her feet and not fancying wearing kids' wellingtons.

"No, they won't. They'll be ruined. What size are you?" Sally tossed a couple of green boots across the floor. "I think these are a pair, failing that I've got an old pair of jodhpur boots somewhere."

If Imo had been at home she would have kicked up a fuss but now she didn't argue. Graham waited for her in the cobbled yard with Marilla the cat matriarch, black and fluffy, weaving around his legs.

They set off up the steep stone steps beneath overhanging laurels, crossed the top yard and Graham pushed open the wooden door in the high stone wall which surrounded the kitchen garden. Flakes of blue paint fell from the wood and the door dragged on the ancient cinders of the path.

Imo saw rows of green stuff, some were lettuces but there were other vegetables and fruit bushes which she didn't recognise. Graham walked ahead and she followed, he didn't say much, often not even volunteering the name of the plants unless she asked.

"Carrots, beetroot, runners . . . . "

Beyond these, up the slope the ground seemed to be still in the grip of brambles and nettles. Apple trees, twisted and unpruned, trailed branches across clumps of docks and meadowsweet.

Graham was uncomfortable, what was he supposed to be telling this girl? She didn't seem to know anything, what use would she possibly be? He clenched his knuckles as they walked.

She asked him why the greenhouses were broken down, why the water in the water butt was 'yucky', why there were nail holes all over the garden walls. Daft questions, what was he supposed to say?

"For the wires." He said about the nails.

"What wires?"

You answered one question and she just asked another. His jaw felt stiff. "For training fruit."

"What sort of fruit?"

"Peaches, mebbe . . . " How should he know? He quickened his pace.

Eventually Sally arrived. They heard her call, "Graham!"

Graham turned and they walked back down between the tall rows of runner beans in scarlet flower, but he did not respond until Sally was within sight. "Lo!"

"I do wish he would be a bit more forthcoming, he does tend to lurk," Sally thought.

"This is all looking good," she said looking round and determining to be encouraging. "You're doing great things here, Graham."

When he still didn't offer a comment she said, "Are those spring onions? Could you bring some down to the house, and a large lettuce?"

Graham nodded.

Relinquishing attempts at small talk Sally said briskly, "You've seen what Graham's been doing here, Imo? It was all overgrown, he's doing wonders." She again addressed him directly, "What can we start Imo on?"

He shifted his feet in heavy boots on the clinkers.

"Weeding?" Sally suggested. "Or maybe clearing out one of the cold frames?"

"'Ez."

"Which?"

Graham loathed being asked to make decisions on the spot, now he thought that he was being made to look an idiot. "Weeds."

"Truly," Sally thought, "poor lad, it's worse than drawing teeth." And yet he clearly knew what he was doing here, the green rows stretched around them, tidy and productive.

"Right," Sally said. "Will you show her what to do?" She scooped up Marilla, who had followed her into the garden and whom Graham was eyeing with disfavour. "Come on cat, leave the birds alone."

Graham stood watching as Sally went, past the parsley and chives and the two rhubarb plants which he had been pleased to find and had cleared of bindweed; behind her she pulled shut the door in the wall. Then he turned and walked towards a small two storey building, a flight of stone steps against the front wall giving access to the higher floor. He had to bend his head beneath the low door lintel.

Imo hung around for a couple of minutes and then when he didn't reappear she walked across to the building and peered inside. It was divided into rooms in the first of which to one side immediately inside the door was a wooden bench with two holes cut in the lid. Imo stared, chalky flakes of white paint had drifted down from the walls.

"Hi!" she called.

Graham didn't answer.

She went further into the building, up a couple of steps into a darkish, low ceilinged room where a fire place with an empty metal grate was set into one wall. There was a heavy table below the small paned window and Graham stood beside this looking at pieces of paper spread across it. There was also a cardboard box containing, it appeared, packets of seeds.

Imo paused in the doorway. "Hi," she said again.

Graham glanced across as if surprised and wondering who was there. What was up with him, Imo wondered, who did he think she could be?

"Where shall I start weeding?" she asked.

CHAPTER 16

JUNE

A few days later Ned was in buoyant mood. Granny Lorrimer had come good, she had given him the money to buy a car and by sheer good chance, parked in a street in Sidmouth near her flat, he had found an open-top Beetle with a hand-written 'For Sale' sign taped to the windscreen.

The deal had very shortly been done. OK, so it was a bit beat up and the clock read 160,000 miles but VWs went on for ever. It was a sludgy yellow colour and he had noticed girls were already looking as he drove it round the town.

Now he was heading off to return to Trevean with the Beetle's roof down.

His mother had phoned and told him to show proper gratitude to his grandmother for giving him the car. Which, of course he had had done – he had listened to her stories of bridge games and hairdressers and chiropodists all through lunch at a hotel on the Esplanade and when she said she looked forward to his visits he had promised to come and see her again quite soon.

This had given him a slight twinge of guilt because the last time he had seen her was over a year ago, but it would, as he had pointed out, be much easier now he had a car.

Also, he thought as he left the main road and neared Trevean, accelerating down a lane with banks ten feet high and occasional passing places for tractors, he was his grandmother's favourite grandson. She had always told him so. It must be so anyway – his brother was less able at everything and not so good-looking and his cousins were small and boring kids. He was special; he deserved a car.

It wasn't until he turned the Beetle into the drive at Trevean where the heavy wooden gate, having slipped on its hinges, leant propped half inside the laurel hedge, that he thought at all about what was waiting for him here. More bamboos. He was overcome by irritation.

For surely estate management wasn't going to require him to spend days on end hacking bamboos? If bamboos needed hacking there would presumably be someone else to do it, he knew enough about it now to be able to tell them what to do.

In fact, Ned thought as he drove onto the gravel in front of the house and negotiated around several battered children's bikes and other wheeled toys, he was beginning to wonder if the Lacocks hadn't got him here under false pretences. The garden volunteers were supposed, weren't they, to be experiencing the restoration of historic gardens and also in his particular case, to be gaining useful work experience for his course at Agricultural College. Clearing half an acre of bamboos with a bill hook didn't seem to satisfy either of these criteria.

The secondary thought came to him that James and Sally

must realise he was of a different calibre to Graham who was probably going to dig dung into vegetables for the rest of his life.

It was another clear blue summer day and the lawn at Trevean where the grass was long and trampled was awash with ox-eye daisies. Warmth caught in the hollow of the hillside enveloped the house.

Ned climbed out of the car and looked at his watch, he had made the journey in quite good time. The Beetle's engine was a bit noisy and it was annoying to have other vehicles overtake him on the dual carriageway but then faces had on occasion stared back and hands waved from car windows.

The house was quiet. This was slightly disappointing because it would have been pleasant if someone had been on hand to admire his arrival in the Beetle. He stood and stretched in the sun and saw that a plastic toy fire engine was sticking out from under one of the car's wheels. He gave it a prod with his foot but couldn't budge it, it didn't seem to have damaged the tyre.

He sauntered into the house.

Graham never used the front door, he always came in through the back porch, and once in he went no further than the kitchen where they ate breakfast and supper. Ned, however, saw no problem with walking directly into the front hall, gazing round now at the stuffed pike and the fox heads, the jug of drooping bluebells on the circular table and the curls of dust and dog hair drifting gently across the floor in the sun patterns cast by the stained-glass window.

No sound. Everyone, presumably, was out.

Actually, this was not the case. Sally and the children were indeed at school and college but James had pulled together some lunch for himself from what was in the fridge, taking it back to the study on a tray to avoid having to make conversation with

Clarissa whom he had found in the kitchen, bent upon the same mission.

Sniffing with disapproval she had now also returned to her room.

While Ned was away Imo had taken, like Graham, to making a sandwich for her lunch and taking it up to the kitchen garden; like him she pulled a lettuce leaf or two and shoved them between the slices of bread.

He habitually referred to this food eaten at mid-day as 'croust' and the first couple of times he used the word Imo looked at him blankly, thinking she had mis-heard. "What's that?" she asked. "Croust?"

"Croust," he said flatly and without elaboration. Briefly he held up the cheese sandwich.

She let it go.

She sat in the sun sketching the bean poles smothered with luxuriant growth or the rows of spinach beside the broken brick paths.

Graham usually read yesterday's Telegraph in the potting shed. He was, as the Lacocks might have been surprised to discover, interested in 'what they think they're doing' by 'they' meaning the politicians in Westminster and locally. Nor were his views on what he read so dissimilar to James's.

Now both he and Imo were back at work, Graham hacking brambles at the top end of the garden, Imo weeding beetroot.

Ned stood in the hall listening to the silence for a few moments and then went through the house, pausing briefly in the kitchen to see if there was anything immediately available to eat. After a desultory check in the fridge and the bread bin he picked up an apple from a bowl on the table and continued out across the yard to the Laundry House.

In his room he saw that no-one had re-made his bed as would have happened in his other life with his parents. Slightly disappointed he tossed some crumpled garments left lying on it onto the floor and then lay down and bit into the apple. A fly buzzed behind the thin curtain, but he couldn't be bothered to get up again and open the window.

An hour or so later Sally phoned James to tell him that she was going to be held up at the college. "I'm sorry," she said, "The Head of Department wants to see me."

"What about?" James asked suspiciously. For him news was most likely to be unfavourable.

"Well . . . " In this case, Sally feared, he could be right. Talk in the college was of redundancy for part-timers in this time of funding cuts; however she didn't really want to discuss this on the phone as she sat now at her desk in the staff room.

"I'm not sure," she said. "I don't expect it will take all that long. But could you collect the children from school? Just Perdita and Claud. I'll go round by the nursery on my way back to pick up Frankie, they won't mind if he stays a bit late, there will be some other children still there."

The word 'late' in relation to Sally's return could make James' heart sink like a stone. He sighed.

Sally could visualise him standing shoulders hunched, by the phone in the dark back hall at Trevean.

"It's a beautiful afternoon," she said encouragingly. "The dogs will love a walk; go across the fields."

"Yes," James said. He didn't say, 'I won't enjoy it by myself; I won't enjoy it without you', but this thought hung heavily between them.

There was nothing Sally could do. "I'll get back as soon as I can," she said.

James set off with the three dogs circling joyfully around him. He paused in the hall to pick a golf club, choosing an iron from the Victorian umbrella stand which was fashioned from dark wood to resemble, horribly, the leg of an elephant. "Good grief, is that real?" Sally had asked when she had first seen it.

Now as he came out onto the granite steps James stared incredulously at the yellow Beetle. "What on earth – ?"

Other people, drawing the conclusion that the car hadn't arrived by itself and that whoever had parked it there was likely to be still around, might have gone back into the house to check this out, but James did not do so. His natural inclination was to avoid meeting people whom he did not know, and indeed most of those whom he did know.

Calling the dogs to follow him across the lawn he set off for the back drive, on the way slicing the heads off one or two dandelions to distract himself briefly from the unattractive task ahead of him. He hated having to collect the children from the Primary School, he felt that he attracted curiosity and probably ridicule among the local parents.

The dogs had neither collars nor leads as James liked them to run free, this regularly resulted in chaos at the school. The dogs would bark, some of the children would want to play with them and some would run screaming to their mothers.

Claud seemed capable of coming through it all smiling but Perdita was left mortally embarrassed and sometimes struggled with the disloyal wish that their father had not come to collect them.

James did not wait, as the few other collecting fathers tended to do, on the edge of the school playground where the children emerged in a sea of navy blue and grey uniforms. He pushed through to the front row of parents where he would have the best chance of seeing Perdita and Claud as soon as they came around the corner from their classrooms, in order to make a quick get-away.

The mêlée of mothers pushing buggies and clutching at toddlers was awful and James loathed having to stand there on the tarmac painted with hopscotch numbers and curly snakes.

The mothers yelled at each other around him and the noise they made was phenomenal. They reminded him of scenes which he must have seen on television of a gannet colony, the constant shifting movement as they nodded and bobbed and waved at each other and then lurched their buggies in a sudden panicky swoop in pursuit of a strayed toddler.

When the children started streaming out it was even worse and the similarity with the sea birds seemed, if anything, increased. The mothers' cries took on a shrill, enquiring note as they questioned their offspring about their day. "Did you find your football boot?" they shrieked in greeting. "Did you hand in your sick note?"

It was amazing, for James, how parent and child could find each other in a matter of moments. All the children looked alike in their uniform, clutching their identical bags and anoraks and art work, and all were white skinned. This last factor still struck him with surprise, his vivid memories being of massed, young, brown faces.

The mothers all looked alike too. In the winter they wore anoraks and boots and in the summer they wore T-shirts and sandals and all the year round they wore jeans.

James himself, despite having fought through to the front of the throng, often failed to distinguish Perdita and Claud until they appeared beside him, claiming his attention.

Which they now did, separately but only a few moments

apart, coming from different classrooms. There then ensued the usual difficulties in rounding up the dogs who had disappeared into the sea of legs in search of crisps and sweets offered them by some of the children.

This was what Perdita particularly dreaded, for James was liable to lose his temper and yell at her and Claud and tell all the mothers standing near him that his dogs were not used to traffic and would be run over if they got onto the road and the mothers would stare at him and then turn away and laugh together.

Once the dogs were retrieved James insisted that they be held until they were clear of the school grounds and the road. This necessitated the children grasping Coal, or Tish or Tash by the scruff of the neck and moving forward crablike and bent double, trying at the same time to hang on to school bags and discarded sweatshirts.

At last they got to the fields and Perdita and Claud and the dogs surged forward across the grass in an excess of joyful liberation.

"Whose is that?" the children asked when they reached the house and saw the yellow Beetle.

"No idea," James said, his brief uplift in spirits at having made it home evaporating in the realisation that the Beetle was the only car on the gravel and that Sally was still not back.

Perdita and Claud circled the car. "I like its yellow," Perdita said.

"Me too," said Claud.

They peered inside.

"Ned's got a T-shirt like that," Perdita said, staring at the tangle of clothes on the back seat.

The car spoke to them of a different lifestyle to their own and it made them feel excited.

When Sally finally got back with Frankie, who was whingeing because he was tired after an extra long day at the nursery, she found James holed up in the study with the dogs. He usually made a pot of tea in the afternoon as he did in the morning, but he had been determined not to do so until she got back. He had not wavered in resolve although he was fully aware that Clarissa, who had her tea on a tray in her room, would think that she had been forgotten.

He had sat, without radio or television, so that he could listen for Sally's return and when he heard the distinctively noisy sound of the car's approach, he took a deeper breath and relaxed into his chair, waiting for her to come to find him and to see how difficult his afternoon had been.

"Hello," she said, opening the door. "All well?"

James sighed. "Hello," he said.

"Whose is the yellow car?"

"I don't know," James said, identifying a sound excuse for lack of cheer. "But obviously it shouldn't be there."

"It could be Ned's," Sally said.

"I didn't know he had a car. Why is he always wanting lifts then?"

"I think," Sally said, "that he may have been hoping to get his grandmother to buy him one." This would make sense of Ned's sudden wish to go to Sidmouth.

"A thoroughly spoilt young man," James said.

"I expect Granny sees it differently." Sally suddenly felt a drop in energy. "I need some tea. Have you had yours?"

"No," James said gloomily. "I was waiting for you."

"I'll put the kettle on."

"I'm coming, I'm coming." James heaved himself to his feet, he did not want to be left alone again. The dogs followed.

"What about Mother?" Sally called back over her shoulder as she crossed the hall. "Has she had her's?"

"No, she has not," James said, "or not from me." His tone conveyed self-absolution form any raiding expedition Clarissa might have conducted on the kitchen on her own account.

He urged the dogs on ahead of him and they began yipping and leaping, in anticipation of getting fed. In the kitchen he pulled the heavy aluminium kettle from the back of the range to the hotplate.

"Let's use the electric one," Sally said. "It's late and Mother will be gasping."

"But not," James said, only to himself, "her last gasp. Unfortunately." Clarissa should not claim precedence in Sally's thoughts; hadn't he also sat tea-less waiting for her return?

Tetchily he banged the mugs down on the table, pushing to one side Claud's school bag and a couple of dirty plates and a half rotten apple which Ned earlier had picked from the fruit bowl and rejected.

Sally unpacked the pasta and bacon which she had brought back for supper. She felt tired and less able than usual to deal with James's black-dog mood and his antipathy to Clarissa. At some stage she was going to have to tell him that she had, indeed, lost her teaching job and so was, until the college funding situation improved, redundant.

CHAPTER 17

JUNE

There are moments in life when realisation comes like a bolt from the blue. Imo experienced such a moment while she was tying up broad bean plants in the kitchen garden, looping them with twine to bamboo canes. She realised that she was going to fall in love with Ned.

Graham had decided that she needed to be shown how to tie the beans and as she didn't question him or argue he had stayed to make sure that she understood and was doing it correctly. Now he had returned to hacking and clearing round the apple trees and she moved slowly up the row of bean plants, lifting and fixing them as he had shown her, taking care not to break the stems. The garden was peaceful and wrapped in the warmth of the sun.

Imo was on the edge of grown up life, she wasn't sure what she wanted or why she wanted it but part of the fog of dissatisfaction which could so suddenly descend to envelope her was a longing for love, or more specifically a longing to be in love.

Not just anyone would do: he should be good looking, he should understand about Art College and he should be prepared to fall in love with her. In effect this had narrowed the field considerably.

There was one boy at college for whom she had pined, but he had shown no interest in her. It is difficult to continue to hold a candle for someone who never looks in your direction.

Graham did not stand a chance with Imo. She was glad that he now seemed less grumpy but otherwise she didn't particularly notice him. If anyone had told her that Graham thought about her a lot she would have been disconcerted.

But now here was Ned and the realisation that her longings had found a focus. She could so easily and so appropriately love Ned. Ned was perfect.

Later on this evening when she arrived in the kitchen for supper and saw Ned, back from Sidmouth and again sitting opposite her, that certainty was only reinforced. The evening sun, shining through the window over the draining board, created a halo of light around his golden hair. She knew then that he was the one.

Ned of course had also been waiting for romance, or more specifically he had been waiting for sex. He frequently returned to the thought that this should have happened already and of course the fact that it hadn't was entirely due to his parents packing him off to a boys only boarding school and then his mother never letting him anywhere near a girl in the holidays. Or not near any girl with whom he might do anything.

One of the irritations of finding himself at Trevean was the continuing lack of girls. He saw girls when he could get to the beach but that was as far as he had got, seeing them. Not being a local surfer and not having transport cramped his style. Having to catch the bus and lug around that clapped-out bodyboard was stupid.

And obviously none of this was his fault.

Now sitting across the supper table Imo and Ned looked at each other and each of them felt this as a moment of recognition.

Sally noticed and inwardly sighed. She thought how tiresome, for hadn't she promised James that Imo's arrival wouldn't cause trouble? What now?

"Is that your vehicle on the front gravel by any chance?" James asked Ned.

"Yes," Ned was pleased that his car had been noticed.

"It needs moving."

Earlier James had said to Sally, "What does he think he's doing – leaving that thing slap bang outside the front door? He's here to dig the garden isn't he, not to make a social call."

"You can put it up in the old cart shed, next to Graham's," Sally said, sorting things out.

There was an uncomfortable moment or two of silence.

Perdita was still captivated by the car's yellow glamour. When it was apparent that neither James nor Sally was going to elicit further information about it she asked Ned tentatively, "Where did you get your car?"

Ned was annoyed by the apparent lack of appreciation of the Beetle. "It's a present from my grandmother."

Claud had been gently pushing a piece of mushroom, which he didn't like, round his plate. "Is it your birthday?"

"No," Ned said without elaboration.

Claud gazed at him, thinking about this.

Imo was intrigued. "What kind of car is it?" Usually she said little at meals, being shy still of the family and her position with them.

"A VW Beetle Convertible." Ned spoke to her directly across the table.

Imo's skin had tanned in the sheltered sun trap of the kitchen garden and her hair had lightened. She stared back at Ned wide eyed.

He thought again, as he had thought when he first saw her, that she was quite pretty and he felt more positive suddenly. Basically, he didn't care what James and Sally thought about his car, they were too old for their opinion to matter. But now this girl was here and things looked altogether brighter; the summer was not, perhaps, going to be totally wasted after all.

"It's my swimming lesson today," Claud said matter-of-factly, he had covered the mushroom with his knife.

"What?" Sally cried, looking at her watch. "Why didn't you remind me?"

"You said put the list on the fridge," Claud pointed to the fridge door where various notices about the children's meetings and activities were stuck in overlapping clumps with blu-tack, masking tape or magnetic letters.

"Oh for goodness' sake," James said, "there's stuff there going back twenty years."

"I think that may be a bit of an exaggeration," Sally said laughing.

"Why? Those bits of paper are yellow with age some of them, they probably go back to Aunt Lavinia's time."

"No, really, darling, they don't," Sally protested. "We got the fridge last year, don't you remember, because it had a double size freezer bit? Second-hand, Jack Richards brought it over in the garage breakdown truck."

Graham shifted in his chair. He disliked it when the Lacocks started arguing at meals, which they often seemed to do; it put him off his food. He didn't know why Sally laughed at the things James said, were they supposed to be funny? Daft more like.

James, Sally and the children did not think they were arguing of course, just discussing facts as they saw them. Sally recognised and appreciated James' vein of bleak humour.

Imo was less unnerved by the Lacocks than Graham for she was used to family disagreements, indeed lately to being the catalyst which caused them. Ned really wasn't interested, he was regretting that there was nothing more to eat on the table except summer cabbage or rice, neither of which he particularly liked.

"Have you got your swimming things ready?" Sally asked Claud.

"I don't know."

"Well, eat up quickly and go and find them and I'll take you. But we'll need to get a move on."

"I think," Claud said, "they might still be in the car."

"Oh no," Sally said. "Not all soggy and smelly in the boot?"

"Maybe."

"Well, you'll just have to put up with it. You should have remembered to take them out."

After this the meal shortly came to an end. "Can you all clear the table," Sally said, not including James. She hurried Claud out through the back porch. "Come on, or it won't be worth going."

James got to his feet, his time with Sally was yet again being curtailed; he headed for the study. He couldn't cope with sorting out domestic details with the children and teenagers. Sally had the knack for it, he hadn't. In Delhi his students had sorted themselves out, sitting politely at their desks and if he was delayed sending one of their number to say that, when convenient, they were ready for his lecture.

Perdita wandered away up to Clarissa's room to collect her tray and answer her questions about what was happening downstairs.

"Why don't you come down for supper Granny?" she had asked once or twice but Clarissa had said, "My legs aren't up to it these days."

In truth the antipathy between Clarissa and James had reduced Sally to suggesting this arrangement in the interests of meal-time harmony. And the stairs with their worn carpet and missing brass rods were a hazard.

Chairs scraped back on the slate floor.

Graham carried his plate to the sink, rinsed it and put it on the draining board. He planned to go up to the Potting Shed while it was still light enough to look through a catalogue which he had picked up from a local plant nursery. Recently when Sally had come to the kitchen garden to collect peas and rhubarb for the house, she had suggested that they might be able to offer him employment at Trevean when the volunteer scheme finished at the end of the summer.

She had said to James privately, "It would be a good idea, don't you think? He's a hard worker."

"Where's the money to come from?" James had asked.

"You never know," Sally was optimistic. "Something may turn up. Those employment grants we've applied for, maybe."

Now Graham was considering autumn planting of brassicas and fruit bushes; he wanted to make a list of plants and seeds to show Sally, there was no point asking James.

Imo and Ned continued to sit at the table, uncertainty about the other's response hung palpably between them. Do you find me attractive? The question was present in both their minds.

Ned despite his positive self-assessment of his own attractions and talents was instinctively disinclined to risk rejection, he remained silent.

Eventually Imo, finding inspiration, asked, "Can I see your car?"

Ned felt relief. So, she did fancy him; things were going to work out. Excellent.

"OK."

Imo followed him down the kitchen corridor and through the green baize door which he jammed briefly open for her with his foot, her heart was beating faster than normal.

Together they crossed the hall and stood on the front steps staring at the Beetle, both with gratification.

Ned was pleased because besides giving him the appropriate independence and image, the car looked good for bringing him a girlfriend. He had known that it would and he had been right.

For Imo the car ticked an extra box on her boyfriend wish list, criteria which she had believed Ned already met so completely; now he was more than perfect.

He asked her, making it casual. "So, do you want to go for a drive?"

Imo took an instinctive, joyful breath. Yes! Ned got into the car and immediately turned the ignition key, she scrambled hastily into the passenger seat.

The seat belt was twisted and as she tried to disentangle it Ned drove off, scattering gravel and bumping over the holes in the surface of the drive. She gave up on the belt and clicked it shut, still twisted, it cut into her shoulder through the thin T-shirt, but she didn't care.

When they came out onto the road which ran through the

wooded valley beside the river and small, rush-grown water meadows, Ned accelerated and although the Beetle's engine did not lend itself to speed, the roof was down and the wind lifted their hair and Imo felt they were skimming the surface of the earth.

"I am happy!" she thought.

Ned decided to drive down to the cove where they could park close to the beach and people could see them. He wished that he had a surfboard in the back of the car, he needed his own longboard. He regretted not asking for the money from his grandmother to buy one, she probably would have given it to him and then he would have been sorted.

The sun was getting low in the sky as they drove down the hill towards the sea. On either side the cliffs were covered with heather, beginning to come into purple flower. Ned drove to the car park above the beach.

As Imo looked down towards the sea, she saw that the tide was far out and the sand stretched away, wide and shining. A few of the local surfers were in the water but otherwise the beach was nearly empty. She and Ned could walk round the rocks where they could be, wonderfully, alone.

Ned found the lack of people mildly disappointing, he had been hoping to show off the Beetle, with Imo in the seat beside him; himself with the car and the girl.

They sat for a while. Imo unlocked the seat belt which was digging into her ribs; Ned glanced around the car park. There were a couple of vans which probably belonged to the surfers and two men were standing by the open boot of their car sorting out their gear to go bass fishing, a family was coming up from the beach carting towels and bags and with a wailing child in tow. All of these people were preoccupied with their own concerns.

Ned stared at the water. "Surf's not up to much."

This was not difficult to deduce because the surfers were sitting far out on their boards, waiting for a wave, but Imo knew nothing about surfing. Her nod of easy acquiescence encouraged him.

Ned had his complications but at a more straightforward level he was also young and healthy and suddenly he wanted to be out there where the evening air was still warm with an edge of freshness blowing in from the sea.

"Come on," he said and the two of them climbed out of the car and went down across the band of stones piled up by the spring tides, onto the pale sand.

Ned glanced back to see if Imo was following him. "OK?"

"Yes," she said but the stones were smooth and shifting and below them a stream fanned out across the sand. She bent to remove her trainers.

Ned, wearing sandals, walked through the water and stood, hands in his jeans pockets watching the line of breaking waves and the black wet-suited figures of the surfers far out beyond them.

The stream water licked cold around Imo's feet; laughing she kicked up a shower of drops. She looked towards Ned, but he did not turn and as she came through the stream he set off walking towards the far side of the beach where the sand spread far out beyond the base of the cliffs.

She ran after him.

They followed the line of the rocks which, dark and limpet covered, sheltered pools filled with miniature worlds of red and pale green seaweed and small darting transparent shrimps. Imo would have paused to examine these but Ned, filling his lungs with air, strode on. He felt he was ridding himself of the cramping, suffocating atmosphere at Trevean where he was unable to do what he wanted and his time seemed set to be wasted, day on dusty, humid day, among the bamboos. So they continued, now walking side by side, far along the beach beneath the cliffs and then Ned turned towards the wave line.

Both knew they needed to discover the possible parameters of their relationship. Neither of them was able to pose directly the question 'Are you free and do you fancy me?' In Imo's case, more specifically perhaps, 'Will you love me?'

"At college," Imo said at last, "I was doing Art and there were more boys than girls, but . . . " she paused, "the boys weren't interesting."

"So you don't have a boyfriend then?" Ned asked, staring at the sea.

"No," she said. She was drawing patterns on the sand with her feet and not looking at him.

"Nor me," he said. "Girlfriend, that is."

Imo's heart sang.

"I've not had much chance to meet people, well, girls." He needed, he felt, to make this clear. His lack of experience should not reflect on him.

She began to tell him then about how utterly boring it was living at home and being stuck in the middle of endless wedding planning.

"Mum and Antonia never talk about anything else, and it's all about flowers on the end of the pews and ivy in the marquee; and shoes, and the photographs, and we're all supposed to be on this diet and Dad's getting really fed up . . . "

Ned stared out across the sea as they walked. One thing which he thought he did know about girls was that they talked a lot and you had to let them, if you wanted anything to progress further.

If you managed to kiss them things were obviously easier, for you could effectively silence them by placing your mouth over theirs.

Ned's mentor in these matters had been a boy at school called Felix who was in the First XV with him. Felix was in the lucky position of having a sister whose friends came to stay at their house in the holidays; he said that one of these girls had succeeded in proving to him that he wasn't gay. Details of the experience which he had gained in the process he was happy enough to pass on to Ned and others.

Now Ned withdrew his gaze from the sea and looked at Imo's face, bright with happiness. He felt the touch of an emotion unfamiliar to him, one which Felix had in fact counselled him against. "Girls go in for falling in love," he had said, "but that just complicates things. Stay clear."

However, what was easy enough in theory was less so when he was with an actual girl. Although Imo was wearing a too large sludge coloured T-shirt and trousers, she was clearly slim and her bare feet were suntanned.

She was talking now about how she wanted to go to Art College and how she had determined to take the volunteer placement at Trevean to escape her family's obsessive involvement with her sister's wedding. Weddings were of no interest to Ned at all, but he found that he did definitely want to kiss her.

When her sand pattern drawing steps at one point caused her foot to touch his he felt a small after shock and on an impulse he took her hand.

Imo caught her breath and stopped talking.

They crossed the sand, cool and ridged, and walked slowly

beside the sea until the frill of water at the wave line lifted and ran towards their feet.

"Is the tide coming in?" Imo asked then.

They stared along the beach and saw that the waves were beginning to fill the pools where the rocks jutted out from the cliffs.

"We'd better go back," Ned said.

"Run!" Imo said on impulse. "Let's run!"

They ran where the sand was damp, leaving their footprints to be washed away behind them. Ned releasing her hand easily outstripped Imo, slowing when they reached the cove and the entrance of a vast cave.

He walked into the shadows beneath the black rocks and Imo, catching up, followed him.

Around them there were pools in the sandy floor and glutinous red blobs of sea anemones among the black mussels clustering on the cave walls, water dripped from the roof far above.

Imo shivered.

Ned looked at her. "Are you cold?"

"I'm all right."

But when he made a quick decision and put his arms around her Imo stayed within them.

CHAPTER 18

JUNE

One particular anxiety lying heavily on Marilyn's heart in the days following their dinner with the Rodmaines was her lack of an outfit for the wedding.

This was now suddenly compounded by Antonia's announcement in a panicky phone call that she was having more doubts about the wedding dress.

"But why?" Marilyn felt her stomach tighten. Maddy the dressmaker would not be pleased – understandably. There had been those endless discussions about the design. The bridesmaids' dresses were already completed, only requiring final fittings but the cutting and sewing of the wedding dress was waiting till last for final post-diet measurements.

And now Antonia wanted to change her mind! Marilyn felt she would cry, there, in the kitchen, holding the phone. From the start everything about the dresses had been stressful. Imo had sulked through each fitting; Antonia had reported that she didn't think Lizzie, Roger's sister, and Petra really liked their dresses.

In fact Lizzie was the cause of Antonia's new anxieties for she was telling people that the pink organza would make her look like the Sugar Plum Fairy. "And we're not thinking The Royal Ballet here; definitely local panto."

She and Petra pretended to go into paroxysms of excitement about the wedding dress. Antonia had made the mistake of telling them about Maddy's idea for the Dresden shepherdess design. "Ooh! We can't wait!" they exclaimed into their mobiles, "Panniers! How hysterical!"

Antonia had lost her nerve completely and despite Marilyn saying that she thought the original design was lovely and a 'real wedding dress' (by which she meant lots of skirt and lots of veil) Antonia wept and said, No, no, no, she'd definitely changed her mind.

The trouble was, of course, changed it to what? She didn't know.

Marilyn bought more copies of wedding magazines and stuck pink stickies on the pages with dresses and at the weekend she and Antonia pored over them and couldn't fix on any one. Antonia brought her own magazines down from London, with yellow stickies, and made a shortlist of the dresses she liked but Clive, asked for his opinion, pointed out that the cost of each of these far exceeded the budget on which they had agreed.

"This whole wedding business is getting out of hand," he said. "I'll still be paying for it in ten years' time. What is wrong with the other dress? If it's Roger's parents who are upsetting you again, then let them pay for a different one. Have they offered to contribute towards this wedding? No, they have not." The memory of the Rodmaines' chilly response to the suggestion returned regularly to annoy him.

"How can this – " he turned one magazine round on the coffee table to look at a photograph of a size six model walking into the sea in Phuket wearing a sheath of cream silk, "cost this?"

Nothing had been resolved but everything was made much worse when Maddy the dressmaker said that unless they stuck to the original design she could not guarantee that the wedding dress would be ready on time.

Marilyn suspected that Maddy had been upset by Imo's behaviour when trying on her pink dress; possibly also she had learned what Lizzie and Petra thought of theirs. Her former pleasant and co-operative manner had cooled considerably.

"And I'm afraid that there will have to be a cancellation charge," she now said, "if you decide not to go ahead."

Marilyn had not dared to tell Clive.

After a week of anguish, it was agreed that Marilyn would meet Antonia in London and the two of them would have a concentrated search for a new dress. The budget had been agreed with Clive and was not to be exceeded. Every time Marilyn or Antonia thought about this each was consumed with worry. London prices!

On the chosen day Marilyn caught the train wearing a pair of low-heeled shoes and with a bottle of Evian water and a packet of Anadin Extra in her handbag. She had woken, as had become usual lately, with that feeling of dread in the pit of her stomach which sent its cold tentacles spreading swiftly throughout her body.

It was all just due to stress, she would be better once the wedding was over. Several of the bridal magazines had pointed out that the mother of the bride carried a heavy burden of responsibility and urged her to 'cosset herself a little'.

Antonia met Marilyn at the station and said that as recommended by a wedding advice column she had booked a consultation with a personal shopper at a bridal boutique. The magazine had advised that this could save much foot-ache and maybe heart-ache too.

The boutique was in a smart street, there were clipped box plants on each side of the portico standing in galvanised buckets. This indicated perhaps that all styles of wedding could be catered for, whether city slick or rural quaint, but not that they would come cheap.

Marilyn and Antonia were welcomed and offered seats by the receptionist, a cool girl in pale grey who was revealed, when she stood up from behind her desk, to be wearing sugar pink heels of great height.

"Are you sure?" Marilyn whispered to Antonia as they sat gazing at glass stands containing embroidered satin shoes, full length buttoned gloves and 'gifts for bridesmaids' – coral and enamel bracelets, single pearls hung on gossamer gold chains. In the window there was a dramatic display featuring fresh peonies.

Antonia's courage had also faltered but desperation made her resolute. Time was running out and she had to have the right sort of dress.

The receptionist introduced them to Stephanie, their personal adviser.

Stephanie was a woman of style, in her well-presented fifties. She gathered up Marilyn and Antonia and as she led them to the inner salon they felt themselves about to be inexorably separated from all their doubts and uncertainties. Soon settled with coffee on an expansive sofa in the soothing glow of the silk-shaded lighting they awaited the arrival of an assistant to take Antonia's measurements.

A portfolio of photographs was produced and the designs discussed for material, length, hemline, waistline, decoration, sleeves and what the dress would look like from the back.

"And also with a veil," Stephanie said, "which is so important."

Marilyn and Antonia nodded in absolute agreement.

"You have," Stephanie told Antonia, "such beautiful skin. We should enhance it."

Antonia glanced surreptitiously at herself in the huge gilt framed mirror.

Then Stephanie's assistant produced selected dresses and hung them on a rail in their voluminous, opalescent protective covers.

Was this the moment, Marilyn wondered, to mention the budget? She bit her lip.

Antonia gazed, enraptured. By now it had been agreed to restrict the choice of dress to floor length, an off the shoulder design in creamy ivory to emphasise her skin tones and to allow a full veil to fall 'like a cloud' around her.

Stephanie was clearly delighted with this image and shortly Antonia was down to her bra and pants in the changing room.

She tried on four dresses and this took a while, as they pondered the pros and cons of satin versus silk, bustier versus bodice. One dress emphasised particularly her high, full breasts, clinched her really quite trim waist and was laced all the way down the back to her well rounded bottom.

"This is the one," Stephanie announced with conviction.

Antonia stared in the great mirror and wondered at what she saw, herself but different.

"Quite lovely!" Stephanie took a step back and spread her

hands to indicate that she rested her case. What more was there to say? "Like the girl who came out of the sea on a shell."

Antonia and Marilyn looked at her, uncertain

"It'll come to me," Stephanie said. "It's a painting."

Finally, as the assistant was poised to take hem and neckline measurements for very minor alterations, Marilyn dared to enquire the dress's price. As she feared, it was calculated to upset Clive considerably.

But it was too late. Antonia gazed at her, her eyes dilated with hope.

"Oh! Well. Yes – " Marilyn said helplessly. "It is lovely."

"We also," Stephanie said, "do of course have beautiful outfits for the mother of the bride. Or – " she smiled at Marilyn as someone, like herself, a woman of good sense and organisational skills. "You have already decided? I expect you have. But perhaps a bag, or gloves?"

Marilyn felt shafted by failure and guilt.

"Well, no – " she said. "I haven't . . . quite . . . well, not a final choice. I don't think – " Her voice faded on a note of apology. There was no doubt, this was a shocking admission to make here, in this shrine to all things bridal. Also, she had been about to mention possible cost, but again her nerve failed.

"But how lovely!" Stephanie clasped her hands. "So we have the opportunity to show you some of our gorgeous outfits. You have a preferred colour?"

"To go with pink, petal pink," Antonia said. "The bridesmaids' dresses – "

"Already chosen?" Stephanie suggested.

"Yes," Antonia's voice was muffled for she had disappeared within yards of raw silk which were being lifted up and over her head by the assistant.

Stephanie nodded, acknowledging Antonia's point, but with regret for the decision already made. "It can be nice to choose everything from the same salon," she said. "Then you can be sure that the materials and the shades go well together. You will be thinking of the photographs, of course."

"Yes! That's what it said in Your Wedding Day," Antonia, emerging, agreed eagerly. She had become an acolyte now to Stephanie, priestess of the bridal temple. "About colours of outfits not clashing."

"But – " Marilyn realised that her voice sounded a bit odd. She had the mental picture of Clive writing a figure with a pound sign on the Cath Kitson message pad in the kitchen at The Rowans and saying, "That's the limit. Don't spend any more than that."

They had already gone above this figure with the wedding dress. If she bought her outfit here as well, imagine the cost! What would Clive say? He didn't often lose his temper, but this time he might for he was already so annoyed about the whole business of the wedding: the Rodmaines, the dress, the hotel, everything.

And yet – she looked wistfully at the cascade of ivory silk over the arm of the seamstress.

"While your daughter is getting dressed," Stephanie suggested. "Perhaps you might like to look at some of our models? I can see you perhaps in a moss rose, you have such lovely English colouring, and there is one particular outfit I'm thinking of."

Marilyn hesitated and all was lost.

"Oh, do have a look, Mum," Antonia said, lit up with relief now that her own dress mission was so successfully accomplished.

Stephanie moved to the wall and opened tall white panelled doors to reveal ranks of colour coded garments; coats, dresses, jackets and skirts. She lifted out, in its plastic sheath, a silk coat and dress in dusky pink.

"And see," she said, unbuttoning the corded buttons, "how the line is so flattering."

"What about . . . shoes?" Marilyn asked weakly as Stephanie helped her slip on the coat.

"Dyed to match. We can arrange all this for you, of course."

"The hotel has said no heels – " Antonia remembered.

Stephanie was in no way fazed. "An extra pair of silk pumps," she said. "And our hats – " she gestured towards a wide brimmed pale grey straw displayed upon a hat stand, "also are colour co-ordinated."

The pink-mauve dress, in its nubbly silk, was spread across one of the gilded chairs.

"Oh, do try it on, Mum!" Antonia said.

Half an hour later it was just a question of which size shoes for dying and for Antonia to receive her complimentary garter with tiny embroidered blue hearts. Emotionally reeling they were ushered down the steps of the boutique to head for the nearest café for a restorative cup of coffee. They both felt this could be a well-deserved break from the restrictions of The Diet.

"I don't know what your dad is going to say," Marilyn felt the euphoria and panic in equal measure.

But Antonia felt that uncharacteristically she didn't care, she was so happy with her dress and indeed with Marilyn's outfit, surely neither of which would now bring down upon her the derision of Lizzie and Petra, that whatever her dad said it would be worth it. All through her growing-up Dad had complained about the cost of things, from people leaving lights on to the over-use of the tumble-dryer, but this was her wedding! He would see that it had to be perfect.

And to an extent she was right because Clive did care that Antonia should have the wedding she wanted. His objections arose mainly from his belief that she, and by default he and Marilyn, were being pushed into unnecessary and gratuitous expenditure by the the Rodmaines, whose attitude he found patronising. He hoped it wouldn't be necessary to see too much of them once the wedding was over.

Initially of course Clive had been pleased that Antonia had found herself a fiancé with a profession, a good salary and perks, that is the house in London, the Porsche, but this pleasure had been lessened by the suspicion that Roger, like his parents, felt superior and was disparaging.

"Do they think they're doing us a favour?" he asked himself and on occasion Marilyn. "Because as far as I'm concerned the boot is on the other foot."

Antonia would make a good wife, she was pretty and she was not bolshie like Imo, she was a professional cook and he and Marilyn had provided her with private education and a good home; Roger should show more appreciation of his good fortune.

"Don't worry, Mum," Antonia said now, "Dad will be all right."

She scooped the froth from her coffee. How many calories? In this moment of delight she had forgotten The Diet.

"We've gone over the budget – " Marilyn said, anxious.

"Yes, but we've got your outfit too, and the hat and the shoes, everything!"

Antonia was feeling sorely tempted by the idea of a blueberry muffin, but the dress had been just a bit pinching under the bust. Stephanie had said that pre-wedding nerves would solve the problem. "Most brides lose that little bit of weight in the run up to The Day," she said. "And of course, the back lacing is accommodating, if necessary." Antonia turned her mind away from muffins. Poor old Mum, she was always in a fuss about something or other.

For the first part of the journey home the train was packed with office workers and Marilyn sat pinched between two men, one of whom read from a folded newspaper; the other, younger, read texts on his phone. Neither of them got up for the woman standing by the doors who had, Marilyn could see, bad varicose veins. She was glad when the woman got out at one of the commuter stations for this meant that she herself need no longer feel embarrassed about having a seat.

Antonia's dress and veil and her own outfit would all be delivered by courier in a week or so's time, by when she would have to have told Clive about them. Or at any rate before he received the credit card bill.

As the train progressively emptied, she made her way to the toilet and gazed at her wobbly reflection in the metal mirror and renewed her lipstick and took a couple of Anadin in a mouthful of Evian water.

Meanwhile Antonia, emerging from the rush hour tube station, found her mobile ringing.

"It's me," Roger said. "I was thinking – perhaps you could ask Lizzie to help you choose your dress?"

This idea had actually come from Penelope. After the rather unsatisfactory dinner with Clive and Marilyn she had phoned Lizzie to voice her anxieties. "Antonia's parents seem to have some quite odd ideas about this wedding. They are not our sort, I'm afraid. Has Antonia chosen her dress? I'm really getting quite worried. What do you think it will be like . . . not too chocolate-boxy?"

"Oh, that's a dead cert," Lizzie said. "It's going to be a crinoline, with panniers and

diamanté detail. Polyester probably – nice and washable. And tiara."

"It's really not funny," Penelope said crossly. "You could help her choose."

"I'd rather not," Lizzie said. Why should she sort out the Apple Dumpling? It would be more fun to have a giggle on the wedding day with her friends, and some compensation at least for having to wear that awful bridesmaid's dress.

So Penelope had phoned Roger at work, to give him a commission which did not please him. "Tell Antonia to ask Lizzie to advise her," she said. "The wedding dress is so important. Whyever has she left it so late?"

Roger felt that he wasn't clued up about women's clothes; his father had always suggested that it was a topic best left alone. Some girls looked nice and some didn't; that pretty much summed it up. The City girls he came into contact with through work could be, frankly, intimidating with their dark suits and high heels and habit of out-arguing people and quoting factual evidence to prove they were right.

One of the reasons that he had picked Antonia was that she didn't argue with him; also mostly he thought she looked nice. She seemed to wear pink quite a lot. Or yellow.

"No, it's all right," Antonia now told him. "I've already got my dress. Actually I got it today."

Penelope had asked Roger to suggest 'not too much material in the skirt, or sleeves' and without an exposure of flesh. Some relief came over him now – if the dress was already bought it was too late, nothing to be done about it.

"It's lovely," Antonia said. "I love it. Mum does too."

This gave Roger slight pause.

"What's it like?" he asked cautiously. Penelope had elaborated her instructions, "Not a long train. Or shiny."

"Shiny?" He had queried, agreeing this didn't sound good.

"I can't tell you!" Antonia said now. "It's a secret, of course. You'll see it on The Day."

Well, Roger thought, that's that then. He was pleased that Antonia was sounding happy, which boded well for tonight, it being Wednesday she would be staying over. She'd been rather emotional lately.

"My yummy dumpling," he murmured tenderly and then realised that three other people in the office were listening to his conversation.

"See you later then," he said hastily and rang off.

Antonia made her way back to the flat. Having taken a flexi-day from work to meet Marilyn and go dress shopping she had time on her hands before Roger came to collect her in the Porsche. Lizzie and Petra wouldn't be back for well over an hour. Because she was feeling so happy the evidence of their possessive occupation of the flat and their casual disregard for her feelings didn't sap her energy like it usually did.

Perhaps they were just being thoughtless rather than actively unkind, perhaps Roger was right, she was too sensitive, imagining slights. She decided to tidy things up a bit.

She picked newspapers and magazines off the floor and lined them up on the coffee table, she put shoes, boots and various garments outside their owner's bedroom door.

She emptied the sink and poured some lemon drain cleaner down the drain, stacked the dishwasher and cleaned the hob, mopped the kitchen floor. In the bathroom she wiped round the bath and basin and sprayed Summer Glade room freshener.

When the others returned, together, Lizzie said, "Heavens! Death by mixed fragrances! Are we celebrating something?"

"Well – I got my wedding dress today," Antonia said, smiling.

Lizzie looked at her. "What do you mean?" she said. "Not off the peg?"

CHAPTER 19

JUNE

Marilyn took guilty receipt of Antonia's dress and of her own outfit, delivered by courier and each boxed within layers of cream tissue paper. Nothing so common or garden as a receipted invoice accompanied them, only a card with an embossed sprig of myrtle wishing her and her daughter the happiest of days. Marilyn was caught at odd moments with a sick-making stab of anxiety when she thought of what Clive would say when he saw the credit card bill, for she hadn't summoned the nerve to tell him the upsetting financial details in advance.

She felt that her life was just one thing after another. When she had returned from the town on Julia's morning, earlier in the week, she had found the washing, including sheets, drying outside and had felt quite panicky. She had protested, but Julia had said that she had put her own washing out in the sun and it was no trouble.

Julia had on previous occasions suggested that it was nice to let the sheets get a good blow in the sunshine until Marilyn had finally had to explain that she didn't think that people on The Glebe liked to see washing hanging out. Julia had looked at her in a way which made her feel foolish.

As soon as Julia collected her bike and left Marilyn hurried out to the rotary dryer and fetched the washing in herself, glancing nervously over the leylandii at her neighbour's bedroom windows, shrouded in net, while she un-pegged the sheets. She then found, maddeningly, that she couldn't get the arms of the dryer to unlock; after struggling for several minutes she had had to retreat indoors leaving them incriminatingly open.

Imo had not had her final fitting for her bridesmaid's dress and this was making Antonia increasingly fretful. She called home on her mobile from the staff changing room at Directors' Lunches, catching Marilyn as she came in from the patio with her arms full of semi-dry pillowcases.

Antonia stressed the urgent need to get Imo to try on her dress. "What happens," she asked, "if she's put on weight?"

"Oh, she won't have, will she?" Marilyn was beginning to feel the familiar tightening clutch of anxiety. She gazed distractedly through the kitchen window at a neighbourhood cat which was purposefully examining the earth in the flowerbed bordering the patio.

"She won't have been sticking to The Diet," Antonia said, her voice rising. "And oh, I've just thought, what about suntan?"

"Sun – ?"

The cat squatted, staring ahead with a rapt expression on its face.

"Shoo!"

"What?"

"Oh, sorry, it's a cat, it's making a mess in the petunias."

"Mum! Listen to me, please! You'd need Factor 50, working outside all the time, like Imo is. And I bet she's been wearing one of those horrid vest things of hers."

"Well – " Marilyn tried to get her head around the implications of this possibility.

"She'll be striped! And the dress is off the shoulder!"

"Oh surely she will have thought of that?"

"Mum! You know Imo only ever seems to think about herself now! Oh, I wish she wasn't being a bridesmaid, she doesn't want to do it does she? Why do sisters always have to be involved in weddings? Or I suppose they can be, but why must they be bridesmaids? Whatever they look like or their hair or something is absolutely awful, which Imo's is, she just does it deliberately, like dreadlocks . . . "

"Imo doesn't have dreadlocks," Marilyn protested. "Not real ones . . . "

"Or she might actually have lost weight," Antonia continued, following her own train of thought, "and then, oh no, the whole dress will need to be altered!" She caught her breath, faced with the enormity of this thought.

Marilyn began to be sure that one of her headaches was settling above her right eye. Antonia was not normally so critical of Imo, in fact she sometimes stuck up for her, saying she would grow out of whatever it was that Marilyn or Clive found so irritating, but since they began arranging the wedding Antonia seemed to be far less tolerant about all sorts of things.

"Well, I could try to phone Imo," Marilyn said, "and ask her to come home. Maybe at the weekend?"

"There's no mobile reception down there. Or she never answers her phone."

Antonia's voice rose towards a note of desperation, which upset Marilyn. Oh why, they both thought, did everything have to be so awkward?

"Then I'll – " Marilyn briefly considered the possibility of asking Clive to phone Imo but a clear image presented itself of Clive's previous response to just such a request from Antonia herself. He had said that having Imo out of the house and not arguing about going to Art College at every opportunity was the best thing that had happened for months and why would he want her back any earlier than was absolutely necessary?

"I could phone Mrs Lacock," Marilyn said bravely.

I expect Mrs Lacock has got children, she thought, she'll understand won't she how difficult they can be? But she hesitated, for would Mrs Lacock understand? The idea of trying to explain Antonia's anxieties about The Diet and suntan stripes to someone who owned an historic garden made Marilyn quail, even as she said she the words.

"Phone now, Mum!" Antonia said. "Will you? Don't put it off, it's really important."

"Yes – " Marilyn pressed her index finger against the groove in her right eyebrow which sometimes helped to lessen the incipient throb of a headache.

"I've got to go." Antonia said, slightly mollified. "We've got asparagus tarts in the oven. 'Bye then." She rang off and hurried back into the kitchens.

Marilyn wondered if Antonia might not have asked, "And how are you?" She found that this conversation had jangled her nerves severely.

This was not least because of Antonia's going on about The Diet. Antonia herself was apparently sticking to one thousand calories a day and power-walking to work. Marilyn was, she felt, trying her best although for the past two weeks her weight had remained stubbornly static, in fact incomprehensibly in the last couple of days it had actually increased slightly. Clive refused to weigh himself on the bathroom scales, but he didn't look as if he had lost much weight, although every day she prepared an easy-seal plastic box of salad for him to take to work for his lunch.

Meanwhile the asparagus tartlets which Antonia was preparing were destined, in a roundabout way, to have an influence on Imo's life at Trevean.

They were to form part of a light, post board meeting buffet ordered by the executive directors of a spread-betting firm in the City. One of the directors who was attending this meeting was Dominic Mason-Poule, father of eighteen-year-old Nicolette.

Nicolette Mason-Poule was now lying on her bed at home in leafy Finchley, smoking a joint. She was bored and beginning to wish that she had agreed to go with her mother and her younger brother to the Dordogne for the summer. But the converted grape processing sheds which were their holiday home would be heaving with family, most particularly with the small French cousins. Every year there seemed to be more of them, more new babies, and last year's babies grown into more toddlers.

There would be mushed up food thrown around the place at meals and along with the puking and screaming everyone would be going into rhapsodies when some kid brought a plastic pot and sat down beside them and did a disgusting great poo.

It was the ghastliness of this prospect which had persuaded Nicolette to apply for the Garden Volunteer Scheme. Chancing upon the Student Union leaflet in the pack of pre-matriculation information from Oxford University she had noticed the ad for the volunteers. Some of the guys in the photographs, engaged in pond clearing or ivy stripping, looked quite fit.

She had recently returned from a pre-university trek to Dharamsala and found that her parents were not inclined to fund any more travelling. There was nobody interesting in London until September and her father would shortly be joining the rest of the family in France. Nicolette went ahead with the Garden Volunteer application and was now waiting to find out if she had a placement.

Today as she lay in her room watching clouds drifting across the open window and at a lower level of her mind listening to the clinking of the string of miniature Tibetan wind-chimes hanging over her bed, she heard the front door bell ring.

In normal circumstances she would have ignored it on the basis that she did not have to concern herself with the domestic details; Cordelia, the Filipino housekeeper, would leave the hoover or ironing board to respond to the caller. But now Cordelia, having at last saved the return airfare was visiting her family in Manila, including her children aged six, seven and eight whom she had not seen for two years. There was no-one else in the house.

Nicolette knocked out the end of the joint onto a plate on the bedside table, on which there was also a half-eaten piece of toast, swung her bare legs over the edge of her bed and sauntered down the stairs and across the large hall. Pulling open the heavy front door she found a postman.

He had been whistling and now stopped. "Too big for your letterbox," he said, proffering a large envelope; he was youngish, cheerful looking and black.

Nicolette looked at him level-eyed. "Thank you."

She held out her hand for the envelope, her palms were still patterned with fading henna designs, legacy of a long and boring wait at Delhi airport. She was aware that the postman's attention was caught by this and by her bare midriff and tumbled hair. For a couple of beats she considered the opportunity but decided on balance to let the moment pass. She smiled and closed the door, but quite slowly, leaving a sliver of possibility for another time.

The postman stood for a moment, gazing at the shiny bottle green paint of the door and the brass knocker which was in the shape of a dolphin and then he stepped down the steps and proceeded along the pavement, continuing his round, but not immediately his whistling.

Nicolette, sitting on the stairs to open the envelope, found that she was offered a six-week placement at Trevean and given a contact number. The enclosed leaflets about historic gardens, suitable clothing and health considerations (tetanus) slid from her lap to the floor as she stood up and made for the phone.

CHAPTER 20

JUNE

On Julia Prentice's next cleaning day at The Rowans she was looking forward to hearing all the latest news about the wedding. She enjoyed the vicarious pleasures of learning about her employers' lives, although arguably her own life was fuller of human interest.

"I'm here!" she called on arrival in the kitchen, pulling her indoor shoes from her bag, all the pale carpets people had these days.

"And how's everything going with Antonia's plans?" she asked Marilyn. "Not so long to go now is it?"

But Marilyn felt that she positively didn't want to talk about the wedding for this would only start her worrying again about all the things, and especially the boutique bill, which she still had to worry about.

"Oh," she said, "yes, it's all – well, it's all getting sorted out."

She cast around for a change of topic. "And how's Sharon and the children?"

Disappointment registered on Julia's face at not getting the chance of a bit of a chat about, perhaps, the new wedding dress.

"She's getting Justin to go for Family Counselling," she said. "She wants to get back in their own place now the baby's started crawling."

"Justin?"

"Her boyfriend."

"Oh, yes."

"Of course, he's not Nyle's dad."

"No – " Marilyn, though grateful for the change of subject felt that on reflection this was perhaps not the best choice of alternative. Maybe it was less stressful to talk about Julia's family than to talk about the wedding, but she had temporarily forgotten how depressing she could find these details.

"And I can't say I'll be sorry," Julia said. "More because of Nyle, he doesn't do too well cooped up with us. At two they need a bit of space to run around don't they?"

"Can't he run around outside?" Marilyn asked.

Julia paused on the way into the utility room to hang up her bag. She sighed. "There's Alan's tomatoes and it's his chrysanths really is the problem. Nyle kicks his ball slap into them every time, like it's fated, and then Alan gets mad at him and Sharon gets upset."

"Oh – "

"The rows," Julia said, "I won't tell you! And our Gary doesn't help with all his mess. Alan says if he'd known what having kids would do to your life we'd never have had any."

Marilyn felt that she had heard enough. She glanced at the clock on the wall. "Oh, is that the time?"

But Julia continued, "And there's me stuck in the middle of it all, can't please one without upsetting the other. Sometimes I'd be glad to be rid of the lot of them, have a little place of my own where I could do what I want for a change."

"What would you do?" Marilyn asked, distracted.

"Scrapbooks," Julia said. "You can get some nice scraps now. I like cats and the Royals."

Shortly after this Marilyn left the house to walk into the town. She put on her sunglasses, they provided protection if she met anyone she knew; neighbours, shop assistants who might ask, 'And how are you?' She would be able to answer, 'Oh fine' without them looking at her, unconvinced.

She wondered as she walked how Julia Prentice could find the energy to live her life, just thinking about it all was upsetting enough.

She stared into a window which displayed children's toys, all made of wood, retro and expensive. The front of a Georgian style dolls' house was invitingly open to reveal a hive of activity. The dolls were in 'period costume', silk and lace for the gentry, flowery cotton and mob caps for the servants. They were engaged in suitable activities on every floor, from the cook preparing mini-vegetables in the basement kitchen to the lady of the house entertaining guests in the – Marilyn hesitated – would it be called the parlour?

She gazed at the dolls' house. She thought that at least all the doll people looked as if they had something useful to do. I've got nothing to do most of the time, she thought, nothing. Or not the sort of things which you should be doing if you lived on the Glebe. Golf? Art classes? Fund raising buffets? These were the sort of things her neighbours talked about on the infrequent occasions when she met them. Behind her dark glasses her eyes

219

filled.

"And why," she asked herself, "why can't I stop crying?"

She walked on past a book shop and a slither of a shop selling French soap and real loofahs and sponges and also, catching her by surprise, embroidered wedding garters and 'honeymoon' lacy bras and minimalist knickers.

There was to be no escape, weddings were everywhere.

She turned away into the chemist's next door and bought a packet of tissues and then headed for The Lemon Tree Café where there was a toilet in which she could tidy herself up a bit.

In The Lemon Tree it was still rather early for the mid-morning coffee break customers and Jamal was leaning on the counter, reading The Times. An elderly couple were seated at a table, with tea and toasted tea cakes, otherwise the café was empty.

"Ah, good morning Marilyn," Jamal greeted her with a smile, folding the paper.

"I'm just – " Marilyn gestured in the direction of the toilets.

Jamal inclined his head. "Of course. Is it a cappuccino? Skinny?"

"Yes. Thank you." Marilyn hoped her dark glasses hid her tears.

In the toilet she managed to gather up some warm water into her hands from the single automatic tap and splashed this onto her face. Shaking the drips from her eyes she realised that the hair dryer was not one of the kind where you can change the angle, so she tried lowering her head into the stream of hot air but this proved not very satisfactory. She prayed that no-one else would come in and find her there, bent beneath the dryer. She ended by dabbing her face with the tissues which she had bought in the chemist's, they disintegrated and removed her make-up.

Giving up, she returned to her table.

This lady, Jamal thought, has been crying again. When she first starting to come to the café he had called her Madam but he liked to use his regular customers' names if they seemed to appreciate it. Generally Marilyn enjoyed the recognition but today nothing seemed to cheer her up.

Once she was seated Jamal came round the counter with her cappuccino and one of the Indian sweetmeats on a small plate.

Marilyn gazed at the sweetmeat, a glutinous but tempting pale pink. "Oh . . . thank you. But no . . . I'd better not."

"Rose water flavour," Jamal said, "to make you happy."

Marilyn hesitated. To mention The Diet seemed inappropriate, maybe even rude. That he should be concerned to bring her happiness caused her breath to catch.

"Oh – " she gave up, "well – "

Anyway, she was beginning to despair about The Diet. Clive hated it and she had not lost any weight for a week. Before her on its plate the pink sweetmeat blurred in a mist of tears.

Mercifully the elderly couple, still the only other customers, got up to leave and Jamal hastened away to attend to their bill and then to open the door for them and to pass a few comments on the delightful summer weather.

"You can't beat an English summer," the husband said jovially.

"When it doesn't rain!" said his wife.

"See you next week!" They stepped carefully out into the passing flow of shoppers, he had a walking frame to negotiate, she had a shopping bag.

Surreptitiously Marilyn dried her eyes. She wished that she had thought to buy a magazine and steeled herself to get up and fetch the complementary newspaper lying on the low table in the window before someone else came in and claimed it.

Having done so she read about a family with seven children and the mother was now expecting twins. In the picture they all looked happy and the mother looked surprisingly young. She said they managed by being very organised and the older children helped out with the younger ones. 'Are bigger families better?' the paper asked and several people gave their opinion.

Jamal returned to his perusal of the political pages of The Times at the counter.

Marilyn tentatively took a small bite from the pink sweet. Indeed it smelled of roses and was something like Turkish delight, sprinkled with icing sugar. Time passed and although she nibbled the sweet as slowly as she might, eventually, inevitably, her cup was empty and she had read several other stories in the newspaper. She glanced at her watch, if she left now she would still have to walk slowly by the longest route possible to avoid finding Julia Prentice still at The Rowans, longing to put away the hoover and have a chat about the wedding preparations.

"And that will get me all worried again," Marilyn thought. "Oh, why am I being so stupid?"

She gazed out through the window at passers-by, soon perhaps The Lemon Tree mid-morning customers would start to arrive. She collected up her bag and made her way to the counter.

"Thank you," Jamal said, accepting her money.

"It's quiet today," she was still delaying leaving.

"Early," Jamal said. "In half an hour, you see, then I will be having some problems."

"Why?"

"Everything to do; the tables, tea-cakes, the coffee. Just me. Difficult."

"Oh – " she glanced round at the tables. Tanis the teenage waitress was missing.

"Is Tanis not here today?"

"Tanis's work-experience has finished. I am alone."

"Couldn't your wife help you?" Marilyn asked, for didn't they live above the café?

Jamal spread his hands. "She is busy with our son. Also she expects another baby. She cooks some things for the café, the cakes, the sweets."

"The pink sweet was lovely."

Jamal bowed slightly. "Thank you."

The street door opened and four young women came in, negotiating high-tech baby buggies to form an encampment by the window.

"You see," Jamal said. "Baby yoga today."

The women were digging into flowery patterned pvc bags for bottles and packets of wipes. One of the babies began to howl, his mother hauled him out of the buggy and peered into the back of his trousers.

"Thought so," she said. "Since he's been teething it's just every single nappy. Mine's a hot chocolate, someone."

She battled her way out from the group, holding the baby aloft and heading for the toilets.

"I must go," Marilyn said.

The woman pushed past calling over her shoulder, "Sorry! Emergency!"

Jamal, picking up his order pad and biro to take the women's order, followed Marilyn towards the door. He held it open for her.

"Goodbye," he said as she stepped out into the sunlight. "Maybe you would like to come and have a job here?"

She gazed at him startled. Of course he was joking.

"No! No!" she exclaimed. Then embarrassed she hurried away. He was joking, of course.

CHAPTER 21

JUNE

The fair month of June was building towards the dangerous dog days of high summer when the roads of Cornwall are full of traffic and for many people, locals and holidaymakers alike, day-to-day routines are put on hold for the holiday season.

The college summer term drew towards an end and James' spirits lifted because Sally would soon be home more. She had not told him yet about her redundancy, hoping as she usually did that 'something would turn up' to alleviate their financial situation.

The children's company outside in the sun and on beach expeditions distracted Sally to an extent from worries about money and how to make some more of it. The gardens plan was progressing more slowly than she had hoped, being realistic it would be next year before there was a possibility of opening to the paying public, and that was assuming that they could get a more effective work force. Ned was only questionably earning his keep and Imo was still an uncertain quantity.

Graham continued to work steadily in the kitchen garden but as the vegetables were now cropping he had less time to spend hacking and clearing the brambles from the area beyond the fruit trees. Sally had arranged for the local green grocer to take some of their vegetables and Graham drove them down to the village and he also left a box of carrots and beans and beetroot by the drive gate with prices marked up on an old roof slate and a tin for the money.

This set-up appealed to passing tourists and indeed to locals, the tin filled up with small change, but let's face it Sally thought it's not really enough to keep our ship afloat.

A lot of the vegetables came down to the house so a sort of ratatouille, depending on the variable ingredients, featured on most days' menus. The children were beginning to whinge about 'vegetable stew'; the volunteers being healthy and working outdoors were always hungry and seemed prepared to eat most things, but Sally did sometimes feel that they should all be getting some more meat.

The vegetable train of thought led her to consider Graham. At one point she had thought that he was becoming more cheerful and forth-coming but now he seemed to have relapsed into his former solitary ways and near-surly lack of communication. It crossed her mind that this might have something to do with the fact that Imo had fallen for Ned.

"I saw that coming," Sally thought, picturing Imo's starry gaze at Ned across the supper table. About Ned's feelings she was less sure.

"Do you think we are in loco parentis with the volunteers?" she asked James.

"Good grief, I hope not," he said. "Why?"

"I think Imo and Ned may be getting involved with each other."

"I knew that fellow would be trouble from the day he arrived here." James felt his irritation levels rising. More trouble, more endless trouble.

"It's all right," Sally said, to calm him. "They're not working together."

"It's not their working together that we have to worry about." James gritted his teeth.

"Well, Ned sleeps in the Laundry House and Imo is up in the attic room."

If she had believed this to be a fail-safe arrangement she was of course greatly underestimating the urgency of youth, but she didn't. She offered it to James to cheer him up, and for herself, she thought, she would keep her fingers crossed. Imo and Ned were only here, after all, for the summer.

"The Garden Volunteers people have offered us another girl," Sally said. "So that may help, it will mean there are more of them and Ned and Imo won't be thrown together so much."

"Another?" James said in horror.

"We need more workers, darling, if we're to get the gardens sorted. She'll be a help."

James sighed.

Sally thanked heaven that they had managed to renew his membership subscription to the golf club. Already since the start of the good weather they had made several expeditions to the coastal links. The children piled into the back of the car and while James played a round she could take the children down across the sand dunes to the beach.

Perdita and Claud would run ahead swinging bags containing

their swimming things and lunch sandwiches and bottles of orange squash. Sally came behind with Frankie while he examined the black and red cinnabar moths on the ragwort or collected feathers and handfuls of dock seeds; it was slow progress.

Back at Trevean, bereft of company, Clarissa took the opportunity to claim the kitchen. She was interested which Sally at heart was not in household matters. When Clarissa lived abroad she liked to think that she had been known for running a comfortable and well organised house but then of course she had had staff.

Now at Trevean which after all had been designed for servants there were no staff. Therefore the state of the house was not Sally's fault, it was James' fault for being a useless provider. The familiar irritation surfaced.

When Clarissa first came to live at Trevean the plan had been that she should take over this side of the family's life, but it hadn't worked out. Laundry for that number was a week's labour in itself if it was to be done as Clarissa considered it should be, that is regularly washed, dried, aired and ironed.

This routine had of course once been provided for at Trevean in the Laundry House and the drying yard. The Laundry House had contained a coke boiler which provided hot water for washing, clothes were aired on wooden racks raised on pulleys, ironing was done with irons heated on a range. The boiler and range were now defunct and Graham and Ned had their quarters above in two small rooms where spare bedding was once stored.

Unfortunately, the mod cons which had replaced the Victorian domestic equipment were fairly minimal and not up to coping with the demands of the family, let alone with the addition of the Garden Volunteers.

The laundry routine which Sally followed was related to her lack of time and enthusiasm: when everyone was running out of clean clothes she would grab armfuls of garments from the overflowing baskets in the bathrooms or from the children's floors and ram them into the washing machine. When washed they went onto the line if humanly possible and it wasn't raining, otherwise she heaved them into the tumble dryer. Currently the tumble dryer was not working properly so it was fortunate that the weather was good. Nothing much got ironed.

Everyone was used to Sally's way of doing the washing and no-one liked Clarissa's alternative which involved sheets and clothes draped around the range in the kitchen and round any other source of heat including when it was lit the open fire in her sitting room. Ironing was done in the kitchen and often seemed to clash with James coming to make the tea or prepare the dogs' food.

Cooking was much the same. With Clarissa the preparation of meals took a long time; with Sally it was a case of 'fling it together and give it a stir'.

Clarissa's domestic reign had ended, acrimoniously, with a show-down about James starting to put together the dogs' food on the kitchen table where she was preparing a meat pie. Clarissa had objected on the grounds that this dog food habit was unhygienic, and James had said various unforgiveable things about the toughness of the meat in previous pies and the house resembling a Chinese laundry.

After this Clarissa had much less involvement in the domestic daily round at Trevean. She sometimes prepared vegetables which Graham brought down from the kitchen garden but this was about all.

Now, it being a Sunday morning, Clarissa and Perdita sat at the kitchen table shelling peas. Sally had taken Claud and Frankie to church on the grounds that they hadn't been for ages. She believed that every avenue to a later life interest should remain open for the children for as long as possible; sport, religion, music or whatever, until they were old enough to make up their own minds about whether they wanted to pursue it. She wasn't quite sure what she herself felt about church although at boarding school there had been virtually compulsory Confirmation.

During the service Frankie had not behaved especially well, dropping a small rubbery dinosaur repeatedly on the floor and scuffling beneath the pew to retrieve it. When they got back to the house Sally put a chicken in the oven and began to chop up some rhubarb for pudding. She was due to go with James to the pub for a pre-lunch drink.

This slice of the weekend when no-one else was claiming Sally's attention and he could also have some manly conversation with Zachariah was important for James, he saw it as an oasis of peace and sanity.

"We could do the rhubarb," Clarissa said, shelling the last of the peas into the colander and loath to go back up to her room, alone.

"Well – " Sally glanced distractedly at the clock. "It's all right, I've got time. Thank you."

Clarissa disappointed sniffed audibly when James appeared at the kitchen door – selfish as usual, she thought, he couldn't let Sally do anything which didn't directly involve him, without making a fuss or interfering.

"I'm nearly ready," Sally could tell that James was beginning to fret; he couldn't help it and anyway she herself liked to go out with him for an hour. They enjoyed each other's company.

James' caustic jokes made her laugh and there were other positive aspects to his character which rarely got a showing in the turbulent day-to-day life at Trevean. He was intelligent and well read; he did also have a better nature to which it was possible to appeal – not many men, Sally reflected, would suffer the continuing attrition of Clarissa's criticism without reaching for a blunt instrument.

James was also not naturally mean with money, but he was defeated by their current state of being always broke. His nervous anxiety about this situation contributed to his bad temper.

"If you get the dogs sorted," Sally said now. "I'll be right there."

A few minutes later the car departed down the front drive with the dogs barking furiously on the back seat, Coal's head thrust out of the window.

"Can you switch the kettle on," Clarissa said to Perdita. "I think I'd like a cup of coffee." It would have to be instant of course, but that was how things were now.

Perdita stood up. Such a thin bony child Clarissa thought, Sally had not looked like that as a girl. She had been athletic and sturdy. Perdita took after James' side of the family; Clarissa pushed this unwelcome thought away. Perdita was her favourite grandchild, she had something of Sally's spirit. Plus of course she was a girl, growing boys in general were hooligans. (This view was rather unfair on Claud).

"Are we going to do the potatoes?" Perdita asked.

Clarissa considered. These days she frequently said, "I know when my help's not wanted. I only do what I'm asked to, then I won't upset anyone." Her demotion from chatelaine still stung and she blamed it all on James.

"Well . . . "

Of course the potatoes ought to be prepared, new potatoes from the kitchen garden, they just needed scraping. Otherwise it would be one more thing delaying lunch when Sally and James returned and the children would be hungry and hanging around, getting under everyone's feet.

Imo would join them for Sunday lunch and Ned too, if he was up and hadn't gone surfing; Graham of course had gone home to help his parents on the small holding.

Clarissa reflected that she was beginning to find Graham a little less sullen since she had started talking to him about his plans for the kitchen garden. But of course he would never compare to Ned, who was so handsome, so public school, so able to make conversation. She liked good-looking young men, in fact she like the company of men, James being the exception.

Perdita looked in the cardboard box where the potatoes were stored. "There's some here," she said.

"Let's do them then," Clarissa said. "Your mother has got far too much to do."

Perdita carried the box to the table, trailing a dusting of earth.

"You'll need to brush that up or we'll get into trouble," Clarissa said.

They both knew that this was unlikely as no-one would notice mud on the floor except perhaps Sally and she would just say, "Oh, for goodness sake, look at that mess!" and rush on to the next thing.

"Where is everyone else?" Clarissa said. "Where have Claud and Frankie got to since they got back from church?"

"I think they are playing trains," Clarissa said. "They might be on the back stairs. That's The Incline."

"And Ned and Imo?"

"Imo was out there." Perdita looked over the sink towards the Laundry Yard.

"When?"

"I don't know. I saw her go past, a bit ago."

"I wonder where she was going?" Clarissa said.

"Maybe – " Perdita stared for inspiration at the scattering of miscellaneous mess on the kitchen table . "Maybe she's gone to find Ned?"

"I hope not," Clarissa said.

"Why?"

Clarissa paused. "I just think," she said, "that it wouldn't be a good idea."

"Because he's still asleep?"

"Well – maybe."

But Imo had gone to find Ned. Heading for the kitchen and the back door leading to the yard and the Laundry House she had heard Clarissa and Perdita talking and retraced her steps to go through the hall and slip round the side of the house.

She had had a bath and washed her hair. The water was as usual not hot and because there was no shower attachment on the taps she had lain, Ophelia like, in the bath to rinse her hair, watching the goose pimples begin to pucker her arms. For a fleeting moment she regretted the quantities of steaming hot water and heated towel rail at The Rowans.

But no, she didn't want to be home. Ned was here and where Ned was she wanted to be.

Ned was sitting in a sunny corner of the yard out of sight from the kitchen, on an old wooden chair. He had made himself a cup of Graham's coffee and had eaten a large slab of the flat currant cake which he had found in a tin.

He was thinking about Imo, or more precisely he was

thinking about what he was going to do with Imo. He had decided that she was quite attractive and certainly she was keen on him which was good because it meant that he wouldn't have to make too much effort. But he sensed that she might become too keen and girls who became too keen were, as he knew from discussions with other people, likely to make life difficult.

Therefore when Imo appeared round the house and crossed the yard towards him Ned did not smile in welcome.

Her heart sank a little, was he not pleased to see her? She had thought of him constantly since he had held her against his chest in the cave and his lips, surely, had brushed the top of her head. She had longed for him to kiss her properly, but he had not; they had walked back across the beach side by side with the incoming tide reaching the pools beneath the rocks; then Ned had driven the Beetle fast, engine revving, up the hill from the cove.

"Hi," she said now, standing awkwardly in front of him.

"Hi." He glanced at her.

"I wondered – "

Ned flexed his bare feet on the chickweed which grew among the cobbles of the yard and waited; he had pushed his expensive duty-free sunglasses up on his head to better catch the sun, now he pulled them down to shield his eyes.

"Maybe we could go for a walk?" Imo said, her voice dipping into uncertainty.

He had noticed the shine on her hair in the sunlight and she was wearing a white T-shirt today, not one of the muddy coloured ones she usually seemed to wear.

"Where?" he asked.

Imo looked round at the high laurels growing up the slope behind the Laundry House. "Maybe the woods?"

Ned paused long enough to appear to be considering this proposal although he had already made up his mind. He put his empty mug on the ground, pushed his feet into his sandals and stood up. "OK."

Imo felt a thrill of joy.

They went down the dark path which ran from the yard under the over-arching laurels, where it narrowed Ned moved ahead. Imo alternately looked down at the piled leaf mould over which she was walking or glanced up and fixed her gaze on the nape of Ned's neck where his hair lay across his suntanned skin. Then a wash of emotion caused the core of her body to feel as if some bright sparkling liquid was flooding into it. "I'm with him," she thought, "walking with him, and he is wonderful and he wants to be with me."

Crossing the front drive, they picked their way around and through overgrown rhododendrons, monstrously tall and some carrying giant mauve pink flower heads, on their way they passed unaware by the badgers' summer sett. Imo, following Ned, started to tell him something of her wish to go to Art College. "This is like a Rackham illustration," she said pushing aside huge pendulous leaves, "all twisting branches where strange creatures live . . . "

It was difficult to carry on a conversation however while climbing in single file over branches and through heavy leaf mould. Ned did not respond.

Finally they reached the crest of the slope and found themselves by a stoned flanked overgrown bank topped with hawthorn and elder; on the far side lay an un-cut hay field. Ned paused, considering, and then pulled himself up through the branches of the bushes.

"Come on." He jumped down into the long grass on the far

side.

Imo followed struggling to gain a foothold on the bank.

When she reached him Ned was already sitting in the warm hollow beneath the hedge, he chewed a soft grass stem and gazed away across the valley to the trees, billowing green on the far side of the valley. Imo, sitting beside him, waited heart-full for him to speak.

Ned however couldn't think of anything to say and wasn't interested in talking anyway. He frowned slightly for he wasn't sure whether this would be a good time to kiss Imo. He had decided that he fancied her enough, for now anyway, while he was stuck at Trevean. He was fairly sure now that she had fallen, or was falling for him, and so there was little risk of rejection.

Imo sat uncertain. She flipped a plantain head, looping the stem around and catapulting the black seed head across a patch of clover. "It's so quiet here," she said at last, "at home you can always hear cars."

He didn't answer.

The silence between the two of them drew on; Imo saw Ned frown and anxiety stabbed her. He was bored, she was saying the wrong things.

Ned glancing at her saw her nipples discernible through her T-shirt, he made the decision and leant forward quickly and kissed her.

Imo had been kissed before but only during alcohol befuddled fumblings at Sixth Form student parties. She hadn't been tempted to encourage the kissers to go any further.

Ned kissing her was wonderfully different.

She felt the warmth of his body as he leaned over her; after a second of emotional shock she kissed him back, holding her breath until the sun motes danced behind her closed eyes and she felt she was almost floating above the crushed grass.

When Ned finally drew back and looked down at her Imo opened her eyes and gazed at him, as if from far off; her pupils were hugely dilated. Involuntarily he said, "Are you all right?"

She blinked and the spaced-out expression cleared from her face, replaced by a smile of such joy that Ned found this almost equally disconcerting.

"Yes," she said. "I'm all right. Yes!"

She knew she would have been happy to lie beneath the hedge in the warmth of the sun for ever, with Ned's arms around her and his mouth on hers.

He slid his hand behind her back and up inside her T-shirt and unhooked her bra. She felt the shock but also there was a delight in his competence. Actually it was largely luck, Ned was not especially handy with bra hooks anymore than with any other practical task. Surprised to have succeeded so easily he hesitated briefly and then moved his hand round under her bra.

Imo saw her breast in that white-hot moment as a green, unripe apple, neat, firm, round, alight with response to his touch.

Yes! Ned thought. He shifted his weight in order to pull down her trousers and get his other hand down over her bottom and into her pants.

Imo was startled; he couldn't, could he, here in the field, in the open, be wanting to . . . ? She opened her eyes, struggling to release her mouth from Ned's; not here, not here!

She saw the pale smooth skin of her stomach, her combats worked down below her hips and her T-shirt rucked up to her armpits.

"No!"

Ned thought, "Sod it! Why do girls do this?"

"No!" Imo cried again, wanting to explain but not finding the words: it must be somewhere private, somewhere safe, somewhere right. She was struggling to pull up her trousers.

"Why?"

But he already knew why. Only tarts let you screw them straight away; girlfriend type girls didn't. This was how, or one way anyway, that you could tell the difference.

He rolled off her.

He could of course have coped with a tart, but the niggling thought surfaced that he was quite glad that he didn't have to; it was not entirely with regret that he sat up and watched Imo struggle to do up her bra. And anyway, if he got it right she wouldn't hold out much longer.

Imo was in love. As they walked back to the house she knew it. She was frightened as they climbed back over the hedge into the rhododendron wood that she'd lost Ned because she'd said no but he took her hand when they reached the laurel path and kissed her again before they emerged into the sunlight of the laundry yard.

Imo, pressed against his chest, felt her heart would be overwhelmed with happiness.

"It must be about time for lunch," Ned said as they drew apart.

CHAPTER 22

JUNE

It had been a bad morning. James and Sally went into the local town, Sally driving, to see the bank about a loan to sort out their problems with the builders. As Sally manoeuvred the Volvo into a parking slot which was barely large enough for it there was an almighty hissing.

"Oh, good grief!" She sat behind the wheel staring as the steam billowed across the windscreen.

James panicked. "What's happening?"

Sally turned off the ignition and when the hissing died down a bit she got out and opened the bonnet. Water was trickling busily onto the tarmac around her feet. "I think it's the radiator," she said.

This did not, Sally knew, help them to the frame of mind to make a positive impression with the Personal Banker dispatched from the bank's regional office to discuss their financial options.

Stopping to talk to Jack Richards at the garage made them several minutes late for their appointment

Sally asked Jack if he could see if the radiator was fixable. "Not terminal, I doubt," he said. "I'll be along drekkly."

Sally handed over the car keys.

James shuddered as they walked away. "Some time next week, I suppose," he said. "How are we going to get home?"

"I'm sure Jack will be able to sort it," Sally said, although this was more a hope than a certainty.

Now they sat in the room at the bank reserved for consultations, a computer on the desk had a small toy rabbit perched on top of it. When she glanced down Sally saw that her fingers were blackened with engine grease.

The Personal Banker was a young woman who introduced herself as Michelle Lowe. On her desk she had a print-out of their account details going back over several years.

James had made an effort when they arrived at the bank to behave as if the situation was what it should surely be: a polite business discussion with a senior member of staff, the satisfactory outcome of which was not in doubt. When the female cashier asked if she could help, James had replied jocularly that they had an appointment to see the person with the key to the coffers. The cashier had looked blank and Sally had quickly explained, "The Personal Banker?"

The confidence to play the role of esteemed client fizzled out in James very quickly. Finding Michelle to be female had set him back immediately, he had imagined talking man to man. As it was he knew as soon as he saw her, tidy in her neat black suit with clip-on badge, that he couldn't cope. Discussing their finances with a woman was all wrong, let alone a woman twenty years younger than him. Sally would have to sort it all out.

Sally knew this too. She felt for James, she knew that it was wretched for him that they should have to go like this, cap in hand, for funds to keep a roof over their heads. And such a large roof too, with holes in it.

She looked at the row of bank statements ranged in neat date order on the opposite side of the desk; although she could not read the upside-down details, she saw the biro rings circling figures in the credit and debit columns.

"Good morning," Michelle smiled, polite and non-committal. "Well, thank you for coming in today, Mr and Mrs Lacock."

She indicated the two strategically placed chairs.

They sat down.

"Good morning." Sally acknowledged the greeting more positively than James. He had dropped his gaze to the laminated veneer of the desk top and sat twisting his signet ring around his little finger.

"The situation we are here to discuss, as I understand it," Michelle said, clicking a couple of times on her computer keyboard and checking the screen, "is that you have had notification from the building company who carried out repairs to the roof of your house, that they intend to take legal proceedings for the settlement of their account."

Sally glanced at James whose face was wiped blank reflecting his horror at having their position outlined by this unknown young woman in such bald terms.

"Yes," Sally said. "I suppose so, yes."

Michelle placed her hands on the bank statements laid beside her computer and separated these slightly with her slim, white fingers.

Sally wondered momentarily if she might have a tissue somewhere in her bag with which to wipe the grease from her own hands but then she pushed thoughts of hand-care, a minor matter after all, from her mind for she knew that she was going to have to steer their side of this conversation if she and James were to achieve financial rescue.

Michelle Lowe proceeded to outline the problems from the Bank's point of view with allowing them a loan. She demonstrated, by neatly turning round the paperwork spread before her so that it was now the right way up for James and Sally to read, that their expenditure had increased while their income had not. Also, their repayment of previous loans had been irregular.

"Do you," Michelle enquired, "at this stage have any new resources?"

"Only if Clarissa falls off her perch," James said, with a flicker of spirit. "Sally's mother," he added in answer to Michelle's look of enquiry.

Michelle pursed her lips as if she found this sentiment to be in questionable taste.

"Please, darling, you know Mother hasn't got any money," Sally said, noting Michelle's reaction. "My mother lives with us," she added, feeling that this might counteract the impression that James was uncaring but James undermined her effort by saying bleakly, "Well, at least it would be one less mouth to feed."

Sally proceeded to outline her plans for the gardens to be opened to the public and the grants applied for and the volunteers already arrived.

Michelle turned to her computer and typed in some brief notes.

"Have you considered functions?" she asked.

James thought he had misheard her.

"Functions?" Michelle repeated.

James glanced in query at Sally. What on earth?

"Corporate functions," Michelle said with an edge in her voice, "or wedding receptions? Country houses are becoming popular venues now."

"No," James said precipitously, this sounded too ghastly for words. The house taken over by hordes of people for some business shindig? Weddings could only be worse.

Sally too was surprised, but less horrified. She had already decided that Trevean had to pay its way and let's face it, she thought, any ideas are better than no ideas.

"Well, that might be worth thinking about," she said, sending James a quick calming glance.

Michelle offered to let them have details of a local PR firm which might be able to offer marketing suggestions.

"Thank you," Sally said. "That would be very helpful."

Michelle then returned to the immediate question of the building debt. Trevean was already mortgaged; by the time James and Sally left the bank James was saying that if they did ever have to sell up they'd be living in a tent for there would be nothing left over from the proceeds to buy another house, however small.

Michelle Lowe had said she would refer decisions about their application to her manager and they would receive an answer from the bank shortly.

Sally felt suddenly tired. "You go to the Lion," she said to James. "I'll see what Jack Richards has managed to do with the car."

Wishing he had Coal with him for company James made his way to the pub which he found empty save for the usual old men in their corner; he gave them a nod as he passed towards the bar.

Zachariah Williams looked up from his morning perusal of the Sports pages. "Morning Sir! Will it be a pint of local?"

James nodded. "Thank you." Refuge! He took a seat alongside the solid, polished wood of the bar counter.

Zachariah held the filled glass up to the light. "They've tweaked the recipe, I do believe, I think it's an improvement. So how's things, Governor?"

James sighed. It was a sad state of affairs when his only chance of male company was talking to the local publican.

He chose in his current negative frame of mind not to recall his small group of acquaintances at the golf club or the various retired former colleagues settled back in the UK, all on the end of a phone. What anyway would they understand of the limitations and frustrations of his current life? None could be as skint, damn it. He realised that he had no money on him.

"My wife will pay," he said, "she'll be here in a minute."

Zachariah nodded in acknowledgement. Odd arrangement he thought, but then the Lacocks were odd by most peoples' standards.

"Banks," James said, launching into a topic which he and Zachariah had discussed on occasion before, "as I understand it they are not interested in the private customer these days." Lifting his glass he added, "This is all right."

"Ah, well . . . " Zaccy acknowledged his approval of the beer and adjusted a towelling bar mat. "There you go, of course. Shower you with plastic cards and offers of loans to cruise to the Bahamas but if you want to do something practical like change the motor they'll get you to sign your name in blood. Not that it's the fault of the people in the High Street branches, they're just following orders from the top." He had local connections to maintain.

"Chance would be a fine thing," James said, caught by the reference to a car loan. "The house takes up cash like a sponge."

"So I would imagine," Zachariah said agreeably, although along with most of the village he admitted privately to the view that the Lacocks should have known what they were taking on when they inherited Trevean and there were plenty who would be happy to swap places with them.

"You're clobbered every which way," James swirled the beer round his glass. "Listed building restrictions, endowments, death duties . . . Lawyers tie you up in knots and charge you a fortune for the privilege."

"Rules and regulations," Zachariah said. "Ruining the brewery trade. Can't move for them. Top up, Sir?"

"We live in the age of the bureaucrat," James agreed, moving his glass after initial hesitation across the bar. "I don't know what's happened to my wife. Gone to see about the car, radiator's blown." He chose when talking to other men to profess to an expected but unsubstantiated acquaintance with practical matters.

"I'm sorry to hear that," Zachariah placed James' refilled glass ceremoniously on the mat. He didn't comment further but James suspected that he thought the Volvo was due for the scrap heap.

"And the trouble with pen-pushers," Zachariah continued returning to his theme, "is they have no knowledge of running a public house, or any other form of business come to that. Not roll up your sleeves and get on with it."

"Absolutely," James agreed. "Nor what it's like trying to maintain an old house. Some of those roof timbers at Trevean were put up in 1590, if they've shifted a bit over time it's hardly surprising. The original drains probably date back to the 1700s and God knows what has happened to the records of where they go."

"Not your average septic tank layout, I dare say."

James in reality knew little more about roofs or drains, either in general or specifically at Trevean, than he knew about car engines. It was Sally who had the discussions with the builders, plumbers and electricians who had to be called in to patch up falling plaster, leaking pipes, out-dated wiring. She relayed their explanations and comments to James, or as much of them as she felt he could take.

"It's a responsibility, taking on an old house," James said, "which is a lot of hassle and for which you get no thanks."

Zachariah's wife now made a brief appearance behind the bar. Nancy Williams always said she was not a morning person. Her make-up had not settled down for the day and to James her turquoise eye shadow and vivid scarlet lipstick looked alarming. Sally rarely wore make-up and if she did and James noticed, he would ask her querulously, "What have you done to your face?"

Nancy greeted James graciously and nodded acknowledgement also to the old men in their corner who had expended their daily quota of talk and were now sitting over their beer, clearly listening to James and Zachariah's conversation.

Nancy cast her professional glance over Zachariah's arrangement of the bar. "A nice day," she said, although she had not as yet been outside to sample it.

"Yes," James agreed. His tone suggested that the sun was shining perversely on all but him and his.

"A spot of car bother," Zachariah said, rubbing a cloth over the immediate polished surface of the bar in case a smear might catch Nancy's eagle eye.

"Radiator," James explained.

"Cars are such an expense," Nancy said. "We had to have two new tyres on the Citroen, didn't we Zaccy? And what was that?"

"I don't remember exactly," Zachariah said. "But they don't make a present of them."

"A car in the country is a necessity, not a luxury," Nancy said. "That's what these politicians don't understand. Zaccy that Bells is looking a bit low."

Nancy departed to gather her thoughts for the day over a cup of coffee, the local paper and a cigarette in the beer garden. A perceptible feeling of relief united the men she left behind in the bar.

When Sally shortly arrived, which cheered James, she brought the news that Jack Richards had patched up the radiator for now and would get hold of a re-conditioned one and fit it.

"When?" James asked.

"Soon," Sally said, climbing onto the bar stool beside him.

"And what can I get you?" Zachariah asked, although he already knew that Sally would have half of the local bitter; again, unusual for a woman, but there you were.

"And how are things here?" Sally asked as he drew off the beer.

"As you see," Zachariah said, "dead as a door nail."

He gazed round expansively, taking in the polished tables, the empty summer fire-place. He nodded to the old men. "Deader," he said, dropping his voice and returning his attention to James and Sally. "I was hearing that you've increased your workforce."

Both James and Sally looked blank.

"A young lady?"

"Oh – " Sally said. "Imogen? She's a garden volunteer. We've got three now."

"I wouldn't describe them as a work force," James said.

"Oh, that's a bit harsh, darling," Sally said. "Graham's doing good things in the kitchen garden."

"Never opens his mouth, to say anything intelligible, at any rate," James said.

"A nice bit of silence can go a long way," Zachariah said speculatively. "Going to get along all right, is she, your new recruit?"

"Haven't seen much of her so far," James said. "Looks reasonably healthy?" He looked to Sally for confirmation. "Which is a start."

He had nearly finished his drink, it was time they were getting back. The dogs would be fretting.

"Oh, I think she'll be fine," Sally said. "She's starting in the kitchen garden."

"Girls and boys together," Zachariah suggested, "a bit of a powder keg, maybe?"

"You don't have to tell me," James said. "Why did they have to go and send a girl?"

"Because we said we'd take either," Sally said, beginning to feel irritated with Zachariah for encouraging James to start worrying. "You have to be fairly flexible and we've got enough accommodation."

"She's probably safe enough with the silent one," James said, "I wouldn't be so sure about the other. What's his name?"

He knew quite well but chose to pretend ignorance.

"Ned," Sally wanted to close the discussion. "Well, they're all eighteen," she said. "I think. Perhaps we ought to make a move?"

James said, "Have you got some money?"

CHAPTER 23

JUNE

During the next few days Imo worked in the kitchen garden. She weeded carrots, thinned out lettuce seedlings and helped Graham mend holes in the ancient netting with which he had covered the current bushes to deter birds from stealing the ripening fruit. All the while she day-dreamed of Ned and did not concentrate properly on what she was doing.

Ned was still clearing the bamboos, it was hot and airless among the dry fallen leaves and tall canes and since his enthusiasm was not great his progress was slow.

Sally came down to see how he was getting on.

"When do you think you'll get this finished?" she asked, staring round.

Ned had no idea, very possibly he would never finish because he was becoming so fed up with the job that he was seriously thinking of leaving Trevean. He would tell his parents that he was learning nothing of any use for his possible career in Estate Management. If it hadn't been for the development of this thing with Imo he would, he told himself, definitely leave.

Each evening after supper Ned and Imo went into the rhododendron woods, or back to the hollow beneath the field hedge. Here they lay kissing until Imo's head reeled. So far however they had not actually done it, made love, had sex. For both of them this was now the preoccupation which filled their thoughts; it caused Imo not to heed Graham's instructions on which seedlings to plant out and Ned to feel increasingly annoyed.

By the third evening Ned had pushed Imo's T-shirt and bra up and stared down at her breasts, her nipples were sticking up, was that not a sign that she wanted sex? He pressed down hard on top of her and muttered through her hair, "Why not? Why not?"

And Imo wasn't sure why not, but somehow she still wanted it to be different, this first time, and not in the open where they might be seen, with rabbit droppings scattered around and possibly stuck in her hair.

"Not here – "

"Come back to my room then," Ned said.

Still she hesitated. "I don't know – "

Stabbed by exasperation he rolled off her and sat up. "Oh well, if you don't want to." He sounded sulky.

"I love you," she whispered but Ned turned his head away impatiently and shortly afterwards he stood up, staring across the field.

Her heart was hammering and her hands were damp. He was angry with her, and wasn't it bad for men not to make love when they had got . . . when . . .

They set off back through the trees, he walked fast and she had to hurry to keep up with him.

Her eyes filled with tears. "Wait," she said. "Please wait."

When he turned to look at her, she said, "All right. Yes, I will. I will come back with you." To herself she sounded defiant, although the defiance was to quell her own doubts. It would be all right.

But it wasn't all right; when they reached the yard and Ned pushed open the Laundry House door Imo, standing behind him, saw Graham was there stripped to the waist and washing at the sink. He looked over his shoulder at them, his expression cold and angry.

For a moment none of them moved then Graham turned on the single cold tap and water cascaded onto the stained white porcelain.

"Sod it," Ned said.

Imo in a sudden panic that Graham had seen her ran back to the house and up to her room. She hurled herself onto her bed and lay there as the light faded across the ceiling. Perhaps Ned would come to find her here? But he didn't and with the window open to the darkening night sky, she lay and ached for him. Slowly the stars became visible. At some point in the middle of the night she woke and creeping downstairs to clean her teeth, stared from the landing towards the Laundry House but it was all in darkness.

The following morning Ned did not appear at breakfast. Imo, wishing him to come, hung around at the kitchen table eating minute bites out of a piece of toast.

Sally said to the children, who were staying at home because the school was running a staff training day, "I'm going to do an inspection of your rooms. They are all an absolute tip."

"For a prize?" Frankie asked.

"What sort of prize?" Sally asked him.

"For the best room?" Claud suggested amiably.

"Best room!" Sally exclaimed. "I just want them to be in a state that you can at least get through the door."

Frankie opened his mouth to howl.

"All right!" Sally said. "If your rooms are tidy, really tidy and that includes toys and clothes and books, I may take you to the beach later. First, can someone run up and fetch Granny's tray please."

"I will," Perdita said.

There was a general pushing back of chairs, the children rushing away up the back stairs.

James, retreating to the study with the dogs, felt oppressed. "When will you be going?" he said heavily to Sally. Was he to be abandoned with the old witch and the gaggle of teenagers?

"Oh, not yet," she said, "This afternoon." She saw the expression on his face, "Could you come and get in a few holes of golf?"

"Doubt there'll be anyone to go round with," but his heart lightened.

Graham stood at the work surface where he was spreading slices of bread with margarine to make cheese and brown sauce sandwiches to take with him to the kitchen garden. He kept the brown sauce up there in the old office building, having bought it himself he saw no reason to let the Lacock gannets get at it.

"Is Ned up?" Sally asked him.

As ever Graham let a few seconds elapse before answering. Would she tell him to go and find Ned? He had already left a mug of coffee outside his door as he did each morning, following her instructions, although why he should chase after the lazy furt he didn't see.

"Ent sure," he said cautiously.

"Well, could you go and give him a shout," Sally said.

Graham's shoulders stiffened. Facing away from Sally and methodically cutting slices from the block of cheddar, he did not turn his head.

Really, she thought, I try to stick up for him with James, but he can be quite Neanderthal at times

"I can go!" Imo pushed her chair back, eagerness in her voice.

Then Graham did turn, to look at her.

So that's the trouble, Sally thought, I knew it. "No, it's fine thank you," she said firmly to Imo. "You both need to get up to the kitchen garden, we're all behind this morning. Graham, on your way can you just call Ned and ask him to hurry up."

Both of them displeased, Graham and Imo left the kitchen via the back porch where the black mother cat Marilla was sitting sunning herself on the jute mat.

Imo made her way reluctantly towards the overgrown steps which led up to the top yard and the kitchen garden. She loitered beneath the overhanging laurel branches, hoping that Ned might appear.

Graham crossed to the Laundry House; he pushed the door open, listened for a few moments and called, "Lo!"

Imo watched. Clearly Ned didn't answer and Graham after a further pause disappeared inside. She climbed a couple of the slate steps and stood, scuffing her shoes on the moss.

Graham hated this sort of commission because it involved trying to communicate with 'one of them'. By 'them' he meant people who sounded like the Lacocks and Ned, who with their up-country way of talking had the ability, without even trying, to trip him up.

Going up the narrow wooden stairs he banged on Ned's door. There was no answer. Graham swore under his breath as anger got to him. He had work to be getting on with, why was he having to waste his time on this harrogant – arrogant, he corrected himself furiously – arsehole. He hesitated, but in the end he turned the handle and pushed open the door.

Ned was sitting up in bed, a couple of pillows propped behind him. "Hi," he said.

Graham stared at him.

"Struck dumb," Ned thought. He had a pretty good idea why Graham was here. He knew what the time was, he just hadn't felt inclined to get up. He had been awake for half an hour feeling dissatisfied with the way things were in his life at present and wondering what to do about them. Imo's behaviour was his current greatest irritation. What was the matter with her? She ought to be grateful for his interest in her and stop acting so stupid and girly. She'd only have herself to blame if he left Trevean now.

But there were other annoyances which were clouding his life and he didn't need them. For a start he didn't have enough money; he could barely afford to keep his car filled up with petrol. It was all very well his grandmother giving him the car but what use was it if he couldn't afford to run it?

How did his parents think he could manage on the pathetic allowance they gave him? If he was supposed to stay on at Trevean the least they could do was give him enough money to buy a decent surf board. He was never going to get anywhere with the Lacocks old bodyboard with which he was stuck at the moment and there was nothing else, other than surfing, to do down here.

This train of thought brought him back to the question of

Imo. Basically, this summer he needed sex. At eighteen lack of sex was bad for you, this was when you were supposed to be getting it. The situation was ridiculous and embarrassing.

He had tried to be reasonable; Imo seemed to be keen on him but he was fed up with lying around on damp grass and having her go all weepy on him if he tried, quite reasonably surely, to go any further.

"Problem?" he asked now, staring at Graham. He yawned, raising his arms and interlocking his fingers behind his head.

Graham saw Ned's well-formed torso and floppy sun-streaked hair and glowered. "You're wanted," he said.

"Who by?" Ned asked, casually.

Graham felt furious, caught by his usual dislike of naming one of 'them'. He sensed a strong risk of making a mistake. "'Er,'" he muttered.

"'Er?" Ned asked deliberately. "Who? What for?"

But Graham was already on his way down the stairs; the stuck-up bastard was taking the piss, he could make his own coffee from now on. In fact, when he came to think of it, the mug which he had left earlier outside Ned's door had gone, so Ned had drunk the coffee and been awake all along and there had been no need for him, Graham, to have wasted his time chasing after him.

By the time Graham reached Imo where she was still hanging around on the steps, the expression on his face was thunderous and he started to climb past her. When she asked, "Is Ned OK?" he didn't bother to answer.

That morning as he tied up heavily cropping broad beans and tomato plants and checked courgettes and strawberries for slug damage, anger pooled in Graham's mind. When he looked across the sunlit rows of vegetables at Imo's slim back bent over lettuce seedlings and saw her occasionally straighten up to push tendrils of hair away from her face he felt the levels of his fury rise. His jaw set as he returned to what he was doing.

At around eleven o'clock Perdita with Marilla alongside her, fluffy tail erect, brought a message for Imo. "Mummy says can you come down to the house," she said and then remembering her full instruction, she added "please."

"Why?" Imo asked her as they went together along the path to kitchen garden gate. "Do you know what for?"

Perdita considered if she knew. "I think your mother phoned," she said.

Imo's heart sank. If her mother was fussing about something then no prizes she thought for guessing what this would be, something of course to do with Antonia's wedding. "It's so boring!" she exclaimed.

"What's boring?" Perdita enquired, intrigued.

"My sister's wedding," Imo said crossly.

Perdita remembered that Imo's sister only ever talked about her wedding; she herself had never been to one but surely it must hold some potential for drama and excitement. She followed behind Imo down the steep steps to the laundry yard, considering.

"Who is your sister marrying?" she asked, to remind herself.

"Mr Giraffe Man," Imo said, stumping ahead.

"Really?"

Imo glanced back at Perdita and saw that she was not trying to be cheeky but was as ever serious in her attempt to understand.

"No," she said, relenting, "he just looks like a giraffe. He's got a very long neck."

"Oh," Perdita said.

Sally was in the kitchen writing a shopping list, helped by

Frankie. "How much milk have we got?" she said. "Can you pull open the fridge door please."

"One," said Frankie, peering inside the fridge, "two, four."

"Three. One, two, three, four."

"Four," Frankie said.

"No, three. There are two big bottles aren't there, and a smaller one."

"Hello?" Imo stood with Perdita in the open doorway.

"Oh, right," Sally turned her head. "Imo. Your mother has rung up and asked if you can go home, for a couple of days. You're needed to try on a bridesmaid's dress apparently?"

"Oh – "

"So – you had better go. There is a train this afternoon, which will be quicker than the coach."

Imo felt a mixture of rage and despair. Why, oh why couldn't her parents leave her alone? She didn't want to go home, she didn't want to be summoned back like a child who must do what she was told. She didn't want to try on the stupid frothy pink bridesmaid's dress and most of all of course, she didn't want to leave Ned.

"I don't really want – "

Sally looked at Imo. She doesn't want to go because of that wretched Ned, she thought, that's what it is. But perhaps he'll get a bit more work done if she isn't here, so this may be no bad thing.

"I think you do have to go," she said. "It's your sister who is getting married isn't it? Family weddings are important."

Imo's face clouded.

"If you go and pack your bag," Sally said, "I can drop you at the station after lunch because I've promised to take the children to the beach."

Even as she spoke Sally realised that this meant that there would not be room in the car to take James to play golf and her heart sank a little. He would be disappointed. I need to split myself in half with a meat cleaver, she thought, to make two of me, and we really need two cars.

Instead of going to pack her bag, for what was the point, she didn't intend to stay at The Rowans for half an hour more than was necessary, Imo slipped out of the house and down the slope to the bamboo plantation to find Ned.

"I don't want to go," she told him, breathless and anxious.

"Go where?"

"Home!"

Ned was feeling hot, sweaty and irritable. Imo, he thought as he looked at her standing tiresomely emotional before him, was adding to the irritations plaguing him. Did she expect him to say that he didn't want her to go? She said she loved him, but she wouldn't have sex with him so where was the relationship supposed to be going?

He had in fact been thinking about taking Imo out in the car that night and driving up to the cliffs and kissing her a lot and then, he was fairly sure, especially if there was a good sunset, all her wavering refusals would cease.

But now he found that his plans had been unfairly upset.

"I've got to go and try on this horrible bridesmaid's dress!" Imo said, finding a catch in her voice. "And I can't bear it – "

Ned half turned away, chucking his bill hook to the ground and pushing his hair back from his damp forehead. "Don't go then," he said.

"But I've got to!" Imo cried. "It's my sister's wedding and I know she'll be getting into a state and so will my mother and they've rung Sally and now she says I've got to go too."

Emotion, unless productively channelled into interest in him, bored and irritated Ned. He thought crossly, well go then, but don't moan at me; what am I supposed to do about it?

"I'll get back as soon as I can – " Imo said.

"OK," he said dismissively. He looked at his watch, surely it must be lunch time?

But when they had toiled up the slope to the house in the hot sun and come round to the kitchen door Ned found yet more cause for annoyance waiting. Sally asked him to pick up the new Garden Volunteer girl at the station.

Both Ned and Imo gazed at her blankly.

"We weren't expecting her yet," Sally said, "but she can fill in while Imo's away, so it's quite useful."

"I'm still fairly busy – " Ned cast about for an excuse not to go. Why should he run a taxi service?

"I'm taking the children swimming after I drop Imo off," she said, "so I won't be able to hang around waiting for the down train. Graham is delivering veg in the village this afternoon so he can't go."

James, arriving in the kitchen to check on the progress of lunch and having learned that his projected golf round was not going to happen, was claimed by disappointment. Realising that Ned was unenthusiastic about his commission cheered him up a bit, that young man needed putting in his place occasionally.

"She's going up to Oxford, this girl," James said, seeing on the table the details sent by the Garden Volunteer organisation. "So she must be vaguely intelligent." His tone implied 'Which makes a pleasant change'.

This information did nothing for Ned. Intelligence in girls was not something which particularly appealed to him. She would probably be solid and confrontational or small and whispy.

He had met girls of both these types, reputedly 'very clever', on the tennis courts of Dubai or the compounds of the other bases to which his father had been posted. Some of them had appeared to fancy him, understandably, but if they were not pretty which they probably were not and if his mother was pressurising him to be nice to them because of their parents being somebody or other then he couldn't, let's face it, be bothered to make the effort. They had usually been rotten at tennis.

The thought came to him briefly that his mother also pressurised him about the pretty girls but that was 'to behave properly' and not give the members of her Bridge Club cause to gossip. His mother was always on at him about something or other.

"I was planning to go surfing," he said now to Sally. Anyway what about his petrol, were they going to pay for it?

"Well, you can go as soon as you get back," she said. "I'm sorry but there is no-one else with a car."

Imo felt that she was going to cry.

CHAPTER 24

JUNE

Imo sat sulking on the train, staring from the window at the passing fields and knowing that each mile took her further from Ned.

So unenthusiastic was she about going home to The Rowans that she had packed only a spare pair of pants and her brown cotton jacket which she now noticed had a pocket coming unstitched. She wished that she didn't belong to her family, for they were all so annoying.

Marilyn drove to the station to meet Imo. She was quite glad to leave the house as Antonia had arrived home in a state of fuss to oversee the trying on of Imo's dress. She had also brought back the other bridesmaids' dresses for minor alterations; Lizzie and Petra had refused to come down with her, insisting instead on trying the dresses on in London. During this process they had managed to make several comments to each other which had been upsetting.

The nearer Marilyn got to the station the more nervous she felt about parking. As she feared, all the 'Twenty Minutes Only' spaces were full which only left the option of parking in a taxi space or crossing the tracks to the Longer Stay. She always avoided the Longer Stay because of the terrifying possibility of the barriers coming down and trapping the car. Now however several taxis were arriving to meet the next train and as she sat indecisive at the wheel one of the drivers hooted at her.

"Oh sorry, sorry!" Agitated, Marilyn reversed at a tangent and drove, her heart beating, across the rails and points and into the old sidings, where she parked awkwardly. It was too late however to move the car again, for the barrier warning was sounding and the tannoy announced the arrival of the next train on Platform Two.

The wooden steps leading to the bridge over the lines were wide and shallow and seemed to Marilyn as she hurried up them to be an awkward height; the train arrived as she reached the turnstile and after a few moments there was Imo sauntering towards her. As ever when she saw her daughters safely arrived, Marilyn felt a lift of relief.

"Hello!" she called, to which Imo made minimal acknowledgement.

"Where's your bag?" The question came from long formed habit, for such questions had been a feature of greeting Imo for years: where's your school bag, sports kit, art portfolio? Antonia always had everything safely with her.

Irritated immediately, Imo said, "I haven't brought one."

Oh why, why does she have to sound so unfriendly, so difficult, Marilyn asked herself. Over Imo's head she saw other people greeting other passengers with welcoming waves and smiles and embraces and her heart ached. But I won't get upset, she thought. Everyone says teenagers can be so difficult.

Imo shifted her small backpack hanging over her shoulder and relented slightly. "All my stuff's in here," she said and then regretted immediately this lowering of her defences. "I won't be staying long anyway."

"Oh – " Marilyn realised that she had assumed that Imo would be at The Rowans for maybe a week and she felt a slight chill pass over her. The house often felt so empty now, it had been designed for a family and the two bathrooms and extra shower room and the dining room and the utility room were little used. It would have been nice to have had these when the girls were young but now really wasn't it too late? This was not a happy thought.

When they got back to the car Marilyn found that because she had parked crookedly it was going to be difficult to get into the driver's seat for a van was now parked close beside her. She struggled to slide in sideways between the van and the car.

Imo stood frowning into the middle distance.

"Can you do it?" Marilyn asked finally, defeated. "Can you get in?"

Imo looked at her mother; she saw that blotchy red marks had appeared on Marilyn's neck and her blouse had pulled up at the back. Why were her parents so embarrassing, why couldn't they just be normal? How would she ever, she thought, be able to bring Ned home?

"Can you get in?" Marilyn repeated.

Imo glanced briefly at the narrow space between the car and the van. "No," she said.

And anyway, she thought, what did Marilyn expect her to do if she did succeed in getting into the car? Couldn't she remember that she, Imo, had not yet passed her driving test because her parents had totally failed to provide her with any driving practice?

"Oh!" Marilyn's voice rose towards a note which Clive would have known presaged upset. Indeed Imo also knew this but she frowned harder.

Marilyn drew a breath. "I mustn't get like this," she thought and momentarily wondered if yoga would be of any use to control this awful panic which made her feel sick as soon as anything went even so slightly wrong. She had thought about yoga before, having seen women going into the Glebe Community Hall wearing lycra leggings and clutching pink pvc mats and water bottles; the trouble was they all looked very fit and purposeful. And thin.

"I'll try the other side," she said and going round the car she found that she could get in the passenger door quite easily and managed, after some manoeuvring past the gear stick, to gain the driver's seat and turn on the ignition.

So at last they were off and Marilyn, finding that her skin felt slightly and uncomfortably damp, opened the window. She drove over the tracks under the now raised barriers with a sigh of relief and a small spurt of, almost, bravado.

"So, how was your journey?" she asked but then before Imo could answer, she was again assailed by doubt. "Where's my handbag?"

Imo stared through the windscreen in front of her. I simply cannot bear this, she thought.

"Can you see it?" Marilyn tried to look down into the footwell around Imo's feet.

"See what?" Imo said shuffling her trainers crossly and then, "Watch out!"

"Oh no! Oh no!" Marilyn pulled on the steering wheel as one of the taxis scraped past, the occupants staring at them accusingly through the window.

"Can you see if it's on the back seat?" Marilyn asked. "My bag."

Imo reluctantly turned her head.

"Is it?" Marilyn asked.

"No."

"It must be! Isn't it? I'm sure I didn't put it in the boot"

Imo didn't choose to answer.

Marilyn tried to think. "When did I have it last? I had to get the car keys out of it . . . "

"Perhaps," Imo suggested, for after all this seemed obvious, "you left it in the car park."

Marilyn's foot hovered over the brake. "I can't have! Where?"

Imo shrugged her shoulders. "On the ground?"

"Oh!"

Marilyn braked, indicator flashing, but someone again blared their horn at her.

"Looks like it's One Way," Imo said.

When they finally got back into the car park the bag was indeed there, on the tarmac beside the still parked van. As Marilyn scrambled from the car a man walking past suggested cheerfully, "Forget your head next?"

The rest of the short journey to The Rowans was silent. Both Marilyn and Imo felt that their nerves were frayed beyond endurance and both planned to seek some peace and quiet when they arrived. Just to get away from her mother, Imo thought, would make her feel better and she planned to go straight to her room. Marilyn hoped that Antonia might, perhaps, have gone out.

Unfortunately, Antonia had not gone out; they heard her talking on the phone in the kitchen as soon as they came into the house. She sounded agitated.

"I don't know what we're going to do!" Her voice rose. "What are we to do? What do you suggest? It's not good enough to just say Insurance, Insurance, Insurance! What about my wedding! No, I don't care about any of that, why should I sympathise? No, I don't ... no, I won't ... Oh, go away!"

She put the phone down and burst into tears.

Even Imo, having reached the bottom of the stairs, paused and Marilyn froze.

For a moment there was a silence and then Antonia appeared in the kitchen doorway; she was white faced and tearful. "We're going to have to cancel the wedding!"

"Why?" Marilyn cried. "What's happened?" Now she knew the day was only going to get worse, not better.

"A fire! There's been a fire!"

Marilyn and Imo stared at her.

"Where?" Marilyn asked. "What do you mean?"

Antonia cried, "At the hotel, at Columb Court – a fire! And that horrible Manager just keeps saying, 'Insurance' but what help is that? We'll never find somewhere else for the Reception at this short notice. And then he said the tragedy was the damage to a listed building, but I don't care! I don't care if it's burnt to the ground ... "

"It was hideous anyway," Imo said.

"Sssh ... " Marilyn said. "Please don't."

"Well, it was. Red brick and turrets; really hideous."

"Oh shut up! Stop it!" Antonia's voice rose in a wail.

"Is it really that bad?" Marilyn found that her knees were feeling weak. "Or – there must be somewhere else?"

"Of course there isn't. Don't you remember the trouble we had trying to find somewhere . . . somewhere that was all right . . . "

Marilyn said, "I'll phone your Dad." I can't cope, she thought, I just can't cope with all this on my own. Clive will have to sort it out.

Antonia paused for a moment as the awfulness of the situation became clear in mental images of her wedding day, ruined. Pushing past Imo, she ran upstairs and into her room where she slammed the door behind her and threw herself onto her bed. Awful pictures of unsuitable reception venues came into her mind and of Roger's parents looking disapproving and Lizzie and Petra laughing themselves stupid.

"And all those horrible great fir trees . . . " Imo muttered, also retreating upstairs.

When Marilyn phoned Clive, he was expecting a call from a client in Oslo. "It'll be sortable," he said once he had grasped what she was telling him. "We'll sort it."

"But how?" cried Marilyn, sounding much like Antonia.

"Later," Clive said. "We'll sort it, but I can't think about it now. Right, that's my call, I've got to go. Don't worry."

Could this wedding, he wondered, cause any more trouble?

Marilyn thought, putting down the phone, 'Don't worry' was an impossible instruction, why had Clive said that?

When Maddy the dressmaker arrived with Imo's bridesmaid's dress Marilyn was sitting alone in the kitchen and both Antonia and Imo were still shut in their rooms; Marilyn had made herself a mug of camomile tea. Sunlight flooded through the open patio doors across the floor tiles and the pale wood units, highlighting the shine on the cream toaster and the too complicated juicer and the flowery patterns on the tea and coffee canisters. Everything, Marilyn thought, looked clean and bright, which was nice, but didn't match how they were all feeling. Tears filled her eyes.

"I've pinned the hem," Maddy said, ushering Imo's dress ahead of her like a giant stick of candyfloss wrapped in cellophane. "So we just need a last check to make sure it's right with the shoes."

"Oh yes, of course," Marilyn said, trying not to let Maddy see her face, which must be a terrible mess. "I've got a bit of a cold I'm afraid, so I won't get too close."

"Oh dear." Maddy thought that Mrs Bradford had been crying. "A summer cold can be quite nasty, can't it?"

Really, she couldn't think of any of her previous wedding commissions that had been so fraught. And yet Antonia had always seemed so happy and easy-going when they were at college together.

They took the dress into the lounge and Maddy began to ease the tiers of pink chiffon from the wrapping. "I think it's ever so pretty," she said. "Different. They've got a bit samey lately, haven't they?"

"Well – "

"Clever of Antonia to get the idea from that china figure, wasn't it?"

Marilyn agreed that yes, it was clever. Antonia had seen the dancing figurine with its petunia frilled skirts and its dainty white feet in the window of the expensive china shop in the high street, among the Royal Doulton pheasants and the fancy glass paperweights.

Both Marilyn and Maddy now recalled the idea for the shepherdess wedding dress which had also come from a china figure, but was now cancelled and had wasted quite a bit of Maddy's time.

"I'll just go and call Imo then." Even as she said this Marilyn also remembered the dreadful argumentative fuss which Imo had made right from the first time she had seen the dress material. Despite attempted persuasion and pleading she had not changed her view, saying that she hated girly, pinky, frilly stuff. "It'll make me look absolutely stupid!"

Also, she thought, Imo had not yet seen the satin shoes which had been dyed to match the dress material. They were in the walk-in wardrobe in the master bedroom, in their box printed with ribbons and wedding bells. She called to Imo as she went past her door but there was no answer. On the way back with the shoes she half-opened the door and said, "Maddy's here to try on your dress."

Imo was lying on her bed listening to her music. Without turning her head to look at Marilyn she said, "Why have I got to keep trying it on anyway?"

Marilyn wondered if she might simply lose all control. I am not going to get upset, I am not going to get upset. "To get the length right," she said, trying hard to keep her voice level, "with the shoes."

"What shoes?"

Marilyn took a breath and held out the box. "These."

Imo looked up, she almost asked to see the shoes but stopped herself, why should she show any interest they were bound to be horrible. What if they were pink too, totally puke?

"What's the point? The wedding's off anyway, isn't it?"

A strange constrictive sensation in Marilyn's chest made her feel that she could not breathe, she reached her hand for the door handle. "No," she managed to say, "of course it's not."

It was difficult to keep her voice level. "Of course it isn't off, your Dad's going to sort it all out. Please come downstairs and try the dress on, and the shoes."

Imo sat up, her mother sounded weird, like she was going to freak out; with reluctance she followed her downstairs.

In the lounge Maddy smiled her professional smile. "Hello!"

If she was set back by Imo's appearance in her creased combats and T-shirt and with her unenthusiastic expression, she managed not to show it.

Imo gazed at the dress, spread on the settee. She thought it was worse even than she remembered, a cascade of pink fairy frills and there seemed to be glitter of some sort edging the tiers of the skirt.

For a moment no-one moved and then Maddy lifted the dress up. "It suits your colouring!"

Imo discovered that she couldn't answer. And in fact she decided to remain silent throughout the fitting. Stiff, like an automaton, she let her trousers and T-shirt fall on the floor and stood stock still while Maddy climbed on a chair and dropped the dress over her head.

"Of course," Maddy said, "you won't have the bra straps."

Imo stared ahead. Her bra was black with white polka dots, the straps had gone stringy.

"You can get some pretty strapless bras," Maddy suggested, climbing down. She was finding this fitting quite stressful; on her previous visits Marilyn had been more chatty and she had hoped that Antonia would be here to admire the dress and maybe they would all have had a natter about the wedding arrangements. However today there was she felt this atmosphere.

"Shall we try it with the shoes?" she said.

Marilyn picked up the box and in the absence of any move from Imo, opened it.

"Oh aren't they lovely!" Maddy said. "Did you have them

dyed to match?"

"Yes."

"And the diamanté detail!" Maddy exclaimed.

"Those are clips, Antonia found them."

"Oh yes! So you can personalise them. It's a clever idea, isn't it?" Maddy took the shoes from the box and their wrapping tissue paper and placed them on the carpet in front of Imo. "I think they'll look lovely on."

Imo's feet were bare, she shoved them into the court shoes and said, "Ouch!" immediately.

"What's the matter?" Marilyn exclaimed, the swirl of panic rising within her. "They're not too small, are they? They're sevens! You are size seven."

"They rub," Imo said, pulling the shoes off. "those glitter bits. They're sticking into me."

She stood listless, dangling a shoe in each hand and then dropped them to the floor.

"Well – " Maddy looked towards Marilyn who didn't seem to be coming up with any suggestions. "Maybe if you put some sticking plaster inside, or you can get those, like, gel patches in the chemists?"

Imo shrugged. "Well, I can't wear them like that."

Maddy said, "If we just take the clips off for now?"

While Imo stood in the clipless shoes Maddy crawled around on the floor adjusting pins. Eventually she stood up and said, "Can you just turn round for me."

Imo rotated, her face wiped of expression. She felt she was experimenting with absenting herself from her body.

"Really," Maddy thought, "she is an odd girl."

Other bridesmaids whose dresses she had made were happy to twirl and exclaim. She glanced round to include Marilyn, "I think that's all right now, don't you? Just off the floor so she won't trip up. You wouldn't want any accidents on The Big Day!"

Imo ignored this pathetic attempt to lighten the mood. She hated everything to do with the wedding, absolutely everything. Why did she have to be involved, why did she have to be here and how could her mother and Antonia expect her to wear this stupid, sugary kid's dress?

This has all got nothing to do with me, she thought, I'll look awful. Why should I have to look awful, and be gawped at by people I don't even know, half of them?

Marilyn held on to the back of the settee. Her knees were definitely feeling wobbly again. "Yes," she said to Maddy. "It's . . . I think it's lovely. Thank you very much."

"Well, it's good to get it all fixed, isn't it?" Maddy, slightly mollified. "One less thing for you all to think about. Such a busy time."

I shall be glad to be on my way, she thought and imagined telling her Mum, with whom she would later be having coffee, "I don't know what was going on, but I felt ever so uncomfortable."

There had already been awkwardness when Antonia changed her mind about the wedding dress and decided to buy one in London, which actually she had found quite annoying at the time but now she was beginning to wonder if she wasn't quite relieved, one way and another.

Antonia, who although being up in her room could tell exactly what was happening downstairs, now decided to check out Imo's dress. Hearing her coming, Maddy and Marilyn looked up expectantly.

Antonia paused in the lounge doorway. She could see that despite Imo's slouching the dress did seem to fit all right, not hideously tight or hopelessly loose, but then the magnitude of the Columb Court fire overwhelmed her again. "Has Mum told you what's happened, Maddy?" she asked, the note of tragedy returning to her voice.

I knew it! Maddy thought, I knew there was something going on. "No?"

Imo didn't want to be involved any further in this discussion, she moved behind the settee and tried to pull the dress zip undone.

"The wedding's going to have to be cancelled!" Antonia exclaimed.

Maddy stared; she hesitated to ask 'Cancelled, why?' but this surely was a natural first question to be followed by, 'Why then am I measuring the bridesmaid's dress?'

"Oh, tell her Mum!" Antonia cried, tears coming again. "I just can't bear it!"

She made a sudden retreat to the kitchen.

"It's the hotel, for the Reception, Columb Court – " Marilyn started.

"Oh, yes, I know," Maddy said, staring after Antonia. "Lovely for the photographs and everything. Don't they have peacocks?"

"Yes, peacocks . . . " Marilyn said, distracted. "But there's been a fire!"

"No! At the hotel? Oh, my, goodness, is it bad?"

"Yes! It is!" Antonia returning, clutched six sheets of yellow patterned kitchen roll.

Imo still struggled with the zip. "Great!" she thought. Here she was, stuck in this hateful dress and they had totally forgotten about her. She kicked off the shoes, bundled up the frothy skirt and exited upstairs to her room where she yanked the dress over her head. Then realising that her trousers and T-shirt had been left in the lounge she crossly pulled a pair of crumpled shorts from a drawer.

She stood staring round her room. Now what was she supposed to do, just be bored? She listened to the voices still rising and falling in the lounge.

Later on, coming cautiously down the stairs to root around in the fridge, she made herself four ham sandwiches with a double whack of low-fat mayonnaise, regretted the lack of crisps and went up the slope of the garden under the apple trees.

Marilyn, Maddy and Antonia meantime instinctively sought the comfort of the white leather settees and an in-depth discussion of every detail of the wedding disaster until after a second cup of coffee Maddy said oh my goodness, was that the time, she was running late.

In the hall they found Imo's dress on a chair where she had dumped it, not wanting to have the reproach of it in her room, in all its horrible pinkness.

Antonia handed over Lizzie and Petra's dresses with explanations of the alterations needed and helped Maddy load them into her car. When Maddy had driven off, calling, "I'm sure it will all come right!" from the open car window Antonia and Marilyn, emotionally worn out, collapsed in front of afternoon TV.

CHAPTER 25

JUNE

At Trevean Ned did not put himself out to get to the station on time to meet the new volunteer but in fact this gesture of casual non-co-operation was wasted because the train was late. He thought about going back to sit in the car but it was too hot so he wandered up and down the platform looking at the posters advertising special deal fares and holidays in scenic locations.

He was not unaware of being a focus of interest for the scattering of passengers on the opposite platform. He had been missing this automatic, reassuring level of notice at Trevean where only Clarissa and Perdita seemed inclined to pay him proper attention.

And of course, Imo.

Imo took notice of him but thinking about her now only caused him to feel the familiar irritation. He had actually been making an effort to be pleasant to her despite her stupid behaviour about sex, so why did she have to go away, just to try on some dress?

He skirted round these ideas in his mind, his expression settling into a slight frown.

The train arrived at last and Ned, leaning against one of the wrought iron pillars which supported the roof, let the crowd of disembarking holiday-makers flow round him. There was not much point in trying to find this girl because he had no idea what she looked like. No doubt, eventually, she would find him.

Coming down the platform pulling one of her mother's expensive French suitcases Nicolette saw Ned, but as he gave no indication of looking for anyone she continued through the ticket lobby and onto the forecourt where people were hassling to claim a taxi. She adjusted her sunglasses in order to consider the mêlée of elderly couples and family groups, all anxiously checking luggage and children. This did not look promising, she had been expecting to be met.

Ned sauntered out a few minutes later when the tide of people had slowed and the few passengers still coming towards him down the platform were manifestly not the girl he had been required to meet. Pleased about this, he pulled his car keys from his pocket; he had done as asked and now he could go to the beach before heading back to Trevean.

Nicolette saw the guy she had noticed earlier, the not-bad-looking one. "Hi!" she called, on an impulse.

Ned turned, annoyed. Was this girl here somewhere after all, and what then of his plan to check out the surf?

He saw Nicolette, slim, startlingly short skirt, her hair twisted loosely up into a clip; he began to walk slowly back, registering as he got closer her skin with an olive shade to it, her legs bare, feet thrust into sandals. He was aware of her watching him and also the realisation that this girl was not as he had expected the new Garden Volunteer to be.

"I've got to get to a place called Trevean," Nicolette said, her voice casual, when he stood in front of her. "Do you know it?"

"Yes," Ned said.

Nicolette said, "Oh good. Are you here to meet me?" Partly her approval was for herself, in confirmation of her assessment of Ned's looks, qualified by the decision that he was too young to be of serious interest. But still . . . her gaze lingered over his salt bleached hair and tanned skin . . . maybe serious wasn't totally necessary.

"Nicolette Mason-Poule," she said, holding out her hand.

"Ned Lorrimer."

She walked beside him pulling her case, the two remaining taxi drivers on the rank stopped their conversation to watch them.

"Nice car," Nicolette said when they reached the Beetle. "Is it yours?"

She stood, apparently expecting Ned to lift her case into the boot, which rather to his own surprise he did.

He found that her presence, sitting beside him as he drove, was unsettling. Although he considered that he was used to girls, and indeed to girls showing they were interested in him, these had been daughters of his parents' friends, sisters of boys at school. Nicolette, he sensed, was not the same, he wasn't sure what she felt. He preferred to be in better control of the situation.

She asked him about Trevean, what were the Lacocks like?

Ned frowned, trying to clarify his thoughts. He gathered a mental picture of the supper table in the kitchen with the Lacocks gathered together.

"There's a lot of kids."

"Oh?" Nicolette said, "I'm not usually that keen on children but they may be all right. How old are they?"

Ned wasn't too sure.

"Like . . . nappies?" Nicolette suggested.

"Oh, not that – " He remembered that girls apparently liked babies and paused.

Nicolette nodded. "Good. Who else? What about Mr and Mrs Lacock?"

"She's a bit of a slave driver."

"Really? Like what about?"

"Like, 'Chop down another acre of bamboos before lunch.'" He allowed his bitterness at the thought to come into his voice.

"Oh? Is that what you do? Am I going to have to chop down bamboos?" She spread her slim fingers on her knees and looked down at them. She had varnished her nails on the train with a tester called Blood Orange which she had picked up in the chemists at Paddington.

"I don't know," Ned said. He was not certain how he would feel if this was the case. "The others work in the kitchen garden, with the vegetables."

"Who are they?" Nicolette turned towards him and he was conscious again of a level of emotional discomfort.

"The other volunteers? Graham's a bit – " Analysing Graham as usual was difficult, as he generally tried to ignore him. "Earthy," he said in the end.

Nicolette laughed. "Do you mean as in mud?"

Ned's glance fixed. If she was laughing at him, he didn't like it. "Rural then," he said. "And a bit thick, probably."

"Not your best friend then?"

"I don't see a lot of him."

"And who else?"

"Imo." Ned said, more reluctantly.

"A girl?"

He didn't answer immediately, glancing in the driving mirror to distance himself from the question. Eventually he said, "Yes."

Nicolette looked at him. "What about her?"

"She's – " Ned tried to think of something non-committal. "Quite young."

Then he wondered why he had said this.

"Oh," Nicolette said. "I thought everyone had to be seventeen, for the Garden Volunteers?"

"She is seventeen, I suppose," Ned said.

"OK."

"But she acts quite young," he said defensively. He wasn't sure, again, if Nicolette wasn't merely amusing herself by questioning him. He found that he didn't particularly want to talk about Imo.

"Is she your girlfriend?"

His hands tightened on the steering wheel and he reached for the sunglasses in the driving well. At the same time traffic coming in the opposite direction meant that he had to concentrate on the road.

Nicolette asked. "These?"

"Yeah."

She picked up the sunglasses. "Nice."

He'd got them in Duty Free flying back from staying with his parents on holiday in Dubai. Her hand brushed his as she handed them across.

"Is she your girlfriend?" she repeated.

"Not – " He wasn't sure what he was going to say. "No."

When they reached Trevean the Volvo was on the gravel and

Sally was unloading shopping from the boot with the children helping her.

"Hello," she said straightening up. "You're Nicolette? How was the journey down? I'm Sally Lacock and here are Perdita, Claud and Frankie." She looked at her watch. "Was the train late?"

"Yes," Ned said; he found he was relieved to be able to get away.

Sally looked at him, catching his tone of voice, and thought, Oh? Let's hope these two haven't fallen out already. She said, "Are you wanting to get off to the beach then?"

"I want to go to the beach!" Frankie said, putting the box of cereal he was holding down on the gravel.

"No," Sally said. "We've got to get all this shopping in and show Nicolette around. Have you said hello to Nicolette?"

Frankie shook his head.

"Can you say it then, nicely. She has come to help us in the garden, with Ned and Graham and Imo."

Frankie shook his head again, frowning furiously.

"I'm sorry," Sally said, "he's having a rather bad day."

Perdita and Claud re-emerged from the house to fetch more shopping. "Hello," they both said, standing gazing at Nicolette. "Hi."

Ned drove away with the unfamiliar sensation of being troubled by his conscience. Imo wasn't his girlfriend, he told himself, they just spent time together. That much of this time was spent kissing was true, but he had made her no promises, not committed himself.

This thought was not wholly convincing but as he reached the road down to the cove he turned to the more helpful argument that she had after all kissed him back, so she must like it, but she still wouldn't have sex so obviously she wasn't in love with him. Clearly.

He hesitated at this point but then pushed the whole question aside and put his foot down, the tide would soon be on the turn and he wanted to get in the water.

Nicolette stood on the gravel waiting for someone to take her case into the house, but as this didn't happen she herself pulled it into the hall. Sally then asked her to fetch one of the bags of groceries and bring it through to the kitchen. "Or even two bags," she said, "if you're up to it."

Nicolette chose one of the less heavy looking carrier bags from the boot of the Volvo and Perdita heaved out one full of dog food.

"It's this way," Perdita said, hugging the carrier to her chest. She looked at Nicolette with admiration and was pleased to be able to give her useful information.

Nicolette saw the stuffed pike in the hall and the twists of dog hair which blew ahead of them over the slates of the floor as the green baize door swung shut behind them. "Gothic," she imagined telling people.

In the kitchen Sally was pushing things around in the fridge. "This could do with a good clear out," she said. "What on earth is this, beetroot? Someone keeps putting bowls back with the spoons still in them, no wonder we can never find any. Who does that?"

"I think it's Ned," Frankie said helpfully accusatory.

"Well, whoever it is, I wish they wouldn't."

Nicolette looked down at the two brown and white spaniels which were sniffing round her ankles, their docked tails trembling. They were making it difficult for her to get to the long pine table to dump the carrier bag alongside the rest of the shopping. There was not a lot of space on the table, despite its size, for on it there was as usual a lot of other stuff. This included a plastic washing basket full of crumpled sheets, a wooden slatted box full of carrots, still muddy and with the greenery on them, and runner beans; used mugs, a toy tractor, a sliding heap of junk mail and opened envelopes.

Nicolette put the carrier bag on top of the sheets.

"Tish!" Sally looked at the dogs. "Tash! In your basket!"

Nicolette didn't like dogs, being an urban dweller, and she failed to understand why people liked having them around. They frequently smelled, these spaniels certainly did, and they made revolting messes on pavements and in parks which their owners left in plastic bags hanging on railings.

She watched Sally and the children continue doing what they were doing around her. Perdita was putting boxes and bottles and tins onto various shelves, going to and fro and squeezing things into spaces and leaning sometimes against cupboard doors to get them to shut. Claud sat dreamily reading the information on the back of a cereal packet, which gave instructions for making a model of an early flying machine. Frankie stood beside the table sticking his fingers into the sugar bowl and licking them.

"Don't do that," Sally said. "It's unhygienic. Right, that's most of it sorted. Nicolette, I'll show you where you're sleeping."

"What about my case?"

"Let's see if we can get it upstairs between us. I'll pull and you lift."

As they reached the first-floor corridor Sally said, "You're sharing with Imo, the other girl, I'm afraid. We've run out of rooms."

Nicolette paused and then nodded. "OK."

The final narrow staircase to the attic was much more difficult to negotiate but with the pulling and shoving they got the case to the hot dusty landing at the top. As Sally opened the bedroom door Nicolette looked round at the two narrow beds and the wooden steps leading up to the open dormer window, at the lime-washed lumpy plaster on the walls, the chest-of-drawers and the wooden towel rail. Unlike Imo she did not decide that she liked the room, it was small and quite dark.

"I think Imo has chosen this bed," Sally said, which was clear anyway because the duvet on the bed beneath the window was tossed back in a heap.

Nicolette dropped her shoulder bag on the blue cotton cover of the bed against the wall.

"And – " Sally opened the door of the cupboard set into the wall, inside which were a pair of jeans and a camouflage sweatshirt haphazardly hung on hooks. "You'll have to share this with Imo. There isn't that much space up here, I'm afraid."

Nicolette nodded. "What about this?" She indicated the chest-of-drawers.

"The same," Sally said, pulling open one of the drawers which contained a muddle of Imo's possessions, a wash-bag with a broken zip, sketch books, an Indian scarf. "Yes, well, can you sort it out between you?"

The room was warm and stuffy, sunlight falling across the wooden steps leading down from the window and across the strip of threadbare carpet on the floor.

"Is there a shower?" Nicolette asked.

"No. I'm afraid not. The plumbing is fairly basic. There's a bath, I'll show you."

They went back down the narrow stairs.

Nicolette stood in the doorway of the nursery bathroom and did not comment but Sally was left feeling defensive. "Too bad," she thought, "they all just have to muck in."

Nicolette's glance lingered on the soggy, ancient towels heaped on the towel rail and floor, the detritus of plastic boats and squirty frogs and toy saucepans, at the tide-line in the bath. Had Sally asked her she would have said that she minded the state of the bathroom more than sharing a bedroom. At home she had her own shower.

"Frankie doesn't always manage to aim straight," Sally said, taking some toilet paper and wiping the seat. "And he forgets to lift it. Remind him if you see him; he's getting better."

Later in the attic, considering the two spare hooks in the cupboard and the lack of space in the chest-of-drawers Nicolette paused with her case open on the bed and thought, "This may not work out."

Sally hurried back downstairs to see if James was waiting to make the tea for he would be impatient, needing to know that she was available to spend time with him before he started the ritual.

"I think," she told herself, "that that girl could cause trouble."

CHAPTER 26

JUNE

Imo agitated to leave The Rowans as soon as possible, which was the day after the bridesmaid's dress fitting, and a Sunday.

She told her parents that she had to get back to work at Trevean, which could have been true, but equally possibly Sally might have agreed to her staying on at home for a few days, had she been asked. But Ned was at Trevean and Imo wanted to be nowhere else.

Clive drove her to the station.

"Can you phone so they'll meet me?" Imo asked.

"Can't you do that yourself?" Clive was not disposed to be accommodating, he felt she had been unhelpful and caused friction in the house.

"My phone needs charging."

"What's the number?" Clive asked with a suppressed sigh. There was no point asking why she hadn't re-charged it before they left, that sort of question got you nowhere except more irritated.

"Mum's got it."

Clive was exasperated. He knew that on returning to the house he would find Marilyn and Antonia still in distressed consultation about the wedding venue and that this would probably involve further protracted phone calls to the Rodmaines, who had now been informed of the hotel crisis.

At the end of the day, Clive thought, when they had all talked themselves to a standstill, he would be the one who had to sort it all out, and of course do most of the paying.

When, he wondered driving home, would Imo grow up and start to take responsibility for her own life, when would Antonia stop letting herself be brainwashed by the Rodmaines and when, when would Marilyn stop crying?

No-one was in the kitchen or the lounge at the house nor, Clive noted, was there any sign of lunch being prepared. Antonia when she was home could normally be relied on to produce something to eat. But not it seemed today.

He went up the stairs and found as he had half expected that Marilyn was in their bedroom; she was lying on the bed with the curtains drawn.

"What's up?" he asked.

"I've got a horrible headache," Marilyn said. "Roger's parents are suggesting Bath."

Clive looked at her. "Bath?"

"For the reception. A hotel in Bath."

"But that's miles away."

"I know – "

"And probably hideously expensive."

"I know!" Marilyn felt blindly for a tissue. "But they say the

Manager knows them. I can't cope with all this! And we could move the wedding."

"To where?"

"To their church."

"But that's ridiculous, we've made all the arrangements, what about all the flowers, and . . . " Clive tried to remember some of the umpteen details to do with the wedding service about which Antonia and Marilyn had been fretting for the past months. "The choir?"

"I know!" Marilyn cried, distraught. "Or George said what about London."

"London!"

"Yes. Because Roger has a house there but it would probably mean changing the date of the wedding because they'll get terribly booked up."

"This is absolute nonsense," Clive said. "All the invitations have gone out. The church is sorted. All we have to do is find somewhere else for the reception."

"Oh!" Marilyn pressed the tissue to her eyes.

Clive thought, I'm fed up with the Rodmaines endlessly causing trouble. To distract Marilyn he said, "Imo wants us to ring the Lacocks and ask them to meet her. Why she should expect us to run around after her when she does nothing whatever to help here, I do not know."

He waited but Marilyn didn't answer.

"Can you do that?" He asked. "Ring them?"

"Oh no!" Marilyn was crying again. "I can't! I really can't, Clive!"

Clive sighed. "OK. I'll do it."

As he crossed the landing and reached the stairs she called after him. "The number's under T in the book."

He paused. "T?"

"That's what Imo gave me. Trevean, the house name."

When Sally answered the phone, Clive explained about Imo being on the train. "She wanted me to ask you if someone could meet her. She gets in at – " he had checked " – one thirty."

"Oh," Sally said, thinking drat that's bang on lunch time.

"If it's inconvenient I'm sure she can get a bus, can't she?" It is certainly inconvenient to me, Clive thought, having to ring this woman I don't know and expect her to go and pick up my daughter on a Sunday morning. He still couldn't convince himself that Imo was any real use in their garden.

"I'm sorry," he said. "Imo can be rather disorganised, she sprang this on us."

"No, it's all right. Hang on a minute." Sally was in the middle of peeling potatoes and she had the kitchen phone cricked under her neck. She withdrew her hands from the sink and dried them on the nearest tea towel, which was hanging on the back of a chair.

Despite the less than perfect reception in some parts of the house the phone situation at Trevean had improved very considerably since the original solitary Bakelite phone with cloth chord had been removed from the back hall and donated as an historical item to the village school. Sally still felt a small thrill of pleasure at not having to run down the slate floored corridor and crash through the baize door when James yelled, "'Phone!" He hated answering it.

Now she stood, walking her fingers on Frankie's head to keep him quiet while she went through possibilities of who could go to fetch Imo. She had already been considering how much of lunch cooking, church, dog walk and pub drink with James she could fit into the morning.

There certainly wouldn't be a bus on a Sunday. It was Graham and Ned's day off, Graham had gone to his parents' small-holding as he always did at the weekend; Ned was presumably still in bed. Sally wondered if the new girl could drive.

"There won't be any buses today," she said. "But we'll sort something out."

"I'm sorry about this," Clive repeated. Curiosity caught him, she sounded a capable woman. "Do you have many of these teenagers with you?"

"One or two. And some younger ones, but they are ours."

Frankie was dragging a chair towards the sink, intent on helping with the potatoes; Sally automatically removed the peeling knife from the draining-board.

"I don't know how you cope," Clive said. He meant it. "Our older daughter's twenty now and getting married and then there's Imo – so only the two of them but I still get driven mad."

"Yes, Imo explained about trying on her bridesmaid's dress. No, Frankie! Sorry, I have a three-year-old here who's into water. How is the wedding planning going?"

Clive paused. "It's not, at the moment. The hotel has let us down for the Reception."

"Oh?" Sally said, watching Frankie stirring the potato peeling water with a spoon. "Be careful not to splash. Sorry – ?"

Clive had realised that there was a lot going on at the other end of the phone. "Oh, it'll get sorted," he said trying to sound as positive as possible. "But we could have done without this. The wedding is next month."

"What happened?"

"A fire." Clive moved into the kitchen with the phone, thinking that overhearing this conversation would cause Marilyn or Antonia, or both of them, to get upset all over again. At the moment the house was quiet.

"Really?"

"Yes, it sounds quite bad; it may have started in the roof. They'd been having renovations done." He had heard this detail on the local radio as he drove home. "Anyway, they've had to cancel all functions."

"What a nightmare," Sally said. "The roof beams in our house certainly weigh on our minds."

"Oh?"

"Several oak trees up there. We lie awake listening for death watch beetle."

Clive remembered that Imo had described her job as working in an historic garden. Where you have an historic garden, it now occurred to him, likely enough you have an historic house. Imo of course had not chosen to give her family any further information about the place where she was staying, or the people she was staying with.

"Your house is old?" Clive asked with a note of caution. Had he unwittingly been talking to the owner of some stately home? Didn't most of those now belong to the National Trust, unless the owners were Dukes or Duchesses or whatever. Was this woman a duchess?

"Yes," Sally said. "It is. Pretty old. Round about 1500, some of it, with Victorian bits added on. But the odd door is probably even older."

"The up-keep must be something – "

"A total nightmare. And the gardens, that's why we need the teenagers."

"But – " Clive thought of Imo, lying for the whole of a summer's day under an apple tree in their garden. "Do you find they're actually much use?"

"Well – " Sally was beginning to think that she must end this conversation and get on. Sad about this man's wedding reception problems but she didn't have time now to chat about them. "Teenagers are better than nothing. They do have certain advantages."

"What?" Clive asked, disbelieving.

Sally laughed, "Young bodies, they're not going to seize up on you and have to take time off. And I suppose the other thing – No! Don't do that Frankie!"

Frankie, taking advantage of her preoccupation, was pushing spoons and knives and other odds and ends off the draining board and into the potato peeling bowl in the sink.

"What?"

"Oh, child problem, sorry," Sally said. "Well, economic. The teenagers come comparatively cheap."

This made sense to Clive, but he mentally readjusted his ideas about Trevean having ducal connections. "Yes, I see," he said.

"Well, I'm afraid I must go now," Sally said. "I hope you can find somewhere else suitable for your reception."

"So do I," Clive said with feeling. "No, we'll sort it."

Sally paused momentarily having recalled the conversation with Michelle Lowe, the Personal Banker. "We had an idea of having weddings here."

"Really?" Clive said, surprised. "But you don't run a hotel?"

"Not officially," Sally said, beginning to pull knives, forks, blades from the electric hand beater and a mug from the potato water. "I wish you wouldn't do this, Frankie. Though sometimes it feels a bit like it."

"Then how – ?" Clive asked.

"Maybe on the lawn," Sally said. "In a marquee, we haven't thought it through properly yet. It's been put on the back burner for this year anyway, too many other things going on."

"Oh – "

"Well – " Sally turned her head to look at the kitchen clock. "I'm afraid I really must go now. I hope your wedding sorts itself out. I'll get someone to pick up Imo."

"Thank you," Clive said.

No sooner had he put the phone down than it rang again.

"Hello?"

George Rodmaine was back from Matins at Church where he and Penelope had had to fend off queries from all sorts of people about, as she described it, 'this wedding catastrophe'. Some people had seemed genuinely sympathetic, but Penelope had denounced others to George as 'extremely impertinent'. She insisted that he phone the Lacocks to ask if they had got any further forward with finding a solution. All the way home in the car he had had to listen to her venting her indignation at finding herself in this position.

"We're being made to look ridiculous," she said several times, "not being able to tell people where the reception is going to be held."

"We have told them," George tried to point out. "On the invitations. It's not our fault if this hotel isn't up to the mark."

"Of course it isn't up to the mark," Penelope was searching in her bag for a handkerchief, emotion had made her eyes run. "Oh honestly, I'm sure I put one in here! Nothing organised by those people is going to be up to the mark. I dread to think what the wedding dress will be like, Lizzie says the bridesmaids' dresses are ghastly. You must ring them up as soon as we get in and find out what they are doing about it."

"We are wondering how your search for somewhere new for the reception is going?" George now asked Clive, irritating him immediately by the implication that they, the Rodmaines, didn't see themselves as involved in solving this problem.

"I'm sure we'll find somewhere."

"Have you got a short list yet? Penelope has suggested that we could look at brochures for you." This was offered as if it was a concession.

We do all the donkey work and they graciously give their approval, Clive thought.

"No, not yet," he said.

Clive could hear Penelope in the background exclaiming, "Only four weeks away! It must be sorted out."

"The point is, as we see it – " George sounded as if he was continuing to follow Penelope's prompt, "the invitations, re-printing. . . Ah yes, the invitations will need to be re-printed."

This had not occurred to Clive. "Possibly," he said.

"Well, they will, of course. We have to let people know where the reception is being held."

"People could be told at the church?" Clive suggested. "If we find somewhere reasonably close."

There was a pause while George relayed this suggestion to Penelope which produced a strongly negative response. "No," he said eventually, "we don't think that would be appropriate."

"Fine," Clive said. "Fine. But being realistic it will be a question of what can be done in the time."

"I mentioned a hotel in Bath to your wife," George said. "I can give you the number."

Clive gritted his teeth but jotted it down.

George said, "They know us there."

Clive felt his irritation increase yet further. At how many hotels did the Rodmaines have personal contacts? Then to avoid having to continue the discussion any longer he said, "Thank you. I'll have to get back to you on this."

Sensing that George was about to say something more he added, "I'm afraid I'm going to have to leave it there for now. I'll get onto it tomorrow, today's no good, it's Sunday." Then he went out onto the patio and breathed deeply.

Meanwhile Imo's train was stopping frequently at minor stations. She sat gazing from the window, firmly ignoring the granny-type woman sitting opposite her who unpacked some sandwiches and started to munch her way through them. If Imo weakened and so much as caught her eye would she proffer one in return for a boring, one-sided conversation?

Imo was thinking about Ned. She had phoned him on his mobile number while she was away but of course reception in the Trevean area was pretty much non-existent. She had thought of ringing the Trevean house number and asking someone to find him, but she wondered if this might irritate him. It was a known fact that boys didn't like girls who were too clingy or chased after them.

She chewed her lip and stared at the passing fields.

The woman with the sandwiches dropped a piece of cucumber and bumped Imo's knee in bending to try and retrieve it. "Oops!" she said. "Sorry!"

Imo acknowledged the apology with a minimal nod.

"It's nice countryside round here," the woman remarked hopefully.

"Yes." Imo tried to sound dismissive. She wanted to stay immersed in thoughts of Ned and in distancing herself from home where her mother and Antonia had been in semi-constant tears. Inadvertently, being distracted by the woman's unwrapping of a slice of fruit cake, Imo let her guard slip and an image of The Rowans awash with panic and upset flooded into her mind. "Even Dad's losing it!" she thought.

When Marilyn and Antonia had emerged from their rooms to say goodbye to her, both clutching handkerchiefs to their blotchy faces, her father had exclaimed, "Oh for goodness' sake, this is getting ridiculous. Antonia, I don't know why you and Roger can't just go off somewhere and get married and save us all this hassle!"

Antonia wailed, "Oh!" and rushed back up stairs and Clive had said, "Seriously Marilyn, I can't cope with much more of this."

Imo ran it all over in her mind. Dad was still in a bad mood all the way to the station. When she had said she couldn't see why Antonia wanted to marry Roger anyway he had told her to try and think of somebody else for a change. Then he hadn't wanted to ring Trevean to tell them when she was arriving.

"Would you like a sandwich?" the woman sitting opposite her asked. "Or a piece of cake?"

Imo realised that she had been gazing for the past few minutes, with her eyes unfocused, at the table top in front of her instead of out of the train window.

"Cheese and cucumber," the woman said. "Or marmite?"

Imo shook her head.

"There's plenty," the woman said, spreading out the cling film around the sandwiches. "I've made too many as usual."

"No thank you," Imo said. She turned her head to stare again at the fields and, briefly, the boats on the estuary as the train passed over the Tamar Bridge and into Cornwall.

The woman did not talk to her again. She got off two stops before Imo, having re-wrapped the sandwiches and returned them to one of the several bags which she had with her, this one a shiny paisley printed pvc.

As the tannoy announced her station Imo caught her breath, her throat felt dry. Ned! He would probably come to meet her, wouldn't he? It was Sunday and so he wouldn't be working.

Her face relaxed. She was back!

But Ned was not there.

Having struggled to open the train door she stood, her bag at her feet, gazing down the length of the platform while disappointment rose and washed over her. The few other passengers to get out at the station hurried away, trundling their cases. Then as she walked slowly towards the exit it occurred to her that maybe Ned was just a bit late, parking the car; he could have been held up on the road. She hurried out onto the pick-up area where a row of taxis waited.

The yellow Beetle was spottable immediately parked outside the proper parking bays which were all full, Imo's heart lifted and she waved. When there was no response she hitched her bag onto her shoulder and set off towards the car across the open space.

As she got nearer she realised that there were two people in the front seats.

CHAPTER 27

JUNE

The roof of the Beetle was down and as Imo hurried across the station forecourt. She could see that Ned's head was turned away towards whoever was sitting beside him in the passenger seat.

There was a girl with him. Neither Ned nor the girl initially made a move to greet her and their reaction to her arrival was concealed as they both wore sunglasses, but neither of them smiled.

She stood, uncertain. "Hi!"

"Hi." Ned only half-turned his head to reply.

When he did open the car door and get out Imo realised that she was expected to climb into the back seat; she pulled her bag in after her. His whole manner seemed to convey reluctance and she was at a loss. What was wrong?

Ned put the car in gear, doing up his safety belt as they drove off.

None of them spoke until after a few minutes the girl glanced back and said to Imo, "I'm Nicolette Poule, by the way."

"I'm Imo, Imogen Broadhurst," Imo said. She caught sight of her own anxious face in the driving mirror.

Nicolette didn't offer any further conversation. They drove the few miles in silence and Imo stared at the sunlight playing across Ned's fair hair, it was beginning to look dryer, bleached by the sun and the salt of the sea and it was longer, falling across the nape of his neck.

I want it to be like it was with us, she thought; I want him. What is happening?

They came up the drive to Trevean beneath the rhododendrons and laurels. Ned stopped the Beetle on the gravel in front of the house.

Imo was surprised, "Aren't you going up to the top yard?"

"No."

She was expected to follow him as he climbed out; he left the driver's door open.

"Thank you for meeting me," she said.

Ned shrugged slightly. "Sally asked me to."

He headed towards the granite arch of the front porch, but as she stepped forward to follow him he said, "I'm just fetching my board and wetsuit."

Imo's disappointment rose and darkened. A hope faded that they, just the two of them, would go down through the woods and to the hollow beside the field hedge which would be warm and studded with the yellow flowers of trefoil and white stitchwort in the afternoon sun.

Nicolette had also got out of the car and was now standing relaxed beside it. Her sallow skin had a blueish tone in the hollows at the base of her neck, her toenails were newly varnished an orangey red.

Imo felt daunted as she watched Nicolette, but she caught at the thought that she had been here first, she knew the set-up, Ned wanted her.

"Are you a Garden Volunteer?" she asked.

"I think so," Nicolette said, she leant back slightly to let the heat of the sun envelope her.

"Are you going to work in the kitchen garden?"

"Possibly, I suppose." Nicolette did not sound engaged with the question. "No-one has said."

Imo found herself compelled to impart information. "I'm working there with Graham."

Nicolette turned her face up to the sun, she yawned slightly.

"We're growing a lot of vegetables," Imo persisted, stung by her apparent indifference. "Ned's cutting bamboos. He's been doing it for ages."

"Yes, she said."

Imo stood, discomfited. Nicolette's dismissive tone reminded her of Sour Face Lizzie with whom Antonia shared her flat, sister of Giraffe Roger.

When Ned returned around the side of the house he was carrying a bodyboard and wetsuit. He had avoided coming back through the kitchen because Clarissa was in there slicing runner beans and she might delay him, asking him where he was going or who with, or would he do something for her.

He had hoped that Imo might have gone inside to put her bag away. But no, there she was still hanging around by the car. This was going to make for some awkwardness and Ned felt irritated. He knew that she was watching him as he opened the boot to sling in the wetsuit.

"OK?" he said to Nicolette.

She nodded and slid back into the passenger seat. She gave no sign of picking up on the current of tension.

"Where are you going?" Imo tried to keep the agitation from her voice as she realised that Ned was taking Nicolette with him.

Ned felt yet more annoyed. Was Imo trying to make him appear in the wrong? It was nothing to do with her where he was going or what he was doing, he could do as he liked. He had had enough of people, like his mother for instance, trying to control his life.

"The cove," he said, switching on the ignition.

"Can I come?" Imo asked quickly.

Ned's face set. "We'll probably check out some boards," he said.

Imo said, "Oh, but that's OK . . . " She meant, don't leave me behind, let me come too.

"Nicolette has surfed in France." Ned said, as if this was an explanation for refusal.

It seemed to Imo that a cold hand touched her heart. Ned had never offered to take her with him when he went surfing; he had implied that it was something he liked to do on his own. He probably met up with other surfers, boys did that sort of thing, went all blokey about sport. It hadn't altered her position as his girlfriend.

Ned revved the engine of the Beetle and as it rounded the sweep of weedy gravel and disappeared into the shadow of the drive beneath the heavy over-arching rhododendrons Imo clutched the strap of her bag; momentarily her legs felt weak.

"Even if I can't surf," she now thought, "I can swim, and anyway I could learn. He could teach me."

Only a few days ago she and Ned had lain together by the field wall and he had crushed her beneath him, kissing her till the late evening dew was dampening the grass around them. Now he didn't seem even to want to talk to her, and he was taking this new girl to the beach.

"Oh!" It sounded like a sob.

She set off towards the attic. She wanted to be by herself, not to have to talk to anyone; she went quickly up the back stairs.

But it was immediately clear that the room was no longer her own. As soon as she reached the top landing she realised that something was different for the door in front of her was open, where she was always careful to leave it shut.

She felt a spurt of irritation for if the children had been in her room, they shouldn't have been and she would ask Sally to stop them. Perdita and Claud and even Frankie were all right, but she didn't want them messing around with her things.

She went into the room expecting to see toys lying on the floor indicating Frankie or Claud as the culprit, or most likely both of them, chuffing up the stairs, being a train coming up the steep incline.

There were no toy trains, no pieces of lego but instead a suitcase open on her bed, the contents spewed out around it: pants, bras, T-shirts, shorts, an orange skirt, a paperback. Someone had slept in the second bed, the one that was further away from the dormer window.

Who? But even as she wondered this she knew the answer: Nicolette. She was now going to have to share her room with the girl who seemed to be taking Ned away from her.

She walked slowly across and stared down at the muddle of clothes. They looked expensive and tangled; possibly not all of them were clean. Initially intimidated by the invasion of her room, she now felt a hot stab of anger.

She tried to think straight. Nicolette was pushy, here she had chucked all her stuff everywhere; she might have mentioned this when they were in the car on the way back from the station, she might even have apologised, but she hadn't bothered.

So probably she had twisted Ned's arm to take her to the beach. He didn't like taking girls surfing, so he surely wouldn't have offered. And he had come to meet her, Imo, at the station. She painted for herself the picture of Nicolette asking to be taken to the beach and Ned saying, "'Fraid I've got to collect Imo."

Nicolette would have persisted, "Afterwards, then?"

It would have been difficult for Ned to refuse. Of course.

Imo squeezed her fingers into the palms of her hands.

But when he got back it would be different! Ned would realise what Nicolette was going to be like, that she was demanding. He would probably want to escape right away and say to her, Imo, if she was there waiting, "Come on, let's go for a walk."

She created this scene in her mind and she imagined Nicolette saying, "Shall I come too?" and Ned replying, "No, just Imo."

She jumped up and began gathering together the strewn clothes and throwing them onto the other bed. Some of the bras and pants were definitely dirty. There was enough of Maureen in Imo to ensure that even when she was wearing her most grunge clothes her knickers were clean on every day. She had been washing them in the nursery bathroom and drying them on the leading of the roof gully outside her room since in her first week at Trevean, her bra and pants had disappeared into the maw of the washing machine along with armfuls of Lacock clothing and had never reappeared.

Things were always getting lost in the wash. Claud and Frankie regularly wore odd socks because the matching ones had disappeared. When the missing garments were important, which was basically only if they were school uniform, there would be a noisy confrontation on Monday morning.

Now when Imo had finished clearing the clothes she pulled the suitcase across the floor and shoved it underneath the far bed. Then she stood by the window and stared out across the slates of the roof. The thought came into her mind that the sky was the blue of the small blue butterflies she had noticed fluttering over the long grass at the edges of the lawn at Trevean, and in the fields.

Thinking of colour led her to realise that she had scarcely done any sketching since she had been at Trevean. Getting up, on an impulse, she collected one of her sketch books from the drawer, and sitting outside the window, she flipped through the worked pages.

The early ones went back to term at college, pencil sketches of other students working in the studio. Then there were a couple of small colour washes of light falling through the branches of the apple trees at the top of the garden at home. The Trevean pages recorded Claud and Frankie building a castle of cardboard boxes in the cobbled yard, she remembered sitting on the steps of the back porch and their coming to see what she was doing. Merilla the black cat had sat beside her. That must have been on a recent evening, waiting for supper, for she had been hoping that Ned would emerge from the Laundry House.

There were a couple of crayon sketches of the vegetable rows in the kitchen garden which she had done partly to record what was planted where, asking Graham for the names and writing in 'Beetroot' 'Celery'. She turned the pages, some of which were interleaved with memory markers – an apple leaf, the torn corner of a seed packet.

There were a series of quick figure sketches of Graham taking a bill-hook to the brambles, she had stood out of his line of vision to do these, he hated being watched.

At college they all made sketchbooks which went on show for their final year exhibition.

"It's a good habit to get into," their tutor had said.

Now Imo took the sketchbook and climbed out onto the roof. With a 2B pencil she began to sketch one of the high chimneys, the stone pelmet around the top serrated like triangular teeth; she became engrossed in getting the perspective right.

As she worked the shadow cast by the roof moved along the gulley but it was not until she heard sounds from the room below that she realised that quite some time had passed and she was no-longer sitting in the sun.

She listened. Definitely there was someone in the bedroom below, they seemed to be pulling open drawers. Cautiously she uncurled her cramped legs.

As she stood up and began to move back towards the window Nicolette's face looked up at her.

Involuntarily Imo caught her breath.

"Do you sunbathe up here?" Nicolette asked; she came up the first step to get a better view of the gulley.

"Yes," Imo said unwillingly.

She saw that Nicolette's hair, pulled up on top of her head and anchored with her sunglasses, clung in wet tendrils to her neck. She had been in the sea.

"I've used a couple of those drawers." Nicolette gestured casually towards them, open and now filled with the clothes from the suitcase. "Hope that's OK."

"Yes – " Imo stopped, uncertain of how irritated she felt. Couldn't Nicolette have asked her first? "Where's my stuff that was in there?"

Nicolette nodded towards Imo's T-shirts and trousers, spare bra and couple of pairs of pants, piled on the bent wood chair; some had slipped or were slipping to the floor. "Over there."

Imo was feeling increasingly certain that she didn't like Nicolette's behaviour, or indeed probably Nicolette herself. She climbed down the steps from the window and pushed the drawers which were open deliberately shut and pulled open the remaining two. Into these she haphazardly stuffed her own clothes. Glancing across at the cupboard in the wall she could see that some of Nicolette's things had also been put in there for the door no longer shut properly and inside her cotton jacket was now lying on the floor.

I know I moved her things, Imo tried to rationalise her anger, but they were actually on my bed. I didn't pull out all her stuff without asking.

Behind her she was aware of Nicolette doing something to her hair in front of the small mirror. The glass was spotted and the light wasn't good now that the sun was no longer shining into the room; this knowledge gave Imo a certain satisfaction.

"Is there really not a shower anywhere?" Nicolette asked.

Pleased to be able to answer in the negative Imo said, "No. We have to use the nursery bathroom." She felt like adding, "And the bath is full of toys and the water is never hot."

"Yes, I've seen that," Nicolette said. "But I wondered if there was a shower somewhere else I could use. Don't Mr and Mrs Lacock have one?"

"No. I don't think so."

"Oh." Nicolette turned back to the mirror. "Well, I'll have to have a bath then. I'm covered in salt."

Imo watched while she picked a couple of plastic bottles from the collection now ranged on top of the chest of drawers.

"By the way," Nicolette said, moving across to the door, "would you mind particularly changing beds?"

Imo paused. What was happening? This was her room, her place, she had come here first. She felt her cheeks flush.

"No!" she said. "I don't want to change, I'm sorry, I like this bed."

"Oh well." Nicolette shrugged, picked the only towel off the towel horse and went away down the stairs.

Outside as shade settled beneath the rhododendrons the badger cubs were waking up deep in their sett and yikking in mock fights.

CHAPTER 28

JUNE

As Imo's train had taken her towards Trevean, Clive at The Rowans remained feeling uncharacteristically rattled. He reckoned that he could generally keep a balanced view on most things but now he had had to impose on Sally Lacock, asking her to collect Imo from the station. This had been topped up by his irritating phone discussion with George Rodmaine about finding a new venue for the reception.

He stayed on the patio for a while considering the state of the lawn which was showing signs of suffering from the continuing dry weather and the perennial hose pipe ban, bald patches were developing on the slope up to the apple trees. After a while he decided that he definitely needed some lunch.

Marilyn was in their en suite bathroom, she had been splashing her face with cold water. Clive stood in the open doorway. "That's sorted then," he said.

"What . . . ?" There was immediate anxiety in Marilyn's voice. "What's sorted?"

"I rang Mrs Lacock about Imo. She sounds quite sane. Heaven know how she copes with those teenagers, can they be any practical use in a garden? As far as I know Imo has never lifted a trowel. George Rodmaine was on the phone too."

"Oh . . . what about?" Marilyn stared at him, her eyes blurred with smudged mascara.

The thing is, Clive thought looking at her, that despite her sometimes driving me nuts I do still fancy her. How many men can say that about their wives?

"What did he want?" Marilyn repeated, her voice catching.

"Of course, what are we doing about sorting out the 'reception problem'? What about re-printing invitations? What they do and don't think is 'appropriate'. It would be good if he offered to do a bit of sorting things out himself. But that's too much to hope for."

"Oh!" Marilyn's voice was immediately heightened. "The invitations!"

"Don't worry about it," Clive said wishing he hadn't mentioned this and wanting to forestall the onset of more tears. "Where's Antonia?"

"In her room I think," Marilyn was holding a towel to her face, "she's so upset."

Clive felt exasperated. "What about some lunch?" he said.

It seemed a reasonable question. If nothing was forthcoming at home they could probably still get a table at the pub if they got a move on, and this had the distinct attraction of having a Sunday carvery.

Marilyn cried, "Oh, Clive!"

Clive felt that she was reproving him. For what? Was it his

fault that the hotel had caught fire? The whole wedding business was being a nightmare, just as he had known it would be, right from when Antonia first went to meet Roger's parents and came back with exaggerated ideas of what sort of thing George and Penelope Rodmaine would find acceptable.

"Well, I need to eat something anyway," he said. "Antonia's not cooking?"

It didn't seem likely, given the apparent lack of anything happening in the kitchen. No smell of Sunday joint, certainly. Oh happy memories! If he was to be offered anything it would probably be smoked mackerel, wonderful for the cholesterol apparently, or some weird salad full of nuts.

Here was something else he could blame on the wedding, and by association on the Rodmaines: this wretched diet which Marilyn and Antonia were so keen on.

Marilyn, her voice still unsteady, said, "She couldn't face cooking today, she's too – "

"Upset?" Clive said. "I know."

Considering that Antonia had lived at home for free while studying for her catering qualifications you might have expected she could knock together Sunday lunch when she came back for the weekend. Surely?

But no. No lunch. And no effort to solve the hotel problem with which she, after all, had landed them.

Usually Antonia did not annoy him, or at least not like Imo did with her half-baked ideas of sitting around drawing naked bodies or making contraptions out of bicycle wheels and coat hangers. Usually in fact Antonia was his golden girl, but not today. Today Clive felt that each of his daughters and indeed also his wife irritated him in equal measure.

He went downstairs to the kitchen and giving up on the idea

of the pub, he looked in the fridge. As he had expected there were two plastic fronted packets of mackerel but also some ham with which he made himself two rounds of sandwiches. He glanced at the Business Section of the Sunday Times while he boiled the kettle.

"Coffee?" he called to Marilyn. "Sandwich?" But she answered with a weak cry which sounded more like a negative than an affirmative. He did not go to check.

Picking up his plate, coffee mug and the paper Clive retreated to the patio to sit on one of the slatted wooden chairs in the sun. In so far as it was possible with the presence, definitely somewhat oppressive, of Marilyn and Antonia both probably weeping behind him in the house, he actively attempted to put his domestic situation out of his mind for a while.

It was peaceful outside. He skimmed an article about the expansion of the market in China for Western prescribed drugs and idly watched a blackbird bathing in the water feature. When after a while he felt restored to some reasonable state of equanimity, he decided to approach the wedding reception impasse as if it were a problem in business: with concentrated consideration, followed by a decision, followed by action. Clive was by nature a sorter and doer. He disliked prevarication and duplicity and, of course, too much emotion.

Then he fetched the phone and the telephone directory and a biro and returned to the chair on the patio. He methodically ringed hotels within a reasonable radius of the local church where Antonia and Roger were getting married, and started to phone them.

Initially he asked the most relevant question: did they do wedding receptions? If the answer was Yes, he then asked if they had a vacancy for the date of the wedding, now barely four weeks away. He had a few more queries to pursue about the number of guests for which they could cater, menu choices, overnight accommodation and, at a pinch, a crèche, but these points he never needed to raise.

Unfortunately, in each and every case where the answer to the general wedding reception question was Yes, the answer to the specific vacancy question was No. None of the hotels had a vacancy for a date so close, indeed some of the managers or receptionists to whom he spoke expressed the opinion that he would be most unlikely to find any suitable venue at such short notice. Wedding bookings were usually finalised six months in advance.

"I appreciate that," Clive said with increasing irritation. "So was ours, but I've explained the circumstances."

Most of the people to whom he talked knew about the fire at Columb Court and were variably convincing in expressing their sympathy. The removal of the major hotel in the area, if only temporarily, from the commercial arena was obviously not bad news for them in business terms and sometimes there was also a hint of, 'See where trying to be posh has got you' in their expressions of regret.

Clive rang eight hotels and drew a blank. Then he fetched his laptop from his work briefcase and continued his search on-line.

After this he was still no further forward. He sat in the sun and thought.

In her room Antonia sensed from the quiet which now filled the house that neither of her parents was actively trying to find a solution to the awful situation which faced her. Her wedding was ruined; she had so wanted it to be perfect, to gain the approval of Roger's parents, to silence the catty comments of

Lizzie and Petra.

Columb Court could have done that, with its acres of mown lawns, giant cypress trees, baronial turrets. No-one would have been able to say that the setting let down the occasion or indicated in any way that Roger was marrying beneath his parents' expectations.

But now what?

Antonia got up, took a damp flannel from the basin, pressed it to her eyes and went to find one or other of her parents, who must be made to concentrate on sorting something out. Marilyn, propped up on pillows on her bed and trying to read one of her magazines, looked up to see Antonia standing in the doorway. She could not help thinking that it was unfair that the young could still look attractive even when they were unhappy. She herself, she knew, had bags under her eyes because crying had made her skin flabby, and her mascara had run.

In contrast someone with a poetic turn of phrase, so sadly perhaps not Roger, might have described Antonia as looking like a flower after a shower of rain.

"Mum!" Antonia's voice was despairing. "What's going to happen?"

"Well . . . " Marilyn wavered, but then tried to summon some conviction into her voice. "I'm sure your Dad will be able to sort something out . . . It will be all right."

"How?" Antonia demanded. "How can it be all right? We've got nowhere for the reception. Nowhere! What are we going to do, tell everyone to just go home after the church?"

This was unusually abrasive for Antonia. Marilyn felt that she really couldn't cope. Antonia however was still untypically persistent. "It's not fair!" she cried. "It's my wedding and now it's being ruined!"

Marilyn pressed her finger tips to her forehead. "Oh, don't go on and on! Please."

"Where is Dad?"

Marilyn realised that she didn't know where Clive was but he would have to talk to Antonia. She just didn't feel up to it all. "I expect he's downstairs."

They found the kitchen empty. Marilyn wished that she had not come down with Antonia. "I think I'm getting one of my headaches," she said, turning to the fridge to get find a bottle of water, she preferred the sparkling. "I'm sure I am."

"Shall I get you an anadin?" Antonia paused, automatically concerned.

Marilyn looked towards one of the kitchen cupboards. "I think there are some in there. It's the stress, it's so awful; it just goes on and on."

Poor old Mum, Antonia thought, sympathising from long habit and momentarily distracted from her own anxiety.

"I'll find them for you," she said and as Marilyn subsided on one of the uncomfortable bar stools she ferreted among the packets and pots of vitamins and herbal remedies. She gets so upset, Antonia thought.

She turned her gaze towards the garden, through the open glass door onto the patio. Here Clive was sitting just out of sight, thoughtfully doodling cross-sections of a plastic tank for use with a water de-salination system for which his company had been invited to tender. He had put his search for a hotel on hold, although he had not given up on it. Now he heard raised voices in the kitchen and sighed.

"Will Dad will be able to do something?" Antonia said, her tone less keyed up.

"Oh, I don't know!" Marilyn with an effort swallowed two

anadin. And it's true, she thought, I don't know. Clive wasn't happy about the wedding arrangements anyway because of Roger's parents not offering to help and he had never liked Columb Court. "All this is upsetting me, really upsetting me. You don't understand!" she said.

But really Antonia did understand. Usually she and Marilyn got on well, they had the same taste in most things, for example things like kitchen blinds or carpet colours. And they both liked mainstream films, books and TV: family sagas, romance or animals; not violence and not aggressive sex. Happy endings.

They went clothes shopping together, had faith in each other's judgement on what looked nice on them.

Antonia was familiar with all this and she knew that her mother had been missing her since she moved away from home. She was less aware of her own dependence upon her parents and put the unhappiness which sometimes entrapped her down to stressful happenings at work, or if at the flat, to Lizzie and Petra being unkind. When she was with Roger she felt better, safer.

Clive, on the patio, had been able to tell from the sound of their voices that the conversation they were having was likely to end in more tears. He hadn't heard the actual words but then he didn't need to; it would all be, quite certainly, about the wedding. He got up and walked back into the kitchen.

Both Marilyn and Antonia gazed at him, hope in their eyes. This could quickly change, he knew, to reproach if he couldn't deliver the goods, solve this wretched reception business. But at the moment he had no goods to deliver.

"I've rung, I think, twelve hotels," he said, slapping yellow pages down on the kitchen island.

"And what – ?" Antonia started to ask.

"None of them can do it."

Now both Antonia and Marilyn exclaimed at once. In Marilyn's case, "Oh, no!" was muffled in wodges of kitchen roll.

Antonia cried, "I knew we weren't going to find anywhere. Now what can we do?"

"I'm going to ring Roger's parents," Clive said. He suddenly didn't see why the Rodmaines shouldn't share in the pain, this problem also concerned them after all, just as much as it concerned him and his family.

"Oh no, don't Dad! Please don't!" Antonia cried, anguished.

"Look," Clive said, "this has got to be sorted out. I'm not particularly struck on your in-laws to be but they have a right to know what the situation is. They might even come up with a workable solution. Though they haven't shown any signs of it yet."

"Oh, but Dad – "

"No!" Clive said. "I've had enough of all this nonsense. It can't be an impossible problem to solve, for heaven's sake. We need a venue for a wedding reception. What's so difficult about that? Where's the phone?"

"Perhaps you left it outside," Marilyn said, her voice still waterlogged but her spirits settling a little now that Clive was taking charge. This was his role, to be a rock in her life; to sort things out.

"Right," Clive retrieved the phone from the patio table, "what's their number?"

Antonia gazed at him beseechingly. She felt torn between hope and anxiety. The hope was that somehow Clive together with Roger's parents would miraculously achieve a solution, the wedding reception would be re-sited to everyone's satisfaction and all would again be well. Anxiety however clawed away at her shaky faith in the possibility of such a happy outcome and made her feel weak at the knees. There might be a row!

Penelope Rodmaine answered the phone.

"We are just about to have lunch," she said to Clive, her tone implying that he should have known better than to ring at this unsuitable time.

"I'm sorry," he said thinking at least you are going to get some lunch. "This is just a very quick call then, to say we're having no joy with finding an alternative venue for the wedding reception and to ask you to help think of a solution."

"I believe George already gave you details of a hotel, in Bath?"

"That's not possible."

"Oh?"

"I thought you might have some other ideas?"

"Me?" Penelope sounded surprised.

"Or your husband. George. Either of you." Clive felt his annoyance levels rising again.

"Well, I don't quite see how either of us can help you any further. Obviously anywhere round us here is out of the question. It's far too far away to re-route people."

And you certainly don't want the hassle of organising anything, Clive thought. He said, "Well, we need to find somewhere. And quickly."

"Quite," Penelope said. "How did this hotel fire happen, anyway? Carelessness in the kitchens I suppose?"

"Wiring fault, possibly."

Penelope ignored this suggestion. "They just can't get the trained staff, though goodness knows why not, every other programme on the television seems to be about cookery . . . "

"Do you know of any other venues?" Clive said, determined to cut short this thread of discussion.

"Venues?" Penelope said sharply as if the interruption and

Clive's choice of word were equally inappropriate.

"Yes." Clive did not choose to search for a more acceptable term. There was a pause until Penelope eventually said, "I'll have to discuss it with George. We'll phone you later. Now I'm afraid I must go and see to the gravy, which has probably boiled dry."

The conversation ended. As he put the phone down Clive said, "That woman is a pain. Plain and simple."

"Oh!" Antonia wailed.

"I'm sorry, but my best advice to you is, if you must marry Roger, see as little of his parents as possible."

"Oh Dad! Don't be so horrible!"

"I am not being horrible. I'm telling the truth. She's stuck up and she's unhelpful. She isn't prepared to do anything at all to sort this out. Nothing. It's our problem as far as she's concerned and her only contribution is, 'I'll discuss it with George . . . I'll discuss it with George'. I've just about had enough."

Clive didn't normally get so close to losing his temper, but his patience today was being sorely tried.

Marilyn and Antonia were now both gazing at him looking distraught; he felt annoyed with himself as well as with everyone else. And he was still hungry.

"Let's see if we can still get some lunch at the pub," he said on impulse and somewhat to his surprise they both agreed.

After roast beef and all the vegetables, plus Yorkshire pudding and plenty of gravy, followed by chocolate brownie and ice-cream Clive found he felt considerably better. Marilyn and Antonia, although they stuck to the vegetarian option with salad, managed not to comment on his choice.

Later in the afternoon Antonia announced that she ought to catch the earlier train back to London, for tomorrow was

Monday and work. Clive drove her to the station. He was still rather irritated with her because of the cumulative toll the wedding was placing upon him and indeed upon Marilyn, of whom he always remained at heart protective. Also Antonia had refused to eat anything other than the salad at lunch despite his suggesting that they all deserved a day off The Diet, and of course this meant that Marilyn had felt she had to do the same. None-the-less he could not help but feel sorry for Antonia as she sat wanly beside him for a moment or two when they drew up in the short stop parking bays at the station. She seemed to be summoning the courage to get out of the car and face returning to her London life.

"It's those two girls she shares the flat with," Clive thought. Roger's sister and the other one. He had not been particularly taken with them from the start. Anyone could see that they had given Antonia the worst room with an outlook onto the blank brick wall of the next-door block of flats and yet she was expected to pay a full third of the rent. Besides which, didn't they say like mother like daughter? Lizzie most probably took after Penelope Rodmaine, not a good recommendation, probably just as stuck up and selfish.

"Don't worry, sweetheart, we'll get it all sorted out one way or another," he said, glancing at Antonia and seeing the slight tremble in her lips. "Here you are – " he took a couple of notes from his wallet and handed them to her. "Buy yourself something nice and try to cheer up. You'll be a knock-out, you wait and see."

"Oh Dad – " Antonia turned her face towards him and smiled weakly. "I wish it could be like that! A lovely wedding!""

"It will be."

"Do you promise?"

"Yes," he said, putting his arm round her to give her a hug.

After she had climbed out of the car, taken her bag and disappeared onto the Up platform, he continued to sit, hands on the wheel, going over possible solutions to the reception problem. All very well to reassure Antonia that he could get it sorted but how exactly was he going to do this?

Finally, noticing the parking attendant watching him he put the car into gear and drove out of the station forecourt and back to The Rowans.

Here he found Marilyn on the lounger on the patio, she seemed to be asleep.

He went quietly back into the house to make another phone call.

CHAPTER 29

JULY

At Trevean the long summer afternoon spread across the lawn and the woods and the kitchen garden. Heat pooled on grass and gravel, the birds were stilled. Perdita had come to see her grandmother. There were two arm chairs in Clarissa's sitting room, wing-back Edwardian chairs covered in a florid chintz, now faded and worn thin on the arms. Once presumably they had belonged to James's Aunt Lavinia, previous chatelaine of Trevean; this thought did not please Clarissa.

Clarissa always sat in the chair to the left of the window and a visitor, in this case Perdita, sat in the chair to the right. In winter the chairs were moved to either side of the fire, which Clarissa fed with fir cones which she and the children collected in the woods behind the house.

Perdita liked coming to her grandmother's room; sometimes she came for some peace and quiet and sometimes for someone to talk to about what she was doing. Her father did not usually seem particularly interested in what was going on and her mother was often in a rush, but her grandmother would listen and did not make it seem that she would prefer to be or needed to be somewhere else.

Clarissa and Perdita's conversations often took place over a game of Beggar My Neighbour. Today the cards were laid out, as they often were, on the wide window seat, under which were shelves where Clarissa kept her Harrods catalogues from which she now rarely bought anything, her occasional 'splash out' copies of Homes and Gardens and her knitting. She could turn heels on socks and knit gloves, the only person Perdita knew who could do so. But Clarissa had a rather ambivalent attitude to these skills for they dated from her girlhood, before she had married and gained a life-style which didn't require her to knit socks. Now, ironically, she was poor again which she felt was unfair and of course James's fault, useless as he was at providing for his family. If he were competent she would not have had to subsidise Trevean and she would not now be living here with no money. "In penury," she said which caused Sally to exclaim, "Oh, really Mother, it's not that bad!"

Clarissa told Perdita, and the boys too, although they were less inclined to stay and listen, about what things used to be like. Sally said that Clarissa lived in the past and it was perverse to see the past as always a better place to be than the here and now. But Perdita liked hearing about Clarissa's childhood, the only girl in a clutch of brothers, having to help with cooking for all of them and cleaning the house. They lived somewhere very cold, where they went skating on a frozen lake, and sledging. Then she escaped into a job in London and met her husband and started to live another life with other people to do all the things which she had previously had to do.

"So then you didn't knit socks anymore?" Perdita prompted.

"No, certainly not. It would have been far too hot for wool socks anyway," Clarissa said. "In the places where we lived." Hong Kong, Kenya.

Today Clarissa was asking Perdita about Nicolette. "What do you think of her?"

Perdita wasn't sure; she moved her pile of cards in a small circle on the window seat. "I think she's pretty."

"Do you?" Clarissa said. "Don't fiddle."

Perdita put her hands in her lap. She considered. "Her hair's nice. And she has nail varnish on her toes."

"Yes," Clarissa said.

Perdita looked at her, uncertain. "She is pretty, isn't she?"

Clarissa said. "Yes, I suppose she is."

Perdita had little experience of grown-ups who looked like Nicolette. Sally did not wear make-up, in the summer she dressed mostly in a cotton skirt or jeans with polo shirts, in winter a thicker version of the same; everything had been through the washing machine many times and lost much of its colour and shape. Clarissa hardly ever wore anything new or bright. The teachers at school were very far from flamboyant.

But Nicolette had a frilled orange skirt and very short shorts and painted her nails and drew smudgy lines round her eyes. Mostly she wore sun glasses and her skin was sun-tanned, her T-shirts slid off her brown shoulders.

"Yes, she's attractive," Clarissa said. "Of a certain sort. And she knows it. I expect Ned and Graham think so, don't they?"

Perdita wondered. "I don't know," she said. "Ned took her surfing in his car; she asked me for a beach towel to borrow."

"What did you say?"

"I said they were a bit holey, but she could borrow one probably, if she wanted."

"And what about Imo?" Clarissa asked.

"Imo didn't go," Perdita said.

"Hmm. And do you think she's unhappy?"

"Maybe, a bit?"

She is a noticing child, Clarissa thought, I think she may find life hard. This thought saddened her.

Perdita shuffled her cards in her lap. "Is she not happy? Imo?"

"I wouldn't know," Clarissa said, "but I'm not altogether surprised if she isn't."

"She said to Mum that she didn't like being a bridesmaid. She's got to be a bridesmaid because her sister's getting married. And she doesn't like her dress."

"Oh," Clarissa said. "I see. But I think there may be more to it than that."

"I would like to be a bridesmaid," Perdita said. "I think I would, anyway. Who chooses your dress if you are a bridesmaid?"

"Usually the bride," Clarissa said. "She chooses. How do you like Imo?"

Perdita stared out of the open window down to the sloping grass bank and the long stretch of bamboos at the bottom, which hid the silt-clogged lake from view. She considered the dress information. "Yes . . . . Do we know anyone who's getting married?"

Clarissa thought. "No, I don't think so. You might be the first one, of your generation."

"Me?"

"Yes. Because you don't have any older cousins."

"I don't really want to get married."

"Well, people change their mind about that, when the time

323

comes around."

"What time?" Perdita asked, although she knew what Clarissa would answer.

"When you meet Mr Right."

Clarissa and Perdita sometimes talked about Mr Right, but they kept quiet about these conversations because Sally was disapproving. She said Clarissa shouldn't fill up the children's heads with all that sort of nonsense but let them be children while they still could.

"Imo might be unhappy," Carissa said, "because of her Mr Right."

Perdita looked at her. "Who is her Mr Right?"

"Who do you think?"

"Graham?"

"Oh no, I don't think so," Clarissa said. "Graham's the wrong type of person altogether."

"Is he?" Perdita asked.

"What about Ned?" Clarissa asked. "He's more Mr Right material, don't you think?"

Perdita pictured Ned and nodded doubtfully.

Ned was taller than Graham and when his fair hair fell across his forehead he pushed it back with his hands which were brown with long fingers. Graham's hands were reddish and always seemed to have bitten, muddy nails. Also Ned now had the shiny yellow Beetle, whereas Graham's car looked old and one of the doors was a different colour red from the rest of it.

But Ned didn't really show any interest in her or Claud or Frankie at all, he wouldn't for instance, when they asked, play cricket with them on the lawn. Graham on the other hand had helped them string their bamboo bows, cutting notches for the string with his jackknife.

Something struck her. "But if Imo has met Mr Right," she said, "why is she miserable?"

"Well, if she was thinking Ned was Mr Right, she may be feeling a bit of heart-ache. He is a very attractive young man, but I don't think you could trust him. And now Nicolette has arrived and I doubt you could trust her either."

"Trust for what?" Perdita asked.

"To behave themselves," Clarissa said.

Perdita considered whether she understood this. Her eye was caught by a movement down the slope below the window, near the bamboos. "There's Nicolette," she said.

Clarissa put on her glasses. "Where?"

Nicolette seemed to have come out of the bamboos. She paused to pull her sunglasses from the pocket of her denim shorts and put them on, she wore a stripey T-shirt rolled up above her waist.

"I'd like some sunglasses like that," Perdita said. "Really big."

"Hmm," Clarissa said. "Where is Nicolette supposed to be working, do you know?"

But Perdita didn't know. "She was weeding in the flowerbeds," she said.

Nicolette made her way up the slope towards the house, her slim brown legs parting the long grass. Sally would have like to get this cut but because of the slope it needed a specialised mower or as originally presumably a man with a scythe. When Nicolette reached the level gravelled area below the house she disappeared from view and Clarissa and Perdita returned to their card game.

A while later James whacked the large brass gong in the hall unnecessarily loudly to signal that he had made the tea and was feeling aggrieved that no-one was paying suitable attention.

Perdita jumped up. "I'll fetch your tray," she said to her grandmother.

She ran along the landing and jumped two steps at a time down the wide front stairs, raising small wafts of dust from the ancient red carpet and being careful to avoid the step where the brass carpet rod was loose.

Sally was in the back hall, talking on the phone.

She shook her head because of the jumping but Perdita ran on across the hall, through the baize door and down the slate corridor to the kitchen. Here James stood guard over the two tea pots, the small metal one for Clarissa's tray and the larger pottery one which was for Sally and him and any children or volunteers who happened to be around.

By and large the volunteers didn't drink the tea. Graham had his flask which he made in the morning and which latterly he had been sharing with Imo. Ned took a bottle of water down into the bamboos with him, preferring to strip off his shirt and do a spot of sunbathing rather than flog all the way back up to the house in the heat of the afternoon. Nicolette was so far not aware of the tea ritual. At this present moment she had gone up to the attic room and was lying on her bed to attempt to reading texts on her phone, the vagaries of the mobile signal had begun to dawn on her. It was too hot to get back to weeding the flowerbeds beneath the front windows.

"Where is everyone?" James asked crossly. Particularly, where was Sally?

"I don't know," Perdita said. "But Mummy's in the hall."

"Well, can you find them. This tea is getting cold."

Perdita went all the way back to the front door to locate Frankie and Claud who she guessed were in their den in the giant rhododendron bush at the edge of the lawn. She stood on the front steps and shouted, "Do you want tea?"

"Is there biscuits?" Frankie yelled back, appearing from the dark interior of the bush.

"No!"

"No, then." He disappeared.

Sally coming from the back hall said, "Do you all need to shout at each other? Why not just go and ask them whatever it is."

Perdita set out Clarissa's tray; she was the most efficient member of the family at doing this, checking that all the required items were in place: tea pot, cup, saucer, special silver sugar bowl and tea spoon. Not milk, as Clarissa didn't like it; really Clarissa preferred China tea, but there wasn't any. Then she carried the tray carefully upstairs, along with a mug for herself.

Sally arrived in the kitchen.

James was dolloping dog food into bowls, which as usual he did at the same time as he made the tea, the dogs wove round his feet. This always added to the confusion and Clarissa said the routine was unhygienic and one reason why she preferred to have her tea in her room.

"Where were you?" James asked Sally. "I rang the gong."

"I know," Sally said, "I was answering the phone." The conversation with Clive Bradford had been drowned by the waves of sound.

"Oh God," James said automatically. "Problems?"

"No," Sally said. "I'll tell you in the drawing room. What about Mother's tray?"

"Perdita's taken it," James said, adding inaccurately, "as far as I know." He did not wish to take responsibility for Clarissa's catering. "The old duck will soon sing out if anything's missing."

"Oh, Darling," Sally remonstrated mildly, "Don't!"

"True though?" He laughed to show he was making one of his jokes.

When they were sitting in the drawing room, he one side, she the other of the huge marble fireplace which was full of dusty dried hydrangea heads and the usual curls of dog hair, and with the dogs flopping around their feet, Sally said, "That was Clive Bradford on the phone."

"Who?"

"Imo's father."

"What did he want?" James asked suspiciously. He had in fact heard the phone ring while he was making the tea, but he had justified ignoring it because he could only be expected to attend to one thing at the time. Anyway it was likely to be someone wanting something.

"They've got trouble with the elder daughter's wedding, the hotel where they were going to have the reception has had a fire."

James wondered if he was required to express sympathy. He liked if possible to take the same line as Sally, or at least not to disagree with her but really he didn't see that they needed to feel sorry for Clive. Who was he anyway, they had never met him, he obviously had money if he was paying for hotel receptions.

Briefly he attempted a picture of Imo in his mind, wasn't she the one with the torn trousers and birds' nest hair? This get-up he considered, in so far as he had considered it at all, perfectly awful. It made her look, as he now said, as if she lived rough. "Eating hedgehogs," he said.

"It's the age," Sally said. "Self-expression." She was aware that James barely noticed what she wore any more, for she was simply herself and filled the frame of his horizon. Perhaps fortunately, she thought, glancing at her creased and washed-out cotton skirt.

"Perdita won't go down that route I hope," James said. "Straw in her hair."

"We'll head her off," Sally said. "I think it's wool in Imo's case, darling. Anyway, he had a proposition, Clive Bradford."

"What about?" James frowned.

"Well – an idea. Which is quite interesting, but I said I would have to ask you."

James felt a stab of foreboding. Sally thought all sorts of things might be interesting but so often they had the potential to cause disturbance to his life to a greater or lesser degree. Lately many of these interesting ideas had related to making some money for Trevean, but none so far had done so. The Garden Volunteers were a case in point, he still believed that they cost more to keep than they had, or would, bring in. Graham did at least produce vegetables so maybe he was a marginal case, but what about the others – eat, eat, eat and nothing much to show for it.

He sighed.

"No," Sally said, knowing him well and as ever wishing to spare him the pangs of anxiety, from which she would shield him if she could. "Really, this wouldn't be too much trouble but it would bring in quite a lot of dosh."

James shut his eyes briefly.

Looking across at him Sally thought that she loved him dearly but she wished that he did not suffer so much from the sensitivity which surely came genetically, down the watery blue line of the Lacock lineage.

James could not bring himself to ask what Clive Bradford's proposition was, he knew Sally would tell him. He reached down to find the comforting head of a dog and stroked it. Coal thrust his damp nose into his palm.

"Good dog," James told him. Coal understood.

"What Clive Bradford wanted to know," Sally said, "was could we have their wedding reception here, at Trevean."

She correctly anticipated James' response to this suggestion. "What!" he exclaimed in horror, transmitting the force of his reaction to his dog stroking hand and causing Coal to produce a small yelp of protest. "There, there," James apologised, "poor dog, poor dog. Master didn't mean to hurt you."

Coal smothered his hand with licks to show that he forgave him absolutely and of course he was ready to lay down his life should James require it.

"I hope you said no," James said. "It's quite out of the question. Clearly."

"Well – " Sally said and James feared the battle was lost.

"We had thought of having weddings here, hadn't we?" she said.

"Had we?" James' voice was dark with doubt.

"Yes, we had. I just hadn't got round to properly finding out about it."

"Then it's no go?" James clutched at the proffered straw. "Anyway, surely you need a licence of some sort?"

"Well, you need a licence to hold an actual wedding, I think," Sally said. "But they just want to hold the reception here. That should be all right, as a one-off. It would just be a party."

"To which we don't invite any of our own guests?"

"Well – a party for friends. Imo's working here after all. And we can use it as a trial run for setting up a wedding business. We can see how it goes."

"Oh God," James said.

"They'll pay quite a lot of money," Sally said, "and we could do with it, you know."

James hated talking about money, the lack of it made him feel sick and inadequate. A decent surplus of the stuff was the only thing if you were to have a bearable life and it was some years since he had been able to say that he had this.

"How much?" he asked.

Sally told him how much and he saw immediately that his deep dislike of the idea was not going to stop it happening. He sighed and gazed past her at some point on the worn carpet, his face featuring extreme despondency.

"How's the crossword going?" Sally asked, to distract him.

"It's not." James in fact had completed most of the Telegraph crossword as he usually did.

"Tell me a clue." Sally put aside thoughts of the Bradfords' reception to concentrate on cheering James up.

Later after supper Imo was disconsolate. Once again Ned had ignored the opportunity for the two of them to be alone, disappearing as soon as the meal was finished. Indeed it seemed to her that he went with even more alacrity than usual, although he never did do much about the clearing of the table or the washing up.

Frankie somehow had succeeded in not having been put to bed earlier. He seemed to have developed a crush on Nicolette and now demanded that she give him his bath and see his squirty frog.

"What's that?" she asked raising her eyebrows.

"It's his bath toy," Sally said. "Would you mind starting him off? I'll be up as soon as I've sorted things out down here."

"Why does Frankie like Nicolette?" Perdita asked, for Frankie had until now sought attention almost exclusively from Sally.

"He thinks she's pretty," Sally said. "Little children like pretty people. Princes and princesses."

"Granny says she's attractive."

"Yes, that's probably nearer the mark."

Imo listening felt a clawing of anxiety. She took the salt cellar and the pepper to the draining board but Perdita picked them up again and said quite kindly, "They go in that cupboard."

Imo went outside into the washing yard.

A light was on downstairs in the Laundry House which had only the one window above the sink. After some moments' hesitation she went across the cobbles to push the door carefully open.

Inside she found not Ned but Graham. He was back from his usual weekend visit to his parents and was making a mug of coffee with the kettle on the draining board.

Imo stepped back quickly but not before he had glanced towards the door with a defensive frown on his face.

"'Right?" he said, questioning.

"Yes," she replied hastily, turning away.

There was no sign of Ned.

CHAPTER 30

JULY

Now that Clive had an idea in his head of how to solve the wedding reception problem he went ahead with checking this out.

In his office at the factory, away from the emotional atmosphere at The Rowans, he sat and thought. He then phoned a couple of local coach companies and asked for timings and costs to transport the wedding guests from the church to Trevean. The answers were, he considered, acceptable since the circumstances left little room for manoeuvre.

He then phoned George Rodmaine and explained the proposed arrangements, which would involve hiring a couple of coaches and a journey of about forty-five minutes.

After a pause George said, "I don't think we would find this arrangement very satisfactory."

Clive, irritated, responded that in that case there appeared to be only two possibilities: either the Rodmaines themselves found an alternative venue and sorted out the logistics involved – there was a further pause at this point in the conversation while the implied 'and pay' hung unspoken between them – or the wedding was postponed until Columb Court had been reopened.

"We will phone you back," George said. "This is all very unfortunate. I don't think Penelope will be happy."

"Unhelpful," Clive told himself as he replaced the phone on his desk. "Of course they won't come up with anything useful."

Next he rang Antonia, although he hesitated before dialling her mobile number for it seemed likely that she too would not receive his news well.

Antonia was in the Directors' Lunches' kitchens wrapping asparagus spears in brown bread and butter for a buffet reception. She was horrified on hearing the proposal about Trevean and the coaches to transport the guests; she said her whole wedding was going to be absolutely ruined.

Clive couldn't get any sense through her head. "I'll ring you about it this evening," he said in the end. "Everything will be fine."

Antonia began to cry and had to be comforted by various of her friends on the prep team until the supervisor, who was normally a capable and unfazed woman, said, "Not again!" and suggested that Antonia might consider whether she was really suited to the demands of a career in catering. At this Antonia wept more, seeing the asparagus and the accompanying rare beef canapés through a mist of tears.

Clive finally phoned home to talk to Marilyn, sighing as he listened to the ringing tone because here was another call which was not likely to go smoothly.

However Julia Prentice answered, for it was her day to clean, saying that Marilyn had gone into town and did Clive think that she should hang the washing out to dry? "Seems a shame to waste the dryer on a lovely day like this."

"Good idea." Clive said.

"She says your neighbours don't like it," Julia reminded him, now cautious in victory.

"Too bad," Clive said. He was well aware of this area of difference between Julia and Marilyn and decided today to side with Julia for hers was after all the sensible view and he was feeling irritated with each member of his family for the trials they were putting him through.

The whole business of drying the washing was ridiculous. "It is not," he had previously pointed out to Marilyn, "as if you were hanging our underclothes over the rose bushes in front of the house. There's a base for the rotary dryer on the patio, so use it."

"Not long to the wedding now?" Julia suggested, made confident by his approval of the drying arrangements and desperate to know the latest. "Have you managed to find anywhere else yet?"

"I think so," Clive said.

"Oh, that's nice!" She paused hopefully but Clive didn't elaborate and said he would try to get Marilyn again later. Julia put the phone back disappointed.

Later that day, when the Rodmaines had decided that they didn't have any other ideas for the reception, Clive rang the Trevean number and suggested to Sally that they should now get down to the nuts and bolts of marquee hiring, coach parking, table seating, timing of guests' arrival and so forth.

"What about the catering?" Sally asked, wondering suddenly how she was going to get all this sorted out.

Clive paused. The wedding catering had been one of Antonia's major pre-occupations, she had spent hours, weeks, considering the menu which they were to have had at Columb Court. Now he would, he supposed, have to check any new catering arrangements with her. Tempting though it was to leave it all to the efficient sounding Mrs Lacock and let her get on with it, he said, "I better get back to you on that."

"Right," Sally said, mentally crossing her fingers. Catering was really not her thing.

With at least some feeling of relief, Clive turned his attention to work matters. People seemed to forget that he had a business to run.

Julia Prentice located the rotary dryer and pegs and hung out a whole white wash.

In The Lemon Tree Marilyn was experiencing a horribly familiar feeling that everything was going wrong and she couldn't cope. She stared hard at the ring of froth on her skinny decaf cappuccino. The mascara on her lower lashes had smudged and Jamal, the Times spread before him on the counter, knew that again she was crying.

The café was still without other customers although soon the shoppers' bus ladies would be in for their coffee and cakes. Jamal cleared his throat gently, but Marilyn did not look up. When she blinked a tear slid downwards on each cheek, carrying a sooty trace. In her hands below the table she crushed a paper tissue.

Jamal drew another cappuccino from the splendid new coffee machine, a recent investment, and poured for himself a cup of chai. Some of his more adventurous English customers were beginning to take to this and in his opinion the aroma from the spices gave The Lemon Tree an individual ambience.

Marilyn, pretending to read the magazine she had brought

with her so as to have something to hide behind, became aware that Jamal was now standing beside her.

"You will allow me?" He placed the cappuccino carefully on the table.

"Oh – but I didn't ask for another . . . " Marilyn hastily lifted the tissue to her face. "I'm sorry, I think I've got a bit of hay-fever . . . "

Jamal placed his chai on the table and gestured towards one of the other empty chairs. "And I will sit here?"

He waited for her approval.

"Oh – well. Yes." Marilyn would have preferred to be able to say 'No. Please leave me. I don't want to make conversation' but she found that, as usual, she was going to go along with what someone else wanted her to do. Why do I always do this she thought but no sensible answer presented itself.

Jamal sat opposite her, across the small square table with the maroon wipe-clean cloth.

"I think," he said quietly after a moment, "you are not happy."

Marilyn pressed the tissue to her nose. Of course he would see that she had been crying, her face must be a mess.

"I'm all right really. It's just – well, my daughter is getting married."

Jamal said after a moment. "Your daughter's wedding is making a difficulty?"

Marilyn might have replied, as on other days, 'No, no. Really, it must be just the pollen . . . ' but today she felt too distressed to carry on with pretence.

"Yes!" she said and gazed at Jamal's calm brown face across the table.

"And so there is this problem? A wedding is, of course, very costly?"

"Oh – it's not that . Though my husband . . . " Marilyn paused, "and the other parents don't . . . " But she didn't feel that she could explain about the disagreements between Clive and the Rodmaines about paying for the wedding.

Jamal nodded and lifted his small handleless cup. "Ah . . . "

"But it's not just the money. It's – " Marilyn was torn between feeling that she should not be discussing Antonia's wedding with someone outside the family and a longing to talk to someone sympathetic, almost anyone.

She was distracted by a movement at the window and turning saw a cluster of elderly women, indecisive, reading The Lemon Tree menu. Any minute now they would push the door open and come in and Jamal would go back behind his counter and polish the coffee machine and discuss with these new customers the sweets and the cakes under the large plastic domes. This moment would pass, this moment when she could try to tell someone what was making her so unhappy, someone who wouldn't react in a way which only made everything seem a bit worse, for this is what usually happened when she tried to talk about it to Clive or to one of the girls.

"They all, you see," she said quickly, "make me feel . . . " How to explain it? "Useless."

"Useless?" Jamal had also seen the women, but he continued to sip his chai. "At what useless?"

"Everything," Marilyn said, and then in a rush, "the house, cooking, meeting people. Everything."

Jamal gazed at her thoughtfully. "This is very sad," he said, "to think this."

"Yes – " Marilyn glanced again towards the women outside and saw that one of them was clearly encouraging the others to come in. "And as well," she said, anxious to complete her explanation, "I don't have any friends here. I used to have friends, where we lived before. And I have nothing to do, and I don't see anyone."

"You do not have a job?"

Marilyn remembered his joke about her coming to work at the café.

"No," she said, despairing. "I haven't had a job since the girls were born . . . "

But the door of the café had opened and a cluster of shoppers stood looking around at the placing of the tables.

Jamal stood up. "I am sorry," he said to Marilyn, "you will excuse me?"

"Tea cakes?" the women's leader was suggesting, her voice rather loud. "Tea?"

"Yes, certainly." Jamal gestured them towards two tables. "Please . . . "

The women came in and settled down, clucking and fussing a little and rearranging themselves on different chairs; they began to tell each other that it was quite nice in here wasn't it?

Watching Jamal take their orders and then go back behind the counter to draw coffee and put tea cakes on plates Marilyn pondered the absence of Tanis the teenage waitress. She thought that she rather missed her. Tanis had added a certain note of drama to The Lemon Tree with her two-tone hair and Cleopatra eyes even if, when the café was quiet, she tended to lean up against the coffee counter radiating boredom.

Picturing Tanis's eyes made Marilyn reach for her sun glasses; she did not want the other customers to notice how she looked. She collected up her bag and the bill.

"Is Tanis not coming back?" she asked Jamal as she waited for him to count out her change.

"Thank you," he said. "No, Tanis has a new job."

Marilyn paused, surprised. "Has she?"

"Yes. Full time. More money. And with a Travel Agency, she hopes to be a Holiday Rep."

Marilyn gazed at him as he picked up a full tray to carry it to the women chattering at their tables. "Oh, I see . . . "

So Tanis, Marilyn thought, who was still in her teens and who only last week was serving her coffee, even Tanis was now moving on, doing things, preparing to travel. This thought of course did not make her feel any better. As she came out of the café and into the full sun on the pavement she wondered whether Julia Prentice would have completed the hoovering by the time she got back to The Rowans.

She walked slowly to make this more likely and indeed when she finally reached home Julia was just pushing her bike round the side of the house.

"I put the washing out, Mr Bradford rang up and he said that would be all right." Julia sounded quite pleased with herself about this.

Marilyn stared at her and found that she simply couldn't manage to say anything. Her stomach churned and in fact she suddenly felt that she might scream. Why did people have to behave like this, going out of their way it seemed to make extra problems and difficulties? Involuntarily she glanced towards her neighbour's netted front windows.

"Mr Bradford said not to worry about Next Door," Julia said. She waited for Marilyn to respond and then said, "Well I must be off I suppose. I got my money, thank you."

She climbed onto her bike and launched herself towards the downhill traffic, calling back cheerily, "It's nice your reception's getting sorted out isn't it?"

Marilyn fumbled in her bag for her key. She let herself into the house and shut the door, wishing that with it she could shut out all her problems. She opened the patio doors and looked at the incriminating washing, snowy white in the sunshine. She knew she ought to bring it all in but suddenly felt that she hadn't got the energy.

Turning to check the contents of the fridge she stared at cottage cheese with pineapple and simply couldn't fancy it. Instead she took out a low-fat strawberry yoghurt and took it upstairs and lay on the bed and closed her eyes.

Before he went home that evening Clive decided to try phoning Antonia again as he had promised to do to outline in more detail the new plans for the reception.

Antonia was alone in the flat for Lizzie and Petra worked further away in the City, and indeed they often stayed after work to have a drink with the analysts and traders who came within their orbit of 'possible men'. To be 'possible' meant they must be young-ish, fit-ish, rich-ish, ex-public school and have a good car and be prepared to spend their money, especially on drinks and meals and weekends away, preferably with people who had houses in the country.

Clive began to explain that he had not been able to find any other hotel locally which was available for the date of the wedding. "And Roger's parents," he said, "have no suggestions, as usual."

"But it's not fair!" Antonia cried. "I can't bear it! It will just be awful, awful, awful and embarrassing. How can we tell everyone they are going to have to catch a bus and drive for miles to some place no-one has ever heard of, that isn't even a hotel? What about the catering? What about – " she gazed round the sitting room at the usual debris of the flat, scattered clothes and shoes and newspapers and a large bunch of dead tulips still wrapped in cellophane which Lizzie had stuffed into a vase without any water. "What about the harpist? And the table decorations? And . . . the disco?"

"Listen," Clive said as Antonia's voice hit a pitch which caused him to feel that his nerves were beginning to react, "all these are details which can be sorted out. The main thing is to get the venue organised. Now this place, Trevean, may not be perfect, but apparently they can cope. We can arrange a marquee, all the rest of the stuff can be transported, or if it can't we will have to find alternatives."

"But it's miles away!"

"It's 45 minutes away. That's not too bad."

"I wish I wasn't getting married at all!" Antonia's voice was filled with choking sobs. "It's all horrible!"

Clive felt tempted to say, 'Well, don't get married then!' for really this would now be a relief: no more Rodmaines, no more expense. No more diet.

Instead he told Antonia that if she wanted to postpone the wedding this would be fine, but if not it seemed to him that Trevean was now the only alternative they had to Columb Court.

"Oh!" Antonia cried.

"Well why don't you have a think about it and let me know tomorrow what you want me to do," Clive suggested.

On this unsatisfactory note their phone call ended. Both of them felt in need of something restorative: Clive fetched a hot chocolate from the coffee machine before driving home and Antonia phoned Roger.

Roger was still at the office and was not pleased to recognise that Antonia sounded distraught. Pudding was becoming very emotional, wedding nerves of course. "It can't be that bad," he suggested when she protested that everything was totally ruined.

"It is, it is! We're going to have to postpone the wedding! Can't you come here now?" she asked. "Can't you?"

Roger felt bound to point out that it was his evening for playing squash.

"Please!"

"Well – " he checked the time. "I won't be able to stay."

"I know, I know! Just for a little while . . . "

Battling his way onto the tube he thought, this is all getting to be a bit difficult. Things would have to be different when they were married, Antonia couldn't expect him to change prior arrangements just like that for no good reason.

He found her alone in the kitchen. That was probably the trouble of course, girls liked company.

"Where's Old Fizz-Up?" he asked. "Or Petra?"

"They're not back yet," Antonia said, switching on the kettle. "Would you like some coffee? Or tea? Oh, what are we going to do?"

Her mascara and eye-shadow had smudged around her large blue eyes.

Roger said without preamble that postponing the wedding was out of the question because the deposit on the honeymoon was paid and it was un-refundable.

"Oh!"

Their honeymoon destination was a secret, but Roger had told her to pack her bikini and have a malaria jab. This was so romantic.

"We can't make everyone sit on a bus for ages to get to the reception!" she gazed at him, a little colour flooding into her cheeks. "Please can't you do something?"

At this point Roger discovered that he was finding Antonia's damp appearance unexpectedly seductive and what he wanted to do was take her into the bedroom now, before Lizzie and Petra turned up. He switched off the kettle and led the way.

Previously each of them had considered that their lovemaking, which still only occurred in Roger's house in Fulham, was quite satisfactory but now they were both taken considerably by surprise at the results of their heightened emotions. Roger unhooked Antonia's bra one handed with a fluid flick of his thumb, which he had never managed to do before.

He recalled fleetingly that he had once gone to a rather good party in a double decker bus and this positive thought was further brightened by seeing close beneath him Antonia's smudgy eyes and parted lips and her absolutely perfect breasts.

The conclusion was swift and satisfactory.

Later on, lying spread-eagled on the Laura Ashley quilted bed throw and recalling the bus, Roger said, "Maybe we should just let your father go ahead and sort everything out."

"Oh – " Antonia's voice filled with renewed consternation.

He rolled back on top of her and explained that when she was his wife she would learn that being an accountant meant that he had to know what he was on about. "And I've got a pretty good record for being right."

Luckily this made her feel secure and desirable. She gazed joyfully up at him and everything started all over again.

When Lizzie and Petra returned to the flat within a couple of minutes of each other they saw Roger's briefcase on the kitchen table and hearing sounds coming from Antonia's bedroom Petra suggested, "Bonk-a-thon?"

They pulled faces at each other but Lizzie wasn't actually

amused. Finding your stuffy, boring older brother acting out of character and screwing in your flat at 5.30 in the afternoon was distasteful enough, but having him screw silly, puddingy Antonia was vile.

The upshot of this was that Lizzie accused Petra of leaving an opened packet of fresh ravioli to grow fur in the back of the fridge and they each retreated to their own room in a sulk.

Later that evening however they rejoined forces to tell Antonia that sex in the flat in the day-time unless by prior agreement was against the house rules, which embarrassed her dreadfully.

CHAPTER 31

JULY

A couple of days after Clive had agreed with Sally that it would be possible to hold the wedding reception at Trevean he was kept late at work making phone calls about a trade show in Helsinki.

Now The Glebe was awash with evening sunlight as he drove up the road and turned in at The Rowans. He felt a sense of satisfaction for the area had a clean, orderly, civilised feel to it and he had done well to succeed in bringing his family to live here. Their occasional dissatisfactions didn't alter that basic fact and after all they were each of them female which as ever explained most things. His expression clouded as he recalled Imo denouncing The Glebe as suicide makingly boring but he suppressed the thought for not only was she female, she was also a teenager.

He found Marilyn in the kitchen examining a boxed set of

diet recipes. She looked up, pleased to see him, it was always a relief to her when he was home and now she wished to defer a decision.

"Would you like spinach and pear salad?" she asked.

"Would I . . . ?" Clive walked across to the open French doors and gazed out onto the pooled warmth on the patio. He noticed that the water feature pump needed un-jamming again, the acid green duck weed registered sub-surface hiccoughs.

"Like spinach and pear salad for supper?" Marilyn repeated hopefully.

Obviously the answer was no, no-one would want to eat spinach with pears for surely this was a very peculiar combination, but Clive didn't really mind because for lunch he had had steak pie and chips in the canteen at work.

"OK," he said, flipping through the sheaf of the day's post which he had picked up in the hall; most of it he pushed into the re-cycling bin.

Marilyn glanced at him gratefully. "Really? It's one of the recipes Antonia sent."

"Fine," Clive said. He went up to the bedroom to change out of his suit. He had had a phone call from Antonia earlier in the day but he decided to wait to tell Marilyn about this.

"It's got walnuts in it too," Marilyn said when he returned to the kitchen.

"Are you sure?" he said, pretending incredulity.

Her face fell. "Yes, it says so in the recipe."

"That's all right then," Clive said, withdrawing hastily from flippancy.

The salad was indeed odd, but he ate it and then Marilyn brought low-fat fruit yoghurts from the fridge and Clive decided it was safe to tell her about what Antonia had said on the phone.

"She wants to come home for the weekend and for us all to go down to Trevean to check the place out. Roger may come too, apparently.

"Oh – " Marilyn found her satisfaction that the supper had been achieved without Clive complaining about The Diet now dimmed.

"And," Clive said, "she's sent her latest list of instructions."

He had in fact said to Antonia, "Don't ring up your mother about all of this. Send me a list of what needs to be done and I'll sort things out."

He fetched his briefcase, retrieved her printed email and read it out:

Hi Dad and Mum,

We MUST go and see this Trevean venue. How can we have our reception there when we haven't even seen it. Roger says so too. Can we go on Saturday.

It's miles away. Can we have champagne and canapés on the coach. And can we have Directors' Lunches do the catering we can get a special rate because I work here. I've already asked but we need to book now.

Also Mum, have you checked with the church flower people that they'll only use white and pink flowers. I wish they'd let us do all the flowers in the church because what happens if they use yellow or something and then they'll clash.

And does Sarah know who to contact at the church because she needs to know about the water and vases and things. Can you ring her. It's Sarah's Flowerbasket and the number is in the book.

Also, what about candles on the tables in the marquee? Will Mrs Lacock organise it? And flowers in the marquee – have you told her pink and white only. And who's going to arrange them?

I'm sorry but I'm really REALLY upset about all this. Everything's gone wrong!!!!

It was all going to be perfect and now it won't be.

Antonia xxx

"Does it all make sense?" Clive laid the print-out on the table.

"I don't know," Marilyn said with a catch in her throat. "I hate it that she's so unhappy."

"Who's this Sarah?"

"She's doing the bouquets and some of the church flowers, she was at school with Antonia, I think she was in the netball team . . . or maybe it was hockey?"

Clive determined to keep to present practicalities. A consideration of Antonia's schooldays and current unhappiness would only make Marilyn more upset and take them no further forward. "But I do think the Directors' Lunches is a good idea. I was going to ask Mrs Lacock to get some catering quotes but if Antonia's firm can do it that will save us a lot of trouble."

"She wants us to go down to Trevean this Saturday," Marilyn said, picking up the email.

"Yes, she does. I suppose we ought to go along with that. She's right, we do need to look it over."

He stood up. "I'll phone Mrs Lacock. She seems to be the one who runs the place, I don't know about her husband." As he dialled the Trevean number he said, "What about these flowers in the marquee Antonia's on about?"

"The hotel was going to organise all the reception flowers!" Marilyn voice rose to a familiar anxious pitch. "Oh, it's all so difficult! I don't know what to do!"

At Trevean it happened that Claud was passing through the back hall. He was always polite on the phone, but he could come across as vague as he didn't like to give the caller a negative response.

"Can I speak to Mrs Lacock?" Clive said.

Claud considered. Mum was Mrs Lacock, she lived here, so yes, this was possible. "Yes," he said.

There was a pause while each of them waited for the other to say something more.

"Hello?" Clive said eventually.

Claud was pleased that the caller had renewed contact. "Hello!"

"Can I speak to Mrs Lacock," Clive repeated. He wished that parents wouldn't let their children answer the phone.

"Yes."

"Well – is she there?"

"I don't know," Claud answered truthfully.

Clive suppressed exasperation. He said, "Can you get her? Tell her it's Mr Bradford about the wedding."

Claud yelled, "Mum!"

Clive grimaced and held the phone away from his ear. Now he'll probably cut me off, he thought.

"Mum!"

They both waited.

"She might be in the kitchen," Claud suggested kindly.

"Can you go and find out?"

There was a slight thud as Claud abandoned the receiver by the stuffed herring gull in its glass case and ran off through the hall.

Clive stared out through the open doors into the garden where shadows were beginning to gather. The grass on the slope towards the apple tree was parched. Could he dare risk the sprinkler? It was the same every summer, banned just when you needed it; what did you pay ridiculously high water rates for? He said to Marilyn, "I should shut the door or moths will get in." She hated moths, fluttering soft winged round the lights.

"Hello?" Sally's voice came on the phone.

"Ah!" Clive sounded as he felt, relieved. "Whoever I was speaking to said he didn't know if you were there."

"Claud," Sally said. "He found me, he's very efficient on the whole."

"How old is he?"

"Nine."

"Well – " Clive explained that they would like to come down on Saturday to discuss details of the reception arrangements. "Will that be all right?"

Sally thought, this wedding is going to be such a hassle. James will hate it; we'll all hate it. Why on earth did I agree to this?

Unfortunately she knew why, and the financial imperative was still there.

She could hear Frankie upstairs, howling and clearly out of bed. Probably Claud had woken him up.

"Yes," she said, "of course. That will be fine."

Marilyn did not sleep well that night, waking finally and irrevocably at five o'clock to the early summer sun sliding beneath the curtains and the garden full of birdsong. By mid-morning when she decided to try to fulfil Antonia's instructions about the wedding flowers, she realised that she was already feeling tired again. "I'm always tired," she thought and tried to remember what vitamin supplement might help, zinc?

First she phoned the competent sounding Mrs Gaston, leader of the Church Flowers group.

Mrs Gaston said that she would just check in her book and then that, yes, her team already had the details for the Bradford wedding. "Although of course our ladies like to provide their own flowers. But we do try to meet any special requests, within reason, but it does depend rather on what we can get hold of."

"I think," Marilyn scrunched a tissue in her hand, summoning courage, "the florist my daughter has chosen would be happy to do all the flowers for the church, if . . . "

But Mrs Gaston's voice became firmer, she said she was afraid this was not possible. The Church Flower group were always responsible for the altar flowers and dear Pat Brinley provided the vase of seasonal wild flowers in the porch and currently she was doing lovely things with campions and meadowsweet.

"But your florist may do the pew ends and the window sills," she said. "Oh, and a standing display, if you wish, by the south chancel pillar as long as this does not cause a safety hazard, so it shouldn't be too spreading. You are welcome to use our containers, but could you please provide your own Oasis. Your florist will need to contact me about the pew-end holders. Who is your florist?"

Marilyn despairing realised that she could not remember Sarah's full name. "Sarah – oh I'm sorry, I'm not sure; I think I've got it written down . . . "

"Well," Mrs Gaston said briskly, "perhaps you could let her have my phone number and then I can give her all the details."

"Oh, yes – "

A pause lengthened.

"Well, goodbye, then, Mrs Er . . . " Mrs Gaston said. She waited a moment and then said, "I'm sure it will all work out very well."

Her determinedly competent tone discouraged any further

queries.

Indeed Marilyn, on putting down the phone, was sure that she must have sounded fussy and disorganised. How was it that everyone else seemed to be so able to cope? If only she knew Mrs Gaston better she could have explained how difficult everything was being, everything to do with the wedding. Mrs Gaston might have had advice, she would have been someone to talk to.

When she rang the number for Sarah's Flowerbasket there was an answerphone message saying Sarah was not available at present but would love to hear from her, so she left the details, as best she could, about the pew-end holders and the Oasis.

Later she drove through the Friday evening traffic to pick up Antonia at the station. On the way home Antonia told her that Roger was arriving at nine o'clock the following morning to come with them to Trevean.

"Oh – " Marilyn tried not to convey her dismay for she had hoped he wouldn't come.

"Of course he's coming!" Antonia cried defensively. "Of course he wants to see the reception venue!"

"Yes," Marilyn said, distracted as she waited for a break in the line of on-coming cars so that she could turn into The Rowans. "Oh, why is this road always so busy?

"Mum, are you indicating the right way?"

"Oh – "

Clive arrived back soon after them determined to keep things positive and with beside him on the passenger seat a bunch of tight furled orange rose buds which he had bought in the convenience shop at the garage. He liked to choose bright, cheerful flowers with, hopefully, some lasting power. Unfortunately they also tended not to open.

Coming into the kitchen he presented the flowers to Marilyn and greeted Antonia, "So – not long now till we get rid of you!"

Antonia gazed at him and burst into tears.

"Joking!" he protested but she had disappeared upstairs.

Marilyn found a vase for the roses, they had no scent whatsoever. "They're lovely," she said sniffing at them sadly.

"What's up with Antonia?"

"I think she's just stressed about the wedding."

Clive managed not to sigh or suggest, "Aren't we all?"

Unfortunately this exchange seemed to set the emotional tone for the evening which later found the three of them seeking solace in different rooms; Marilyn watched TV in the lounge, Clive checked business emails on his computer and Antonia spent some time scrubbing her skin with apricot kernel exfoliate in the bathroom. Nobody slept particularly well that night and sadly when the next day dawned they were still feeling pretty much the same, that is, on edge to varying degrees.

Roger Rodmaine arrived slightly later than he had intended in the Porsche and blocked Clive's Jag in The Rowans' driveway. He too was feeling out of sorts because he would have preferred not to have to drive down the motor-way and half-way across south-west England on a Saturday morning. He could have been having a lie-in and maybe later a game of tennis or, had Antonia stayed in London, sex. Also, he hadn't had any breakfast.

He rang the musical door bell which, he remembered, had produced disapproval from his mother on his parents' only visit to The Rowans, for Sunday lunch. This had actually turned out to be a barbeque. "Had we known," Penelope had said, seating herself on one of the slatted garden chairs on the patio, "we could have worn something more suitable for being outside."

Clive, who hadn't noticed what they were wearing and was

turning chicken thighs on the grill, said, "Don't worry, you're fine!"

"The whole thing," Penelope said discussing it later with Lizzie on the phone, "was most peculiar."

"Daddie's sauce I hope," Lizzie said.

Clive now opened the door, seeing the Porsche. "Good to see you," he said, "but you'll have to move that car if you're driving with us."

Roger hadn't considered the logistics of the trip to Trevean but he knew that he didn't, if he could avoid it, want to travel with Antonia's parents. For one thing the discussion of the wedding details would be unavoidable and likely to be tedious.

"I was thinking of taking my car," he said scrabbling for an excuse; perhaps a need to visit old friends or an Ikea branch on the return trip? But this proved unnecessary.

"Fine," Clive said without comment, retreating into the house. "Anyway, come on in."

In the kitchen Marilyn and Antonia were still eating cereal.

"As you see," Clive said, "we're ready to leave. Would you like some breakfast?"

Roger eyed the cereal bowls and regretted the fry-up he might have had if he had stopped, as he had considered doing, on the motorway.

Antonia, her face brightening, slid down from her stool; she came to stand beside him, taking his hand and whispering, "I'm so glad you're here."

He wished she wouldn't do this. Such displays of affection were really quite difficult to cope with in front of other people and certainly in front of her parents; his arm stiffened instinctively and while trying not to make this too obvious, he sought to disentangle his fingers from hers. Sitting carefully on one of the bar stools he unenthusiastically accepted slimmers' muesli with tropical fruit bits which he extracted and ringed around the bowl, and black coffee.

The next twenty minutes were spent in familiar preamble to family travel: exhortations to get a move on from Clive, questions about whether Roger knew where to go from Marilyn and Antonia, concerns about how far it was exactly and what they would need to check on when they got there. And what should they do about lunch?

When finally they left Antonia travelled with Roger but neither the occupants of the Jaguar nor of the Porsche found the journey particularly enjoyable. Roger, but not Clive, chose to continue by the motorway route.

Antonia realised that in the flurry of departure she had forgotten to bring the directions to Trevean which didn't please Roger and necessitated stopping to ask, twice, once they got into Cornwall.

The longer she and Clive drove the more Marilyn got wound up, worrying about how Antonia, Roger and probably George and Penelope Rodmaine might complain about the length of time it would take the wedding guests to reach Trevean by coach.

Clive, determined to forestall an irritating conversation along these lines, switched to the cricket on the radio and strove to give the impression that his attention was fully engaged.

On arrival at Trevean the potholes in the drive and the tunnel of rampant rhododendrons were not encouraging. Someone, Clive thought, needed to have a go here with a chainsaw and a few lorry loads of bitmac.

But the house itself did not disappoint them. In the late morning sun its pleasing human scale, the mullioned windows, the slightly yellowish local stone, the small hand-cut slates on the roof, the wisteria and the very way the house appeared settled into its surroundings, belonging to its site, soothed and lifted their spirits. There is surely a magic which very old buildings, long occupied, can acquire and which in Trevean's case had saved its bacon more than once. Sally had on occasion thought that, without this quality, it might have suffered any of numerous calamities down the years, being torched by Cromwell's Parliamentary forces perhaps, or more recently being rejected by James and herself to who knows what fate, to be horribly over-renovated perhaps by someone with a lot of money. Although to be fair to people with a lot of money they would at least have been able to get the structural problems, like the roof leaks, properly sorted out.

So the Bradfords' first impressions were generally positive, although Marilyn felt her fear of meeting the Lacocks heightening, for what should she say to people who lived in this sort of house?

As Clive parked under the yew trees on the edge of the lawn they heard the Porsche approaching up the drive. Roger, on rounding the giant rhododendron, was not amused to see that he had been beaten to it by his prospective in-laws.

Earlier that morning, when Sally had stood on the front steps, she had noticed the proliferation of dandelions and chickweed around her feet. She had therefore, bearing in mind the Bradfords' visit, set Ned and Nicolette to weeding the front gravel. "Imo's sister may be having her wedding reception here," she said, "and her parents are coming to have a look."

She instructed Graham to mow the lawn. This meant using the erratic petrol mowing machine and was a laborious business since much of the grass had grown to hay length.

Nicolette was intrigued by the information about the reception and by the suspicion that Imo had been trying to keep this from her. Here was an opportunity to do a bit of stirring and so alleviate some of the daily dose of boredom.

It had begun to occur to her that if it were not for this Ned thing she probably wouldn't be staying at Trevean: there was considerably more digging involved than she had anticipated. Also sharing the bedroom and bathroom was unsatisfactory; no-one ever seemed to clean up, provide dry towels or clear the kids' toys out of the bath.

"Well – get the Porsche!" she now said to Ned. "The Imo family, I guess?"

She wiped the back of her hand across her forehead. "Sweaty work, weeding. What do you think, shall I go and find out?"

Ned, who had felt a twinge of annoyance at Nicolette's drawing attention to the Porsche, didn't respond and stared deliberately at Antonia as she emerged from the passenger seat.

The Bradfords and Roger stood a little uncertainly looking about them with their attention fixing, as she approached, upon Nicolette.

"We're here to see Mr and Mrs Lacock," Clive explained when she reached them. "About the wedding reception?"

Nicolette smiled. "I'll try and find somebody." With no indication of urgency, and so allowing their appreciation of her shorts-clad bottom and sun-tanned legs, she strolled away.

Antonia, who identified a deliberately provocative version of Lizzie and Petra, felt discomfited. She reached her hand for Roger's but he ignored it.

Nicolette found Sally in the kitchen; she was peeling potatoes and mopping down Frankie who had been engaged in making mud porridge in the water tank against the Laundry House wall.

"Bother, I hoped they wouldn't be here just yet," Sally said. "OK Frankie, you'll do. No more mud. Where's Claud? Can you go and play with him please."

"Don't want to." Frankie frowned ferociously.

Sally dried her hands and left the kitchen; Frankie, feeling that he had been made to lose face in front of Nicolette, stamped crossly after her.

Nicolette thoughtfully paused to drink a mug of cold water.

"Good morning!" Sally called, coming out onto the gravel and noticing in passing that Ned also was no longer weeding. "I'm Sally Lacock," she said. "How do you do?"

The Bradfords gazed at her. She was wearing a crumpled and, because of the scrubbing of Frankie, a rather mud splattered denim skirt and a washed-out blue T-shirt.

Sally thought they expected someone grander as many people did. This was, she had found, one of the minor burdens of living somewhere like Trevean.

"What here for?" Frankie asked, peering from behind her.

Sally, from experience, knew it was best to ignore him.

"And did you," she asked, grasping Frankie by the arm, "have a reasonable journey?"

"Yes, fine, straight through." Clive remained determined to avoid any adverse comments about time taken.

Roger felt another flicker of annoyance; fine no doubt if you had had the right directions including a postcode, without which the Porsche's sophisticated sat-nav couldn't be expected to function.

"Well," Sally glanced across the lawn to where in the distance and with difficulty, Graham was turning the ancient mower, "we've got things in hand here, as you see."

The Bradfords looked unsure, but then they had not seen the

state of the lawn before Graham started to cut it.

"Is that," Clive asked, "where the marquee would be?"

"Yes," Sally said, "we thought so."

They all walked onto the grass.

"And the tent for the caterers," Sally said. "The toilets can go over there, behind the rhododendrons."

Roger frowned slightly, "Really?"

"Yes," Sally said firmly. "Really. Porta-loos."

If they think we are letting their one hundred and twenty guests use the loos in the house they've got another think coming, she thought, James would have a fit. And there was no way the drains would cope.

Antonia searched in her bag. "What about," she said, flipping pages in her notebook which had 'Your Wedding' embossed in silver on the cover, "the cocktail bar?"

"The local pub could run that, if you like. The publican – " Sally wondered if this would add credence in some way to the suggestion " – was in the navy."

"And the flowers for the tables?" Antonia said anxiously. "They need to be pink and white."

"Yes." Sally nodded. Something else to get sorted.

"Come and have some coffee," she said. The wife was looking fraught poor woman as well she might in the company of the organising husband and fussing daughter and the snooty fiancé.

They followed her towards the house.

None of us is quite what the others were expecting, Sally thought. She was not what the Bradfords had imagined but they were not what she had guessed either, less arty certainly. Perhaps the way they were had something to do with Imo's lack of joyousness, but Sally still believed the main cause of this to be Ned.

Ned himself reappeared with Nicolette who had decided it would be amusing to get another look at Imo's family.

"Two of our Garden Volunteers," Sally introduced them.

Ned chose to smile, mostly at Antonia; Nicolette's eyes flicked.

Marilyn and Antonia both looked at Ned. Each remembered that Imo had uncharacteristically mentioned his name several times at The Rowans and they now suspected why; but he was unsettlingly glamorous and here anyway was the provocative and probably competitive Nicolette.

Marilyn at least feared that here was another cause for upset.

"And that's Graham mowing the lawn," Sally indicated into the distance. "Imo mostly works with him, we have an old walled vegetable garden which they are reclaiming from nature."

Clive almost asked what Imo actually did but he decided to wait, now perhaps was not a good time to express his surprise at the thought that she was achieving anything productive in the vegetable line.

"Anyway, come in," Sally said, guiding them into the hall.

Clarissa was coming down the stairs.

CHAPTER 32

JULY

Clarissa knew from Sally about the wedding reception and about Imo's family coming today to Trevean and she found that she badly wanted to see them and later be able to enjoy discussing the visit with Sally or even the children.

So hearing the arrival of the cars she peered down from her sitting room window. She watched Nicolette greet the Bradfords and saw Ned put down his rake and slope off round the side of the house.

Her eye was drawn to Antonia, could this be Imo's sister? How unlike her in looks and dress, if she was. Clarissa was also surprised by the parents: 'tidy and suburban' she thought rather summed them up; how had they produced Imo, all messy hair and grubby trousers and emotion?

And the young man with the sports car was presumably the sister's fiancé.

She looked down at Roger who she decided was not terribly exciting to look at but probably a few rungs up a well-paid professional ladder. So money would be marrying beauty, which was not unusual after all. On an impulse Clarissa took her stick and set off along the top corridor and down the front stairs to meet up with Sally guiding the Bradfords through the hall.

"Oh, hello Mother," Sally said, trying to avoid sounding negative. She introduced her, "My mother, who lives with us."

"Well," Clarissa said, "I hear you've come to arrange a wedding reception. Didn't you have a problem with your arrangements somewhere else?"

Sally said quickly, "I explained, Mother. A fire at the hotel."

"They've had to close for a while," Clive said. "And we were having the wedding reception there."

Clarissa said. "And so what do you think of Trevean?"

Marilyn had been gazing round the hall and now as her glance rested upon the stuffed pike in its glass case, she found Clarissa's question apparently directed to her.

She said weakly, "Oh . . . it's very nice." She felt that everyone found this reply inadequate.

"How old is this house?" Clive asked into the following pause.

"Well," Sally said, gathering her thoughts, "bits of it, possibly, eleventh century. Mostly later though, and some rather unfortunate Victorian plumbing."

At this point Frankie and Claud rushed through the front door, explaining that they had been helping Graham to cut the grass. They had a lot of green stuff in their hair.

"And have you been rolling in it?" Clarissa asked, proprietorial. I am their grandmother she thought, I belong here.

"No," Claud said factually. "We emptied the grass onto the pile. To help Graham."

"And we jumped on it!" yelled Frankie.

"And now we're hot," Claud tried to clarify, "so we've come in to get some water."

"Don't shout," Sally said. She had realised that the probable state of the drawing room made it unsuitable for the discussion the Bradfords wanted about their wedding reception. Too much dog hair, too many newspapers; torn chair covers.

But the kitchen perhaps needed some explanation as an alternative choice. "There's a large table," Sally said, "where we can all sit and plan. And – " she cast around for another good reason, "I can show you the Norman arch."

Claud and Frankie raced ahead.

When they reached the kitchen, Sally thought that really it wasn't that much better in here. She pointed out the possibly Norman stonework and moved a cardboard box of muddy veg, Ned's cereal bowl, various bits of junk mail and an empty jar of strawberry jam from the table.

The Bradfords stood doubtfully in front of the low granite archway leading to the larder.

Clarissa moved towards the fridge.

"She is trying to help," Sally told herself, gritting her teeth, as Clarissa nearly dropped the milk. "Let me take it Mother, it's heavy."

"I can manage," Clarissa said, making it across to the table.

"They weren't tall in those days, were they?" said Clive, still looking at the arch.

"I believe that is an established fact," Roger said. He had said nothing else so far, his eyes resting on the piled plates beside the sink, the children's clothes overflowing a couple of washing baskets and the medley of dog bowls on the floor.

"Do find somewhere to sit," Sally said, pulling out a couple of chairs. "The round backed ones are more reliable."

"So the marquee isn't going to present a problem?" Clive asked as they found seats. He had a copy of the details which he had forwarded to Sally and he now spread this out on the table. It was necessary to get on with sorting things.

"I don't think so," Sally said making coffee.

She was aware that news of a wedding reception had got out into the village and was causing quite a stir of interest, for Trevean was still after all the big house of the neighbourhood. Local feeling was that the Scouts' mess tent would suit for a wedding and the hire fee would help funds. It had been good enough for the vicar's daughter when she got married.

Sally herself tended to agree but she was fairly certain that the scouts' tent wouldn't meet the Bradfords' wedding ideas. Therefore going further afield, into the local town, she had found a marquee company which miraculously could cope with the booking, could provide tables, chairs, dance floor, DJ stage, flounced tent lining and poles which could no doubt be wound with ivy, as per Antonia's specified requirements.

"And the tables and chairs," Antonia asked uncertainly "will they be . . . ?" The reality of Trevean was unnerving her. She glanced at Roger, anxious for his approval but his expression was non-committal.

"I've got a brochure, I'll just go and fetch it." Sally went quickly to find in the study the cardboard envelope file which she had appropriated for the wedding details.

James was sitting, as she knew he would be, tense shouldered in his wing back chair. He was trying to contain the knowledge that the house had been invaded by strangers.

"The Bradfords are here," she said, going along with the idea that he hadn't heard all the commotion earlier in the hall.

"About the wedding reception arrangements."

James said, "Oh God."

"Oh, they're not too bad." Sally began to turn over the papers, books, string, empty envelopes and dog combs piled on the circular mahogany table. "I'm looking for the wedding file."

Why, she thought, can't we have empty surfaces? We never manage it.

"What wedding file?" James asked.

"It's green," Sally said. "This one."

"That's not the dogs' file is it?"

"No," Sally said; she showed him 'Wedding' written in black board-marker on the cover.

James shook out pages of the newspaper he was holding. "Well, this doesn't need to concern me, does it?"

"Not if you don't want it to," Sally said. "But why don't you come and meet them?"

James felt that he had no desire whatsoever to meet the Bradfords.

"Please?" Sally said. "I think it would be a good idea."

She wished always for people to perceive James in an appropriate light, playing what should be his natural role as decision maker and master of the house. Not, anyway, as procrastinator and avoider of contact with outsiders.

"Just for five minutes?" she suggested. "You needn't stay."

James supported Sally in her decisions always no matter what, that was understood between them, but the cost sometimes as now weighed heavy.

"Oh, all right," he said, heavily and Sally appreciated the worth of this gesture.

"I'd better get back," she said. "Heaven knows what Mother is saying to them."

"Oh God," James said, "is she there too?" But Sally had gone.

Clarissa was enjoying talking to the Bradfords. She had discovered fairly quickly that Clive ran his own business, something to do with plastic; that Roger was in finance in London, that Antonia worked for a catering company and that Marilyn didn't have a job and didn't play bridge. Some of this of course she had already gleaned from questioning Imo, but she liked adding the extra details.

"I thought everyone played bridge," she said to Marilyn. "What do you find to do with yourself in the afternoon?"

She disowned the knowledge that Sally didn't play bridge, on the grounds that she did not have the time, James' fault of course, and that she herself had not been able to play since she had come to Trevean.

Marilyn gazed at her. She couldn't think of anything she did that this formidable old woman might find acceptable.

"Sally and James got married in India," Clarissa again took up the reigns of the conversation, for really Imo's mother had so little to say for herself. "Sally had a beautiful wedding dress, it was made of sari silk."

She hadn't actually seen Sally wearing this dress of course, only in a photograph, for she had not been told about the wedding until they came back to England on honeymoon. She suspected that this was because Sally thought she would be horrified, which indeed she was.

"With silver embroidery," she said firmly, looking at Antonia.

"I did think of embroidery," Antonia said, realising a response was expected of her. "But – " she couldn't think quite what else to say.

"You need to be able to carry it off," Clarissa said. "A wedding is great fun. I haven't been to one for a long time."

Antonia, now feeling constrained to offer some invitation, looked for help to her parents. "Maybe you would like to join us for – the evening party?"

They couldn't ask all the Lacocks to the Reception proper, it would upset the numbers hopelessly.

"Of course," Clive said.

Marilyn nodded, anxious to be seen to agree.

"Thank you," Clarissa said. "I don't go out much in the evening, but I'll see."

There was a further uncertain pause during which Frankie, who in a far corner had been loading plastic farm animals into the trailer of a toy tractor, could be heard encouraging the pigs and sheep to fit into the space available. They continued to fall out but he was being patient with them. Claud had wandered away.

Sally arrived back with James. He continued to maintain sufficient distance to indicate his reluctance to be involved in this meeting and on seeing Clarissa seated at the table this resolve strengthened. Stirring up trouble as usual, he thought, the old bat was in her element.

Sally said, "My husband, James", and briefly introduced the Bradfords. Holding up the wedding file she said, "I've found it, all the marquee details."

James sank into his chair at the head of the table, his almost palpable reluctance causing Clarissa to consider that as usual he wasn't making a proper effort.

Sally opened the marquee company brochure on the table. They examined the proportions of marquee, table shapes and chairs.

"There seems to be a choice, white chairs or gold," Sally said.

"Oh – " Antonia peered at the illustrations. The gold chairs had a touch of rococco flourish.

"What do you think?" she deferred to Roger.

Roger felt that he shouldn't be asked this question. Girls should know about this sort of thing, Lizzie would know.

He was uncertain about the whole set-up at Trevean and this made him cautious. The house was OK but certainly run down; the Lacocks sounded all right but were very possibly skint. The place was certainly a mess, he visualised his mother's likely reaction. He frowned slightly and didn't answer Antonia's question about chairs.

"Will they do?" Clive suggested looking at the white chairs and wanting to get a decision made; they were of a plain frame-stacking design which he quite liked.

Antonia preferred the gold. Marilyn, when Clive asked her, also chose gold in order to agree with Antonia.

Clive thought and said, go with whichever they liked; it certainly wasn't worth an argument, chairs were chairs. Roger did not express an opinion. They went for the gold.

Clarissa pursed her lips, had she been asked she would not have chosen the gold chairs, they looked flashy, but then the white ones might be made of plastic.

Frankie, hoping to gain some attention, pushed his tractor forward so that the grown-ups could become involved in his game, but no-one noticed. The discussion was moving on to table dimensions.

Antonia said anxiously, "I have to know exactly how big the tables are."

Everyone paused and looked at her. Her cheeks flushing a light peony pink she tried to explain, "I've got to tell my boss at work because they're going to do the catering. The table cloths must reach to the ground. And they will be round, the tables, won't they?"

More consultations of the brochure followed. Frankie's boredom levels rose, he brought the tractor and the animals under the kitchen table and began to negotiate them with appropriate sounds around people's feet. He was especially attracted by Antonia's painted toe nails in her white sandals and arranged the sheep in an admiring semi-circle around them, moving one forward to gently nudge a toe.

"Oh!" Antonia exclaimed. "There's something under here!"

"Have the dogs got out?" Sally asked James. He might have left the study door open, he rather enjoyed the mayhem they caused, barking and licking. Animals were always preferable to visitors.

"No" James said gloomily, "not unless someone let them out." He sent a laden glance towards Clarissa.

Sally didn't react to his joke, it was nonsense of course for Clarissa had met them in the hall while James and the dogs were in the study and anyway she wouldn't have done anything with the dogs. They and golf were James' concerns and as such she chose to ignore them.

"Come out, Frankie," Sally said, peering under the table.

Frankie frowned.

"Well, if you're going to stay there you must be good. Don't annoy people."

Frankie frowned more seriously.

"I think he's taken a fancy to you," Sally, straightening up, said to Antonia. "He rather likes girls with blonde hair."

"Oh – " Antonia was startled.

The Bradfords and Roger then made attempts to see Frankie, he scuttled away from them crab-like.

"Have you got a den down there?" Clive asked but Frankie

chose not to respond.

The interruption caused the discussion to splinter into separate conversations. Antonia wanted to ask Sally about flowers on the tables and, inspired by an illustration in the brochure, twining ivy round the tent poles. "And maybe . . . it says here . . . honeysuckle? Scented . . . like a sort of woodland glade?"

"Ivy is probably all right," Sally said, avoiding looking at James. She thought there's masses of the stuff in the wood, I can send Graham and Ned out for it. "I'm not sure about honeysuckle." Weren't wild flowers protected in some way from the depredations of trend-setting florists and wedding designers? She realised that Clive was now asking James about the power supply for the disco and the lighting.

"Good grief, don't ask me," James said.

"At Columb Court of course they had the necessary power supply, but sometimes these guys can bring their own generator," Clive suggested.

James gazed ahead of him. "Sounds a good idea then," he said, washing his hands of the matter.

Sally turned from the tent pole discussion to say that she would phone the DJ and find out what was needed. She tore the lid off a cereal packet and on the inside of the card wrote 'Elec' and 'Ivy'.

Clarissa had taken the opportunity to appropriate Roger. She liked to talk to men, other than James, and she rarely got the chance.

"And where will you live when you are married?" she asked.

Roger, who was well used to being cross-questioned by women, specifically by his mother and sister, explained that he owned a house in Fulham.

"Fulham?" Clarissa said. "Do you find that a pleasant part of London?"

Roger shifted cautiously on his seat. He had told himself that he would maintain a low profile during these negotiations, that he was only here to support Antonia and, a less congenial idea, to head off decisions which would upset Penelope, but he realised that he was cornered.

He agreed therefore that yes, Fulham was a good area in which to live.

"And what about property values?" Clarissa persisted.

"Oh, well, yes, still moving – "

"Upwards?"

"Oh, yes, upwards."

"How clever of you," Clarissa said.

Roger had managed to buy the house with the pay-out from a trust fund set up by his grandparents and a hefty tax avoidance package from his firm, which pretty much anchored him to them for life. Obviously, he chose not to discuss this with Clarissa.

The main lines of conversation were coming to a close for the Bradford party was individually beginning to think about lunch and so clearly were Perdita and Claud who had turned up to hover, shifting their feet, around the table.

"Well, that seems to cover most things," Clive said. It would hopefully work out all right he thought, although James Lacock's attitude had seemed odd. Did he always leave all the decisions to his wife?

Time to go.

Marilyn had hardly spoken.

"Would you like to see Imo?" Sally suggested, suddenly realising she should have thought of this before. "She can show you where she's working."

After just a brief hesitation the Bradfords felt that of course they should, and Sally sent Claud up to the kitchen garden with this message.

Imo, disliking intensely having the Lacocks meet her family, came unwillingly. She stood sulky and monosyllabic in the kitchen, emitting such bad humour that Marilyn did not dare express horror at the mud-caked state of her clothes and trainers.

After a few minutes of awkward exchanges about what vegetables were currently growing and since Imo gave no indication that she would like to show these to anyone Clive looked at his watch and felt that he was hungry and Marilyn was looking tired. He said they'd better be on their way and they could perhaps see the garden another time.

Sally orchestrated goodbyes; James, every fibre of his body expressing relief, swiftly removed himself to the study. Clarissa hoping to indicate her disapproval of this behaviour, followed the party to the hall and made a point of wishing them a safe journey home.

The two cars departed down the drive. In the Jag Clive said firmly, "Well, I think that went quite well."

He turned the radio on to the cricket to pre-empt any risk of further discussion of the Trevean arrangements for Marilyn would only end up getting herself fussed. He had had enough of wedding details for now and he wanted to get to the pub which Sally had suggested for lunch.

Unfortunately in the Porsche Roger did not do the same. He expressed the opinion that the Trevean set-up was a bit peculiar.

Antonia turned to gaze at him, her eyes wide with anxiety. "Oh . . . "

"It all looked a bit run down," Roger said.

Despair overwhelmed Antonia: he didn't like it. "Oh, do you think so?"

"That lawn was like a hay field."

Antonia's eyes blurred with tears. Roger's parents wouldn't approve, Lizzie and Petra would be horrible. "Oh . . . I can't bear it!"

Roger glanced at her; he felt exasperated, why did she always have to get so emotional about everything?

"What's the matter?"

"I so wanted," Antonia searched her bag hopelessly for a tissue, "I so, so wanted everything to be perfect!"

Roger felt he had heard this before. He also realised that he was feeling hungry, but if they stopped for some lunch this would surely provide the opportunity for a further prolonged, irritating discussion about tablecloths and honeysuckle.

He drove on, the insidious thought returning to him, as it had once or twice lately that maybe he was making a mistake. Should he actually be getting married at all?

CHAPTER 33

JULY

As darkness and moonlight came over Trevean the night following the Bradfords' visit Perdita, Claud and Frankie slept soundly, their hair full of salt and their limbs stained green from cut grass. Few other members of the household slept as easily.

Clarissa lay awake, propped against her pillows. She tried to find a position which lessened the pain she felt in arthritic joints, from which she was now never entirely free.

She smoothed the creased top of her sheet; she couldn't do the ironing, not anyway the bigger things and Sally certainly did not have time. The house needed staff, I've said it before she thought and it's true.

She regretted the linen cupboard she used to keep, Egyptian cotton sheets and pillow cases folded in piles on separate shelves, white wool blankets bound in satin, quilted eiderdowns. The family now used a collection of sheets and blankets which had been in the house in James's aunt's day and which had suffered a lot of wear since, the children had duvets with rather hideous covers.

Sally slept as she usually slept on first closing her eyes, fallen deep into a pit of physical exhaustion. She lay close to James to bring him security. Sometimes he would stir, surfacing to face uncertain fears; both of them were used to this, Sally trying to wake herself sufficiently to murmur something reassuring. She hoped always to return to sleep but sometimes she lay awake doing financial calculations in her head.

Imo crouched on the back stairs staring out through the window into the darkness towards the Laundry House until eventually she got stiffly to her feet and went to the attic room where she lay on her bed and cried.

In the Laundry House Graham listened to Ned and Nicolette's voices and the intermittent episodes of thudding on the bed in the next room, from which he was separated only by a thin lath and plaster partition. He failed to block the sounds out. "Bugger it," he said in the end and getting up pulled on his jeans and gathering the blanket from the bed went out.

Some while later, when the moon had long set, Nicolette returned to the main house across the cobbled yard.

Imo, waking groggily, saw her silhouetted in the dawn light from the open attic window and watched her cross to sit on the bed by the far wall.

Nicolette yawned, pulled her green cotton dress over her head, slid under the duvet and apparently immediately slept.

Imo turned away to stare at the brightening sky above her head; she listened to the first tentative notes of bird song which soon increased to fill the gardens and woods around with an orchestrated chorus. She was rigid with misery.

She knew that she would not sleep again. She went down the stairs to wash and get dressed in the nursery bathroom. Her reflection in the mirror looked wan, her eyelids were pale and puffy; she splashed her face with cold water, avoiding the scummy tide line in the basin and the squashy pellet of abandoned soap.

In the kitchen the dogs looked up briefly from their baskets. As she was not James and her arrival did not signal the start of their day they stayed put.

Imo paused, she thought of making a cup of coffee but feared that this might actually set the dogs off into their normal morning cacophony of barking. Instead she went outside into the clear morning light where she found the vegetation drenched heavily with dew; the sky was a high, pale blue and wheeling far above was a buzzard. Tentatively she touched the damp cobbles with her bare feet, instinctively responding to the sweet clarity of the morning before heartache claimed her again. Ned!

But now she did not want to meet Ned, as she had always hoped to do as she went to and fro across the yard, so she went quickly past the Laundry House and up the steps to the top yard. Here to her surprise she found Graham emerging from the back seat of his car, clutching a blanket.

She stared at him blankly.

He glared in response, angry at being found like this where he might have to explain what he was doing. One of the sad things about Graham was that he habitually looked at other people as if he was angry with them when in fact he was more angry with himself.

He had not slept much in the car and he was furious now that he had let himself be driven out of his bed. He was aware of Nicolette's physical attraction and although he might attempt to deny this, telling himself that she was a stuck-up tart and he wasn't interested, this increased the level of his loathing for Ned, smug bastard.

Graham did not attempt self-analysis, but had he examined his reactions he could have concluded that what infuriated him was not that the two of them had denied him a night's sleep, or even that Ned had got to have sex with Nicolette. It was Ned's assumption that he could behave like this if he felt like it. Arrogance. Graham turned the word over in his mind, habitually giving it an initial 'h'; the recognition of his mistake made him yet more angry with himself.

Imo in fact was almost as unnerved at being discovered by Graham as he was at being found by her, and like him she did not feel up to explaining why she was in the top yard at this very early hour of the morning.

"Hi," she said weakly. Why did Graham look so furious? Tears filled her eyes again, why was everyone and everything being so horrible?

Graham saw that Imo was crying but didn't credit himself with having this effect upon her, he assumed the cause of their shared discomfort was Ned.

"I woke up early – " Imo tried to offer an acceptable explanation for her presence.

Graham nodded and then lowering his guard a bit in an attempt to indicate that he also found Ned a total waste of space, he added, "Didn't get much sleep myself."

Imo gathered a wobbly breath. "Did you sleep up here?"

Graham hesitated. "Yeah."

Immediately he regretted the admission for it invited further questioning. His face again assumed an angry distancing stare.

"Why?" Imo asked.

He could think of no plausible excuse and indeed why should he cover up for them pair of smart-arses? They'd caused him enough grief.

"Don't want to listen to that bloody racket all night, do I?"

Imo stared. "What racket?"

Exasperated because although his intention had been to avoid giving a full explanation of what Ned and Nicolette had been up to, he now found coping with further prevarication beyond him Graham said, "Them two at it."

He then felt yet angrier. Of course the likes of Ned despised him and Imo probably too, he showed himself up all the time, couldn't say things right.

Imo felt her heart lurch. "Who?"

He looked away. "That tosser," he said, "and her. The tart."

It was brutal, he knew it was brutal because he could not kid himself that he didn't know that Imo was keen on Ned but at that moment he didn't care. They were all alike, they all thought he was an idiot and without feelings so why should he show them any different?

Imo stared at him and then uttering a single "No!" she turned and ran back to the path leading down from the yard.

Graham watched her go. After a moment he muttered, "Torn it, then." He kicked a stone skittering across the ground and after a while went up into the kitchen garden and vengefully mixed up a bucket of garlic and onion insecticide. He was not about to sit through breakfast with the Lacocks all yelling at each other about the kids' stuff and Sally telling him to go and wake Ned.

Imo ran down to the house where in the kitchen the dogs, surprised by this second early morning visit, rose from their beds stretching and shaking themselves. Coal uttered an explorative bark. "Oh, be quiet!" Imo cried. "Be quiet!"

She went up the back stairs as far as the nursery landing and then remembered that she couldn't retreat up to the attic room because Nicolette was there. She stood irresolute trying to think of somewhere to take refuge, perhaps the toy-scattered bathroom or nursery but even as she listened she heard Frankie call out and Claud answer. They were awake and would soon be out of bed and running around so there was nowhere in those rooms to safely hide.

She pushed open the door leading to the top corridor.

Clarissa, wearing her old silk dressing-gown, was returning to her room from the bathroom. She was aware that she did not wish to meet James and it must now be getting towards six thirty, the time when he went downstairs to make the morning tea.

"Come here," she said imperatively when she saw Imo. "Come here."

Imo came through the door and it swung to behind her; she approached unwillingly.

"I need you to help me," Clarissa said. "Let me hold your arm."

Imo hesitated and then raised her arm awkwardly.

"No," Clarissa said, "not like that, bend it so I've got something to lean on. My hip is playing up."

Imo was surprised at how awkwardly Clarissa moved. How horrible to be all crippled up like that, surely it wasn't being properly alive?

Together they made their way up the steps to Clarissa's bedroom door. Once inside Clarissa let go of her arm and moved to sit on the bedside chair.

"It's worse some mornings than others," she said, reading

Imo's expression. "It'll happen to you one day. We all grow old in the end."

"It won't," Imo thought. "It won't ever happen to me; if it does I'll jump off a cliff."

"And there's nothing you can do about it," Clarissa said, looking for her pills.

Imo didn't want to hang around and give Clarissa the chance to register her tear- blotched appearance.

"What's the matter with you?" Clarissa asked. "Why are you crying?"

"I'm not," Imo said.

"You have been. What is it?"

Imo stared at the carpet, which was circular and old, of pink and green Chinese silk. Clarissa had had it shipped back from Hong Kong when she came home and now these many years later it was worn and badly needed cleaning.

To Imo's horror tears once again began to slide down her cheeks. "I can't – "

"Sit here," Clarissa said. "Yes, here on the bed. Tell me what the matter is."

Imo was so unhappy and so in need of consolation that she did as Clarissa instructed.

"So what is it?" Clarissa asked. She was interested and starved of human drama and naturally inclined, to an extent, to be sympathetic. Although, she thought, the sorrows of youth were transitory and the pain they caused would fade. Youth still had plenty of that cure-all, time.

Imo wept.

"Is it to do with that young man?" Clarissa asked. "Ned?"

Hearing his name Imo experienced shock; she bowed her head and nodded, drowning in grief.

"He is good-looking," Clarissa said. "Too good looking, probably. So there's always likely to be trouble."

Imo found her voice and the words escaped, not spoken before. "I love him," she said.

Clarissa thought, she will lose the capacity to feel grief like that, all those tears and emotion. One day she will feel grief only as an ache, maybe a continuous ache, but it's not the same. I think I would like to be able to cry again like that, but I can't. Not any more.

She observed Imo. If only the girl would sort her hair out.

Imo drew a shuddering gasp.

"And does he love you?" Clarissa asked, to move the conversation on.

"Yes! I don't know!" Imo cried. "I thought he did!"

"But did he say he did?"

Imo stared through her tears. "I don't know!"

"Well there you are," Clarissa said, as if this uncertainty explained quite a lot.

Imo was provoked to justify herself. "Sort of. He sort of did."

"And so what has happened?"

"I think he loves someone else now!"

Of course, Clarissa thought. Of course that is what it is. "Who?" she asked.

"Nicolette." Imo didn't want to say it. It was the first time that she had admitted this fear to anyone else; just voicing it made the reality grow stronger in her mind. She caught her breath.

"Ah, the new girl," Clarissa said and paused. "Well, I don't suppose he loves her."

"He does!" Imo pushed strands of damp hair from her face. "They were – I think they were together last night. They were. I know." She gazed at Clarissa. "I do know."

Clarissa considered. "That doesn't mean he loves her, though, does it?" she said.

Imo stared at the floor. "No . . . they were together all night. Nearly. In his room." She hated having to clarify her meaning. "I think they were in bed."

"She's very young," Clarissa thought.

Imo sniffed helplessly.

"There is a handkerchief in the top drawer over there," Clarissa said. She still preferred her small white handkerchiefs to those paper tissues.

She watched as Imo found the handkerchief and held it to her face, "Never mind, it will wash. Even if that is what happened, with Ned and Nicolette, it doesn't mean that he loves her. People do foolish things."

"No," Imo said, implacable. "Ned wouldn't do that. He isn't like that."

"How do you know?"

"He must love her!"

"Men are not always reliable," Clarissa said, "if girls make themselves available . . . "

"I hate her!" Imo cried.

"Well. The saying is, it does take two."

Clarissa paused. She suspected that Ned would not be inclined to put too much effort into seducing a girl but then he wouldn't need to, with his looks it was more a question of having the moral fibre to resist and she doubted he had that. She had always found human beauty appealing, she liked looking at Ned. But I wouldn't, she thought, trust him.

"I'm sorry," she said now to Imo. "It does hurt, but you will get over it."

"I won't!"

"Yes, you will," Clarissa said firmly. "You have all your life to live, so you will have to."

Imo was silent, she folded the handkerchief into a damp oblong and turned it over and over in her fingers. "Sometimes boys – " she suggested as Clarissa began to listen to sounds indicating that Sally and the children were up and about at the other end of the corridor, "well, men, don't care about girls, if they . . . afterwards . . . "

Clarissa looked at her. Oh dear, she thought, now she'll persuade herself into thinking he'll see the light and come back to her, but it's not going to happen. "Possibly," she said. "But that doesn't stop people doing it, just sleeping together."

"Oh!" Imo again was stricken.

"The best thing you can do is ignore them," Clarissa said. "Don't give them the satisfaction of seeing they've upset you. Nicolette is selfish and probably spoilt, but I am afraid that she is attractive to men. You can tell. So they are two of a kind; leave them to get on with it. If you want a boyfriend, you need to look for someone quite different."

Yes, Imo thought, provoked, she means boring; a boring, ugly, safe boyfriend who nobody else wants.

"I hate boring!" she said, burying her face in the handkerchief.

Ah, Clarissa thought, a spark. "I didn't say boring, I said different. Unreliable people are exhausting and really not worth wasting your time on in the long run."

"But – " Imo stared at the reality of what Clarissa was saying, which was that she had lost Ned. "I can't bear it! I'm so, so unhappy!"

This sounded pathetic, she thought, even to her.

Clarissa shifted in her chair, feeling the rise of irritation. "That is part of life," she said. "Being unhappy is part of life. You'll learn that. Now I need to get dressed because someone will be bringing up my tray soon. You can leave the handkerchief."

Imo knew that she was dismissed. She stood up and put the handkerchief on the dressing table in front of the mottled glass of the mirror, then she went to the door. "Thank you," she said, on impulse, turning to look back towards Clarissa.

Clarissa nodded. She thought I can give advice on life to a girl like this, but what about my life? I tread on eggshells all the time. I see my daughter overworked, and it upsets me, but I can't do anything to help. I'm getting old, maybe I should keep my advice to myself.

Imo went to the nursery bathroom and once again for several minutes splashed her face with cold water. Then she sat on the edge of the bath and stared at Frankie's green frog lying on the floor. Downstairs she heard the phone ring.

Later when Imo came down to the kitchen, Sally was mopping up the dogs' water bowl into which Frankie had dropped his shoe. The children were eating Weetabix at the table and James was about to retreat to his study; there was no sign of Graham, Ned or Nicolette.

Sally, looking up from wringing out a cloth into the sink, said to Imo, "That was your father on the phone."

Clive had rung on arriving at work, apologising for the early call but needing to confirm the coach parking arrangements and discuss the cocktail bar upon which Antonia was insisting so much depended. He asked Sally to release Imo a few days before the wedding; this also was at Antonia's request. Clive himself had little faith in Imo proving much use at The Rowans but at least it would stop Marilyn and Antonia panicking about her arriving at the last moment and not fitting into her bridesmaid's dress or not submitting to having her hair sorted out, both of which possibilities were still the subject of much anxious repeated discussion between them.

"If they need you, you better go," Sally said to Imo. "Would you like to go today?"

She thought she's been drooping around the place since Nicolette arrived, maybe it's better if she has a break.

Imo realised that this was just what she would like, to get away. "All right," she said, cutting her toast into small pieces, she wasn't hungry.

"It'll have to be the train," Sally said. "If you get packed I could get you to the station for the 10.10."

Nicolette arrived, yawning; Imo pushed back her chair and left the kitchen. Nicolette shrugged slightly, yawned some more and asked if she could have some coffee.

"The kettle's just boiled," Sally said. She suspected that she was not getting to like Nicolette much, the girl gave the impression of being self-sufficient and contained within her smooth, sallow skin. But, Sally thought, it's not so much that she doesn't care about other people, more that she is indifferent to them.

Nicolette looked around for a clean mug and made herself some instant coffee. She did not ask if Sally wanted any.

Claud took his empty cereal bowl to the draining board and then wandered out of the kitchen.

Frankie sat over his Weetabix which had been an attractive island floating in a milky sea and sprinkled with sugar snow but was now a soggy mass. He gazed at Nicolette whom he was considering marrying, when he was older. He had used to say that he wanted to marry Sally but now knew that this was not possible. He liked Nicolette's hair.

"Eat up your cereal," Sally said, giving the floor cloth a final wring.

"No," Frankie said thoughtfully.

Sally sighed. "Well, you must eat some of it," she said.

Perdita, competent child that she was, took charge of the situation. "Shall I make a bargain with you?" she suggested.

Frankie's' eyes narrowed. "What like?"

Perdita pulled his cereal bowl towards her. She manoeuvred it round the usual collection of flotsam on the table which today included a rhythm stick made from a cardboard tube filled with some dried lentils.

"Did you make this?" she asked Frankie, "in Nursery?"

Frankie nodded.

"It's very nice," Perdita said, picking up the tube and shaking it.

Frankie snatched it. "It's mine!"

"Don't shout," Sally said, now engaged in trying to get the bottom rack of the dishwasher back on its rollers. Second hand from an ad in the local paper it had not been a good idea and tended to flood. So much for trying to keep up with the modern trend, Sally thought.

"Look," Perdita said to Frankie, dividing the Weetabix in his bowl into quarters. She moved a nearly empty jar of jam out from behind a vase of drooping vetch and ragwort further down the table.

"No more sugar!" Sally said automatically, her head still in the dishwasher.

Perdita raised her finger to her lips. Frankie's eyes brightened. Carefully Perdita spooned some jam onto one of the quarters of weetabix, which Frankie then ate. He gazed at Nicolette, wanting to make sure she was impressed.

"He's eating his weetabix," Perdita explained.

Nicolette nodded. "Oh."

Her thoughts were elsewhere, recalling details of the night with Ned in the Laundry House. Repeats would now enliven the summer; she might stick around.

In the attic Imo dragged her back pack out from under her bed and began haphazardly to stuff things into it, pants and bras and sketch books and pencils; a paperback and socks. She pulled her jacket out from the cupboard, having to push Nicolette's crumpled green dress out of the way on the floor to get the cupboard door open. She stared at the dress.

Nicolette knew what to wear, and she seemed to have the money to buy what she wanted to wear.

I don't know what to wear, Imo thought, not really; she looked down at her combats. In two weeks' time she was going to have to appear here in a hideous pink sugar puff of a dress with rose buds stuck in her hair and Ned would see her and she would look like a freak. But Nicolette had already stolen him from her, so it didn't matter. Nothing mattered any more.

Nicolette, drinking her coffee in the kitchen, pondered the fact that she had almost finished weeding the front flower beds. She thought that she might absent herself to sun-bathe for a while or maybe go down into the bamboos and find Ned. To avoid Sally asking her plans for the morning and giving her some other job to do she wandered out of the kitchen and returned to the attic to swallow her contraceptive pill and collect her sun-tan lotion.

Here she found Imo, looking a mess. What on earth had Ned seen in her? Obviously it hadn't been, couldn't have been, anything serious. However, the knowledge that he had seen something brought with it a small frisson of excitement in nabbing him for herself.

"Hi," she said, glancing round the small untidy room, "what

are you doing?"

Imo kept her face turned away. "Packing," she said.

"Really? Why?"

"I've got to go home," Imo said.

"Oh?" Nicolette moved across to the chest-of-drawers to rummage on top among the moisturisers, hair conditioner, nail varnish. "You haven't seen my sun screen stuff have you?"

"No," Imo said.

Nicolette found the sun lotion; she sat on her bed and began to rub it onto her arms.

"Anything interesting?" she asked. "That you're going home for, a party or something?"

"My sister's getting married," Imo shortly. You know that, she thought, so why are you asking me stupid questions?

"Oh, yes . . . What is she called again?"

Imo frowned. "Antonia."

"And are they really going to have the reception here?" Nicolette idly flipped the top back on the sun lotion.

Imo hitched her rucksack over her shoulder and turned to leave.

"It doesn't matter," she said.

Nicolette raised her eyebrows and stretching out her legs surveyed her varnished toe nails, which needed re-painting. "I don't care where or how your boring sister is getting married," she murmured as Imo's footsteps receded down the back stairs, "why would I?"

Imo's heart was leaden as she sat, silent, beside Sally on the way to the station and while she sat on the train, staring at the passing fields and small stations.

"I don't feel anything," she told herself. "I don't even feel alive. Other people think I'm alive but I'm not. I'm like an empty packet of something."

CHAPTER 34

JULY

The last two weeks leading up to Antonia and Roger's wedding were, for those most involved, not the period of happy anticipation which ideally they might have been but all things considered this was not really surprising.

Penelope Rodmaine was most alarmed by what Roger told her of the new reception venue. She reported to George, "Apparently this place is quite run down and the husband sounds rather peculiar. And honestly, putting everyone on a bus! I've had to spend hours on the phone explaining it to people and some of them are not at all happy. Aunt Gwen is worried about Lionel."

George sighed for he really didn't want to talk about Penelope's Uncle Lionel and his bladder problems. He said that in his opinion the whole thing had been wrong from Day One, right back to Roger's choice of a bride.

"Roger hasn't got much get up and go," he said. "Let's face it.

He needed to choose a girl with a few useful connections and a bit of money behind her."

Penelope demurred slightly at his assessment of their only son's character but agreed with George in finding Antonia and her family wanting.

"I fear the worst with the wedding dress," she said. "Lizzie says the bridesmaids' dresses are all pink flounces, she hates them. I know you're not supposed to talk about good taste these days, or the lack of it, but it's ridiculous to put Lizzie in pink flounces. Don't you think?"

"No. Yes," George said accommodatingly. He hadn't a clue and preferred to steer clear of commenting on women's clothing, this being a principle to which he had been raised and which had stood him in good stead down the years.

Penelope gazed reflectively out of the sitting room window at their well mown lawn. "The Atkinsons are having Chinese lanterns hung in the trees," she said, "for their daughter's wedding. Rather a nice idea."

"Oh?" George said.

Meantime at Trevean the reception preparations were far indeed from being orderly and trouble free. Most problems Sally, as chief organiser, had to try and sort out.

The phone seemed to ring constantly, people making appointments, changing appointments, checking the address, checking access to the house itself. The DJ wanted to confirm that dance space and flooring would be organised by the marquee company. Directors' Lunches wanted to ensure premium location for their catering tent and covered access to the diners' tables; they said that they had been informed by the bride that a floor plan for the marquee would be provided and this they had not yet received. The portable toilet company threatened to cancel delivery unless they received payment upon booking.

Clive Bradford phoned to ask if Chinese lanterns could be strung around the lawn and down the drive. "It's a quarter of a mile long!" Sally protested.

"I know," he said. "I'm afraid Roger's mother is responsible for this idea, but Antonia is desperate to keep on the right side of her."

"Please, Dad, please!" Antonia had begged. "Will you try to fix it?"

Nicolette, despatched by Sally into the woods surrounding to house to check out the availability of pink and white rhododendrons with flower heads which could be used for the table decorations, returned after a desultory search to report finding only the weed-like mauve variety in flower.

"Tough," Sally said. "Mauve it will have to be. If we start ordering florist's' flowers and lights and all these extras we'll lose money, not make any."

Clarissa meanwhile, having elicited an invitation from the Bradfords for herself, and indeed the whole Trevean household, to attend the 'evening party' was exercised over what to wear.

"Maybe my blue frock?" she said to Sally who came to see her in her sitting room. "I haven't bought anything new for such a long time, I can't remember when – I would have had a choice of half a dozen outfits in the old days. What will you wear?"

"I haven't even thought about it," Sally said. "Are you sure they will want us to come?"

She suspected that Clarissa had backed the Bradfords into a corner from which they couldn't escape without seeming rude. But then why shouldn't Clarissa go to the party, she so rarely got a chance these days? She herself would really prefer not to have to go and James would rather be anywhere else but there. But we may have to put in an appearance, she thought.

"Maybe you could wear that nice grey dress and jacket you had?" Clarissa suggested.

Sally was regularly exasperated by Clarissa's clothes conversations for which she herself never seemed to have the time, or indeed the inclination. I go for things that will wash, she thought, and which don't look too odd. The grey outfit had been for another wedding and a last-minute purchase in a summer sale. She hadn't liked it even then and had not had any suitable shoes.

"Oh goodness, I don't know where that is," she said now.

"I thought it was rather nice," Clarissa sounded wistful. Sally had always been considered to look attractive as a girl, when she, Clarissa had the buying of her clothes. And she still is attractive, or could be, she thought, if she didn't have to spend all her time working so hard, ruining her hands and never having her hair properly styled.

It was, she thought as ever, James's fault; of course he should be providing a decent income for his family, not sitting around all day reading the paper and talking to the dogs.

Sally could follow Clarissa's thoughts fairly easily down this well worn path and as always they irritated her considerably. However, she thought, there was no point in having an unnecessary row with Clarissa; things which needed doing for the reception were piling up thick and fast.

"I must go," she said. "I'm sorry. I've got things to sort out."

"To do with the wedding?"

"Yes."

Clarissa clearly would have liked to talk about the wedding but Sally, although this again made her feel ungenerous, extricated herself.

"If Perdita isn't busy," Clarissa called after her, "maybe she's like to come and have a game of cards with me."

"I'll see if I can find her."

Sally hurried down the stairs. The phone was ringing again and James hovered in the study doorway, not wanting to answer it.

The caller was Antonia, anxious to reinforce the importance of the Chinese lanterns. "Down the drive? And round the lawn? We think they'd be really pretty."

"It is rather short notice," Sally said, stalling. She had hoped that this particular request would go away.

Antonia was persistent. "Roger's mother thinks lanterns will look nice."

Indeed, Sally thought, but she doesn't have to organise them.

"They may be quite expensive to buy. If we can get them in time."

"Oh!" Antonia sounded panicky. "But will you let me know? If you can get them?"

"Yes, all right." Sally felt a stab of sympathy for the girl. Thank goodness, she thought putting the phone down, that we got married abroad; I couldn't have coped with all this palaver. And the mother-in-law sounds a pain.

"Who was that?" James asked.

"The girl who's getting married. They want Chinese lanterns."

"What?"

"Hanging round the lawn and down the drive. You know those small round paper lanterns? They have candles in, or maybe there's an electric version. Which come to think of it, might be a bit of a problem. Can you plug them into the mains?"

"Heaven help us," James said.

The phone rang again and the portable toilet company

representative, a young woman with a take it or leave it attitude relayed the information that having received payment they were now prepared to deliver six chemical toilet cabinets, but a water supply was required for the hand basins.

"I thought you could provide water?" Sally said.

"At such short notice," the girl said, "our bowser trailers are all booked out."

"Right," Sally said. She didn't pass this information on to James, for the water supply at Trevean came not from the mains but from a large slate holding tank beside the kitchen garden and thence via the original Victorian pipe work to the house. It was not always reliable in the summer.

Sally looked at James; he was looking depressed. She glanced at the hall clock, it was eleven thirty. "I've got to talk to Zaccy Williams about the bar for the reception," she said. "Why don't we go to The Lion now for a quick drink?"

Escape! James gave an audible sigh of relief.

"I just need to find Perdita and send her up to play Patience with Mother."

"Oh." He was again deflated.

"I'll only be a couple of minutes, if you get the dogs into the car? I suppose we'd better take Frankie and Claud, stop any uproar."

But the boys were occupied in the Laundry yard building an Adobe African Village with mud and water from the water tank.

"We did it at school," Claud said.

"You're much too filthy to come with us," Sally said. "You'll have to stay here with Granny."

In The Lion Zachariah Williams was reading the local paper, which he had spread out on the bar counter. "Morning, Guv'nor," he said, looking up as they came in. "And your good lady, equally welcome. Dog, welcome if he behaves himself."

James had brought Coal in with him, Tish and Tash had been left in the car.

"He'll behave himself," James said. He and Zachariah had had this exchange many times before.

"That'll be all right then," Zaccy said, moving to pull two pints of local bitter.

James and Sally sat at the bar; Coal subsided on the floor beside them.

The old regulars were in their corner.

"I'm reading here," Zachariah said, indicating the newspaper, "that a nasty great hole has opened up where they're building that new stretch of by-pass."

"Will that be mine workings?" Sally said, taking an exploratory taste of beer.

"Oh, for sure," Zachariah said. "There they are, see, all those clever engineers scratching their heads, but they don't think to ask the locals, do they? Ey, Bazz," he lapsed into the local intonation as he called across to one of the old men, "up Japhet's corner, where they're working on the new road, wasn't that where a cow was lost down a shaft a while back?"

"Ez, that's right," the man agreed.

There was a reflective pause and then his companion stated, "Never did get 'er back. They thought 'er would wash out the adit but 'er never."

"Left a dumper-truck parked up over night," Zachariah, reading, paraphrased the newspaper story, "came back in the morning and found it twenty foot down. Dear, oh dear."

He paused for his wife to make her morning appearance in full fig, hair up and lipstick on. "Greetings, beloved."

Nancy Williams swept her glance along the bar to check that

all was in order and adjusted a towelling drip mat in front of the beer pumps. She inclined her head towards James and Sally and then called, "Good morning, Gentlemen" to the corner group. There was a murmur of response.

"And how are the wedding preparations going?" Nancy enquired.

James gave a quiet sigh and bent to pat Cole's head.

"It's all coming together," Sally said, "but we did just want to check with you about the bar. Is that going to be all right?"

Nancy looked at her husband. "Zaccy?"

"Oh, 'ez. Right on."

"They are talking about cocktails now, I'm afraid," Sally said.

"From up country, aren't they?" Zachariah suggested.

"Yes."

"Fancy tastes, then."

"Will that be OK?"

"Have to see what we can do."

"I'll find out a bit more what they have in mind," Sally said.

"Don't you worry," Zaccy said, "blow them away, we will."

"That's what I'm afraid of," James laughed his 'we men understand each other' laugh, which seldom got an outing these days. He cheered up a bit as he recalled that for this half-an-hour or so there would be no tiresome phone calls, no bills, no children, and he had Sally to himself.

Sally herself felt cheered by this indication that his mood had lightened. "Good brew this time, Zaccy," she said.

"We aim to please."

Too soon, however, it would be time to get back to get lunch organised. Otherwise Clarissa would be standing reproachfully in the kitchen saying, "I could have done something about it if you'd asked me."

CHAPTER 35

JULY

The day had arrived, the day of Antonia's wedding, the day upon which everyone had expended so much anticipation, anxiety and general fuss.

At Trevean although the dew still lay heavy on the shaded slopes of the marquee fox and badger prints had faded from shorn grass of the lawn.

There was a problem with the electric cabling for the coloured lights which Sally, in an epiphany moment, had thought to borrow from the village Christmas Decorations Committee. Graham and Ned had strung these around the lawn and down the drive and although they were not Chinese lanterns, they had looked quite attractive among the rhododendron branches at the trial switch-on the previous evening.

Now however, possibly affected by the heavy dew during the night, they had blown a ring circuit in the house.

The DJ and his sidekick, who arrived in a van painted with flames and wearing T-shirts identifying them as Belial and Dagon, said the power arrangements were inadequate. Currently they were setting up their generator and had had a confrontation with Jonathon from Directors' Lunches, whose staff were laying up the dining tables.

Half a dozen members of the local rugby club were setting up the cocktail bar for which Zachariah had commandeered the Mid West set built for the pub float in last year's carnival.

"I think not the bullock horns," Sally said, standing in front of it. There was a risk, surely, of Trevean presenting an image of a shoe-string and slightly dotty theme park rather than a romantic, historic setting for a wedding. At least the disco was the choice of the bride and groom, odd though this was.

"Local," Zachariah pointed out. "That's what these up-country people like, isn't it? Horns came from Wheal Damson slaughter house."

"Still – "

"How's about we decorate them up a bit? Silver wedding bells maybe?"

"No," Sally said. "I know you're taking the mick, Zaccy."

"Would I?"

You certainly would, Sally thought, and what's more you would probably have a crack at James and me too. I'm not sure we are ever going to be really accepted here.

"Unscrew the horns," Zachariah said to one of the rugby club. "I never argue with a woman."

Nicolette was attaching ivy around the poles of the marquee with parcel tape and there were mauve rhododendron flower heads in a bucket of water, from which she was to make the table decorations. She yawned a lot having spent the previous night in bed with Ned. Her arrival, none-the-less, had galvanised the rugby club recruits into greater efforts stacking beer barrels and boxes of wine bottles.

Sally had had her suspicions about Ned and Nicolette; even so she had not been pleased to discover that she was right. Earlier that morning she had gone across to the Laundry House to ask Ned to help move the catering gas cylinders. When calling up the stairs and banging on his bedroom door had got no response she had looked in to find the pair of them sprawled on the bed asleep. But, she thought, as they were technically adults there was really nothing she could do about it.

She had not told James.

Clarissa couldn't resist the atmosphere of hustle and bustle. When Perdita brought up her breakfast tray she found that her grandmother was up and taking clothes from her mahogany wardrobe.

Perdita stood holding the tray.

"I'm trying to choose something suitable to wear with all these people coming here today," Clarissa said.

"Where shall I put this?" Perdita asked.

"Oh – " Clarissa glanced at the tray. "Over there on the table."

She took a navy blue and grey dress from the wardrobe, on its hanger. "This was a very good dress," she said. "I think I may have got it in Harvey Nichols, but it's dreadfully old now."

Perdita nodded. She had been told this before.

"And what are you going to wear?" Clarissa asked.

Perdita looked down uncertainly at her T-shirt and shorts.

"I wish you had a nice dress to wear," Clarissa said. "It will be a big party today you know, a wedding party."

Perdita thought about if she had a dress which would fit.

"If you come with me later on, we can see what we can find,"

Clarissa said.

"But what?" Perdita was doubtful.

Clarissa said, "Maybe your skirt with the flowers?"

"It's got a hole," Perdita shook her head, sorry to provide bad news.

She's such a serious child, Clarissa thought, as she often did. "Well," she said again, "we'll see what we can find."

Meanwhile up the road a dumper truck driver, working weekend overtime, was emptying his twentieth load of subsoil down an old mine shaft into the Wheal Japhet Deep Adit. People on the beach in the surfing cove below found that the stream which flowed across the sand from the base of the cliff was becoming a mere trickle.

Nicolette, in a desultory way, was now sticking rhododendron flower heads into various small jars, cups and Clarissa's Chinese glass finger bowls which Sally had found in the back of a cupboard. She was upsetting Jonathon's staff by dropping water and mauve petals onto their pristine white table clothes.

"I'm afraid I must ask you to stop doing this," Jonathon told her.

Nicolette was pleased to comply. She abandoned the remaining rhododendrons in their bucket and wandered away to chat to the rugby players, en-route to sitting in the sun in the Laundry yard and tanning her legs.

Sally found James in the study. "Come and have a look at the marquee," she said, as ever wanting him to be seen and recognised as head of the house. Knowing so well his reaction to domestic decisions she added, "Everything's ready now, just about."

And indeed the marquee was looking delightful with meters of fluted silk overhead, country sisal carpeting underfoot and tables laid up with Directors' Lunches best: Kings' pattern cutlery, white china with platinum band, linen napkins, lots of glasses.

Sally said, "What do you think?"

"Very nice," James said, to please her. He looked at the mixing desk and lighting rig and his face fell. "What is that?"

"For The DJ. The disco."

"Heaven spare us!"

"Not till this evening," Sally said, calming. She looked at her watch. "And there's supposed to be a harpist."

"A what?"

But at that point, perhaps fortunately, the children arrived to have a look.

"Why are you wearing that skirt?" Sally asked Perdita. She noted a hair ribbon too, saved from a birthday present wrapping.

"Granny said – " Perdita gazed around the marquee wide-eyed.

Sally made herself suppress a comment that the gaudy ribbon and frill of a skirt, last worn for the village carnival, were not suitable. If it gave Clarissa pleasure to dress Perdita up like that, did it really matter? But she still felt the prickle of irritation.

Frankie, excited by the glamour of the surroundings, went into train mode. He set off chuffing round the tables. "You too," he commanded Claud.

"Be careful!" Sally called to them as Jonathon, martyred, completed the placing of the last table decorations with elaborate care.

"And you too!" Frankie commanded Perdita as he chuffed past.

"No, no!" Sally said. "You'll cause an accident, and the wedding people will all be here soon. Out! Go out and play on the lawn."

She moved to liaise with Jonathon, who reported that his team was now fully prepared.

"We have tried to make a bit of a special effort, as the bride is one of ours. And in the unfortunate circumstances."

Sally wondered if the Trevean arrangements were included, in Jonathon's view, in what was unfortunate. Should she feel annoyed? Again, she decided that it wasn't worth it.

Instead she said what was clearly expected of her, "It's all looking beautiful."

"The lighting," Jonathon pointed out, indicating the strings of fairy lights and the bank of disco strobes, "is of course not within our control."

"Well," Sally said, "we'll just have to keep our fingers crossed."

She saw a ripple of disquiet pass over Jonathon's face and added quickly, "Please will you thank all your team. Don't you think so, James? They've done a wonderful job."

James nodded, if without much enthusiasm. "Oh, yes."

In the house again Sally thought, 'Well, I suppose I'd better make a bit of an effort about clothes, to please Mother if no-one else.'

She said to James: "I'm just going to tidy up a bit."

"Why?" He found himself so actively disliking all this change to routine. Why must Sally make ready to meet and greet these people who were strangers and obviously not their sort.

"Nothing major," Sally said. "But I'll just get out of this skirt, find something clean."

"What about me?" he called after her, preparing to stage resistance.

"No, you're fine," she replied, placatory.

The harpist, a nervous young woman, was being driven

by her mother who unfortunately had decided to take the cross-country route, to avoid possible traffic hold ups on the trunk road. The dumper-truck driver was even now trying to phone his boss to tell him the B road at Japhet's Corner was flooding and would have to be closed.

CHAPTER 36

JULY

Antonia's wedding day!

At The Rowans everyone had been awake since first light. In fact most of them felt that they had barely slept.

Lizzie and Petra had been collected from the station by Clive. They had declined the invitation, relayed by Antonia, to spend the previous night at The Rowans. Petra had suggested to Lizzie that this might be an easier option than getting up to catch the early train, but Lizzie had been adamant in refusal. "We're giving up a whole day of our lives to this ghastly wedding," she had said, all ice, "isn't that enough?"

But now Marilyn stood in front of the full length mirror in her bedroom and realised that it was ten o'clock in the morning and contrary to all that she had feared, on this day of days, nothing of consequence had so far gone wrong.

Those who felt like it had eaten scrambled egg and smoked

salmon for breakfast. There were glasses of champagne, several glasses in Lizzie and Petra's case.

Imo had submitted to having her hair re-styled without protest. In fact since her return from Trevean she had barely spoken and mostly stayed in her room.

Everyone was now dressed. The bridesmaids' dresses fitted. The hairdresser had arrived with the girl from the beauty salon, who had advised adding 'a little glow for the photographs'.

Although Lizzie had murmured, "Too sweaty!" Petra had not responded and this difficult moment had passed.

The bouquets had arrived.

Marilyn considered her reflection in the mirror. She thought how strange it was that the worries and upsets which she had suffered lately were not, somehow, more apparent in her appearance. The privations of The Diet were reflected only in the smooth hang of the rose-coloured dress and jacket. Her heart lifted.

Meanwhile at the church the bell ringers started the peel and the choir master was counting heads in the vestry.

George and Penelope Rodmaine had arrived and were being shown to the front pew on the right side of the nave by one of the ushers, who had been at school with Roger. Penelope thought goodness, he's losing his hair already.

Sunlight floated through the stained glass of the windows to lie across the chancel floor in glowing lozenges of red and blue.

Sarah of Sarah's Flowers, having decided that Antonia's wedding presented an opportunity to launch her business locally with a flourish, for word would get around, had made every effort to bond with Mrs Gaston's flower ladies. The result was that massed white and pink lilies filled the church with scent; the pew ends and pillars were garlanded with myrtle and ivy.

Penelope, settling herself, murmured to George loudly enough for several other people to hear that the flowers were really too much but in this instance George didn't agree with her, he thought the lilies looked rather good.

He therefore chose not to respond. Sniffing she sought for a handkerchief in her handbag and then turned her critical attention to the appearance of the congregation.

The demarcation line between the family and friends of the bride and those of the groom, which is sometimes only too apparent in the unequal numbers present in the left- and right-hand pews or in the mode of dress chosen by each party, was not in fact as marked as it sometimes is or indeed as Penelope had expected it to be.

This was partly because Roger and Antonia's London friends, who over the past couple of years had been regularly invited to each other's weddings at the rate of about one wedding a month, had got the whole matter of their clothes and the church seating totally sorted.

Many of the men wore morning dress.

The girls were resolutely wearing pastel, fluttery dresses and hats and high heeled sandals, telling each other that it had better not rain, had it? And what about this bus trip? They had decided to enjoy themselves.

They ignored the ushers' attempts to guide them to one side of the church or the other with dismissive explanations that they knew both the bride and groom and headed, waving and exclaiming, for places saved for them by people already seated.

Those who were young parents and whose children were being cared for by the staff of the pre-school toddler group in the church hall anxiously consulted their phones for messages about the welfare of their offspring. They had been a little disconcerted to discover that the children would have access to the sand and water trays and all the pedal tractors.

Roger arrived with his best man Gareth. They walked up the aisle accompanied by encouraging acknowledgement from the friends. The girls smiled and the men pulled 'Good Luck, Mate' expressions.

Memories revived for some of the stag party, a wet but uproarious weekend at a surf school in Rock. Antonia's hen party, when she had found herself lying next to Petra in an expensive Berkshire spa, covered in Dead Sea mud and cling film, had not been so much fun.

Everyone was now looking forward to the serious business; a gentle rustle of anticipation passed through the congregation.

"I hope she's not going to be late," Penelope said to George.

"Bride's prerogative?"

"Quite unnecessary. I wasn't late."

"No."

Penelope was never late. He suppressed the insidious thought which questioned why he had proposed to the youthful Penelope instead of one of the other girls whom he had known at the time. He actually couldn't remember.

Marilyn arrived escorted, in the absence of any closer relations, by Clive's second cousin Ian, an IT specialist based in Dublin whom she did not know very well.

Penelope had to allow that Marilyn's appearance was quite acceptable. Of course, she thought, withholding judgement, I can't see her shoes.

George, inclining his head in greeting across the pews, thought that his future daughter-in-law's mother was actually rather an attractive woman. Maybe Roger wasn't such a fool after all, like mother like daughter, what?

The bells fell silent, the choir filed in. The vicar who had been waiting to greet Clive and Antonia in the porch, now strode, cassock flowing, up the side aisle to stand beside one of the pyramids of lilies on the chancel steps. He motioned the groom and best man forward.

The organist, who had sat watching over his shoulder, turned back to pull out the stops and the church filled with Clarke's Trumpet Voluntary.

The congregation, pleased to be given so familiar a cue and craning their necks to glimpse the bride, rose to their feet.

Everything now, somehow and rather miraculously seemed to come together.

The church, which long pre-dated the roads of suburban houses like The Rowans, had certainly witnessed many weddings since it was built by the inhabitants of what was then a small market town surrounded by the slopes of wooded hills. With its lichened stone and stubby tower, it provided a setting reassuringly on a human scale.

It might have seemed, had anyone been thinking about it, that generations' worth of ordinary human emotions had been expended here and absorbed into the fabric of the place. So when Antonia appeared, on Clive's arm, blushing and smiling within yards of misty veil, it was apparent that she was, for this place and for this summer's day, the perfect bride. She looked like the Queen of the May and in the age when the church was built might have inspired a sonnet.

Roger turned and gazed and his heart lurched; the doubts which had undermined him over the past few weeks with insidious whispers that Antonia would prove too needy for his marital comfort, vanished into the dust motes dancing in the shafts of sunlight. She was sweet and young and golden and thank heavens showed no signs of becoming hard boiled, like his sister Lizzie (for he could no longer deny spotting the occasional sourness in Old Fizz Up).

Lizzie herself had had her hopes dashed, for she had planned to mock her way through the whole day, from the dressing of the bride to the coach ride to the distant reception, but she had taken one look at Antonia in her wedding dress and known that every man present would willingly lay his heart at her feet.

Compounding Lizzie's annoyance she had found that even the sulky Imo was transformed by a radical haircut and being extracted from her sewage coloured dungarees, although no-one, she reminded herself, could fully rise above the horror of those pink powder-puff dresses. Gritting her teeth Lizzie followed Antonia down the aisle and later took care not to smile for the photographs.

Clive found himself more emotionally charged than he expected to be as he relinquished his eldest daughter to her new station in life. He came to sit beside Marilyn, noticed her brimming eyes and squeezed her hand.

"Will you take this woman?" the vicar asked Roger, who without hesitation assured him that he would.

The vicar turned to Antonia. "Will you – ?"

She gazed at him, eyes wide, cheeks peony flushed. "I will."

The vicar was not unimpressionable; he felt able to dwell on the satisfactions of matrimony in his address with more conviction than he sometimes found to be the case. None-the-less he reminded them, "Marriage is a serious business, not to be undertaken lightly . . . "

The choir sang during the signing of the register, the younger members anyway cheered by the realisation that the end was in sight and an envelope containing their fee awaited them in the vestry.

And so it was done. Roger and Antonia, man and wife, came down the aisle to Mendelssohn's Wedding March, smiles following them all the way.

The photographs were taken in showers of the right coloured rose petals and the parents of the toddlers rushed off to collect their offspring, some of whom wailed loudly as they were reluctant to be removed from the sand pit and the tractors.

The bride and groom were despatched to the reception in the Porsche, retrieved from its safe parking place by one of the friends and garlanded with dancing streamers of white ribbons.

Clive with Marilyn and George with Penelope also drove ahead in their separate cars.

Some of the guests also chose to drive themselves but most climbed aboard the two coaches. The parents of the children and the carers of the very elderly relations were reassured to find that there were toilets on board. All were delighted to find Directors Lunches staff ready to serve them with canapés and champagne or orange juice and biscuits (no E numbers). The mood was set to become merry.

"I suppose we couldn't give it all a miss?" Roger said suddenly, as they drove, glancing at Antonia beside him. Her hair was delightfully disordered, framing her face, for she had taken off her veil which was now bundled on the minimal back seat in a shifting snowy heap. He had had an uncharacteristically wild thought of stopping at a Travel Lodge and taking a room.

"Not go to the reception?" she gazed at him amazed. "Why?"

Roger thought: all those speeches, my parents, her parents, hours of saying the right thing to everyone. He said, "I just thought we could be together."

But then he had a mental image of how Penelope would respond if they didn't turn up. "I suppose it wouldn't work out."

"But we couldn't not be at our reception – "

"I know."

"Oh!" Realisation of what he had been thinking dawned on Antonia. Happiness welled up within her. He loved her, he hadn't changed his mind as she had begun to fear he might have done over the preceding fraught weeks. She blinked back tears, remembering her so expensively applied make-up.

Roger nudged the Porsche speedo up a bit.

"Well, so far so good," Clive said to Marilyn as they headed onto the motor-way. "I think that went OK, don't you?"

Marilyn was feeling light headed with relief and lack of food for she had not been able to eat any breakfast. "Yes!" she said.

Imo by contrast, seated on the first coach, was feeling increasingly miserable. She was now going to have to face Ned and Nicolette while trapped by her bridesmaid's role and unable to get away and hide. Anyway she had no-where to hide, for Nicolette had taken over her room at Trevean.

"I can't stay there," she thought, "I can't bear it now."

CHAPTER 37

JULY

Clive and Marilyn were the first of the wedding party to arrive at Trevean, ahead of George and Penelope Rodmaine.

Roger and Antonia had made slower progress for Roger had on a romantic whim stopped in a lay-by with a view of the wide azure sweep of the sea.

"I'm so happy." Antonia rested her head on his shoulder.

Roger found he felt the same. "My lovely wife!"

"Oh!"

A further delay resulted and a couple of passing cars hooted encouragingly.

As the Jag bumped up the drive Clive said, "They've put up those lights Antonia wanted."

"Oh," Marilyn said, "That's nice . . ." She peered doubtfully at the lanterns looped through the branches. Was there something rather odd about them?

"They need to get this resurfaced before it gets any worse," Clive said, not listening as he slowed the Jag to avoid the worst of the pot holes.

Marilyn realised that she was feeling wobbly all over again at the approach of the social trials which now lay immediately ahead: the greeting line, the meal, the speeches. The numbing need for everything to go well. The Rodmaines.

As they drew up on the gravel in front of the house the air was throbbing with the beat of heavy metal impressively amplified.

James appeared on the front steps as they got out of the car.

"Bloody awful din!" he addressed them in an obvious fury, as if he held them responsible.

They gazed at him.

"Sally!" James called, and repeated this twice more with increasing urgency. "Sally! For God's sake!"

Sally eventually emerged from the marquee onto the lawn. She was wearing a blouse and a skirt in different shades of green which in all honesty did not go too well together. Now she took in the three figures before her, James agitated and the Bradfords standing uncertainly beside their car. She walked across the gravel towards them.

James said, "You can't hear yourself think!"

"Hello!" Sally greeted Clive and Marilyn with a determined smile. The morning had been a run around of sorting problems and chasing after people and she had only just finished completing the table flowers, abandoned by Nicolette. "The DJs are testing their kit," she said to James, "that's what it is."

"Well, they've got to stop!"

"They will in a minute."

"The dogs are being driven mad."

Sally said, "They'll stop now with people arriving." She turned to the Bradfords. "How was your journey down?"

"Straight through," Clive said, bringing his attention back from the beat of the music. He was still determined to minimise any problems to do with the rearrangement of the reception.

"That racket's not stopping," James pointed out.

"My husband is not a big fan of loud music," Sally said.

"That is not music, it's just noise."

"Go back in," Sally laid a consoling hand on James' arm. "I'll sort it out."

A vehicle approached up the drive, driven faster than was probably wise given the state of the surface. They all turned to look, expecting more of the wedding party, but it was the post van. The postman who wasn't keen on dogs and was always reluctant to get out of the van at Trevean, wound down the window and waited for someone to come across and take the letters. James moved to do so and for a moment Sally was distracted by her familiar instinct to get there first to protect him from finding anything disturbing in the contents, but she realised Marilyn was trying to ask her something. This turned out to be where might she find a toilet?

"The loos are beyond the marquee," Sally said levelly. "Come through and I'll show you."

She added for James' benefit, "I can have a word about the music at the same time."

In the marquee Jonathon of Directors' Lunches had marshalled his catering staff, two of whom now stood waiting with trays of filled glasses, white wine or guava juice.

"Here are Mr and Mrs Bradford," Sally introduced them, "parents of the bride. I'm sure they would like a drink after their drive. I'm going to ask the DJs to tone it down a bit."

Jonathon, registering relief, rallied to his professional role.

He bowed slightly to Clive and Marilyn. "I hope you will find everything satisfactory."

"It was good of you people to step in," Clive said, sensing this was expected of him.

"Well . . . I won't deny that we haven't had our problems," Jonathon said, glancing meaningfully towards the disco stage where the strobe lighting was flashing on and off, "but of course you had such unfortunate circumstances. We felt for Antonia."

Marilyn was gazing round inside the marquee, her anxiety centring on whether Antonia would be happy and the Rodmaines would approve. And surely they would approve? The tables receded into the distance with fold upon fold of heavy white linen and every piece of cutlery and every glass gleaming in the oddly watery light, which was reflected perhaps from the grass outside.

The rhododendron flower heads on the tables struck a slightly quirky note, compounded by the assorted cups and so on which contained them. These, fortunately, Marilyn did not notice.

She realised that Jonathon was waiting for her reaction. "It's . . . I think . . . it's lovely."

He inclined his head in acknowledgement.

But now there was the sound of George and Penelope's BMW approaching up the drive and Marilyn cried, "Oh!" and gazed at Sally anxiously. Sally ushered her between the tables and out to the rank of portaloos. Then she went to ask Dagon and Belial to cut the music and the lights, or perhaps on second thoughts to play something quietly 'background' as the harpist had not yet turned up.

They looked at each other and Dagon, identified by the logo on his T-shirt, shrugged eloquently; the beat died.

Returning to the front of the marquee Sally thought that she should perhaps have taken Marilyn, who was looking stressed, into the house but the only loo on the ground floor was James' private domain, out of bounds to females and it would have upset him greatly. The upstairs bathrooms were inadvisable because of the state of chaos up there which was, Sally suspected, considerable. She had had no time for cleaning up the house over the past couple of weeks. Anyway it was too late now.

Roger and Antonia had also arrived. The Porsche came to a halt on the gravel and Roger still gripped by uncharacteristic elation sprang from the car to open the door for Antonia who emerged in a cloud of white silk and a scattering of rose petals.

"I think she's probably quite a silly girl," Sally thought, "but she does look rather lovely."

Clive saw his favourite daughter transformed now into a married woman and felt his heart tilt. Maybe all this trouble and expense was worth it, if she was happy?

"Hello, you two!" He walked towards them. "All well?"

"Yes!" Antonia cried.

"Happy?"

"Yes!"

"Absolutely!" Roger said, surprising himself with the positive strength of his response.

"Church went off all right?" Clive suggested.

Roger agreed. "Fine."

"But I expect you're glad to have got that bit over and done with?" Clive looked at him. "Probably could do with a drink now?"

"Good idea!"

"Oh, but it was a lovely service!" Antonia's pansy eyes gazed upon them both reproachfully. "And the flowers and everything were lovely, weren't they?"

Roger looking at her felt a quickening of the pulse. "Yes," he said, taking her hand.

"You did enjoy it didn't you?" she persisted.

Roger said, "Yes, of course I did."

"And now he could do with a drink," Clive turned resolutely towards the marquee. "Come and see if we can find one in here."

"Where's Mum?" Antonia asked.

"Doing women's things," Clive said. "Be here in a minute."

The Directors' Lunches team greeted Antonia with joyful exclamations, some of the girls envious of the transformation of one of their less flamboyant members into this cloudy vision of eternal young womanhood. Dagon and Belial raised cans of lager in tribute.

Marilyn found her way back to the group, Jonathon hastening forward to offer her a glass of wine. By and large he preferred the mothers to the daughters, his professional role having brought him into contact with too many examples of the young corporate female. Bossy, demanding and un-charmable he thought, they seemed to have thrown femininity out of the window. In this he and Roger, had they known it, had rather similar views.

"Oh thank you!" Marilyn accepted the glass.

By this time George and Penelope Rodmaine had located Sally. She had been hoping to leave the meeting-and-greeting to the bridal party themselves and was about to go in search of Ned to organise the parking and ensure the coach drivers took their vehicles up to the top yard.

"That drive is in a terrible state," Penelope said.

"I'm so sorry," Sally said coolly. "We did have an estimate for re-surfacing, but it was exorbitant. So for now it's on hold."

Penelope directed her glance at Sally's blouse, from which a button had come adrift, and then down at her Birkenstock sandals.

"Rodmaine," George said, establishing their status. "Parents of the groom."

"Sally Lacock," Sally said. "Welcome to Trevean."

Penelope, without making a response, concerned herself with adjusting her hat and her handbag.

"Which has been in my husband's family for several generations," Sally said, provoked.

"Really?" George was looking up at the front of the house with its small haphazard mullion windows and mellow stone.

Sally indicated the marquee. "I believe everyone is over here."

Penelope gave a summoning glance to George and headed across the gravel.

"Ghastly woman," Sally thought. "Still – " she told herself, "I should have kept a better grip." None-the-less she was pleased, watching as the Rodmaines moved away, to see that the backside of Penelope's slub silk skirt was considerably creased.

Standing next to Roger, in her bubble of happiness, Antonia greeted George and Penelope with effusive delight, kissing them both. "Mops and Pops!"

She was buoyed up. "Did you have an easy drive down?" she asked. "We did – we just came straight through, didn't we Roger? No hold ups, nothing at all. Except we stopped to look at the sea, it was so lovely and blue! I hope the coaches arrive soon, I can't wait to see everyone. Don't you think everything is looking nice? There will be lights later on, look – all those fairy lights. I wanted it to look like a fairy grotto . . . Roger drove so fast! I was expecting a police car at any minute and I thought what will they say when they see me in this dress! But they wouldn't have stopped us on our wedding day would they?"

George raised a hand to greet Clive and Marilyn and lowered

it to accept two glasses of wine from one of Jonathon's hovering staff. One glass he passed to Penelope, who although ostensibly in conversation with her son and newly acquired daughter-in-law, was letting her eyes travel round the interior of the marquee. "Are those rhododendrons?" she asked.

Antonia followed Penelope's glance to the nearest table. "Oh – " she said, "are they? I asked for pink flowers but they're more sort of mauve, aren't they?"

"I don't object to them not being pink," Penelope said coolly.

"Oh – " Antonia paused, uncertain.

Penelope turned her attention to greeting Clive and Marilyn and pronouncing judgement on the reception arrangements. "Well, things seems to be reasonably all right," she said, "in here."

Were they, Clive wondered, intended to feel honoured by her approval?

"Now that we are actually here," Penelope continued, "but of course it was a long drive down for people. Some of our guests are quite elderly, which can present problems. And then there are the children."

Neither Clive nor Marilyn could immediately come up with a response. There was a lengthening pause in which people sipped their drinks until with a degree of relief they saw the first coach rounding the giant rhododendron by the lawn and drawing up on the gravel. The seats were full and on board were Imo, Lizzie, Petra and Gareth the best man.

"Well, now we'll see how they got on!" George said.

Imo was, as she had anticipated being, feeling increasingly wretched. The day had started at The Rowans with her mother and Antonia working themselves into a state about the need for her to get up, and the arrival at the house of Lizzie and Petra.

While they were getting dressed Lizzie had made it quite clear how much she disliked the bridesmaids' dresses. Imo heard her talking to someone on her mobile, "Nightmare! Think candyfloss, frills – no, shut up, it's not funny."

Although Imo had also always hated her dress she was now surprised to find that she felt a bit sorry for her mother who kept trying to say that they all looked lovely and offering Lizzie and Petra champagne, or scrambled eggs, or biscuits or coffee, of which they only accepted champagne.

The visit of the hairdresser was very fraught with Lizzie refusing point blank to wear her rosebud garland. "All we need now is the may-pole!"

Antonia, on the verge of getting weepy, had said that then Petra and Imo couldn't wear theirs either because they all had to match.

As she had guessed they might, Imo's shoes pinched; on the coach she had kicked them under the seat as she tried to avoid talking to the man who had sat next to her. He said he had been at school with Roger and asked whether she minded if he took his jacket off. He had beige crinkly hair and a loud, self-deprecating laugh and she didn't care in the least what he did with himself. "And will we enjoy this fête champêtre?" he asked.

She looked at him blankly. Her mind was filled with thoughts of Ned.

When they finally reached Trevean she was feeling slightly sick. She had drunk several glasses of wine and eaten only a few of the filled olives, anchovies in snippets of puff pastry or bite-sized smoked salmon sandwiches on offer on the coach. The sun shone on her seat for the whole journey and she had not wanted to unhook the pleated orange curtain and pull it across the window because this would signal to the irritating man beside her that she was not, as she was pretending to be, engrossed in the passing scenery and he might then have become more persistent in attempting to talk to her.

As she now got down from the coach she was feeling disorientated and sticky. Her scalp hurt where her hair was unfamiliarly pulled back and spiked with a few of the rejected rosebuds.

Ned, sulky in a surf label T-shirt and board shorts, was on the gravel. He was not pleased to be stuck with the role of parking attendant.

Imo's heart beat, she stood still. The other guests scrambled down the coach steps exclaiming and staring about them at the house, the lawn, the snow-blindingly white marquee. They eddied around her until to escape the flow of moving bodies she was forced to step aside.

She gazed at Ned as he stood beside the driver's window, his hand on the sun-warmed paintwork of the coach, staring through dark glasses into the middle distance.

The sick feeling curdled in Imo's stomach as she became aware of the interest he was generating among the London girlfriends who headed across the gravel on a wave of nudges and giggles.

Eventually, when everyone had moved away the driver began, slowly, to back the coach. Imo waited, for now surely Ned would acknowledge her.

But he didn't. His gaze passed over her, refusing recognition, as he turned towards the cars appearing at the entrance of the drive.

"Shift yourself, please, darling," the driver called down to her as he began to move off.

Meanwhile Gareth, recalling his role as Roger's best man and having downed quite a few glasses of wine en-route, had sprung from the coach. He crossed the gravel rather in the manner of a young and bouncy Labrador newly let off the lead.

"Hello, happy couple! Hello happy parents!"

"Hi Gar!" Roger said, relieved to see him. "Journey OK?"

"Pretty girls, nice wine! Good time guaranteed!"

Those in the reception line now found themselves deftly shunted into position by Jonathon, who had taken upon himself the role of maitre d' which was not, his experienced eye informed him, likely to be satisfactorily filled by Gareth.

Past them filed the aunts in navy and turquoise or navy and pink and their husbands, some of whom, if wearing their own morning-dress, were finding the trouser waistband rather tighter than they remembered it to be. Penelope Rodmaine's ancient Uncle Lionel who walked with a frame and had blood blisters on his lips, was escorted by his daughter, who had the fixed smile of reluctant sainthood.

The harpist meanwhile, who should have been playing, had not turned up. Her mother, driving her and the harp in their old camper van, had come up against the flooded adit at Japhet's corner and had to retreat. They were now hopelessly lost.

And so the reception got under way, the guests clustering round the seating plan, which Sally had forgotten until rather late in the day, hence it was pinned to the nursery blackboard, propped on a chair.

Having discovered where they were sitting the guests circled and settled like a flock of multicoloured birds descending on their feeding grounds.

The parents of the toddlers, who had been sorting things out in the crèche tent and explaining to the Nursery Nurse students whom Sally had recruited all about allergies and the contents of specially prepared lunch boxes, hurried back to the marquee not wanting to miss anything and dying for a drink.

The London girlfriends pronounced the style of the flower arrangements to be 'so country' and exclaimed excitedly, comparing with each other across the tables the sugar bowls, finger bowls, mugs or whatever contained the flowers. Some of the girls, with their own weddings coming up, alert for ideas to pinch, announced that this was just what they had in mind for their own receptions.

Clive rose to his feet; borrowing a microphone from Dagon and Belial he thanked the assembled company for braving the rigours of the coach journey and invited them to eat, drink and be merry.

"Hear! Hear!" cried the London friends.

In the catering tent the Directors' Lunches staff were poised for action, starters plated up.

Jonathon gave the signal and in a miraculously short time all the guests were served with chilled gazpacho, paté or goat's cheese filo parcels.

Gareth seated with Lizzie, Petra and Imo was in danger of forgetting that he still had a speech to make. He raised one of the bottles of wine which were already on the table, "Drinkies for all?"

Lizzie who had known him since they were both eleven had discovered on the coach that old Gar had miraculously become quite sexy and surprisingly, since everyone knew there were no decent single men in London, he wasn't currently attached.

People clinked glasses and compared their choices of starters.

Marilyn was seated between Roger and George on the top table, she had accepted her third glass of wine and now found that the tightness in her jaw which had earlier almost prevented her from speaking had lessened. She seemed to be saying the right things to George as he talked about his and Penelope's plans for their garden, which included a bog area to encourage newts, about which Marilyn admitted to having little knowledge.

George himself found he was enjoying Marilyn's uncritical acceptance of the information he passed to her and finding the soft glow which suffused her face rather attractive. He suspected that Penelope was solidifying with disapproval beneath her pinky beige wedding hat, but seated as she was next to Clive and on the far side of the bridal couple, she was out of his line of sight and so he put her out of his mind. He allowed his hand to brush against Marilyn's as he refilled her glass.

When their conversation moved on to foreign travel Marilyn had to admit to never having visited Machu Picchu or Vermont in the Fall or Reykjavik. "I think," she said doubtfully, "that I'd like to see a bit more of the world. We usually go to Spain for our holidays."

In fact they hadn't even gone there for the last few years, since the girls stopped wanting to come with them and Clive had got so tied up with the business.

"A shared holiday?" George boldly suggested. "Joint parents-in-law? Good for us all to get better acquainted before the arrival of the grandchildren, what?"

"Well – "

"Penelope and I know of a rather nice villa in the Dordogne, belongs to a former colleague of mine as a matter of fact, a bit off the main tourist route . . . plenty of room for all of us. Roger and Antonia too."

"It sounds – " Marilyn wasn't too sure what it sounded. She was feeling rather warm. "Nice?"

"Yes, indeed." George bent towards her and she was quite relieved when the waiter arrived bringing the vegetables for the second course. Gratefully she leant away from George to accommodate the serving dishes being handed over her shoulder. George became distracted by wondering whether he had made the right choice with the salmon.

When the time came for speeches Clive got to his feet, coped with the microphone and told them how Antonia had always been an easy child to raise, never been wild or kept rodents, never painted her bedroom black. When she had decided that she wanted to work in catering she had done the sensible thing, got the right qualifications and then a job with this splendid company who were doing such a good job of looking after them all today. Everyone clapped.

"And how lucky is Roger for all this?" Clive said. "For don't they say, the way to a man's heart is through his stomach?"

A couple of ribald suggestions for alternative routes surfaced from the London boyfriends, but the girls told them they were tasteless and never knew when to stop.

Marilyn had a moment of doubt; was Clive making reference to her own lack of culinary skill? But truth be told Clive was not, he had trawled the joke, plus a couple of others, from a wedding speech book he had spotted in an airport shop when he was en-route to meet a client in Oslo.

He proposed the toast to the bride and groom.

"The bride and groom," everyone echoed.

Roger, taking over the microphone and pressing the wrong button said that the bridesmaids had done a fine job in getting Antonia to the altar on time. Clive turned the sound back on, rather too loud, and Roger said it again. "The bridesmaids!"

"The bridesmaids!" everyone dutifully chorused.

Gareth had been playing thumb boxing with Lizzie.

"You're on!" she said, kicking his foot as Roger stood waiting to hand over the microphone.

Gareth felt in his waistcoat pocket for his notes, which he had definitely put there, but they had disappeared. Momentarily non-plussed, he ploughed ahead anyway. Only a short speech among friends after all. Most of them had been best man in their time, knew the full horror.

"I've known Roger, I've worked out, for twenty-two years," he said. "That is, all through school, university and now we live in London half a mile apart, and through all that time I can tell you that we have never had a cross word. Or not many. I can also tell you that our relationship has always been purely platonic. Scout's honour!"

"Hurray!" cried various people. Penelope pursed her lips.

"But to be serious," Gareth said. "Roger is a good mate, and a good guy. If I was ever in a real hole . . . "

"Shame!" shouted a couple of the boyfriends.

"Don't even think about it!" warned the girlfriends, kicking ankles.

" . . . I know I could go to Roger and he'd give me good advice. I wouldn't expect a cash loan mind you," laughter rippled, "he's careful, our lad, very careful."

He told them how on the night of the Freshers' Fair when the rest of their group had been set on discovering the university drinking dives, Roger had been discovered in his college room working out his term's cashflow forecast.

"And now look where it's got him," Gareth said, "all this planning, all this carefulness, all this tight-fistedness: it's got him a junior partnership, a nice house, beautiful wife. . ."

"Hear! Hear!

"And so it was all obviously a complete waste of time!"

They all laughed.

"The bridesmaids!" Roger hissed at him, "you're supposed to reply to the toast!"

But Gareth, flushed with success at how well all this was going down, was beginning to lose his way.

"One of the best things about Roger," he said, with his gaze slightly unfocussed, "is that he has a very attractive sister! Yes, Sir! And she has a very attractive friend! Lizzie and er ... Petra." A certain amount of foot stamping ensued here. "Who have both carried out their bridesmaids' duties in a totally ... er ... totally ... very well!!"

Lizzie and Petra giggled and Imo realised that he had clearly forgotten her existence.

"I give you The Bridesmaids!" Gareth cried joyfully, grabbing a glass.

"The Bridesmaids!" everyone cried and some of the friends added, "Again!"

"You made a complete cock-up of that," Lizzie said amiably as Gareth returned to their table. Her fingers interlaced with his upon the white tablecloth.

Informality now began to overtake the mood in the marquee. Jackets and wraps were tossed over chair backs, at one table they were playing shove ha'penny with the sugared almonds which were scattered among the rose petals on the table cloth. Zaccy's bar was increasingly busy.

Outside the full heat of the afternoon was lessening, the white rose straggling over the terrace scented the air around it and somewhere in the tangled bushes above there was honeysuckle.

Jonathon's staff were beginning to pack china and cutlery and the queue lengthened for the portable toilets.

Now as the sun dropped behind the beech trees on the edge of the lawn and midges rose above the shorn grass, a camper van came up the drive. The harpist and her mother had finally made it.

CHAPTER 38

JULY

Once the food and speeches were over and the shadows were lengthening across the lawn the inhabitants of Trevean began to join the party.

First in, by sliding under the canvas towards the back of the marquee were Claud and Frankie. They stood for a moment staring around them until they were spotted by one of the girlfriends.

"Oh look!" she cried. "How cute!"

Frankie, impressed by Perdita's change into her flowered skirt, had dressed himself up in his Thomas the Tank Engine T-shirt and green fleece dinosaur hat; Claud had limited himself to his archery belt which was in fact a pony girth, and brought his quiver of homemade arrows.

The friends, now mellow and looking forward to some dancing, called the boys over to offer them sugared almonds and spoonfuls of summer pudding. Frankie ventured across and was soon preening himself in the petting he received from the girls and stuffing his cheeks full of sweets.

Claud's arrows attracted some attention and so encouraged he went back to the house to collect his bamboo bow. Two of the young men who had taken a fancy to girls on a separate table tightened the bow string and fired arrows with messages attached written on business cards. This caused a certain amount of disruption.

Clarissa had also come across from the house, drawn irresistibly to a party. She had been watching proceedings for much of the day from her sitting room window and had twice walked around the marquee, having recruited Perdita as attendant, 'to have a look see'. She had, in the process, struck up an acquaintance with some of the Directors' Lunches staff whom she had found taking a breather between courses, on the grass bank behind the catering tent.

Clarissa welcomed the chance to be recognised as having a certain position at Trevean, one of the Family. She was used to dealing with staff and indeed she felt she had been good at it in her former life abroad, no need to dwell now on how times had changed.

"It is not easy," she said to Jonathon, "to cater for this number and have everything ready at the right time, as I know having lived abroad and done quite a lot of entertaining. And you are operating from what is really a field kitchen, aren't you? I think you are to be congratulated."

Jonathon had been charmed and so was galvanised when he spotted her later as she watched the dancing from the marquee entrance to rush over and offer to fetch her a chair. Clarissa had been gracious and now, leaning upon her ebony stick, waited for the chair to arrive.

Penelope Rodmaine had regrettably been forced to queue at the portable toilets. Not at all pleased, she was making her way back and had reached Clarissa when they were jostled together by the sudden noisy arrival of some of the friends who had decided to explore the garden. A group of them were now returning, rather creased and picking leaf mould off each other.

In their mutual disapproval of this sort of behaviour Clarissa and Penelope sensed a likeness of mind.

"Good evening," Clarissa said, making the first conversational move.

Penelope, thrown off kilter by the toilets and the brashness of youth, was inclined to accept this overture although not prepared to cede precedence as mother of the bridegroom. She noticed Clarissa's stick. "Can I help you back to your table?"

Clarissa's comment to counter Penelope's proprietorial tone, that she was not a guest but lived at Trevean was all but drowned out in the waves of sound.

The harpist had found that her planned recital had to be cut short after her late arrival and feeling unappreciated she and her mother were now re-loading the harp into the camper van. A couple of the boyfriends gave them a hand.

Dagon and Belial who turned out to be more prepared than they looked to adapt to suit the punters had launched into club music and the centre of the marquee was now filled with people dancing to Madonna.

Through mutual grimacing she and Penelope understood that they both found it all a bit much. When Jonathon arrived with the chair, Penelope suggested that they sit outside for a while.

Perdita was transfixed by the glamour of the scene in the

marquee and had stood quivering beside Clarissa. She trailed over the lawn after her and stood behind her chair, when Jonathon placed it at a distance across the grass. She jigged from one foot to another.

"Do you need the lavatory?" Clarissa asked.

"No!" Perdita exclaimed. She was overcome with horror at the question which Clarissa asked without tact just as two Directors Lunches staff arrived with more chairs, followed by George Rodmaine who had also been driven to escape the dancing.

"I believe there is a children's tent," said Penelope, who had kicked up such a fuss about the need for a crèche, but had not so far gone to look at it.

"They're really young," Perdita said for she had made a trip round earlier with Sally when they had found only three toddlers being looked after by four Nursery Nurse students. The babies had been smuggled back into the marquee by their parents and were either being passed from hand to hand among the friends or were asleep under the tables in their travel seats.

"What do you want to do then?" Clarissa asked.

"I don't know."

"Well, you can't just stand there fidgeting." Clarissa was dying to chat to Penelope, an opportunity for proper grown-up conversation which she so rarely got. "Think of something."

"Claud and Frankie are in the marquee," Perdita said, staring at her toes.

"Is that what you want to do too?"

"Mummy said we musn't."

"That was earlier I expect," Clarissa said, relieved to discover this solution. "I think it'll be all right now that they've started the dancing."

Penelope felt that she should offer her endorsement of this

suggestion. "Yes, do," she said, "if anyone says anything to you, say I said you could, and I am Mrs Rodmaine and mother of the bridegroom."

She said this as much for Clarissa's benefit as for Perdita's.

Perdita looked at her for a moment and then ran off towards the marquee.

"Bit of a racket in there?" George suggested, sitting down beside them.

Penelope in her turn was not best pleased by his arrival for undoubtedly it would limit the scope of her conversation with Clarissa. She had begun to think that since he retired George was getting under her feet more than he used to and her daytime social life which mostly involved W I activities and afternoon bridge with girlfriends was suffering.

She sent him off again to find glasses of wine, then complained because he had spilt some on the journey back across the grass, then largely ignored him.

"Do you play bridge?" she asked Clarissa.

"Oh, I used to play a lot when I lived abroad." Clarissa paused. "Hong Kong, where my husband was in business. But not so much now." She was regretful. Her explanation that she did not often have the opportunity to play, which she hoped would imply more pressing social or family commitments blurred the real facts. In truth no one else at Trevean was interested in bridge and she had no realistic way of getting anywhere to play. She certainly wouldn't ask for a lift from James who was of course, in her opinion, far too selfish to offer. Nor could she ask Sally who had too much to do already, and petrol was so expensive.

Penelope, who was capable occasionally of moments of insight, said, "But you must come up and stay with us. I play

435

with some girlfriends on Tuesday and Thursday afternoons, we stop for tea – it's quite civilised."

"Oh – " Clarissa was overcome with longing. "I don't know if I could manage the journey . . . with my hip." And she also thought, "Money? Clothes?"

"The trains are convenient," Penelope said firmly, "and we'd meet you at the local station."

"This poor woman," she imagined giving her friends Clarissa's credentials, "is marooned down there with her really rather odd daughter and the daughter's husband who is most anti-social and I'm not sure how many children but there seemed to be a lot of them, all rather scruffy. I felt so sorry for her because she is clearly used to a very different sort of life. Abroad – Hong Kong I believe, yes rather interesting."

It was of course always necessary to be able tick the right boxes with new people.

George meanwhile, sitting on the uncomfortable folding chair beside Penelope, was feeling excluded. If the music had been something more reasonable, he would have asked Marilyn to dance but all that hopping about wasn't his style and meantime he had been pipped at the post by Clive who had taken her away to the overfull dance floor. George saw them leave the table with regret, watching Marilyn disappear into the crush, a flushed and slightly crumpled rose.

Now he noticed that James had appeared on the front steps of the house. He rose to his feet for here perhaps was an opportunity for some masculine conversation, something which he was beginning to miss. Retirement, he was starting to suspect, could bring with its inherent gains some unforeseen losses.

James, unexpectedly, was feeling positive. He had imagined

that he would spend the day of the wedding loathing every minute of it and seeking refuge in the study. However, after weeks, months, in which nothing encouraging had ever arrived in the post, on this day of all days, something had: a letter had come from India.

He did not, as he more usually would, do a bunk when he saw George strolling towards him. He wanted someone with whom he could discuss his news and Sally had been rushing around all day so that he had scarcely been able to do more than give her the bare facts as presented in the letter.

Now he even found himself unfamiliarly relaxed about George's expressed wish to see some of the older parts of the house. He took the lead round the back of the building to look at the supposed medieval window arches and from here their natural progress was into the kitchen to examine the larder doorway, probably of earlier date.

George strolled, glass in hand, his comments demonstrating to James an educated but not too stressfully intense level of interest.

In James's mind had been the thought that he should probably offer George a proper drink, along with the depressing knowledge that there was no gin or whisky. This problem resolved itself however when they found two spare bottles of wine from the reception on the kitchen table.

"What have you got there?" James asked, looking at George's now empty glass. "Fancy a top up?"

George accepted for the only apparent alternatives were to sit out Penelope's conversation with Clarissa or return to the marquee. He had earlier done the round of the family guests, which had involved fielding comments about the 'inconvenience of the conveniences' as one of Penelope's aunts put it, with grim archness, referring to the toilet arrangements in the coaches and the portaloos.

"Not easy to manage," said the aunt. "I gather Lionel may have had a bit of an accident."

The image this information conjured up was distressing. George had no wish to return to the marquee so he helped James to clear a space at the kitchen table among the toys, wet drying-up clothes, plates, dirty mugs, dead buttercups and other flotsam scattered across it and they opened the bottle of Bordeaux red.

"Not too bad?" James suggested, tasting the wine.

"I had some input into that," George said, with satisfaction, especially as the input had been informative rather than financial; Clive had paid for the wine.

They proceeded to finish the first bottle and talk about golf, a shared enthusiasm. The discussion moved on to life experiences.

James found to his surprise that he was quite enjoying the conversation. Having outlined his teaching career in India he introduced the suggestion broached in the letter which he had received that morning.

"The head of the college in Delhi where I used to teach has got in touch with me," he said. "Nice chap, he wants to know if I would consider mentoring their students who come over here on exchange placements, or to complete post-graduate research."

"Sounds interesting?" George suggested

"Well, yes . . . " James paused. It is interesting, he thought, to me it is interesting because this is what I know about, these are people I enjoy working with. It will mean that I am still connected with the college, with India. He felt his jaw tighten from the sudden anguish he felt. India! "The students might require accommodation in the vacations," he said.

"Could you manage that here?"

"Oh, I should think so," James glanced round vaguely and then paused to give the idea some attention. We might be able to get rid of those gardening people, he thought, which would be a blessed relief. The girls especially, the one in a boiler suit with a bird's nest in her hair and the other miss who goes around semi-naked.

"Not as easy as you might imagine, being retired," George said speculatively.

James was uncertain. Was George suggesting that he wasn't coping too well at Trevean? But he got the impression that George, who was staring thoughtfully at his empty glass, was talking more generally.

"No," James conceded. "Has its drawbacks, retirement."

"You can," George said with sudden frankness, "find yourself getting into a state of petticoat rule."

James looked at him.

"The woman of the house," George pointed out, "is Queen Bee."

"Oh, yes – "

James felt a twinge of guilt for he needed Sally to sort things out at Trevean, but then wasn't he stuck with Clarissa – perhaps more wasp than bee? "'The monstrous regiment of women . . . '" he murmured. (Excluding Sally of course).

"So what's to be done?" George gazed through the kitchen window.

James didn't have an answer, so he re-filled their glasses and they both sat in reflective silence for a while.

CHAPTER 39

JULY

When Clive and Marilyn left the dance floor they found their table deserted, cleared even of their glasses by the efficiency of Jonathon's team.

"Why don't you go outside and get a breath of fresh air?" Clive suggested. "I'll see if I can find some more drinks. I'll bring them out."

Marilyn left the marquee and stood on the grass. She had enjoyed the dancing. "We used to dance a lot," she thought. "We used to go out and dance ... "

That was years ago, before Clive's business had become so time consuming, before they moved to The Rowans. They used to swap babysitting tokens with other parents from the children's primary school and go out in a group.

As she waited it struck her that she always did what people told her to do. Clive had just said, 'Go outside' and she had gone out and now was waiting for him. She fulfilled other people's expectations.

Some of the friends were playing a make-shift game of cricket with Claud and Frankie in the fading heat of the evening. Around them the light shimmered over the grass, clouded with pollen particles.

Their ball seemed to have gone into the giant rhododendron bush bordering the lawn and the batsmen were lolloping to and fro as yells of protest rose higher from the fielders. "Hey! Lost ball, man!"

Claud had crawled into the undergrowth like a terrier going down a rabbit hole; Frankie stood waving his arms.

As Marilyn watched them a breath of air cooled her skin and involuntarily she shivered.

Sometimes in such brief moments a sudden clarification of thought and conviction will fuse, enabling a decision to be made.

"What are these?" Marilyn accepted one of the glasses with which Clive had returned.

"Cocktails," Clive said. "Ought to give them a try, I suppose, they caused enough trouble to organise. Lamorna Sunset, this is called, apparently. I think that guy on the bar makes it up as he goes along, sunsets aren't green."

"I'd like to sit down," Marilyn said, suddenly.

Clive looked at her. "Not feeling ill are you?"

"No," Marilyn said. "I just want – " I want to say something, she thought, now while I have the courage.

"Well, where – " Clive's glance rested doubtfully on the chairs where Penelope and Clarissa sat.

Marilyn turned towards a short flight of granite steps leading up to the terrace. "Over there."

The stone of the steps was mottled by orange lichen, they sat with the white flowers of convolvulus trailing around their feet.

Clive paused, uncertain of her mood. Was she getting upset again? When she didn't speak he said speculatively, "So, it's gone off quite well, this wedding, all things considered?"

He himself was feeling relief that none of the things which might so easily have gone wrong had actually done so.

Also he had taken the opportunity when fetching the drinks to check his messages and found the agent in Qatar had confirmed payment for the roof panels. He now stretched his legs and leaned back, breathing in the fresher air and half listening to the music drifting from the marquee. Dagon and Belial were, perhaps by request, cooling it a bit.

"Ok?" he asked Marilyn, realising that she had not responded.

Marilyn linked her fingers together in her lap. She had set down her glass, the cocktail had an odd taste, it was sticky on her lips. "I want to get a job," she said.

This Clive had not expected. "What?"

"A job," she repeated, still gazing ahead of her.

He looked at her, non-plussed. "But you've never wanted to go back to work have you?"

Admittedly he hadn't really wanted her to work either, certainly not when the girls were younger. It would have meant having to juggle child-care and school pick-ups, both of them getting overtired, the house in a muddle.

"Well, now I do," she said.

"But why?"

"Because there is nothing for me to do at home." It was a statement of fact.

Clive tried to get his head round this. "But there's – " he hesitated to say 'housework' as women could get stroppy about housework these days but still someone had to do it. "What about – shopping and the garden? Seeing people?"

Marilyn stared into the darkening evening, still laden with the sun's warmth on stone and grass and the scent of some mauve and self-seeded stocks nearby.

I haven't got anyone to see, she thought, that's half the trouble and it's not that there is nothing to do, it's that there is nothing interesting to do, nothing that has to be done by me, nothing that I enjoy doing, that I'm good at doing.

There's no point me doing things because it's better if I don't. I don't need to cook because everyone likes food from the supermarket better and I don't need to shop for that because they deliver it. I don't need to wash anything because it goes in the washing machine and the dryer or it goes to the laundry. I don't need to clean anything because Julia does it better than me. Clive would never let me redecorate and do the painting.

"Office work has changed," Clive said, thinking of the various tasks to which his secretary could be asked to give her forceful attention. "Computer programmes and so on."

"I don't want to work in an office," Marilyn said.

"But what then?"

Marilyn's fingers tightened. "There's a restaurant in the town, well, it's just a café really. It's called The Lemon Tree and it's run by someone called Jamal. I want to ask him to give me a job." She was winding her engagement and wedding rings around her finger. She said the words in a rush.

Now Clive was totally bemused. "In a café?"

"Yes."

"What, as a . . . ?"

"Waitress."

For a moment or two he remained surprised into silence. "But why?" he then asked yet again, for it seemed such an unlikely and indeed inappropriate choice.

"So I can meet people," she said, "and talk to them."

"But you don't like meeting new people!"

"That's why," she said.

He didn't understand.

"And maybe learn how to cook different things," she said.

"But you don't like cooking."

"That's why"

There was an edge to her voice. Neither of them said anything further for a while, Marilyn felt exhausted with the effort the explanation had cost her, in so far as she had been able to make it, Clive was lost in incomprehension.

"But will he give you a job?" he asked eventually, for he was doubtful. "This café owner?"

"I don't know," she said, "but Tanis has left, the waitress, and there's no-one else."

A further moment or two of silence followed and then a sudden thought occurred to Clive. "Is he married?"

"Jamal? Yes."

"Then can't his wife help in the business?"

"They're Indian," Marilyn said. "And they have a little boy, quite small, and she's expecting another baby. She does do some of the cooking, but in their flat."

Clive considered. Might Marilyn learn to cook a decent curry?

"Oh."

In the marquee the dance track ended and quiet flooded in. A cheer rose raggedly from the cricketers who were having to call it a day in the fading light.

Marilyn squeezed her palms together; they were slightly

damp. "And as well – " she said.

Clive looked at her. What more?

"Imo – "

"Imo?"

"Yes. She must to go to Art College."

Now he was beginning to feel annoyed; where had all this come from? "But we've been through all that. It would be a total waste of time."

"No – "

"What?"

"It wouldn't be a waste."

"Why not?" Clive asked exasperated. "I thought we'd agreed?"

"Because . . . " Marilyn stared at the white convolvulus flowers on the granite step and tried to explain. "Then she can be out there, where things happen and . . . seeing things and doing things , and not . . . " she struggled for the word, "be stifled."

He stared at her. "Stifled?"

"Yes," she said, clutching for more conviction than she in reality yet possessed. She took a breath to fill her lungs with air.

Clive, hearing the strain in her voice, decided to say nothing more. Anyway he had to get his head round what she had said, ideas which seemed to have come out of nowhere.

Meanwhile Imo herself was feeling that she had had enough. She had sat virtually silent throughout the meal and the speeches, isolated on her table with Lizzie, Petra and Gareth. As he got more drink inside him Gareth found it amusing to tease her, addressing her as The Little Sister.

"And ow is Little Sister enjoying Big Sister's wedding?" he asked, returning from a foray to find another bottle of wine. He noticed the untouched chocolate mousse still before her on the table. "Aren't you tempted?"

Involuntarily Imo drew back and said, "No."

Lizzie laughed. Imo felt herself flush, she clenched her hands beneath the fall of the linen tablecloth.

"And still all alone?" Gareth said, for Petra had gone to check out spare men at the cocktail bar.

"I've got to go," Imo said, pushing her chair back.

"No!" He pulled a sad clown face.

Imo felt she hated them. She blurted out, "I've got to find my boyfriend."

"Oops!" Lizzie cried. "Who he?"

"Ah!" Gareth was refilling their glasses. "Absolutely! What is it you do here? Gardening? Is he a gardener?"

Lizzie was convulsed. "Love in the greenhouse!"

Imo left, threading her way between the tables with the groups of laughing, chattering people, beneath the fairy lights and the trails of now wilting ivy, towards the marquee entrance.

At the cocktail bar the friends had discovered Zachariah. The girls were begging him to sing them a sea shanty. "Oh please, Zaccy! Please!"

"I could maybe sing you a good Cornish song my handsomes," he said. "Got to keep it decent. It's a wedding after all."

"Oh yes!" they perched on the bar stools, flushed faces, hitched skirts.

"Everyone got a drink in?" he suggested. The girls turned to the boyfriends to get this sorted out.

Outside the marquee Imo found people milling around in the soft evening air. There was nowhere here, in her ridiculous dress, where she could escape notice. On an impulse she ran into the house.

She went through the hall, along the slate flagged corridor and into the kitchen. She had half intended to go up the back stairs to her room but remembered that Nicolette might be there, doing her hair or asleep on the bed.

"And I can't stand it," Imo thought, "I can't stand her always being there. It's not my place anymore."

She stood in the kitchen, recently vacated by James and George who had transferred themselves, plus wine, to James' study to look at some early Trevean estate records.

She saw but barely noticed the usual clutter, now with extra layers because of the reception. A bucket of unused rhododendron flowers had been left beside the sink; odd mugs and glasses, rejected for holding the table decorations, were piled on the draining board; the dogs' drinking bowl had again been spilt and water pooled across the slate floor, trailed with footprints from different feet.

"If – " she forced herself to say the words in her mind and a harsh ache lodged beneath her heart. "If Ned doesn't love me – "

She knew for certain, in that moment, that if this was so she must get away. It was too terrible, too much to bear. She couldn't stay.

But it couldn't be true, it couldn't be true.

Her mind kept replaying the awful moment when she had got off the coach and Ned had turned away from her, when he hadn't seemed to want to recognise her. Surely, surely she had been mistaken, surely there was an explanation. In her dress, with her hair different? Maybe he really hadn't recognised her, was that possible?

On an impulse she went out quickly and across the cobbled yard to the Laundry House.

In the cool dim interior she stood listening. Initially silence seemed to fill the building, then she thought she heard a sound of movement above, up the bare wooden staircase which led to the two small rooms under the roof where Ned and Graham slept.

Graham rarely spent any spare time in the Laundry House, his bolt hole was the potting shed where he kept a lamp so he could sort seeds in the evening. This was far more likely to be Ned.

With her heart beating she moved to climb the staircase and gazed upwards, a sliver of light from a slightly open door fell across the white-washed plaster of the wall and she distinctly heard a bed creak as someone turned over.

Reaching the small boarded landing she paused again beside the door leading to Ned's room. Her lips unconsciously formed the single syllable of his name; she tentatively pushed the door slightly further open.

There were two figures on the bed and both were naked.

Imo froze. She reached for the edge of the door-frame for it seemed in that brief moment as if her knees would lose the strength to support her. What she was seeing was not real, she felt detached, almost as if she watched a few sharply illuminated frames of film.

They were unaware of her. Ned lay on top of Nicolette; her fingers pulling at his damp hair.

"Don't do that!" he jerked his head away.

She laughed and said something, maybe, "Sulking . . . ?" but this was cut short in a gasp as Ned's marble perfect buttocks began to rise and fall above her. The she wrapped her thin brown legs around him and hooked her feet behind his arching back. "Better . . . "

Imo felt so weak as she retreated down the stairs that she resorted to leaning against the wall, causing small particles of flaking paint to drift down around her feet.

CHAPTER 40

JULY

When Ned and Nicolette came down the Laundry House stairs, having decided they felt like joining the party in the marquee, they discovered Graham standing stripped to the waist at the sink. He had spent the first half of the day as instructed by Sally helping to shift and carry kit for the DJs and the Directors Lunches team. As soon as possible, to avoid further involvement in the fuss and bother or contact with any more people he had retreated to the Kitchen Garden.

Now as he always did after work he was having a wash and shave. He could of course have used the nursery bathroom, but he chose not to go into the house any more than was necessary.

Nicolette paused staring. "You scrub up well, Graham," she said. "Don't you think, Ned?"

Ned pushed her so that she stepped off the bottom step. "Get a move on, I want to get a drink."

They went away laughing across the yard. Loathing them, Graham dragged the towel roughly across his chest, picked his clothes from the floor and went up to his room. Passing Ned's door he found it had been left wide open affording an unwelcome view of the tumbled bed.

He pulled on his non-work jeans and a shirt and stood for a while staring through the open window. He could hear the beat of the music from the marquee.

Dagon and Belial had turned the volume up again, causing the jackdaws to rise in a circle above the tall serrated chimneys of the house. The torpor of the hot afternoon had faded and the sky lightened from its clear high blue. Clouds strung thinly behind the beech trees were touched with pearl.

Graham stayed where he was for a while until hunger drove him across the yard, but the kitchen was empty and there were no signs of any food preparation. This indication that no-one had thought it worth telling him what he was supposed to do for his tea did nothing to improve his mood, which as so often kept him captive in curdling anxiety and suppressed anger, partly with himself. Why did he let these people walk all over him? And they wouldn't call it tea, he remembered, another annoyance, they'd say 'supper' and as usual make him feel inferior.

He opened the fridge door but possessing a strong territorial sense he hesitated to take the sausages or bacon which he found inside and saw as belonging to the Lacocks. Instead he took out the chunk of cheddar with which he made his crous, it was dry and cracking, stuffed behind the bowls of left-overs and the opened tins of spaghetti hoops. He turned to look for some bread.

When Sally came to the kitchen to fetch a glass of water,

for she had been dancing energetically in the marquee with Perdita and the boys, she found Graham sitting eating alone. He appeared to have been reading a copy of the Telegraph left lying on the table but this was now pushed aside, possibly when he heard her coming. He had a closed frown on his face.

Sally reflected as she looked at him that Graham had been born in the wrong time and the wrong place. He would have been well-suited to the life of, say, the early pioneers to America for he was practical, physically strong and inclined to be stoically satisfied with his own locality and limited human contact. In fact in such a situation he would for some girl have been a good catch, her log cabin would have been sturdier than most and her vegetable patch double dug and well dunged. But as it was, in this age, in England, girls by and large wanted something different.

Sally looked at Graham's brooding face and felt sorry for him. If life was fair he should be the one going to Agricultural College, not idle Ned who wasn't interested and would probably make nothing of it.

"Have you thought of getting some qualifications, Graham?" she asked. As usual he didn't answer at once but being used to conducting conversations with strongly silent teenagers, Sally waited until eventually he replied.

"What would that be?"

"Well – " she considered. "I know that they run Horticulture courses at the college where I teach, day release."

Graham stared at the remaining sandwich, which he didn't feel able to eat with Sally standing there watching him.

Sally decided that a fuller discussion was going to have to wait until she had more time, she went to the sink for the water. On an impulse as she was leaving the kitchen she said, "Come and see what's happening in the marquee. You might actually enjoy the music, you're more the right age group than we are."

She waited in the doorway.

Graham interpreted this as a command. He got to his feet hating the thought of mixing with these people, the Lacocks' sort of people. But he couldn't express his reluctance, putting it into words was beyond him, so he followed Sally down the slate corridor and through the hall.

Imo meanwhile had gone down the slope below the house; she sat amongst the long grass and ox-eye daisies where the last of the sun's rays slanted through the leaves of the large lime tree. She felt desolation surround her cutting her off from everything and everybody, she was trapped within a misery which was personal and particular and felt thick enough almost to be tangible. The sun dropped behind the tree and the ground had begun to pick up the slight damp of evening.

Not until bats appeared swooping overhead did she finally get to her feet and climb the bank, for she found their erratic flight frightening. She had decided to find her parents to tell them that she did not want to stay at Trevean. She wanted to come home with them, in the car, when they left that night.

Clive and Marilyn were still sitting on the granite steps beside the terrace and so when Imo reached the marquee she stood slightly inside the entrance gazing round in an unsuccessful attempt to locate them.

Meanwhile Graham had followed Sally unwillingly to where the children had commandeered a table.

Normally James would much rather have been in his study but mellowed by his drinks with George he had come looking for Sally to explain to her the news he had received from Delhi. He had not had a chance earlier because of, as he saw it, the chaos which had been going on all day.

The children had ceased leaping about on the dance floor and were flopping in their chairs. They were now hoping to persuade someone to buy them something to drink from Zaccy's bar, they had already finished up some glasses of guava juice abandoned on other tables. They knew better than to ask James for he never had any money on him.

"We are really thirsty," Perdita said now when Sally and Graham arrived.

"What, all of you?" Sally asked.

"Yes!" Perdita looked for confirmation from the boys. "Aren't we?"

"Quite thirsty," Claud attempted to combine support for Perdita with his natural inclination not to be too demanding.

Frankie wasn't bothered about such politesse. "Thirsty!" he yelled. "I want a juice!"

Not impressed, Sally said, "There's plenty of water in the tap. Go and get some in the kitchen like I've just done. What do you think, Graham, do you like this sort of music?"

Graham had occasionally been to the Fish Cellar in the nearby town which was the dance venue of choice for local youth; he tagged along with boys he had known at school, having met up with them in the pub. These evenings had usually involved the rapid consumption of alcohol followed by an approach to any unattached girls present by some of the bolder or more inebriated members of the group, of which Graham was not one.

"I s'pose," he said now, in unenthusiastic response to Sally's question.

Except for Frankie, who grasped Sally's arm, clamouring monotonously, "Thirsty, thirsty, thirsty . . . " they all appeared to be looking at him, expecting him to say more. This type of attention always unnerved him. As a way to escape he took up the children's idea and muttered that he had to find a drink.

Frankie's eyes brightened. "Me!" he said.

"No," Sally said. "Graham is only getting a grown-up drink. You can get some water, like I said. Perdita will go with you."

Frankie flung back his head and howled.

Graham moved away hastily, heading for the narrow strip of space along the side of the marquee and avoiding the more open route between the tables.

James said, "Why does he behave like that?"

"Shy," Sally said. "You can be a bit anti-social yourself, darling."

"Not if I'm in civilised company."

"I know. Frankie shut up or you'll have to go to bed. It's way past your bed-time."

Graham had decided that he wasn't staying and was in fact making for the exit when he saw Imo standing forlorn, scanning the dance floor for her parents.

In that moment, as he watched, her face changed for she had caught sight not of Clive and Marilyn but of Ned and Nicolette.

Roger and Antonia had not yet left and when they were on the dance floor the other couples instinctively gave them, as the bride and groom, a shifting but significant area of space. Neither Ned nor Nicolette felt the need to demonstrate such restraint, they moved into the clearer area and proceeded to show off.

Nicolette swayed in front of Ned. She had practised a lot of yoga and was quite startlingly supple. The message was easily read as she moved close against Ned's body and slid down the length of it.

Graham made his way deliberately, refusing to watch them, which others were now gathering to do. Imo ran precipitously.

Up in the attic room she got her backpack out from under her bed and stuffed into it all of her clothes from the chest-of-drawers and cupboard and whatever other possessions she could see lying about. She paused then wanting to get out of the hateful bridesmaid's dress but unable to reach the zip. Distracted she gazed at her reflection in the small mottled mirror, wondering in that moment how her appearance despite the heartache she was feeling could seem so little changed.

She pulled the rosebuds out of her hair and then in despair with the dress she tore the zip apart. Once off she pushed the cascade of foolish, frothy, pink frills under the bed.

Anguish once more engulfed her for this was now finally and certainly the end; she had lost Ned, lost love. Tears filled her eyes.

Dragging her backpack behind her she made her way down the narrow stairs. As she went she paused from habit to gaze from the window into the cobbled yard below but she missed seeing either Graham or Ned, each of whom was at that moment making their way towards the Laundry House.

Graham had had enough of being messed around at Trevean for one day; he was going to drive to his parents' small holding. He suspected that if he stayed Sally would ask him to work the Sunday too, helping to clear up.

Ned had left the marquee to fetch his wallet, with some reluctance but at Nicolette's insistence, after they had jointly failed to persuade Zachariah to serve them with free cocktails. Clive, in the knowledge that he was footing the bill for the champagne and the wine, had refused point blank to fund the bar. Nicolette had expressed her opinion that a pay bar at a wedding was naff.

"So it may be, darlin," Zachariah said to her, "but that's the way it is I'm afraid. You pays your money and takes your choice. Or not, as the case may be."

"Have you got any money?" Ned asked Nicolette.

"My handsome," Zachariah said, "we may be living in the sticks down here, but we still don't expect our women to buy our alcohol for us. Or their own, either."

Ned frowned.

"So hop it," Zaccy said amiably, "and find some ackers."

"How well you put it," Nicolette said, hitching herself onto a stool beside the bar, allowing her skirt to ride up across her thighs.

"That seat," Zachariah said, observing her, "is reserved for paying customers which as yet, unfortunately, you aren't."

She stared at him. "Are you saying I can't sit here?"

"'Ez."

She didn't move immediately but he continued looking at her until she slid down and stalked across to the nearest empty table.

"And fetch my cigs," she called clearly after Ned.

Zachariah returned his attention to giving the friends a lively rendition of 'Going up Camborne Hill, coming down' of which they soon got the hang and the chorus.

Graham, having collected his car keys, was leaving the Laundry House as Ned reached it. Both of them were in an excessively bad temper.

Ned deliberately pushed ahead.

Rage engulfed Graham. "Watch it!"

"What?" Ned demanded incredulously.

"Get out of the road."

Ned advanced a step. "What do you think you're playing at, you thick oaf?"

The right words as ever deserted Graham, in frustration he shoved Ned hard in the chest so that he fell backwards into the large water tank which stood beside the Laundry House wall. Then he turned and strode towards the yard steps; he did not look back.

"I'll kill you," Ned shouted after him.

The water in the tank was soupy with rotted leaves and it smelled, mud and glutinous bubbles glugged to the surface; it took Ned a couple of minutes to haul himself out. Looking down at his filthy clothes he was consumed with fury.

"I've had this sodding place!" he said, kicking at the tank. "And these sodding people!"

Shortly afterwards Graham's battered Vauxhall was the first of a succession of vehicles to depart down the drive at Trevean as the summer dusk deepened into night and the honeysuckle scent hung beneath the trees in the cooling air.

The Directors Lunches' van followed towing its matching trailer and with Jonathon at the wheel. A general sense of satisfaction prevailed among the staff crammed on board. They had given a potentially difficult job their best shot and now they looked forward to being shown the wedding photos; after the honeymoon Antonia could pay back favours by swopping shifts.

Ned drove the yellow Beetle with scant attention to the pot-holes in the drive or their effect upon the suspension. "This place is sodding crap," he said. "and I'm sodding out of it."

Nicolette sitting beside him in the passenger seat, laughed.

Roger and Antonia leaving at last in the Porsche, which had somehow become hung about with rattling tin cans, 'Just Married' balloons and more white and silver streamers, drove in a more restrained manner. Once however Roger had stopped in the drive to remove the cans and they reached the road he boldly put his foot down on the accelerator. Their hotel with its bridal suite securely booked was only ten miles away.

They didn't recognise the harpist and her mother whose camper-van had broken down and who were waiting for the arrival of Jack Richards' call-out truck, which at this time of night was not likely to be soon. It had not been a very successful gig for them, one way and another.

The departure of the bride and groom signalled to the wedding guests that they might now, with the niceties observed, leave. The coaches were brought down from the top yard and the elderly relations and the parents of the babies and toddlers were soon queuing to board.

The friends followed, carrying shoes and bottles and having mislaid various ties, jackets and bags. Although Petra had saved a seat for her Lizzie chose to sit with Gareth.

The Rodmaines and the Bradfords stood on the gravel to see the coaches off.

Marilyn's relief that the wedding was safely over had been buoyed up by champagne and adrenaline which had carried her earlier through both the reception and her attempt to explain to Clive that she must work at The Lemon Tree and Imo must go to Art College. Now she felt drained.

George wondered if he had imagined the rosy bloom he had seen in her face. Perhaps it had been the light, in any case he must have been mad to think that Penelope would let him get away with anything of that sort. He needed a decent hobby. The golf club committee?

Imo had lugged her backpack up to the parked Jag in the top yard and she sat on the ground against one of the wheels until Clive found her.

"What are you doing here?" he asked.

As she climbed into the back seat of the car he missed the sense of her short muttered reply but he got the impression that she had been crying. Leave it for now then, he thought; he had had enough emotion for one day.

As she waited for George to bring down the BMW Penelope turned to Sally, "I have invited your mother to come and stay with us. She will enjoy some bridge. It must be so difficult for her giving up the lifestyle she was used to."

Sally was tired, it had been a very long day; she wondered again how Penelope managed to be quite so consistently irritating.

James had gone to take the dogs for their last run, leading them out the back of the house into the woods. "They'll all be going home soon," he assured them, "all these people."

The dogs didn't care, they rushed joyfully out to pursue rustlings and night smells in the undergrowth.

"Ah, here's George at last," Penelope said as the car rounded the rhododendron bush, her tone giving no indication of regret to be leaving. "Is your husband here? I think we need to be going."

"I'm afraid James is having to deal with something at the moment," Sally said with finality.

"Well, it's going to take us quite a time to get back to our hotel. It's not like motorway driving round here is it?"

Sally thought, no fortunately it was not.

"And do you know where the Bradfords have got to?"

But Sally didn't.

Marilyn had in fact retreated to sit at a table in the marquee which was empty save for Dagon and Belial who were packing up their kit at the far end.

"Well, all the same I really think we must be off," Penelope said.

George came to make his own his own farewells. "Considering the problems I think we can say things didn't go too badly." His glance lingered briefly on Frankie's trike with its bent wheel, sticking out of the flowerbed in front of the house,

"George !" Penelope's voice had edge as she stood waiting for him to open the car door for her.

"Right. Well, goodbye then, Mrs ... er ... "

"Lacock," Sally finished for him as the BMW disappeared down the drive.

Finally when Clive had returned to find Marilyn the Bradfords also made ready to leave, their thanks on the whole more convincingly expressed.

Clive said, "It's all been a success, I think. People enjoyed themselves."

He looked around with satisfaction at the house, the lawn, the marquee; it had been his decision to choose this place.

Marilyn felt she must make an effort to keep smiling although she was definitely now feeling a bit wobbly. "Oh yes, I think so ... "

Clive, checking off the problems he had been faced with said, "The buses worked out fine and those catering people of Antonia's did a good job. I think they've left the place reasonably tidy haven't they?"

"I haven't had a chance to look yet," Sally said, "but hopefully, yes."

As they set off for the top yard and the car and Imo, about whom he had still to tell Marilyn, Clive remembered to add, "You'll let me have the final bill?" There might yet be a chance yet to get a contribution out of George Rodmaine.

"Yes, of course," Sally said, quailing slightly at the thought of the paperwork this would involve. Never mind, tomorrow would be another day.

As the Jag passed down the drive through the dark tunnel of rhododendrons the branches were suddenly illuminated with Father Christmases and jolly reindeer. Sally, returning to the house, had belatedly remembered to switch on the lights.

Later in the marquee a badger, attracted by dropped scraps of food, came upon Dagon and Belial asleep on the sisal matting beneath their disco decks; the badger beat a hasty retreat.

After that the night settled over Trevean.

THE END

CHARACTERS IN THE STORY

Peter Trewin	30	garage mechanic
Zachariah Williams	59	local publican aka 'Boy Zaccy'
Nancy Williams	58	Zachariah's wife
Michelle Lowe	30	Personal Banker
Alec Sancreed	78	Local in The Lion pub run by Zachariah
Bobby Grose	78	Local in The Lion pub run by Zachariah
Ivor Morton	65	newsagent

The Bradfords at The Rowans in Somerset

Name	Age	
Clive Bradford	44	owner and MD of small plastics moulding company
Marily Bradford	40	Clive's wife
Antonia Bradford	21	Clive and Marilyn's elder daughter, junior chef at Directors' Lunches, Mayfair, London; shares flat with Lizzie Rodmaine and Petra Colyton
Imogen (Imo) Bradford	17	Clive and Marilyn's younger daughter, would-be art student

Others in Somerset

Name	Age	
Maddy Cooper	22	dress-maker, was at technical college with Antonia Bradford
Sarah Batchelor	21	proprietor of Sarah's Flowers, was at school with Antonia Bradford
Julia Prentice	47	twice weekly cleaner at The Rowans
Alan Prentice	49	Julia's husband , council employee on county roads

CHARACTERS IN THE STORY

Sharon Prentice	19	daughter of Julia and Alan Prentice, unmarried mother
Gary Prentice	17	son of Julia and Alan Prentice, 'trouble'
Nyle Prentice	2	son of Sharon Prentice
Finn Prentice	3 months	son of Sharon Prentice
Justin Larne	26	boyfriend of Sharon Prentice and father of Finn
Jamal Akbar	42	proprietor of The Lemon Tree café
Peter Fullerton	50	Function Manager, Columb Court Hotel
Lisa Heyworth	23	Receptionist at Columb Court Hotel

The Rodmaines at The Old Granary, Worcestershire

Name	Age	
George Rodmaine	65	semi-retired solicitor, owner and senior partner iwn firm
Penelope Rodmaine	60	wife of George Rodmaine, President of local WI
Roger Rodmaine	33	son of George and Penelope Rodmaine, chartered accountant and financial analyst in City firm
Lizzie Rodmaine	26	daughter of George and Penelope Rodmaine, Personal Assistant to partner in insurance company in City, London
Petra Colyton	26	Personal Assistant in London based head office of estate agents

Others

Name	Age	
Jonathon Smythe	42	Team Leader, Directors Lunches
Dagon and Belial	42, 39	aka Steve and Craig, DJs with disco 'Fire and Brimstone'
Edward Skimmins	64	Receptionist at hotel in Somerset used by George and Penelope Rodmaine
Henry Hobden	68	Waiter at this hotel

POSTSCRIPT FROM THE AUTHOR

A friend of mine with a kind nature asked me if those two disaffected young people, Imo and Graham, were ever destined to meet again.

Well I can tell you that yes, they were. But that was some time later and part of a different story.

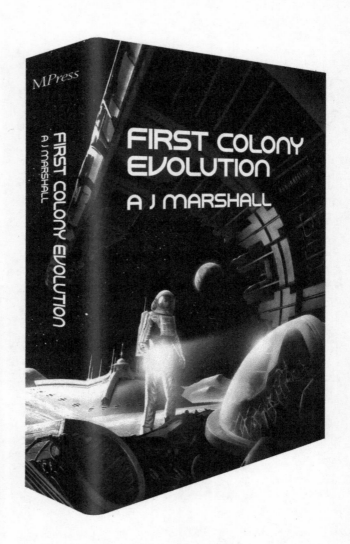

FIRST COLONY

EVOLUTION

Read an extract now . . .

The science fiction work *First Colony* is a series containing five novels. Together, the books span the century and more of unprecedented change immediately after the first human 'off planet' birth. By 2050, Moon base Andromeda had expanded from its initial, tentative, portacabin-like modules, into a sprawling labyrinth of double and triple storied architectural units built from materials mined on the Moon's surface.

After the Proclamation of Independence in May 2050, the new 'Senate of Lunar Colonisation' removed the military-like regime under which Andromeda's two thousand inhabitants lived and worked and implemented a self-governing, self-sustainable democracy based on the charter of the American Declaration of Independence. Those who would return to Earth amid its energy calamity and climatic strife did so, but those who remained formed the populous of the First Colony. The strict rules governing male and female fraternisation in Andromeda and the immediate return to earth of women falling 'illegally' pregnant whilst on space duties was abolished. Cohabitation was allowed, even encouraged, and the first baby was born nine months after lunar independence. His name was Aaron Wu, born of a British mother and a Chinese father.

First Colony charts the life and legacy of this first so-called 'Luman' – a human born in the lunar colonies. Aaron Wu's life begins innocently enough – the result of unique events entwined with fate. Each of the five books form a chronological framework for an extraordinary life; events being both astonishing and shocking in unequal measure. The novels will set out the trials, tribulations and interactions of this character as he rises through the Lunar Senate to the highest office of this and perhaps other independent space colonies.

The novel *First Colony* is a work composed of five volumes and the storyline, by nature of being set in the future is essentially science fiction. Fantasy, however, it is not, as the science described in the books is either fact, based on fact or expectation. Indeed, the author's style and his previous works reflect highly believable scenarios.

First Colony is about man's inevitable pursuit of the unknown and his innate necessity to colonise; driven in this case as much by environmental calamity as by instinct. It is about the relentless advance of technology and the misuse of knowledge.

First Colony is about high adventure and love, about deceit, greed and the unexpected. It is about the dissolving power of governments and the emergence of the all-consuming 'Corporation'. It is an intelligent crime thriller as well as an emotional rollercoaster. It is about Neil Armstrong's legacy and the immortal words he spoke as he stepped from the landing craft *Eagle* on 20 July 1969 as mankind held its breath.

The *First Colony* Series:	Availability:
First Colony – Evolution	2019
First Colony – Forgotten Gods	2020
First Colony – Quantum	2020
First Colony – Planets	2021
First Colony – Thoughts	2021

AUTHOR'S COMMENT

First Colony is a futuristic novel about man colonising the Moon. As our neighbour and partner in the vastness of space, the Moon's close proximity dictates much more than just the rising and ebbing of our ocean tides. Since time began, the Moon has influenced the very fabric of our existence. Indeed, without the presence of this apparently inert body, the Earth would not have become an oasis for any species, least of all ours.

The predictable and eternal passage of the Moon through the night sky has etched its form into the subconscious of each and every generation that has preceded us. And so too, whether in desperation or not, it was just a matter of time before man viewed this familiar place as an achievable goal, with a frontier to be crossed like any other and subsequently a new land to be settled. Like the Americas centuries before, a new world beckoning, with new opportunities and with new dreams over a distant horizon. However, as is often the case, the old lessons learned are quickly forgotten as humankind rushes to stake its claim – except that the irradiated cold of space and the desolate Moon are far less forgiving than any frontier that has beckoned before.

BOOK 1: EVOLUTION

Lumans are essentially the same as the humans that preceded them; however, by nature of the changed environment in which they live, minor genetic anomalies are to be expected. When the first of their kind – some say 'subspecies' – visit Earth in 2069, their welcome is euphoric. Such elation is, however, short lived. Suppressed racial intolerance rises again, bolstered by hardship and food shortages.

Born on the same day as Aaron, but in a small American town in Arizona, a young woman closely studies a one-metre diameter hologram of the Moon in her bedroom. A little above the floor, the surreal image slowly rotates and the young woman encircles it transfixed. In her nineteen years of life – mainly below the earth's surface – Jessie Parker has never seen the Moon with her own eyes. This because the dense suffocating layer of contaminated cloud that surrounds the Earth has neither lifted nor dispersed in her lifetime. She instinctively knows, however, that her destiny lies on that neighbouring planetoid, where immigration is illegal and political accord with Earth's teetering governments is strained at best.

FIRST COLONY
EVOLUTION

A J MARSHALL

MPress Books

First Colony
Evolution

First published in the United Kingdom in 2019 by MPress Books

Copyright © Andrew J Marshall 2019

MPress Books Limited Reg. No 6379441 is a company registered in Great Britain
www.mpressbooks.co.uk

British Library Cataloguing in Publication Data
A catalogue record for this book is available from the British Library.

Where possible, papers used by MPress Books are natural, recyclable products made from wood grown in sustainable forests. The manufacturing processes conform to the environmental regulations of the country of origin.

ISBN
978-0-9565077-2-3
Electronic book format 978-1-9996531-6-3

Typeset in Minion
Origination by Core Creative, Yeovil 01935 477453
Cover design by Tomislav Tikulin
ePublication produced by MPress Books Limited
Copyright Protected

PROLOGUE

Everyone experiences grief at some point in their lives, although its intensity, I now know, is subjective. My first recollection of this debilitating emotion was not my own, but my mother's, and I remember exactly when it occurred. At that precise moment in time, and because of an accident, this 'melancholy' flooded into our lives like water through a breached dam and for years after I fought to shore up the damage. It was an emotion I tried enormously to forget – to relegate to the recesses of my mind. Perhaps that's why my primary school teacher reported me as hyperactive, amongst other things.

The day before my fifth birthday started innocuously enough, but by midday we knew that my father was dead and thereafter the hell that contains all the sadness, all the wretchedness, all the misery of people, opened beneath our house. My mother immediately fell into that fiery underworld and soon she had dragged me down with her. I didn't kick and scream, for at the time I had no idea where I was going. Hindsight truly is a wonderful thing, but I can't help feeling that even at five I should have flailed my arms and grasped something – that I should have held on for dear life, seizing any and all opportunities before we both vanished into that pit. A purple tree . . . that man Jesus from Earth . . . my pet robot . . . anything – or at least shouted for help or left a trail, like Hansel and Gretel did in the Brothers Grimm story. For longer than I care to remember we floundered beneath that house, or 'module' as it really was. Looking back, it was three years before I climbed high enough to get a hand-hold on the edge of the precipice. At eight years old I looked eleven – at least that's what people told my Mother – but inside I felt like I thought a fifteen-year-old would, weighed by the pressures of growing up in the colony: forthcoming exams, a hopeful place at the Mare Ingenii Academy, aspirations of a career, image, girls . . . in so doing and whilst participating in the inevitable, accelerated social changes, still trying to make a statement about myself. During those years people often commented on my manner, unintentionally or otherwise reminding me of my responsibilities. I was merely eight and the man of our house.

My father died in a mining accident. I'll fill you in on the details later. Although 'accident' was the immediate, official explanation, the term was used so flippantly, so upsettingly off-hand thereafter that it aroused not only my anger but also my suspicions. Subsequently, the casual, careless indifference that was handed to my mother by way of an explanation eventually became the catalyst for my espionage. I can tell you that it is not the word I would use *now*.

My father had worked for Epsilon-Rio, the mineral conglomerate, since gaining a First from the Chinese University of Mining and Technology. After leaving Xuzhou at the age of twenty-three, he had spent a further year studying in Beijing and then five specialist years in Brazil before gaining a converted place on their Helium-3 extraction team. His subsequent, ill-fated, appointment to Andromeda arrived in the spring of 2048. He was thirty-seven years old when he died, as was my mother at the time. In fact, their birthdays were just a week apart. An Earth week I mean, not a lunar week, because, unlike me, they were both born on the Earth. They were both sixty seconds in a minute, sixty minutes in an hour, twenty-four hours in a day, three hundred and sixty-five days in a year, and so on and so forth, type people – again, unlike me. Because I grew up in a different time reference, although my mother would never admit to it.

My early life was disorientating, and not because of my father's absence – although that didn't help – but because life revolved around 'Earth' time from as early as I can remember. Of all the clocks in our home, only one was on lunar time. That was the school clock, and even then it was one of those antique, twin-faced, battery-powered models that stopped periodically and with the other face always set on Greenwich Mean Time – always!

GMT was and remains at odds with Lunar Corrected Time, creating a sort of bio-antagonism, and it served to confuse. All of my friends at school were so young when their parents transitioned that they never experienced the 'terrestrial effect', that was only for the 'oldies'. Retrospectively, however, one helpful thing did result from all those years of disturbed biorhythms: at the age of eighteen, when I first visited the Earth to start my university education, I did not suffer from lunoxia – not once, never: no dizziness, no diarrhoea, no insomnia. And believe me, with all the other things going on at the time that was charmed.

To explain further, my parents were human, one hundred percent born and brought up on planet Earth. As such, their bio-clocks were fixed. Indeed, even after thirty-three years as a colonist – and in her last twenty she never left the Moon – my mother's biorhythms hardly changed. She was subconsciously tied to the terrestrial calendar, as with most of the 'oldies' . . . the First Generation. There were a few who adapted, I recall – those who were still in their teens when they came across – but they were the minority. Most FGs arrived when they were in their thirties, were in stable relationships, usually with their partners back on Earth, and they had had their intended quota of children prior to taking up a lunar appointment. In those days an 'appointment' meant three years. 'Maturity' and 'stability', they were the key words when recruiting the lunar workforce. In reality, of course, back then, in the First Decade, it was NASA's call as to who was accepted into the programme and who was not, and they, the NASCALS – NASA's decision-making secret fraternity, I mean – were shit scared of being sued over excessive radiation exposure. Body defects, early death, child deformities – radiation had a lot to answer for. Of course, it was never the problem they believed it would be. Yes . . . hindsight is a wonderful thing.

The lunar colony claimed its independence on 21 May 2050, and on that same day, after the old rules had been 'dispatched' back to Earth on the 'last' shuttle, banished, along with any sentiment for the home planet, all the brewing, brooding relationships surfaced like bubbling lava from a volcano. The strict, military-style regulations on cohabitation, the segregated accommodation, the threat of being sent home the moment a pregnancy was detected – and a hormone check was compulsory every month – the no-fraternising and no-touching rules, the authority's obsession and anxiety regarding birth defects, everything . . . it all simply dissolved into oblivion. There was a lot of bed-hopping that first night by all accounts, and my mother and father were no exception: free love, like the hippy movement on Earth almost a century earlier. Apparently, it was mayhem, total chaos; a twenty-four-hour party. Ten lunar months later, to the day, I was the first out. Others soon followed, but I was the first. They called me a 'Luman' – a human born in the lunar colony. I was the first Luman. A fact that would enhance and haunt in varying measures each and every day of my life. With more to come, I assume.

There were twenty-eight of us, I remember, in Class 1A. The first class in the first primary school in the 'First Colony' and of course, due to the confines of our world, we not only knew each other like brothers and sisters we shared something special. Again, I'll come to that later. All the same, Stefanie was my best friend. I loved her even then, I think – in my primary years, but more so later. I was certainly over protective and I wouldn't let another boy sit next to her – not if I could help it. After a while it became an unwritten rule. I was pleased about that. No more squabbles, no bickering, no stand-offs.

Stefanie Elin Olson, with her blue, blue eyes and palest of complexions was, undoubtedly, the most beautiful girl in the school. Even when I knew nothing about anything, she would make my heart race – that's why I learnt to control it, for childish excitement was, on the whole, discouraged. She would occasionally leave something on the chair next to hers. A protein bar, or a carbcube perhaps, so confident was she that I would sit there. At home, and with several daily chores to do before leaving for the school module, I was so often running through the sky portal as the bell sounded that knowing precisely my place in that classroom was not only very helpful, but repeatedly a lifesaver. Stefanie, with her long blonde hair was a beacon, and me – seemingly two places at once – often exhausted, but happy. Because of this most fortunate prestige, some standing among my classmates and a few other things, like sport for example, people said I had a natural ability to lead, although my mother never mentioned it. Her indifference on this subject was often confusing and to some degree inconsistent, but many people, particularly other parents and close family friends, spoke of my mother's pride at me leading the Triteam six times in as many seasons.

Stefanie lived in the module next door in those early years, before her family moved to the new Insularum Estate over on the east side of Andromeda. We both arrived for our first day of primary school in pristine white uniforms, I remember, like thinly padded spacesuits with raised collars and elasticised sleeves. Saying goodbye set my mother crying again. I was used to it and I could deal with it like a nonchalant teenager would, even though I was only six years old. But I wasn't immune. I would always put an arm around her and provide some comfort – as best I could as an infant; perhaps a little better later, as a junior. Those years of pre-school, three of them, lower, middle and upper, were more a playgroup affair and half days. I remember always wanting to stay longer. Just to be out of that module was a joy, but to me Stefanie made each day there seem like the one before Christmas.

Ah yes . . . that day . . . the one before Christmas. A happy time for me; always was and always will be. Why? Because my mother was too – happy, open, sharing and talkative. Actually, it was more the anticipation of the following day that excited my mother and she would smile freely and communicate. Make calls. Invite people over.

Christmas Day itself, on the other hand, was a particular and peculiar 'Earth Day', and I learnt early that such Earth Days had the opposite effect on her. Christmas Day was, in fact, one of the 'special days' they tried to slot into a niche in the lunar calendar. 'They' on this occasion being the Lunar Senate. Of course, there was no niche, in fact there was no place for it at all – never has been, and in my view, never will be – except, perhaps, as a Remembrance Day. To remind me of it, however, so that it stands out like a radiation burn, my mother always cried on that day – perhaps more than on any other.

As my mother was essentially a Christian and I was brought up with their beliefs and values – beneath that somewhat misplaced 'planetary umbrella' so to speak – Christmas was one of 'our' days, but there were similar, equally significant days for the other great 'terrestrial' religions. And there were also other days they tried to integrate. These were deemed less important and so didn't warrant 'Colony Day' status, which was a day off, like a bank holiday on Earth. Easter Day, Boxing Day, Shrove Tuesday, Palm Sunday. Clearly, they meant something to the Oldies, but to us Lumens . . . me . . . they were just annotations on the first calendars that gradually vanished over the years. Scientology had a niche, however, if you could call its brief popularity that. For our neighbours in Module 101 it was important. I remember heated discussions over the dinner table between my mother and her friends and articles in the *Lunar Times*. But again, by the Second Decade that too had petered out – at least that was the case here in the Colony.

After my mother had sent me to university on Earth – in her home town of Oxford in the Royal Kingdom, which is England and Wales combined – and against my wishes, I might add, I found forgetting my mother's ever-lasting grief much easier. Upon reflection, it was just because other emotions quickly welled to replace those of my missing father. I'll come to the story of Stefanie in a moment. But for now, at the home planet age of twenty-one years, nine months and three days, and as I recount my life to this point, I can honestly say that I understand what my mother went through when my Dad died.

CHAPTER 1

FIRST AMONG THE NEW

To begin, let me give you a perspective on those early years and later explain a little of Andromeda, the first celestial colony of our species. Let me tell of the exodus, the minerals, the misinformation and of the inevitable conflict.

Not long after my father's death and during the months that followed, my mother was so troubled by what people were saying that she wrote directly to the Senate and asked for clarification. I can recount one particular afternoon vividly. There had been another core slip occurrence earlier that day – the forth in the space of a month, or 'phase' in lunar speak – and people were nervous, as, needless to say, was my mother. I remember her pacing backwards and forwards in our living module as she dictated into the séance program. She raised her voice at times, as if reinforcing the points and even shouted periodically, as if she was addressing the Home Affairs Committee directly. I remember glancing briefly at the primary bio panel after one such outburst: her blood pressure was overreacting and her pulse rate peaked at one hundred and sixty-six on more than one occasion. She wanted answers. No more side-stepping, no more delays and no more deception. Information specific to the events leading to my father's irradiation and no matter how incriminating. As a scientist, a mineralogist, she wanted to know the reason why seven failsafe bridges – two being reliable electromechanical devices – had offered little or no resistance, not even a basic level of protection, before effectively collapsing; why layer upon layer of external alarm protocols failed to activate and how and why the circumstances allowed the phosphor portal to open with those fatal results. Their answer, however, a good while later and amid their usual procrastination was more of the same. They said the investigation would take some time, a number of phases, ridiculously even a few years – they would get back to her. They never did, and my mother died not knowing – bless her . . . yes . . . bless her and bless my dad.

I'll tell you that there were whispers though, troubling things, they surely troubled my mum. I didn't understand the reasons, the rational, the ramifications, not then, but I began to when I was a teenager.

We were all good at science, that first class of lumens, gifted some said. I knew my way around a tranquillityite-powered reactor by the age of twelve and could theoretically engineer a Helium-3 fusion cell by the 9th Grade *and* purge the resultant troublesome proton. So when Oliver came back from the Seventh Reality, the first human – I should say luman – ever to make the crossing, and told me what he had seen, and then later, after he had guided me into that realm and then into the eighth, where I was simultaneously electrified with fright and astonishment at what was happening there . . . *and* I might add, incensed, I began to fill in the gaps. But it was after Guy, who had accompanied us on that third foray into that desperate realm and foolhardily stepped off into the darkness that things really began to fall into place. Then I began to realise the full implications of the deception and it went all the way to the top – both in the Colony and on Earth.

Time passed. We all grew up, perhaps faster than we should, encapsulated both by life enhancing and protective technology. It was three days after my seventeenth birthday; we were eleventh graders. By then most of the class were veterans of the banned Inca matrix and its associated recitals. Just knowing about the programme was regarded as an offence; interference would incur ruination for one's entire family; we all knew the risks. Only a few of us, however, knew how to write the necessary coding sequence and construct a bridge to the highest level. It was safer that way, Oliver had argued, and we agreed. His abilities were and are astounding. On that day we went there for the first time, the three of us, Oliver, Guy and me, hardly prepared. We used the college facility, generally deserted after fourth phase lectures and the interface is amazing. We saw, we interacted as much as we dare, and we left with not so much as a ripple. Their realm, the twelfth, so called, unknown to but a few and by nature, impenetrable. How could this insidious, malicious, threatening dimension have happened? The answer . . . look towards the Hadley Crater Recycling Facility . . . how short-sighted we remain. Discarded without a second thought, most not even powered down; a mechanical scrap heap seething with artificial intelligence.

For our second visit we were better prepared and after that excursion I knew without question that my father's death had not been a tragic, freak accident. It was on that day I vowed that when I was able: older, wiser, qualified, perhaps in a position of authority, that I would find out exactly who was responsible and why. I will do that for my mother. Clearing my father's name and removing the perpetrators, however, would prove more difficult than one could ever imagine. So let me start by telling you something of those early days, of the first official extraterrestrial disclosure, of the technologies and of the advancements that I, we, were accustomed to . . . *and* of the mistakes. Before we go further, however, make note of this name: Pierre Charles Sanderton. I urge you to commit it to memory and not to mention it again, not even in passing. My chance meeting and subsequent involvement with this unlikely Mancunian changed everything.

CHAPTER 2

THE GAME CHANGER

To be continued . . .

FIRST COLONY
EVOLUTION

ISBN: 978-0-9565077-2-3